# EVERYTHING WE DREAM

# The Hamilton Series

# EVERYTHING WE DREAM

## KATE SMITH

*sometimes unexpected ... ends up incredible — Kate Smith*

# CHAPTER 1

## Brandon

V ISITING HIS MOTHER AND STEPFATHER was far from exciting or even pleasant. For Brandon, the boisterous group of guys surrounding him made the long flight from Boston worthwhile. Their friendships made life bearable over many years in the small Montana town he'd once called home.

"Congratulations, Dr. Reynolds." His best friend, Rory, lifted a glass. "Both on earning your MD and on the new job. When do you start?"

"July." He tapped his drink against his friend's, smiling at the memory of the day he'd accepted the hard-won honor of calling himself a doctor.

"This bum, living the good life." His friend, Jayce, elbowed him in the ribs. "You'll soon be rich."

"I wish," he said under his breath. The numerous zeros on his loan statement far exceeded the few pathetic zeros accompanying his new salary as an intern. Four long years of intense training were in store before he'd earn more than a minimal income.

"… can't wait to meet this girl of yours. When are you bringing her for a visit?" Jayce asked.

Brandon brought his gaze upward, forcing himself to re-engage in the conversation. He curled his lip, taking another swig from his beer. "I like her. Why subject her to my mother?"

A round of laughter erupted around the table.

His mother was notorious among his friends. Brandon rarely introduced girlfriends or even mentioned the women he dated within the four walls of her house.

Jayce reached for Brandon's phone, which lay face down on the table. "I haven't seen a picture."

Brandon grabbed for the device a split second too late, kicking himself for leaving it out.

"Is this her?" His friend peered at the screen as a new text notification appeared at the top. "No wonder you decided on a little cradle robbing. Awww, sweet. She sent you a picture. And she's about to call." The guy turned the phone, showing Brandon the name *Savannah* displayed across the screen. "This must be her now."

"Give me that." Brandon snatched at the phone.

"Uh-uh." Jayce cleared his throat as he tapped the answer button. "Well, hello there. What's that, darling? You wish to speak with our boy, Brandon? Might cost ya."

"Don't be an ass." Brandon wrestled the phone from his friend's grasp. "Sorry. Ignore Jayce," he said, throwing his friend a dark look.

"Sounds like you're having fun."

He let out a sigh, relieved she sounded more amused than upset at being addressed as darling. "Just drinks with the guys. How about you?" He exited through the front doors, reveling in the light summer breeze and silence.

"We climbed three hundred and eighty-seven steps to the top of the Notre Dame bell tower. Our reward is a scoop of the première crème de glace in Paris," she said. "The gargoyles are amazing. Did you see the picture of me with the bell?"

"Not yet, 'cause Jayce hijacked my phone." He swept a hand through his hair. "What flavor?"

"Caramel au beurre salé. I've gained ten pounds from eating ice cream and gelato."

"I bet you look amazing." Brandon closed his eyes, picturing her sweet smile. "I miss you."

"Me too," she said softly. "I hear you've been busy saving lives."

"That was an intense day." The major pile-up he'd attended with Aiden had been a nightmare. "Your dad kept his cool."

"Not much phases him," she said. "Have I ever told you how I met my dad?"

Brandon frowned. "No, actually."

"I'll tell you someday."

"Deal. How are you and Tiffany getting along now you've spent more than two hours together?"

"Another thing to fill you in on," she said.

"She's right there, huh?"

"Sure. But it's all good. Hey, I have to go. We're meeting Stefan for dinner. Only ten more sleeps, and I'll be home."

"Can't wait to see you. Enjoy that amazing French cuisine. Bye, sweetie." Brandon hung up and leaned back against the building, propping the sole of one foot flat against the brickwork. He stared at the wisp of clouds floating across the bright summer sky, wishing he was there with her.

Their weeks apart had been more difficult than anticipated. Even his busy work schedule, hanging out with Nate, and multiple dinners with Aiden and Emily hadn't soothed the ache of missing her.

"There you are." Rory tipped his head back, squinting skyward before focusing on Brandon. "How's Savannah?"

"Having a grand time in Paris." He sighed, watching as the wisps changed shape. It reminded of him of when they were kids. The hot summer days filled with adventure, far from the worries of adulthood. Those distant times were simple and easy, at least compared to now.

"Man, you have it bad." His friend furrowed his brow. "You're never like this about a girl. When do I meet her?"

"When can you visit Boston?" Brandon lifted one shoulder. "Bad enough Piper's a complete bitch about the relationship. I don't need Carol or Jeremy adding their opinions," he said with a sideways look. "You know how they get."

"Enough said." Rory patted his shoulder. "Sorry about Piper."

"The girl's ridiculous. Why does she assume calling dibs on Vanna's friendship gives her the right to interfere in my relationship?"

"You've heard my opinion."

"She's my little sister." Brandon grimaced.

"Who isn't blood-related, dude. At least consider her ulterior motives."

"I seriously hope you're wrong." Brandon shuddered. "Piper's too close to being related. And too young."

"Says the man dating her friend of the same age."

"Savannah doesn't act eighteen. She's more mature than most women our age."

"How long have you been dating?"

Brandon squinted. "Define dating." He struggled to calculate their relationship timeline. It had started as a passionate, amazing week, followed by a hiatus after the revelations rolled in. That his *Zoe* was eighteen, not twenty-two. His stepsister's friend. Real name Savannah. Followed by the complete awkwardness of discovering her last name was Hamilton. The beloved daughter of his ER supervisor. Not his finest moment. Or hers.

"That right there is a big ole red flag." Rory's lips twisted. "When did you date for real? Not some no-strings-attached week of hot sex with a random chick you rescued from the big bad ex-boyfriend in a bar, Brandon. A real, honest relationship, where you called her by her actual name?"

"April?" He'd been entranced by Savannah by the end of their first week together. Those amazing days they'd spent in late January before things went to hell. Maybe that didn't count. His friend didn't seem to think so.

"Three months, bud. That's nothing, even if it's challenging your record. Autumn was only ten." Rory smirked. "Bet she'd love to see you."

"Not a chance." Brandon shook his index finger at his friend. "I'm with Vanna."

"Kidding."

"More like testing."

"I hope Savannah is committed to you." Rory tilted his head. "A month apart is a long time. That's a third of the relationship, and she's a long way from home."

"She's traveling with her mother. I doubt she's club-hopping and picking up French dudes." Brandon kicked at the thin layer of grit on the sidewalk.

Rory threw a light punch against Brandon's shoulder. "Watch out, or she'll have you picking curtains."

"Shut up, asshole." He shoved his friend even as a grin twitched his lips.

Rory feinted another couple of punches, laughing as they roughhoused.

"I give." Brandon held up his hands.

"Getting soft, are you?" Rory asked. "Hey, there's a barbecue tomorrow afternoon. You should come. You don't even have to talk to Autumn."

"We'll see."

"No excuses. It'll be the last time we see you for months." Rory observed him steadily. "Sorry for not making your celebration. I'm super proud of you, man. You worked your butt off."

"It's a long and expensive flight." Brandon hadn't expected his friends to show, given the distance. "Savannah made the trip with her family."

"But not your mother or anyone else from that household." His friend shook his head.

"Story of my life." A vague edge of disappointment bit him at his family's lack of support, but it was for the best. "Carol's embarrassing. She would have gotten loaded or done something stupid. Though, I'd have loved to have seen Mia. But," he said, smiling, "I had a great time and a celebratory dinner with Nate and my ER supervisors. It's all good."

"Wish your residency was closer. Hey, let's play some pool and have a few more drinks."

"You're on." Brandon followed his friend inside, glad the inquisition was over.

"Up." The stern voice dragged Brandon from his peaceful dreams.

"Tired," he mumbled as he burrowed deeper into his pillow.

"You wouldn't be if you came home at a decent hour." Her shrill tone sliced into his brain.

Brandon winced as a waft of cool morning air hit his bare skin. "What the hell?" He grabbed a wisp of the sheet, tugging it free from her grasp.

"Put some clothes on. Get your ass out of bed." His mother loomed over him, hands on hips. "Later, you're on a plane to Boston. I've hardly seen you."

He smothered a scoff. The only thing she ever wanted to do was get drunk and enjoy using him as a convenient emotional punching bag. "I'm up. Just get out of my room. Don't know who's worse, you or Piper," he muttered, cringing at the memory of his immature stepsister barging in on him and Vanna.

Half an hour later, after a hot shower, he entered the kitchen and poured himself a cup of coffee. He grimaced at the bitterness biting his tongue. Had it always been this bad? Maybe he'd become spoiled in Boston.

"What's that face about?" Jeremy shifted in his seat at the shabby, pitted kitchen table.

"Nothing." He dumped in a liberal dose of sugar to disguise the taste. Critiquing anything would invite a lecture on gratefulness.

Jeremy peeked over his shoulder, clearly scouting for Carol. "I hear you have a new girlfriend," his stepfather said in a low voice.

Brandon rolled his eyes toward the ceiling. "What did Piper say?"

"That you got involved with someone you shouldn't." Jeremy leaned back, leveling his gaze at Brandon over the rim of his cup. "Your supervisor's daughter? That doesn't sound smart."

"Did she tell my mother?" Brandon sighed before he downed a slug of foul brew, hiding his disgust.

"No, and neither did I." Jeremy drummed his fingers. "Eighteen? That's dangerous territory. It could affect your career if your supervisor finds out."

"Give me some credit." Brandon frowned. "My supervisors are aware of the relationship. Besides, Savannah isn't a child."

"It's true?" His stepfather's eyebrows flew upward. "You're having sex with her?"

"She's a grown woman." Brandon quirked his own brow. "We're not ..." Teenagers. A half-truth. Though she acted mature, Savannah was five years younger than his age of twenty-three. "It's not an issue."

"So you're not?" Jeremy contemplated him. "Or you'd prefer I shut up about it?"

He eyed the man over the rim of his cup. He liked Jeremy, but on occasion, his stepfather crossed boundaries. By the time the man had come into his life, Brandon been an adult. Far too late to dish out fatherly advice or to be the role model Brandon wished he'd had during his tumultuous and wild teenage years. Anyway, he suspected his stepfather was too weak and easily domineered to be a good example for anyone.

"Right. Be careful, Brandon. She's a young impressionable girl, not a woman. I'd take exception to a man your age sleeping with my eighteen-year-old daughter." The man emitted a deep sigh. "When are you planning to tell your mother?"

Brandon scoffed. "Since when does a grown man report his relationships to his mother?"

"Coward." A low laugh rumbled from his chest. "Keep on Carol's good side if you expect continuing support for your career."

Brandon bit back the retort. Neither Carol nor Jeremy offered much encouragement. His accomplishments were his alone, earned through hard work and the burning desire to escape this oppressive house and backward small town. The barbecue looked more and more appealing, even with the high probability he'd run into his ex-girlfriend.

⌒

Two hours later, Rory arrived at his house, practically dragging him into the car and driving them to the park.

"Brandon." Nick charged across the grass, hopping up and down, waving a mitt in one hand. "Play ball with me."

"Hey, Nick. You have an extra one of those?" He pointed at the glove, ruffling the boy's sandy blond hair.

"Yup." A grin spread across his face as he produced one from behind his back.

"A regular Boy Scout." Brandon followed Nick to a clear spot in the park and spent the next hour fielding catches and coaching the preteen boy on his pitches.

A willowy dark-haired young woman intercepted a pass. "Time to pack it in, Nicky. They're serving burgers."

Nick cheered. "Are you coming, Brandon?"

"In a minute, buddy. Check out the selection and save me some of the good stuff."

The boy nodded and raced toward the food-laden tables.

Autumn's gaze trailed after her younger brother before she shifted her focus to Brandon. "You're great with him. You've been missed." She extended a frosty bottle. "Your reward for being …" The woman lifted one shoulder.

"Thanks." Brandon swallowed a mouthful of icy beer, which soothed his throat after the exertion in the late-afternoon heat. "I love that kid. Next time I visit, he'll be a teenager, and far too busy chasing girls to play ball with me."

"Thirteen next month. I'm not sure about the girls. He's quiet." She tossed the ball into the air, catching it with ease. "How's Philly? Or is it Boston now?"

"Boston. It's good." Brandon offered a faint smile. "How are you?"

"Same as always. Nothing's changed around here," she said as they wandered toward the fire pit. "I hear you're seeing someone."

"Word travels fast."

"It's a small town."

"Mia tell you?" Though he hadn't gotten into the details with anyone but Rory, his sister knew he was dating. At one time, Mia and Autumn had been close.

"Mia never says much to me about your big life in the big city." Autumn caught her braid and twisted it around her finger, fidgeting with the hairband securing the end. "What's her name? And how long?"

"Savannah. I met her in January."

"Savannah," she said in a low melodic voice. The corners of Autumn's mouth quirked down. "A proper southern belle."

He smirked. "She's a West Coast girl from Oregon."

"But it's serious? Is that why you chose Boston for residency? Didn't you have an offer closer to home?"

"It's a wise career decision, and where I matched. Savannah has nothing to do with it." Brandon refused to discuss the convoluted situation brewing with his new girlfriend. Especially not with his ex-girlfriend, no matter how long they'd known each other. Besides, he'd set his sights on Mass General during medical school and had jumped at the offered opportunity to intern at a top hospital. "Anyway, there's nothing positive about living close to home, aside from seeing Mia."

Autumn's eyes grew shiny, and she looked away.

He sucked in a breath. "Sorry. I didn't mean …" He turned toward her. "We ended things before I left, and you know how it is being around my family."

"I get it, Brandon. I just thought … never mind." She shrugged as a tiny smile appeared. "You'll be amazing. Dr. Reynolds. That title's kind of trippy. You have a fantastic future ahead." Autumn motioned toward the buffet table. "Better get in there before it's all gone. You have a long flight home."

Leaving Montana once again came as a relief. He never managed more than three days in a row before he itched to leave. To return to his reinvented life, far, far away from the negative influences of small-town life.

After a flight delay and the crowded conditions in economy, Brandon couldn't be happier to arrive in Boston, or as happy as one could be, given his current living situation.

He entered the apartment, wrinkling his nose at the rank odor of garbage. The bedroom was even worse. Dylan's dirty clothing littered the floor, his unmade bed a tangled mess, and dirty dishes and discarded takeout containers formed a grimy layer over top.

Brandon used one foot to shove the piles to his roommate's side before opening the window. The books spread across his bed landed on the floor with a thump as he gave them an unceremonious push.

He eyed the disarray of his covers and groaned. His sheets needed washing. The unsavory thought Dylan had entertained some girl he'd picked up at the bar made him shudder. How the guy even managed to entice a girl home, he'd never understand. Any woman with a modicum of sense would run.

One of his dresser drawers hung open. The guy had stolen clothes. Again. As he closed it, a note tacked to the front of a glossy medical journal on the top of the dresser caught his eye:

Another present for you, doctor's pet.

Dylan never tired of commenting. Even though Will Kavanagh acted as his supervisor, it only took one mention that he planned to earn chief resident, and he'd received valuable tips plus a stream of extra reading from Aiden and Emily.

After years of medical school, he'd become accustomed to exhaustion, so he tucked the journal under his arm and hauled the sheets and duvet off the mattress. He slogged downstairs and crammed them into washing machines, adding generous doses of detergent and cranking the dial to the hot setting. He glanced at his watch and headed into the street, intent on finding dinner.

The pizza joint a few doors down offered quick and decent fare, so he ordered two slices and opened the medical journal. He'd barely managed three bites before a clatter of plastic against tile made him look up.

A young woman offered him a smile and retrieved a tray from the floor before she continued cleaning the nearby table.

Brandon bit into his second slice of Hawaiian, focusing on the medical terminology, which wasn't easy. The occasional loud clatter, along with the growing feeling of being watched had him sending a covert glance toward the offender.

She looked away, but tipped her chin, a sideways look coming his way as her smile reappeared. After tucking a lock of dark auburn hair behind her ear, she turned to the soda machine. Moments later, she approached his table. "I thought you might need this." She set the drink in front of him with a napkin tucked underneath. "On the house," her voice dropped to a whisper, "but don't tell my boss."

"Thanks." Brandon looked into wide hazel eyes as another smile twitched at her rosebud pink lips. Definitely cute. And flirtatious.

"What are you reading?" Her eyebrows rose. "I'm Naomi."

"Just a medical journal."

"You're a doctor?" Her eyes widened further as she twirled a finger in her hair.

"A resident." He loved the way the title sounded, even if he hadn't officially changed roles at work. Brandon motioned to the drink. "I hope you don't get into trouble."

She shrugged before she hurried behind the counter as another customer arrived.

Brandon ate the last bite and sipped from the drink. A flash of red caught his eye. A name and phone number written in red ink on the napkin, complete with a tiny heart over the *i* in Naomi.

He glanced toward the counter, but she was busy filling her current order. After setting the cup on top of the napkin to hide the writing, he scooped up his journal and made a speedy exit. He didn't want to hurt the girl's feelings, but his days of collecting phone numbers had come to an end. All he could think about was Savannah.

# CHAPTER 2

## *Savannah*

S**AVANNAH TAPPED ON THE DOOR** of the tiny apartment, scanning the dimly lit hallway. The door opened, her relief fading at the sight of the tanned, bare chest of the blond man looming in the doorway.

"Well, look who it is." Dylan gave her a cool look and wheeled around, presenting her with a view of his broad back. "Yo, Brando. Your squeeze is here."

"I have a name," she muttered as she stepped inside, pushing the door shut.

"You sure do," Dylan said under his breath. He dropped onto the couch, propping his feet on the coffee table and guzzling from a silver beer can.

A combination of smelly gym bag and old food assailed her nostrils, making her gag. The pile of dirty socks underneath the kitchen table, along with the litter of empty pizza boxes and fast food bags made Savannah cringe. She'd bet a perusal of the fridge would turn up sour milk and some wilted lettuce or moldy fruit, but little else.

Brandon appeared from the bedroom. "Vanna."

Vanna met him halfway, leaping into his arms and wrapping her legs around his slim waist. She sighed against his soft lips, sinking into a long, deep kiss, enjoying the shiver that ran through her.

"Do you never quit?" Dylan muttered.

Brandon threw a dirty look in Dylan's direction before refocusing on Savannah. "I missed you. How was the trip?"

"Better than expected." With a touch of apprehension, she'd agreed to the European holiday with Tiffany and subsequent meet up with Stefan in Paris toward the end of their tour. They'd culminated the trip with several days in Chicago. "I missed you too." She sneaked a look from the corner of her eye, noting Dylan's leer. "Want to get out of here?" She glared in his roommate's direction.

"Yeah." His gaze turned in the same direction. "Hey, Dylan, quit being creepy. And why don't you toss your garbage and fumigate those socks?"

The surly glower from his roommate spoke volumes. "If it bothers you, then clean it." Dylan returned his attention to the drone of the sportscaster on the ancient TV.

Brandon scowled. "I'm not your fucking maid." He latched onto Vanna's hand, snagging his keys and wallet from the counter as they breezed through the exit. "That guy. It's embarrassing to invite anyone over."

"It's foul. I don't know how you stand it." Savannah wrinkled her nose. "It'll be over soon, though. Where did he match?"

"Boston? Nate and I are looking for another apartment. Hopefully, we'll find something less slummy, but rent is exorbitant."

"Are you sure Dylan's staying in Boston?"

"What do you know?" He quirked a brow. "Some happy news, perhaps?"

"I overheard something, but I could be wrong." She shrugged. "Do you want to stay over? Aiden and Emily are working the late shift."

"What about Iona and the rug rat?"

"Iona's in Ireland. Kellan's staying with Jenna and Tom. We have the place to ourselves."

"Enough said. I should have packed a bag."

"I have a drawer full of your clothes. If you're stuck, we'll raid Aiden's closet."

"Doesn't he get tired of it? I have a growing pile of stuff to return, but Dylan's a thief, so who knows if half of the stuff will ever find its way home. Aiden's going to ban me from entering the premises. Or padlock his closet."

"We'll schedule a recovery mission when Dylan's at work and fumigate as required. If they look anything like his clothes today"—she shuddered—"we might torch them."

Brandon snickered. "Your dad would be thrilled if you burned his clothes."

"I dunno. Dylan's a slob, so Dad might appreciate it. Anyway, he hasn't mentioned his missing clothing." She pursed her lips. "That doesn't mean he hasn't noticed. Not much gets by him."

"Don't I know it." He wrapped an arm around her shoulders. "Hey. What's that? Did you hurt yourself?" His gentle touch to her shoulder made her smile.

"We made a visit before I flew home."

"The tattoo?" He pulled her out of the flow of pedestrian traffic. "Can I see?" Brandon slid her flowing blouse aside, tugging at the adhesive at the edge of the light dressing. He whistled as he peeled it back. "That's incredible."

"Right? Tiffany knows this amazing tattoo artist, so I got this and we both got butterflies on our ankles." A happy feeling bubbled to the surface as she remembered the day they'd shared while getting tattooed.

"Mother-daughter butterflies?"

"Tiffany designed them. I learned so much about her. We spent time at her gallery and I saw her work. And she took me to meet a photographer friend of hers, who gave me some fantastic pointers to improve my composition. I remembered him. He took wedding photos for Dad and Emily as a special favor."

"And who was he?" Brandon lifted a brow.

"Bailey. A fashion photographer."

Brandon nodded as he entwined their fingers and tugged her into motion. "The trip went well, then."

"I had serious doubts, but I'm glad I went. I mean, who'd turn down weeks of touring Italy and France, but any trip with Tiffany would have been good, you know?" She searched his face, hoping he understood her inability to explain the emotions coursing through her.

"You discovered who your mother is. That's a big deal. I'm happy you're forging a connection."

"I'm sorry," she said, squeezing his hand. "I'm yapping on about my fantastic travels, but you haven't said much about yours. How was Montana?"

Brandon shrugged. "Nothing new, though it was great to see the guys. Rory is dying to meet you, but it's not a good idea."

A frisson of disappointment lingered in her belly at those words, but she'd learned her lesson in New York. Don't expect too much, too soon. "And your mom?"

"Intolerable."

"What did she do?"

"Spent the entire time criticizing and ordering me around like I'm five."

"That doesn't sound like much fun," she said. "Did you tell her about me?"

His lips twisted. "Piper told Jeremy on her last visit."

"But not your mother?" Savannah exhaled a long slow breath at the slight shake of his head. "So Jeremy hates me? He thinks I'm a little tramp, just like Piper does?"

"How could anyone assume that?"

"I bet Piper didn't provide a flattering picture."

"She focused on my cradle-robbing."

"Oh, so much better." Her stomach lurched.

"It is for you," he said. "I can handle his concerns. But enough about my depressing family. Tell me about the amazing things you did on your holiday."

She shook her head. "More about Montana first."

"Just the usual small-town stuff. Drank beer, played pool, went to the beach, and spent time with Mia."

"Ahh, the little monster Piper bitched about."

"Piper's a spoiled drama queen, especially compared to the meager attention my little sister gets." His expression softened. "I worry about Mia, but not much I can do, aside from spending time with her when I visit."

"I'd love to meet her." Savannah peered at him. "And your friends." She squeezed his hand. "But it's too soon."

"It's not that. I've met your family and friends, except for the infamous Justin," Brandon said, his eyes narrowing almost imperceptibly.

She wrinkled her nose. "Don't be jealous. He's my friend."

"He's your ex-boyfriend." He pressed a kiss to her lips. "I trust you."

She smiled and nodded, pushing down her disappointment. His resistance to telling his family or allowing her to meet his friends burned. She'd remain patient and hope he changed his mind.

⁓

Over the next week, they reconnected, and it soon felt like they'd never been apart. They settled into an easy and comfortable routine, with Brandon spending most of his free time with her.

"You're an angel." Brandon rubbed at the stubble on his jaw, shifting on his perch at the counter. "Kayaking this morning was fun. We should do it again."

Savannah set a plate in front of Brandon. "I told you it would only take a few minutes." She brushed her windswept hair back from her face, hoping her cheeks weren't sunburned. "I enjoyed our adventure too."

"Your dad and Emily will get tired of feeding me." He sliced into the steak with a sigh, digging in with apparent satisfaction at the sumptuous meal.

"Half of the time, they're the ones inviting you. Look at how often you were here while I was away." She slid onto the stool beside him, sipping a glass of water. "You've been adopted."

"I'm a lucky guy." He grinned, obviously pleased at the easy and natural routine that had developed. "Or they've taken pity on me. Did they tell you they allowed me and Nate to stay a few nights? The apartment was so bad after I got home—"

"Aiden!" Emily's voice rang down the hall. "I need you. Right now!"

Brandon frowned at Savannah. "That doesn't sound good."

"Nope." Savannah leaped from her seat and dashed into the hallway, stopping short at the sight of her stepmother.

Emily hunched with one palm flattened against the wall, the other resting on her lower back as a puddle formed around her feet.

"Ohhhh." Vanna slapped a hand over her mouth.

"Move." Brandon grasped her shoulders as he slipped by. "Are you in pain?"

"My back aches." Emily peered at the floor. "My water broke. Where's Aiden?" She grimaced. "Another one."

Brandon pressed a hand against the small of her back. "Does the pressure help?"

Emily nodded and sucked in a breath before forcing it out between clenched teeth. "Our baby girl is eager to join us."

"Dad took Kellan to the park. I'll call." Vanna fumbled for her phone as Brandon supported Emily, leading her toward the bedroom.

Savannah trailed down the hall, looking away as she skirted the puddle in the middle of the floor. "Answer … answer …" When Aiden's voice mail picked up, she hit disconnect and redialed his number.

"Hi, honey—"

"Come home. Now. Hurry up. There's a big icky puddle on the floor." Savannah followed Brandon into the bedroom.

"Is Emily okay?" Aiden sounded breathless. "Kel. Come on, buddy. Time to visit Auntie Jenna."

"Brandon's here, but it's happening."

"I'm on my way. Can I talk to Em?"

Savannah extended the phone to Emily. "It's Dad."

Emily accepted it. "Aiden. Only a couple of minutes. I need you." She smiled, her eyes shiny. "I love you."

"Vanna, can you find dry clothes?" Brandon motioned to the closet. "I'm timing, Emily. You can relax."

"I'm fine. Aiden's on his way, and it's not my first baby." Emily smiled faintly. "I've even delivered a few."

Savannah hurried into the closet, finding a summer-weight maternity dress and the hospital bag. She returned to find Emily leaning against the wall while Brandon talked her through another contraction and rubbed her back.

"Anything I can do?" Vanna asked.

Brandon shook his head, turning his back as Emily peeled her sundress over her head.

"You don't have to look away, Brandon." A smile fleeted across Emily's face. "I'm not shy. And you're probably seeing more of me in the photo." She slid the clean dress over her head.

Savannah smothered a laugh as Brandon looked up, a rueful grin appearing as he realized he stood under the large framed boudoir photo of Emily mounted above the fireplace.

Emily rubbed her belly, ambling across the room and back.

Savannah paced back and forth on her own path, glancing at her watch every few seconds. "Where's Dad?" She wished she had something productive and helpful to do, but Brandon seemed to have it covered.

"Someone else needs to relax more than I do." Emily laughed softly before a furrow appeared between her brows.

Footsteps resounded in the hallway, and a moment later, Aiden dashed into the room. "How you doing, Em?" He strode across the floor to join his wife, cupping her cheeks in his palms as he pressed a kiss to her brow.

"The contractions are two minutes apart." Brandon glanced at his watch. "And thirty to forty-five seconds each."

"Showtime," Aiden said. "Vanna, can you take the bag and grab my car keys? You're driving."

"On it." Savannah scooped up the bag and hurried out the door, tugging Brandon along with her.

"I'll deal with the mess." Brandon pointed at the puddle on the floor.

"Thank you." Savannah grimaced. "How can you stomach it?"

He snorted. "You should see what we deal with at work. If you get me a mop …"

"There's one in the laundry room."

"Find the keys." He winked and gave her a gentle push. "That baby isn't planning to wait."

After parking the car, Savannah rushed upstairs to the delivery unit, making a stop to ask for Emily's room number. At the entrance of the suite, she took a deep breath before opening the door. She peered around the edge and froze.

Her dad sat on the bed behind Emily, supporting her while she groaned. "You're doing amazing." Aiden brushed her stepmother's sweaty hair back, not moving an inch.

Emily leaned against him, panting. "Kellan didn't take this long."

The midwife at the end of the bed patted Emily's calf. "Almost there."

Tears pricked at Vanna's eyes as Emily smiled at Aiden, accepting his kiss.

"You made it." Her dad spotted her hanging out by the door. "Come in."

"I don't know. Maybe this isn't such a good idea." She'd begged to be included, but now she felt queasy, her knees trembling as the drama unfolded.

"Hold Emily's hand." Aiden beckoned as Emily tensed up. "Breathe, Em. You can do this."

Savannah moved across the room, offering her hand to her stepmother.

"You're crowning," the midwife said from her place at the end of the bed. "Aiden, you know what to do."

"Sweetie, let's sit you up." Aiden helped his wife reposition, remaining on the bed as her support.

"You can push when you're ready," the midwife said.

Aiden grasped Emily's hand, totally focused on his wife. "Ready, Em?"

"Get this baby out of me." She panted and then let out another low groan.

"Hang in there. You've got this, Em."

Emily gritted her teeth and clenched her eyes closed, her face scrunching in pain.

"Ohhh," Savannah said. Complete fascination warred with absolute terror as the baby's head appeared. "Wow."

"One more good one. Push, now."

Emily gasped for breath, then bore down with a groan, her chin pressed to her chest.

Savannah peered at the tiny red infant making her entrance, a loud squall emitting from the baby after a few seconds of silence. The midwife rubbed the little girl with a towel before placing her across Emily's chest.

"She looks great. Pinking up and a fantastic set of lungs."

Savannah reached out. "Can I touch her?"

"Yes." Aiden grinned as he caressed the top of the baby's head with one finger. "Meet your sister."

A tear tracked down Emily's cheek. "Aiden. Look at our baby girl."

"You did great, Mommy. She's perfect."

Savannah couldn't keep the smile from spreading across her face. "That was freaky but amazing." The baby wrapped her tiny hand around Savannah's index finger, a strong grip for someone who'd only appeared in the world moments earlier. "She's tiny."

"Does Dad want to cut the cord?"

"Absolutely." Aiden slid from behind Emily, settling her against the pillows before accepting the scissors. He snipped between the clamps and the nurse carried the baby to the warmer for her first exam.

Aiden kissed Emily, running the back of his hand over her cheek before advancing toward the bustling group around the baby.

"How is she?" Emily propped herself up and peered across the room at the clear plastic warmer.

"She's perfect." Aiden received the swaddled infant from the nurse. "She's a beauty, just like her mother." He sat on the side of the bed, tucking an arm around Emily as she cuddled the bundle against her chest.

Savannah perched on the opposite side and peeked at the tiny face. Dark serious eyes stared at her. "Do you think she knows who I am?"

"Definitely." Aiden beamed. "She'll know your voice because you're around so often. And you talked to the belly."

"That I did." The first time she'd talked to Emily's growing belly, she'd felt silly, but Aiden did it all the time, asserting that babies could hear before they were born. He believed talking increased the level of bonding and was adamant his daughter would recognize his voice.

"What are we naming her?" Savannah brushed a fingertip over the soft down of hair, anticipation building as Aiden and Emily exchanged looks.

Emily peered at the tiny baby with a gentle smile. "Meet Cierra Marin Hamilton."

"You used my name."

"A beautiful name, for a beautiful girl," Emily said. "Do you want to hold her?"

"Yes." Savannah cuddled her precious new sibling. Having a younger sister was something she'd dreamed of, and now, that dream had come true.

~

Savannah hurried into the ER, searching for Brandon. She flagged down a young woman she didn't recognize, though her lab coat signified she was a medical student. "Dr. Reynolds around?"

"I'm sorry, but you'll need to wait over there. Have you checked in with the triage nurse?"

"I'm not a patient. I'll wait in the doctor's lounge. Could you tell Dr. Reynolds where to find me?" She knew he was on shift, so he couldn't be far away.

"The lounge is for doctors." The young woman narrowed her eyes. "Please wait there." She pointed at the family room.

"How are you?" Will Kavanagh appeared from one of the exam rooms and pulled Vanna into a hug. "Savannah is Dr. Hamilton's daughter," he said to the medical student. "How's it going upstairs?"

"I have a completely adorable baby sister."

"I'll pop in when I have my break. Congratulations, Vanna." He hugged her again. "I have a patient waiting." He waved and hurried down the hall.

"I'll just ..." Savannah motioned toward the lounge, turning away from the glaring young woman.

"Vanna," Brandon appeared behind her as she pushed into the lounge.

"Hey. You done with the trauma?"

"The patient is off to surgery, but I can't be long." He captured her lips in a kiss. "These shifts are murder. I can't wait until I'm done for the day, but I have another three hours. How are things with Emily?"

"I almost ran out of there it was so scary. How do you watch stuff like that?"

He shrugged. "You get used to it. I don't know how to explain it. You almost disassociate and concentrate on the patient, not how you feel. Does that make sense? It's about them, never about you."

"It does." She nodded.

"So, a girl?"

"Yes. She's sweet. You should visit after your shift. Then if you want to come over, I'll make you"—she glanced at the clock with a frown—"breakfast? The time really flew by in the delivery suite."

Brandon snickered. "Bet Emily didn't think so. I'll come by once I've finished my shift. I'll text when I'm on my way." He bent down to claim another long kiss. "I'd better get to work, or I'll be hearing about it."

"See you soon, then." Savannah bit back the words that wanted to escape. Whenever she said goodbye to this man, she longed to blurt out *I love you*. But she simply couldn't. Not after New York and their long discussion. The worst thing would be to appear clingy or needy. That would surely send him running, just when things were progressing.

With a happy smile, she strode toward the stairs, intent on having another cuddle with her baby sister before they kicked her out and sent her home.

# CHAPTER 3

## Brandon

BRANDON PEEKED INTO THE SUITE. The bed stood empty, but Aiden sat in one of the chairs, a blissful look on his face as he snuggled the little bundle against his chest.

"Hey," Brandon said in a low voice. "Congrats. Vanna told me everything went well with the delivery."

"It was amazing. Thanks for your help."

"Have to put my medical training to good use." Brandon peered at the baby, amazed at how tiny the little girl appeared. It seemed odd to be so in awe as he'd attended births during his rotations. He'd even delivered a few babies himself. "Can I hold her?"

"Sure." Aiden stood, allowing Brandon to take his seat before transferring the teeny girl into Brandon's arms. "See? You're a natural."

"Yeah, right." He inhaled the sweet baby smell, brushing a fingertip over her downy head. "She's adorable." He grinned and relaxed against the back of the chair. "Babies are cute until they start to cry, then I like to give them back."

"Ahh, they're worth the trouble even if they are a major commitment."

"It'll be years before I consider my own crying, eating, poop machine." Brandon laughed softly as he inspected her perfect tiny fingers. "She has quite a grip," he said as her small hand wound around his and her tiny mouth stretched in a wide yawn, her eyes closing. "She's sweet."

"I'm betting Cierra takes after her mother." Aiden rested against the side of Emily's bed, rubbing at the stubble on his jaw. The man's eyes appeared red and tired, reflecting a mixture of joy, but also a touch of sadness. "Times like these, it makes it even harder to remember how much I missed with Savannah."

Brandon cuddled the little girl against his chest. "I don't know how you dealt with it. Being so …" He lapsed into silence, not quite knowing how to phrase his thoughts.

"Young?" Aiden's faint smile combined with a lift of one shoulder. "We'd have managed if given the chance. But Ross and Jayde were great parents. Perhaps Vanna was lucky to escape the messy dynamics of our families."

"Vanna never told me how she found you."

"A picture, and a train derailment," Aiden said as he shifted his position on the bed.

"What?" Brandon hadn't expected those words. The usual story consisted of phone calls, letters, and contacting adoption registries or social workers. At least the few stories he'd heard.

"Vanna was on the train in Chicago when it derailed. Em and I were sent to the scene, and Savannah was my patient."

"Was she hurt?" His heart lurched at the thought his girlfriend had been involved in a serious and potentially deadly accident.

"Her injuries were minor. A bruised shoulder and some lacerations requiring stitches."

"How did she figure out that you were her dad?"

"Tiffany hid a picture in Vanna's baby blanket with my name written on the back. Jayde found it, kept it, and passed it on to Vanna, and she heard my name in the ER. A strange set of coincidences."

"Or fate?" Brandon considered the odd circumstances and how it had shaped their lives. "She's a survivor. No wonder she's so mature."

"Nothing has been easy. I hope her future is happier than her past. I guess all parents wish that for their children."

The bathroom door opened and Emily appeared, wrapped in a fluffy robe. She padded across the floor, smiling at Brandon as she wrapped an arm around Aiden's waist. "I feel much better after my shower."

"I thought you might." Aiden pressed a kiss to his wife's temple.

"Thanks for your assistance, Brandon. Poor Vanna seemed a touch anxious."

"Happy to help. Congratulations, she's beautiful." He peered down at the sleeping baby in his arms. "Vanna invited me for breakfast. Can we bring you something later?"

"My lovely husband already sneaked me in some decent food." Emily tipped her head against Aiden's shoulder, giving his belly a light pat. "Thanks, though."

"I'll make something later," Aiden said. "I'll help Em for another couple of hours before I head home for some sleep."

The baby squawked, her face screwing into a displeased moue.

"That's my cue to return this munchkin to Daddy." Brandon rose, transferring the baby to Aiden.

Aiden propped the baby on his shoulder, cradling her head with one hand and rocking gently while waiting for Emily to settle herself on the bed. "Shh, sweetheart, it's okay." The tiny girl sputtered then fell silent as her dad continued to shush her. "I bet you're hungry."

"I should go, but I'll see you later?" Brandon waved as he headed out the door, happy to be on his way to what he considered his second home.

~

The walk through the Boston Commons and into Back Bay only took a few minutes. He waved at the doorman as he crossed to the elevator and stepped inside, relaxing as it rose toward the top floor.

"There you are." Savannah peered around the corner as he hung his hoodie on the rack. "How was the rest of your shift?"

"Not bad. I did a cool procedure." He laughed as Savannah grimaced. "Sorry, I'm breaking the rules. You don't want to hear the gory details at mealtime."

"Nope. I formed my own visuals. Being in the delivery room was incredible and terrifying all at once." She stood on tiptoe to give him a kiss. "Did you meet Cierra?"

"She's sweet, and both Aiden and Emily looked super happy." He wrapped his arms around her from behind, nibbling on her neck. "I heard the short version of how you met Aiden. You never told me you'd been in a train derailment."

Savannah shrugged. "I don't dwell on it. Those were some scary moments. Leanne ended up in surgery for her leg and there was blood everywhere." She shuddered. "People died," she whispered.

He gripped her shoulders, turning her toward him. "I'm sorry. It was thoughtless of me to bring it up. Have you considered counseling? Lots of people find it helps."

A deep furrow appeared in her brow as her chin lifted. She fixed an intense stare on him. "I've been to a million therapy sessions. Aiden's a damn ER doctor. You think he doesn't understand PTSD? Or he missed my obvious issues after my dad died and Tiffany refused to acknowledge me?"

Words failed him. He'd become used to doling out the advice, and the mixed reactions to the suggestion, but her defiance, tinged with something he couldn't identify, stunned him. "I didn't mean anything by it." He cupped her face between his palms. "I'm glad you talked to someone."

"Are you?" She searched his face. "It doesn't scare you that your girlfriend has a therapist on speed dial?"

"I'd be more worried if you didn't." He offered a faint smile. "It doesn't have to be a secret."

"Except people judge me for seeing a therapist. Like I'm"—she circled her index finger beside her temple—"crazy."

"I'd never judge, and you're not crazy. You've persevered despite difficult circumstances. I'm happy you sought help." He slid his arms around her, rubbing her back until she relaxed against his chest. "You can trust me," he murmured against her hair. "There's no shame in seeking help."

"Can I?" she whispered, her words muffled by his sweater.

His heart went out to this woman who'd experienced unthinkable heartbreak. "I won't hurt you, sweetheart."

Savannah's embrace tightened, her fingers digging into his back. A tiny shiver ran through her.

"What?"

She gave the slightest shake of her head as she inhaled a long breath, but she didn't pull away.

Brandon bent his head, pressing his lips against her temple. The faint scent of her lotion and the warmth of her body caused a flicker of desire. This woman drew him in, captivating his mind and body, and she didn't even seem to know it.

She lifted her chin, nibbling on her lower lip in her sexy enticing way. Savannah sighed against his mouth as he captured her lips, one arm wrapping around his neck while her fingers ruffled his hair.

He scooped her up and carried her through to her room, shoving the door closed behind them. He deposited her on the bed, stopping only to strip off his sweater before he joined her.

⌒

Brandon rolled and reached for Savannah but was greeted by an empty space. He hadn't meant to fall asleep, but he'd been warm and relaxed with her curled against him. This bedroom, with its plush queen-sized bed, combined with the blissful peace of this home, always provided the opportunity for deep, restful sleep. Comfort and privacy was a rare commodity in the cramped dwelling on the other side of the river.

His stomach rumbled, reminding him he hadn't claimed the promised meal. He negotiated his way to the bathroom in the familiar room and splashed water on his face before combing his fingers through his hair, patting down the bits that stuck out at all angles.

Locating his jeans was easy, but he gave up on a shirt within moments, more concerned with the hollow feeling in his stomach. He reconsidered his decision halfway down the hall when he heard the two voices.

"Uh, hey," Brandon said as he wandered into the kitchen. "Sorry, I fell asleep."

"Good nap?" A bright smile appeared on Vanna's face.

"I was beat after that shift. It was crazy in the ER."

"Anything interesting?" Aiden asked after finishing a mouthful of eggs.

"Will let me do a new procedure." He caught the slight frown on his girlfriend's face. "Any more, Vanna?" Brandon slid onto his usual stool, trying to ignore Aiden's smirk. The man had clearly read the silent order from Savannah.

"Yup." She served a liberal helping onto a plate and set it in front of him. "Emily and Cierra are coming home tomorrow. And my grandmothers will arrive too."

"Ah, the family descends. I'll make myself scarce." Brandon dug into the pile of food, eager to satiate his protesting stomach.

"You might enjoy being here. Well, except for all the crying." Aiden grinned, clearly thrilled about the prospect of having his wife and new baby home. "Nina makes a mean Paella."

"Dad loves her Spanish cuisine, so Abuela commandeers the kitchen every visit."

"I won't be in the way?" Brandon glanced at Aiden.

"Might make you change a diaper or two, but you don't have to disappear."

Brandon relaxed, considering himself lucky to be welcomed so warmly into her family's home. When the time came for Vanna to meet his family, he feared things wouldn't go so smoothly.

Brandon found the visiting relatives to be warm and welcoming, aside from Caroline Hamilton, who only stayed overnight before returning to Chicago. Still, it was a relief when they all left for home, followed by Aiden and Emily packing up the two kids for a summer of relaxation in the Vineyard.

Their departure was followed by an invitation to move into the penthouse. After a moment's protest, he gave in. His girlfriend assured him she'd cleared the arrangement with Aiden and Emily, so he accepted. Escaping the depressing department was like a mini-vacation.

Three weeks into his new living arrangements, Brandon had become spoiled. He could concentrate on work and avoid Dylan's constant moodiness and slovenly habits.

On the third sunny Saturday of the month, Brandon settled on a bench near the hospital, opening the lunch Savannah had delivered earlier in the day. He only had a half-hour, but the interns were encouraged to escape from the ER for their breaks as part of their mental health initiative.

An involuntary, heavy sigh broke free as Piper slumped onto the bench beside him. He hadn't seen or heard from her in weeks, which he considered a positive, given how she'd treated Savannah.

"How are you, Dr. Reynolds? That's crazy." A giggle escaped from her lips. "Doctor."

"You missed my graduation." Not that he cared. It had been easier to avoid dealing with Piper and her excessive, needless drama.

"I'm interning at a new firm. They don't permit time off unless you're practically dying." Her expression soured. "I don't get special treatment by working in a nepotistic environment."

"Still hanging onto that, huh?"

"Doesn't matter, does it? The relationship will expire soon. You only managed six months with Autumn."

*Ten, but did it matter?* Brandon scoffed but didn't bother to correct her. What was the point? "Thanks for your vote of confidence."

"Any time." She smirked. "Since she hasn't met your crazy-ass mother or your bratty sister, you're safe for now."

He narrowed his eyes. The girl seemed a touch too smug. "You've been tattling to Jeremy."

"I didn't say a word." She bestowed an innocent smile on him.

*Liar.* "Don't you dare ruin this."

"How's living in luxury?"

"How did you know?"

"Boston is a small town." The smug grin widened. "Word gets around." She inspected her claw-like nails. "Moving in with your girlfriend is newsworthy. That might come up in conversation with my dad. If he asks."

"It better not." He infused a note of warning into his voice. "Why do you hate Savannah? You went from her bestie to complete avoidance."

Piper folded her arms across her chest. "Do you know what it's like to be your sister? I finally escape nowheresville, Montana, and guess what? Even then one of my so-called friends goes stupid and drools all over my stepbrother. Worse, Savannah's sleeping with you." She shuddered. "At least my other friends never did that." She squinted. "Or did they?"

"Don't be ridiculous. Those girls were barely legal, not to mention incredibly annoying and juvenile." Brandon's lips twisted in disgust. "It's your own fault for not trusting Vanna. Or maybe it's me you don't trust. Whatever. She didn't have a clue who I was when we met." He shoved his lunch back into the bag and rose from his seat.

"Like it would have made any difference." Piper glared. "You two would have hooked up at some point."

"You owe her an apology for your behavior."

Her lips twisted into a grimace. "I'll never forgive her."

"Your choice." Time to walk away. Arguing the point was exhausting and futile. The move to Boston had changed his stepsister. Or maybe it allowed her shallow and decidedly unsavory traits to rise to the surface.

Nate fell into step beside him as he approached the sliding glass doors at the front of the hospital. "You look rather pissed off for someone living the good life."

Brandon waved a hand. "More Piper bullshit. She's keeping tabs on me and feeding select tidbits to her dad. I'm sure they get back to my mother, so that should be fun."

"Teenage girl drama." Nate nodded as they reached the locker room. A grin twitched at the corner of his mouth. "Speaking of drama, you're rarely home. Does Dr. Hamilton know you've moved into his penthouse?"

He located his lab coat and stethoscope. "Aiden prefers me to be at his place, rather than have Vanna anywhere near Dylan."

"What a shocker. He doesn't like the miscreant close to his beautiful daughter." Nate chuckled. "What are you doing on your days off? Heading to Montana?"

"Hell no. Why torture myself needlessly? I accepted an invitation to the beach house."

"Lucky bastard." Nate smacked Brandon's shoulder before heading into the lounge.

Brandon followed, smiling in anticipation of the upcoming holiday, as short as it would be. Two more days and he'd be lazing on a sandy beach.

～

"This isn't a beach house." Brandon stared as the gravel on the long driveway crunched under the car tires.

"Sure it is." She grinned as she parked beside Emily's Cayenne.

"So this is beach house, Vineyard style." He'd seen no shortage of massive homes from the moment they'd disembarked from the ferry.

"It's a shack compared to many of the homes on the Vineyard." She slid from the seat, stretching her arms skyward.

"It's practically falling down." Brandon snorted as he opened the hatch. "This summer home is nicer than our full-time house in Montana."

Savannah wrinkled her nose as she gathered the items from behind the seat.

"It is," he mumbled as he hefted their bags and closed the hatch, trailing behind Vanna onto a spacious flagstone patio. "Damn. This is sweet." He eyed the cozy arrangement of furniture around the outdoor fireplace and the kitchen setup with the large gas grill. Bright flowers overflowed two massive stone planters, transforming the space into a lush, private oasis.

"They must be sailing," Vanna said, scanning the waterfront. "*Maya's* gone."

"Who?" Brandon drew his brows together.

"The boat." A soft smile touched Vanna's lips. "Her name is *Maya*." She tapped the code into the electronic door lock, which opened with a whir and a click. "I'll show you our room."

Brandon trailed her inside, grateful for the cool interior of the house. The drive from Boston had been long and stifling hot. Savannah had opened the sunroof but remained adamant in her refusal to resort to air conditioning, insisting they, but him in particular, spent too much time in climate-controlled environments at work.

He nodded in approval as they arrived in the bedroom. The well-appointed space seemed more like a high-end bed and breakfast than a beach house. The soft neutral tones along with the fresh sea breeze wafting through the open window encouraged the tension to drain from his body.

"This was Aiden's room, though it's been updated. You should see the deck off the master." She grabbed his hand, tugging him into the hall. "That's Kellan's bedroom"—she pointed—"and there are a couple of guest suites. And this," she stepped inside the large airy room, "is Aiden and Emily's retreat."

His eyes widened at the beautiful suite, complete with walk-in closet, luxurious bathroom, and gleaming wooden floors. A bassinet sat near the inviting king-sized bed, and a changing table was positioned against one wall. He understood the couple's eagerness to spend the summer in this little slice of paradise.

He followed Vanna through the French doors onto the well-appointed deck, lifting his face to the sun. "Gorgeous."

She shielded her eyes against the flashes of light reflecting off of the waves, searching the expanse of blue. "There." She pointed. "That's *Maya*."

"How can you tell?" Brandon ducked his head, peering down her arm in the direction she'd indicated. Given the number of sailboats dotting the water, it seemed impossible to distinguish one from another. The particular boat she indicated was only a triangle-shaped spot on the horizon.

"The sails. I chose the replacement material when Aiden dry-docked her for maintenance," she said as she bounced on her toes. "Let's change and meet them at the dock."

Her excitement combined with the thought of being near the water brought a broad smile to his face.

By the time they changed and arrived at the waterfront, Aiden had secured the sailboat. He waved before removing Kellan's life jacket and lifting the boy onto the dock. He offered a hand to Emily, who had Cierra snuggled in a baby wrap slung around her body.

"Cariño." Emily leaned in to hug Vanna. She turned to Brandon, stretching to plant a kiss on his cheek. "Hijo mio. Sorry for not being here for your arrival, but Aiden can't get enough sailing."

"How do you manage with two kids?" Brandon swung Kellan onto his shoulders in response to the boy's insistent tugs at his arm.

"Easy enough for now, as it's two against two. Cierra sleeps for most of it. And it's beautiful and relaxing on the water. We stopped in a small cove for lunch and a swim."

"You'll love sailing." A sparkle appeared in Vanna's eyes. She looked at her dad. "Is the forecast good for tomorrow?"

"We'll check tonight. Let's find some shade and cold drinks." Aiden grabbed their gear from the deck and motioned toward the house.

"This place is amazing," Brandon said once they were ensconced in plush lounge chairs on the flagstone patio. "How long have you owned it?"

"It's been in the family for over fifty years. The original cabin burned down when I was a kid, so my grandparents built this house." Aiden lifted Kellan onto his knee and the boy leaned against his chest, closing his eyes. "Our own bit of heaven."

"And private." The absence of the usual cacophony of traffic, horns, and sirens prevalent in the city soothed him. The only sounds to be heard were waves lapping onto the beach, the calls of seabirds, and the soft shush of the breeze through the leaves on the trees surrounding the property. This entire home was bathed in peace.

"We love it," Emily said, a contented smile on her face. "I couldn't believe it when I first visited. It's so restful and secluded."

"Our waterfront is deeded, so we enjoy privacy on the beach. I entertained selling this place, but now we're using it several times a year."

"You can't sell." Vanna's eyes widened.

"I said the same thing." Emily laughed softly. "Our family will enjoy summers here for many years."

"We will, Em." Aiden grasped her hand, looking as content as his wife. "I'm happy you love it as much as I do."

The next morning, Savannah woke Brandon with a gentle shake. "Up, sleepyhead."

"It's vacation," he muttered, cracking an eyelid. "It's dark."

"You can nap this afternoon." She prodded him again. "Sunrise over the water is breathtaking."

He forced his eyes open in the dim room, noting she was fully dressed with her hair still damp from the shower.

She smiled and disappeared into the hallway.

By the time he'd dressed and made it downstairs, the fragrant aroma of freshly brewed coffee infused the air, accompanied by the rattle of pans on the stove and the murmur of voices.

"Morning." He slid onto a stool, smiling as Savannah set a steaming cup in front of him. He sighed after the first sip and focused on Aiden, who tossed the pan of sizzling veggies like a pro. "You're up early."

"I work out before the kids are up, otherwise it doesn't happen." Aiden motioned to the pan. "Want one?"

"Yes, please." The moment Aiden set the savory omelet in front of him, he devoured it.

Savannah added several containers and two ice packs to the cooler and snapped it shut. "Everything's ready. As soon as you're finished, we can go."

"Have fun," Aiden said and kissed his daughter on the cheek. "I'll take breakfast to Em." He picked up the tray he'd prepared and headed toward the stairs.

"He spoils her rotten."

Savannah shrugged. "Emily had a baby only a few weeks ago. She's up several times a night, so he ensures she doesn't lift a finger around the house." She slung a bag over her shoulder. "Let's go."

He followed her through the door. "We're going alone?" Brandon asked as he lugged the cooler toward the dock. The first rays of light glinted off the water, a magnificent golden glow igniting the sky as the sun peeked over the horizon. The woman was right. Sunrise over the ocean was incredible.

She wrinkled her nose before hopping onto the boat and untying lines. "Don't you trust me?"

"Do I have a choice?" He gave her a saucy grin. "I'm being kidnapped."

She rolled her eyes and tucked in the bumpers, shoving lightly against the dock. She pointed the bow toward the open water. "If you object, you'd better swim for it. We'll be out for hours." The boat picked up speed as she hoisted the sails.

"I'll take my chances. What can I do?"

"Man the helm."

Brandon admired her lithe tanned figure as she moved easily about the boat, adjusting the lines. Soon they were skimming across the waves. "Amazing idea," he said as she perched nearby. "I can't believe you're allowed to take the boat out alone."

"I'm not alone. I have my own doctor." She tipped her chin, her lips twitching. "I'm certified, so you're perfectly safe." Her hand covered his as she adjusted their course. "The weather should be fine all day."

Brandon relaxed and tucked an arm around her. The refreshing breeze negated the effects of the bright sun beating down upon them, and the water sparkled as they skimmed along the coastline. He understood her eagerness to spend the day on the water. This was heavenly.

At lunchtime, Savannah directed him into a small protected cove and dropped the anchor. "Time for a swim and lunch." She peeled off her t-shirt and unfastened her linen shorts, sliding them down her toned thighs, revealing a candy-pink bikini. She executed a smooth dive into the water, surfacing and flipping onto her back. "Are you planning to join me?"

He stripped off his own shirt and kicked off his shoes before performing a cannonball from the side of the boat, creating the largest splash possible.

Vanna laughed as he surfaced. "Elegant." She cupped her hand and flung water at him.

"You'll pay for that." He lunged after her, grabbing her ankle as she paddled away. He pulled her toward him, wrapping his hands around her slim waist. "Caught you."

"Only because I wanted you to." She bit her lip as she wound an arm around his neck, her legs twining around his waist.

He smothered a laugh as he grasped the side of the boat with one hand, capturing her bottom lip between his teeth, nipping it. Her passionate response took his breath away, and he wondered who'd done the catching.

She pulled away with a coy smile and flipped onto her back, gazing up at the cerulean sky as she floated.

Brandon sighed. This woman was irresistible, wavering between sweet and delectable, and sexy and unpredictable.

"Interested in lunch?" she asked.

"I'm starving." He hauled himself over the side of the boat and extended a hand to help her aboard. His gaze remained locked on her as she wrung the water from her long hair and patted at the droplets glistening on her golden skin.

"Here." She handed him an icy bottle from the cooler before retrieving their lunch. "You're allowed one." She lowered herself onto the deck, patting the blanket beside her.

Brandon sat and drank a slug of the icy beer. "None for you?"

"We'll share." She snagged the bottle from his fingers, taking a dainty sip. "I'm responsible for a safe sail home."

"Right, captain." He bit into half of his baguette then scooped a serving of salad onto his plate as he munched.

"My mom and dad spent summers here when they were teenagers." Savannah chewed slowly, staring over the water. "They sailed this boat."

"Sweet way to spend holidays. Mine were always spent slogging for minimum wage." He stretched his legs out, emitting a contented sigh.

"I've visited for at least two weeks every summer since I turned fifteen." She swallowed another gulp of Brandon's beer before eating a few more bites. Expressions fleeted across her face. "Do you ever wonder how your life would be if your dad hadn't left?"

"Why waste energy?" He took her hand, pressing a kiss to each finger in turn. "I'm happy with where I've ended up." Brandon studied her. "Are you?"

She graced him with a smile. "I love my life. The struggle was worthwhile."

"Same." He leaned in, pausing briefly before kissing her. "This feels like a fantastic alternate universe," he whispered against her hair, inhaling the enticing beachy scent clinging to her skin. He sank into another kiss, cupping her cheek, focusing his complete attention on the wonderful woman in his arms.

Savannah trickled her fingers down his chest, breaking their contact with a gentle smile on her lips. "Finish your lunch." She blinked and lowered her eyes. "Store up some energy."

"Tease," he said under his breath, unable to contain his grin. His eyes traveled over her as she dangled her slim legs over the bow.

At the end of the meal, he helped her stow the empty containers and fold the blanket.

Savannah scanned the calm sparkling ocean before she slid her hand into his, linking their fingers. Without a word, she tugged him toward the cabin, turning the moment they were inside.

Brandon lost himself in the dark pools of her eyes, welcoming her warm lips against his as she curled an arm around his neck, pulling him onto the small bed with her.

# CHAPTER 4

## Savannah

T HE GENTLE KISS PRESSED TO her brow made her long to be awoken this way every day. "Morning." Savannah wrapped a hand around Brandon's neck, wrinkling her nose at the damp hair at his nape and the musky smell of sweat. "Go shower."

"Time to get up." He prodded her side. "Join me," he murmured, nibbling her earlobe.

"Stop." Vanna giggled.

"Suit yourself." His finely toned muscles appeared as he peeled off the damp tank top, tossing it into the hamper on his way into the bathroom.

The urge to follow became irresistible, and moments later she slipped into the shower. His golden skin enticed her to press herself against him and taste the saltiness, dropping light kisses that raised goosebumps—not only on him, but on her. "Those morning workouts are paying off."

"You should join us," he said as he turned. His eyes widened. "Not that you need to. You look great."

Savannah poked him in the ribs. "Why interfere with male bonding time?"

"Have to ensure your dad likes me," Brandon said with a grin.

"Mission accomplished." Vanna accepted his kiss. "When do I get to meet the rest of yours?"

Brandon smoothed his hair back, brushing the water from his eyes. "Why would you want to?"

She jutted out her lip and performed a long slow blink. "Are you ashamed of me?"

"Don't be silly." He pulled her tighter against him. "My mother is crazy. She'll scare you away."

"I don't frighten that easily."

"Can we forget my family? Relax? Have fun?"

The gentle kisses he placed on each tender spot on her neck almost made her forget the discussion. *Almost.* There would be plenty of time for her to convince him later.

By the time they arrived on the patio an hour later, she felt happy and relaxed. "She almost asleep?" she asked as she peered at her baby sister nestled in Emily's arms.

Emily nodded, brushing a tender finger over Cierra's cheek. "She's been up for a couple of hours." She shifted her position in the padded wicker chair, propping her legs on the ottoman.

Brandon headed straight for the buffet-style meal set out in small stainless steel warmers. "Where does he get the energy?" His gaze traveled toward the back lawn where Aiden kicked a soccer ball with Kellan. "You'd think he'd be exhausted after rising at dawn for a morning swim followed by an intense workout."

"Topped off by a long walk on the beach with me and the kids before he whipped up breakfast." Emily laughed. "Lounging isn't his thing, even during vacation. I figured you knew that by now."

Savannah accepted a plate from Brandon. "Thank you, sweetie." She rewarded him with a kiss before he returned to select his own food.

Aiden chased an exuberant Kellan while they ate, the boy's shrieks and giggles echoing across the lawn. After half an hour, he caught the red-faced boy and tossed him over his shoulder. Aiden set his giggling son onto a lounger and offered him a glass of water. "Who's interested in a sailing trip to town?"

"Ice cream, Daddy." Kellan bounced to his feet, sloshing water down his t-shirt and shorts. His eyes widened, his lips turning downward as he tugged at the wet clothing.

Aiden ruffled the boy's hair. "It's only water, Kel."

"Ice cream?" Kellan's brow wrinkled, his eyes glistening with tears.

Savannah crouched in front of her little brother. "If we change super fast, Dad will reward both of us with ice cream," she whispered. "What do you think?"

The small boy nodded and skipped into the house without a backward glance.

"Quick thinking." Aiden sent her a grateful look.

She stretched to kiss his cheek. "You need a break too, Dad. I'll get him ready."

After helping Kellan change into a fresh outfit, she gathered their beach totes. The thought of several hours on the water thrilled her. She would take advantage of every moment of sunshine and ocean.

"Can I sail *Maya*?" Savannah asked her dad as everyone boarded and stowed their gear.

"Why don't you and Brandon crew?"

"Deal." Savannah took over the captain duties, giving direction to Brandon. Soon they were skimming over the waves. "You're a natural."

"It's strangely addictive." He wrapped an arm around her waist. "And, you're an excellent teacher."

"Take us in." Savannah pointed to an empty slip as they approached the harbor, helping him guide the boat alongside the dock.

Kellan jumped to his feet to flip the bumpers over the side.

"Someone else is excited to learn to sail," Brandon said.

A huge grin spread across Aiden's face as his son helped with the process, but a crew hoisting a sailboat from the water a short distance away caught his attention. "No way." He shielded his eyes and squinted. "Hal's selling?" He scooped up Kellan and strode toward the man operating the hoist.

"Don't mind me," Emily muttered as she rose from the bench, cuddling Cierra in a baby wrap. "Men and their toys."

Brandon chuckled as he assisted Emily to the dock. "For me, it's sports cars."

"Well, he's into those too." Emily shook her head. "You've seen the garage."

"He can afford to be," Brandon said under his breath.

Savannah frowned at her boyfriend before heading toward her dad who was now in deep conversation with an older white-haired man with ruddy cheeks.

One summer, Aiden had pointed out the boat, sharing the story of Hal and Jeannette who owned it, and how he'd learned to sail. The wonderful stories from her dad's childhood had contributed to Savannah's own growing passion for boats and life on the water. As had the tales of the amazing people who'd filled a void in his life, even if temporarily.

"I hadn't heard," Aiden said in a sad voice. He rubbed a hand through his hair. "How's Jeannette holding up?"

"She's getting by, but the stress is showing," the older man said. "It's terrible. They're buried in medical bills and desperate to sell. Some guy from New York sniffed around and threw them a low-ball offer. He heard about their predicament from the local gossip and tried to take advantage. They refused it on my advice, but Jeannette won't hold out long. I'd buy this beauty myself, but Tilly would slaughter me."

Aiden rubbed his jaw. "What's the valuation, Sam? Jeanette's list price seems low."

"The boat's mint, so …" The man wrote a figure on his clipboard and tilted it toward Aiden. "That's what Jeanette should sell for. This beauty is less than ten years old and well-maintained. You know how Hal babies his boats."

"Hmmm. Great lines … sails like a dream …" Aiden set a squirming Kellan onto his feet. "Wrap 'er up, Sam. Call Jeanette and prepare the bill of sale for," he said, pointing to the clipboard, "that number. I'll transfer the funds this afternoon." He held out a hand.

Sam grinned as he shook it. "You're a good man for offering market. You won't be sorry, Aiden."

"Hal taught me to sail, and who will ever forget Jeannette and her fabulous crab rolls."

Both men nodded and smiled.

"My family will love this boat. With the kids, we need more space."

Savannah sneaked a look at Brandon.

"Did he just buy a boat?" Brandon whispered. "Without even going aboard?"

"Yup," Savannah said. "But he's sailed with Hal many times. And he trusts Sam." She perked up as bits of the conversation between Sam and Aiden drifted down the dock.

"… put the word out on yours." Sam pivoted toward where the smaller boat bobbed in its slip. "I'll run an appraisal while you're in town."

"No." Savannah dashed across the rough planks. "You can't sell *Maya*." Tears sprang to her eyes. It seemed impossible to have happy visits to the Vineyard without *Maya* moored in front of their house. "Please, Daddy. Don't do it."

"I can't sail two boats." Aiden slung an arm around her shoulders. "Does it mean that much to you?"

She nodded, the lump in her throat choking off the words.

"How much do you have on you?"

Savannah frowned, but she dug into the front pocket of her shorts, coming up with a single crumpled bill. "Five dollars?"

"I accept."

Her eyes widened.

"You just bought yourself a boat." Her dad kissed her temple. "We'll draw up the papers when we get back to the house. Ready for ice cream?"

Brandon caught her hand as they strolled down the street toward the waterfront. "Unbelievable. It's not even your birthday."

"I bought *Maya*." She nibbled at her ice cream.

"For five bucks? That's a gift." He leaned in and stole a bite from her scoop of caramel swirl. "Why is the sailboat so important? You almost cried."

"Memories." She leaned on the railing overlooking the beach, closing her eyes and absorbing the calls of the gulls and salty breeze. "I'd lost both of my parents and left my friends to move to the opposite end of the country with a father I barely knew."

Brandon slid an arm around her and squeezed.

Vanna rested against his chest. "Aiden had complete responsibility for a confused, distraught teenager dropped onto him. Something happened between him and Emily, and we were struggling to attain balance. Being on the water eased the pain." She tipped her chin, soaking up the warm rays of the sun, recalling the amazing summer she'd spent getting to know her dad. Those sunny days on the water had revealed an entirely new side to the young and seemingly privileged doctor. "I understand why my parents fell in love here. On that boat. It's magical."

Brandon rubbed her arm.

"It's dumb to be emotionally attached, right? I love *Maya* but didn't know how much until that moment. A stranger having her is unthinkable."

"I wish I had sweet memories of my parents."

"I'm incredibly lucky, even though I've experienced the pain of losing parents and the uncertainty of what would happen next. Without Aiden, I might be in foster care. He wasn't obligated to rearrange his entire life and sacrifice his career in Chicago, but he did."

"Why does that not surprise me?" He wrapped her in a warm embrace. "It makes me sad for Mia. She never knew our father, has a crappy mother, and a series of disinterested ex-stepfathers." A smile twitched his lips. "I miss that little pain in the ass."

"She has a great brother." Savannah patted his cheek. "I'd love to meet her."

"Ha. We're back to that again?"

Savannah blinked, tipping her head a touch. "We've been dating for months." Another slow blink. *I have him.* "Isn't it time I met the important people in your life?"

He puffed out a stream of air. "Carol and Jeremy aren't like Aiden and Emily, or even Tiffany and Stefan." He rubbed the back of his neck. "You might regret it."

"I'd love to meet your friends. See where you grew up. Meet that little pain in the ass you miss so much."

"Meeting my family means that much?"

She graced him with her sweetest smile.

His answering laugh was deep and low. "I give. We'll visit Montana on my next days off. I'll see who'll be in town, and you can meet the guys."

"Perfect. I'll pay for the flights." She linked their fingers. "Let's sail my boat home."

# CHAPTER 5

## Brandon

SAVANNAH'S GRIP ON HIS FINGERS tightened as they leveled off at cruising altitude.

"Why the nerves?" Brandon asked. "You've flown a million times."

"What if they hate me?" Her eyes widened. "What if Piper's been telling them horrible things?"

Sadly, Piper hadn't softened on her stance one bit, leaving Savannah hurt and saddened by his stepsister's attitude. He couldn't imagine how anyone wouldn't love this sweet, kind woman. "It's impossible for them to hate you. You're amazing."

"You have to say that, or I'll cut you off." A tiny smirk appeared. She sighed as the seatbelt light went out, and the pilot announced they could now move around the cabin. "Hold that thought," she said, pressing a fingertip against his lips, "while I visit the ladies'."

She rose from the roomy seat and moved toward the front. Those long shapely legs peeking out from under the skirt of her sundress along with the gentle sway of her hips kept Brandon riveted to her every step.

As she disappeared into the closet-sized bathroom, he swirled the ice in his drink, hoping what he'd said about his family wouldn't prove to be a complete lie. Maybe they'd make an effort to like his girlfriend and make her feel welcome. Put their pettiness aside and see how important Savannah was to him. *Right. I'm screwed.*

"Can I offer you a refill?" the flight attendant asked.

"Please."

The woman smiled and retreated, returning moments later with a fresh rum and coke. She handed him his drink along with an extra napkin and returned to the galley, glancing over her shoulder.

Brandon swallowed a large gulp and set his glass on the tray, turning the napkin to read the words written in blue pen. *Business or pleasure?* A phone number and the name *Geneva* had been added in neat script.

He shoved the note into his pocket as Savannah exited the cubicle and swayed toward their first-class seats.

She motioned to the cup as she slipped into her spot. "You didn't order me another?"

"Sorry. What would you like?" He motioned at the flight attendant.

"I'd love what you're having, but I'll settle for a soda."

"What can I get you, sir?" the woman asked. "Something for your little sister?"

A saccharine smile appeared on Savannah's face. "A Coke, please," she said as she entwined her fingers with Brandon's, bringing his hand to rest on her well-toned thigh. "Sister. You wish, honey," she muttered under her breath as the flight attendant returned to the galley.

"Easy, tiger." Brandon squeezed her hand. "I'm sure she didn't mean anything by it."

Savannah scowled. "The woman practically crawled into your lap. It's disgusting." She shot him a look. "I recognize those moves. I'm surprised she didn't slip you her number while I was in the bathroom."

Brandon gulped a swig of rum and Coke, avoiding her gaze.

"Wait." She scoffed. "She did." The sweet smile reappeared as the flight attendant served Vanna's drink.

Brandon bit his lip. He'd never considered that his girlfriend would nail it down so quickly, accurately reading the other woman's body language in mere seconds.

She tugged her hand free. "Why the guilty look? Because her number is in your pocket?" Vanna's chin tipped down as she shook her head. "Ohhh, Brandon."

He drew in a breath, gripping the arm of the seat. *Complete calm required, with a side of immediate confession.* "I never planned to call, but I didn't want to create a scene. You're already on edge about my family." He retrieved the napkin and held it out, not daring to even look her way. The momentary lack of judgment might end them, right here and now, no matter how pure his intentions. He couldn't bear to see her anger or pain.

Savannah's brows drew together as she read the note. "Wow. Does that cheesy crap actually work?" She scoffed, sprinkling shredded bits of filmy paper into his empty cup before waggling it in the air.

Brandon kept his head down and avoided looking at either woman as the flight attendant appeared to retrieve the cup.

"Can I get you another, miss?"

"No, thank you. You've done more than enough." Savannah's voice sounded bright and cheery. "You'd probably spit in it," she muttered as the woman retreated.

He shot her a sideways look before he focused on his hands, fighting the smile. "A touch passive-aggressive, don't you think?"

"Did you expect me to attack with claws out and provide today's in-flight entertainment? Make mister air marshall earn his salary by forcing a landing so they could eject us from the fight? Why bother with a scene? Geneva got the point."

He cleared his throat, wishing he could order a double, but he didn't dare. The flight attendant might just spit in his drink too.

The soft pressure of Vanna's palm against his face forced him to turn his head. "Dating a guy like you means accepting that other women will show interest," she said in a calm, low voice. "They'll flirt, give their numbers, or make inappropriate offers, even when you're unavailable."

"A guy like me?" Brandon quirked his brow.

Savannah's piercing gaze was accompanied by the slightest narrowing of her eyes. "What I won't accept, *Brandon,* is you hiding it. You think I haven't seen this play before?"

He clenched his jaw.

"Women flirt with my dad, assuming I'm too naive to realize they're hitting on him." She spun a piece of her honey-blonde hair around her fingertip. "I appreciate the appeal of a good-looking man, but slipping a guy your number while pretending to mistake his girlfriend for the little sister is insulting. It's the equivalent of those guys who assume a woman should fall to her knees in gratitude when they serve up gross over-rehearsed pickup lines."

"I'm sorry. Putting it in my pocket was the wrong choice. I promise it won't happen again." He studied her. "Women try to pick up your dad in front of you?"

"Regularly. It's revolting and quite disturbing, especially since he always wears his wedding ring." She tipped back the last swallow of her drink. "Why do women insist on preying on men who are clearly in a relationship? And why don't guys grow a pair and ask a girl out? Why don't they talk to us like people instead of a set of boobs?" She peered at him from the corner of her eye. "Sorry. I'm ranting."

That viewpoint place a new perspective on their first night together. "Where does that put us on the scale? Things just … happened."

A warm, genuine smile appeared. "You think I'd have gone home with just anyone? A girl needs standards."

"Nobody could accuse you of having low standards."

Her brows shot upward. "Seriously? Your bitchy stepsister suggested exactly that. And people judge. Dylan makes creepy little comments, implying I'm a dirty whore. And look how he treated Rochelle. Now she's labeled as a trashy little tramp."

"I'll deal with him." He reached for her hand. "Are we good? I know the phone number thing was stupid."

She nodded. "I understand why you did it, so we'll let it go." A determined expression appeared as she leaned in close. "Never do that again."

⁓

"Damn." Brandon whistled as he viewed the sleek red Mustang convertible waiting for them in the airport parking lot. "How did we score that?"

A huge grin spread across Savannah's face. "I asked the travel agent to book something fun."

He tossed the keys lightly into the air before hitting the unlock button on the remote. "Sometimes I love that you're only eighteen." He'd known she'd assigned him as the driver on their rental car, but not that she'd booked them a premium ride.

"Enjoy it while you can." She smirked.

After stowing their bags he opened Savannah's door, allowing her to settle into the leather seat before sliding behind the wheel. The car purred to life, and he retracted the roof, throwing a glance at Vanna as he gunned the engine, peeling out of the lot.

"Easy, tiger." She winked. "Don't want a speeding ticket five seconds into the trip."

"Now I know why you refused Jeremy's offer to pick us up."

Savannah rested a hand on the back of his neck, running her fingertips through his hair. "I didn't want to be beholden or dependent for transportation." She gazed at him steadily. "Maybe it's silly."

"Nope. That's good thinking." Brandon captured her hand, kissing the back before resting their entwined fingers on his thigh. "It's best we have a planned escape. I don't want you overwhelmed." He never forgot that Vanna attended therapy. Now he'd become aware of her anxiety issues, he tried to spare her undue stress.

"I'm not made of glass." She accompanied the squeeze to his fingers with a warm smile. "But thank you for understanding." Vanna leaned back, draping an arm over the side of the car. She twirled her wrist and made wave patterns with her hand. "I love highway driving in convertibles. Something about it gives me a sense of freedom." She turned her head, tendrils of her long blonde hair dancing around her face in the wash of air sweeping over the top of the car.

To Brandon, she'd never looked more beautiful. This felt like how life should be but had rarely been. Vanna had introduced him to an entirely new world, so far from his current reality, there were days when he feared he'd awaken to find nothing but remnants of a wonderful dream. He focused on the pitted pavement, content with the silence between them.

But the magic of the open road had to end. The closer they drew to his home, the tenser he became, the inevitable moment of truth drawing nearer. He pulled onto his street, tightening his grip on the steering wheel, anticipating her reaction. The home he'd grown up in was a modest bungalow in a middle-class area, bordering on shabby without the slightest hint of chic. He drew in a long breath as he parked on the street in front of the house. "I apologize in advance for anything my mother may say or do to offend you. And I'm sorry, this place isn't much."

"I'm here because of you, not your family." Savannah dropped her chin as the corners of her mouth tugged downward. "I can only imagine how this visit will play out."

"I have no idea, but you wanted to meet my friends and family, so it's your own fault."

She turned, taking both of his hands. "Whatever happens, we can't let anyone get in between us." Her eyes widened. "Deal?"

"Deal." He rested his forehead against hers. There were so many things he wanted to say, but it seemed the wrong time and place. "Let's get it over with." He drew back, giving her an encouraging smile before he hopped out to open her door.

Savannah accepted his hand, swinging her legs out and rising from the low-slung convertible with remarkable grace before smoothing her light sundress. Her gold sandals added a splash of color, as did the Kate Spade bag hung over her shoulder.

Her clothing emphasized that she wasn't a child as implied by Jeremy, and she looked every bit the cherished daughter of a well-to-do doctor who'd had every advantage in life, even if the surface appearance was misleading.

He popped open the trunk, sighing as he retrieved her Louis Vuitton bag. *Damn, he'd hear about this.*

"Do I look okay?" She raked her fingers through her curls, brushing them over her shoulder.

His inspected her from head to toe, lingering for a moment on her slim, toned, and tanned legs. "You're beautiful." He dug his nails into his palm as the screen door banged and slung his bag over his shoulder before picking up her suitcase, motioning for her to precede him.

"We thought you'd lost your way." His mother's eyes narrowed before an icy scowl appeared. "You must be the girlfriend."

"Savannah." She smiled and extended her hand. "Nice to meet you."

Carol blinked and focused on the bag in Brandon's hand, her lip curling. "Let's go inside."

Savannah tipped her chin down, hiding the glimmer of tears with a silky curtain of hair, and Brandon clenched his fist. *Disaster loomed.*

"You made it." Jeremy appeared in the hallway. "You must be Savannah." The man grasped her hands and placed a kiss on her cheek. "I'm Jeremy."

Vanna greeted the man with a shaky smile. "Hello," she said in a barely audible voice.

"Let me take that." Jeremy claimed Vanna's bag. "I'll show you to your room."

Brandon watched as Savannah trailed down the hallway after his stepfather.

"Don't just stand there." His mother arched a brow. "You know where your room is." She pointed toward the basement door. "Don't even consider any of that nonsense in my house."

"Whatever," he muttered, yanking open the door and trudging downstairs. He loved the privacy the basement offered, but right now he wished he could be upstairs protecting Savannah. This promised to be an interminable four days. In the end, he might be minus one girlfriend.

~

During dinner, Jeremy tried his best to make conversation, asking Savannah questions about school and her family.

Carol pushed her food around her plate, throwing the occasional dark look at his girlfriend. "So." She sipped her wine. "You met my son in a club?"

Brandon gritted his teeth.

"That's right." Savannah straightened, meeting his mother's gaze without flinching.

"You're eighteen. That's a bit young to be hanging out in bars. Our Piper isn't allowed to visit clubs."

Brandon smothered a snort. The woman rarely had time for her own children, let alone her stepdaughter. "And you never do anything wrong."

Jeremy shoveled in his last few bites of potato, his fork clattering against his plate as he set it down. "I'm dying for some Rocky Road. Brandon, would you mind running to the store?"

"No problem." He kept his voice even and controlled, ignoring his mother's glower.

"Let me grab my purse." Savannah pushed away from the table and hurried down the hallway.

As he dashed downstairs to retrieve his wallet, the Carol's caustic tones cut through the air. Brandon couldn't summon even an ounce of pity for his stepfather, who was surely her intended victim.

Once they were in the car, Vanna tipped her head back, staring at the houses flashing by, her hands clutched in her lap.

"Vanna."

She shook her head, a small sniffle escaping. "Piper told them everything." Her eyes shimmered. "About how we met. About my fake ID. Your mother hates me."

Brandon pulled onto the gravel shoulder. "Hey." He held her chin in a gentle grasp, turning her head toward him, saddened by her shiny red-rimmed eyes. "Ignore her, please? Once she gets to know you, it'll be fine."

"Big fat liar." She smothered a small laugh. "But thanks for trying to make me feel better about that complete disaster. I wish I could cuddle with you tonight. That would be some consolation."

"Wait about half an hour after bedtime, then sneak downstairs. Carol's never out of be before eight, so you can be back in the traitor's room before she even realizes you were gone."

"If she catches us, she'll be livid. Besides," she said, smirking, "I bet she padlocks my door and strings trip wires down the hall with little bells on them to keep me from taking advantage of her precious son."

"Well, she couldn't be any ruder, so I'm willing to chance it." A wicked grin quirked his lips. "If you don't come to me, I'll sneak into your room. The basement has more privacy." He wiggled his brows.

"You wouldn't."

"Don't test me." Brandon leaned in, capturing her mouth in a deep kiss. "My room by eleven, sweetheart, or I raid yours," he said against her lips before kissing her again.

A genuine smile appeared for the first time in hours, lighting up her entire face. "What, are we twelve?"

"Nope, I'm *allllll* grown up," he said. "So are you. Don't let her make you feel bad. She's testing you." He winked. "The guys will be much easier to take."

"I sure hope so, or I might run away to visit my friends. At least they like me."

Brandon put the car in gear and pulled onto the roadway. "My friends will love you. Don't you worry, sweetheart." Even as he said it, he hoped it was true.

"Go back to sleep," Brandon murmured as Savannah lifted her head yet again and squinted at the clock. "She won't be up for another four hours."

"I hate to give your mother more ammunition." She rolled toward him. "Tell me what to do."

Brandon brushed a stray wisp of hair back from her face with his fingertips. Already he regretted the trip and how his mother's coldness tormented Savannah. The poor girl never had a chance, given that his mother lacked even a sliver of warmth or speck of compassion. The woman had continued on her quest to drive his girlfriend away until last night's bedtime.

"It's great you've tried, but it's an impossible feat to earn anything even resembling approval." He moved closer, bringing her head to rest on his chest. "Remember our deal. Nobody gets between us."

"Does she treat all your girlfriends this way?"

"I never bring girls home."

"That must be difficult. Dad has met every single one of my boyfriends, and he's always nice to them, which is saying something. Most of them have turned out to be complete assholes."

"I'm sorry." He tipped her chin. "I'll try not to be one of those guys."

She nodded and closed her eyes, burrowing against him.

The next time Brandon dragged his eyes open, light streamed in through his window. He bolted upright, staring at the clock. *Nine.* "Vanna." He rubbed her back. "Time to get up, sleepyhead."

"Mmmm, I'm so … wait. What time is it?" Her eyes widened as she spotted the time. "We slept through the alarm?"

"Don't worry. I'll scout out the situation. Then you can sneak back to your room while I create a distraction." He allowed a grin to surface. This small act of rebellion against his mother was long overdue.

"If she catches me, you're in big trouble, mister." She wagged her finger, but a tiny smile shone through.

He tiptoed through the basement and up the stairs, opening the door a crack. All seemed quiet, so he beckoned to Vanna, kissing her lightly before motioning her into the hall.

Brandon crept back to his room to have a quick shower and pack a bag for the beach. He ruffled his sister's hair as he arrived in the kitchen twenty minutes later. "Hey, Munchkin. We missed you last night."

"I had to work." She untucked a long slim leg from beneath her and rose, wrapping equally long arms around her brother. "I'm free today."

He hugged her before taking hold of her shoulders and studying her face. His sister had grown from child to girl to young woman during the years he'd been away at university. His short and sporadic visits meant he'd missed much of it. "Where are Carol and Jeremy?"

"Out, I guess."

He nodded, grateful he didn't have to fight with his mother over spending the day with his friends. Or listen to any further criticism of his girlfriend. "I promised to meet the guys. We're having a cookout at the park so they can meet Savannah."

"Can I come?" A hopeful smile lit her face.

Vanna appeared in the doorway looking lovely in a soft shirt and light linen shorts, her hair still damp from the shower. She nodded, clearly having heard the question.

Mia's eyes widened, but she grinned as Brandon made the introductions.

"Grab a swimsuit and pack a sweater. It'll get chilly later."

"Five minutes." Mia bounced toward her room.

"Thank you," he whispered, "for being okay about including my sister."

"She's cute. I'd like to get to know her." Savannah lowered her voice. "If you believe Piper, Mia's a little troll, but I'd better form an unbiased opinion."

"She's incredibly immature, but kind of sweet. I think you'll get along."

"Mia's a teenager. I wasn't mature at that age either, and I suspect you weren't either." She poked her index finger into his belly. "Admit it, you love your sister."

"You caught me." His grin faded. "She's had it rough, not having a dad, putting up with my mother's boyfriends, and you'll see how our mother is with her. Speaking of Carol … if we grab our things, we can disappear before she comes home." He nudged her toward the hallway.

Within a few minutes, they both reappeared, toting small packs and they headed to the car.

"A convertible." Mia clambered into the back seat. "Put the top down."

"Seatbelt, munchkin." Brandon lowered the roof while the girl buckled in. "We'll stop for our contributions to the picnic. And we'll pick up breakfast and visit the liquor store."

"Will you buy me something?" Savannah's brows went up.

"Of course." He winked. With a glance over his shoulder, he said, "You keep your lips zipped, munchkin. If you say anything to Carol …" He slashed a finger across his neck.

Mia mock saluted, a sassy grin crossing her face.

"Fill me in on everyone who'll be there," Savannah said.

"Rory is my best friend, and there's Jayce, who you talked to on the phone. And Noah, he's the jock of the group. Liam said he'd come after work." He noted her intense frown. "Too much testosterone?"

"It's fine. I'm looking forward to meeting your friends."

They made their stops, picking up soda for Mia along with snacks for the picnic, followed by a quick visit to the local deli for breakfast sandwiches and coffee. While Mia and Savannah ate, Brandon ran into the liquor store, fulfilling the list of drinks.

"Thanks." He scooped the full bag from the counter and exited. The sight of Mia and Savannah perched on the trunk of the car, chatting while Savannah braided his sister's hair made him smile, as did the sound of joyful laughter carrying across the lot.

"Don't scratch the paint," he said in a light tone, setting the bags on the ground. He lifted Mia off the shiny red car before placing his hands on Vanna's hips.

A cheeky grin appeared. "We won't hurt the precious paint job."

Mia giggled. "Guys always get so uptight about their sports cars. You should have heard him when he lived here. Mom used to make him pick me up from soccer practice. 'Mia, pick up your gum wrappers.'" Her voice rose several octaves into a high-pitched falsetto. "'Mia, don't slam the door. Mia, watch the paint.'"

He scooped up the girl, tickling her before he deposited the giggling teenager in the back seat. "Be good, or I'll make you walk home. And you," he said, turning to Vanna, "teaching her bad habits." He wrapped an arm around her waist and swung her to her feet, his pulse increasing as her sweet warm breath caressed his cheek.

"So?" Her eyes sparkled. "What are you planning to do about it?"

"You'll find out," he said under his breath as he waggled his brows. Ideas on how he'd repay her insolence tumbled through his mind. Not that she would complain …

"I'd better behave," she said as she strutted to the passenger door, her hips undulating in a seductive sway.

He reclaimed the bags, taking several deep breaths to calm his pounding heart. After stowing his purchases in the trunk, he slid behind the wheel. If they were alone, he would capture those luscious, sweet lips and lose himself in those feelings that never failed to surface every time he held the woman in his arms.

The coy look sent his way told him she read exactly where his mind had wandered. She wrapped a stray strand of wavy hair around her finger, crossing her smooth tanned legs. "What are you waiting for?"

Rising eyebrows accompanied his panicked look toward the back seat.

"Are we meeting everyone at the park?" Her smile widened as she arched a brow.

"Right," he muttered as the engine roared to life. "The park."

By the time they reached the beach, the guys were already setting up at a premium picnic site. His heart sank at the sight of the lithe figure with her dark hair upswept in a ponytail.

Rory appeared the moment Vanna stepped from the car. "Ahh, none of that." He waved aside Vanna's hand and wrapped her in a tight embrace. "This guy wouldn't shut up about you on his last visit."

"Oh?"

Brandon covertly checked out Autumn's reaction. From the way her eyes narrowed, he guessed she was calculating the age difference.

Rory looped an arm around Vanna's waist and lead her away. "I'll do the introductions."

~

"Damn." Jayce's gaze kept wandering to Savannah as he helped Brandon unload their purchases from the trunk. "That picture didn't do the girl justice. Better watch out or someone might steal her away."

"Over my dead body," Brandon muttered. "Sure, she's gorgeous, but she's more than that." He focused on his girlfriend's animated conversation with Mia and Rory, and the lukewarm greeting from Autumn and her younger brother, Nick.

His friend snickered. "Someone's in looooove."

"Shut up, idiot." Brandon shoved him.

Noah joined them. "We should play touch football. You've been slacking off and getting all pudgy hiding in the hospital." He jabbed at Brandon's belly before he looked toward Savannah. "Never pictured you dating a high maintenance princess. Bets that she sits on the sidelines so she doesn't risk breaking a nail."

"She's not a prin—"

"Ha!" Noah snorted and crossed his arms, eyeing Vanna from head to toe. "Keep telling yourself that, dude."

Brandon observed his girlfriend with a fresh perspective. The long blonde waves cascading over her back. The impeccably manicured nails. The perfectly arched brows and flawless, even if understated, makeup. The clothes that *might* qualify as beach-casual, but fit her shapely curves to perfection. The sparkling heart pendant surrounded by glittering diamonds. Everything about Savannah screamed privilege and expensive taste.

"Fortunately, you'll be making buckets of money, Dr. Reynolds." Noah snickered. "Have fun keeping that one satisfied." He loped off to gather everyone for the game.

"She's *not* a princess," he muttered.

"Ignore him." Jayce clapped him on the back, pushing him towards the group.

"I've never played, but I'll try," Savannah said to Noah as they congregated on the field. She twined her hair into a loose braid as she listened intently to the explanation of the rules.

"Should I go over them again?" Noah asked. "It's not hard, but if you're not into sports, it can be confusing."

Vanna sent an uncertain glance toward Brandon. "No, let's play. I'll pick it up."

"Suit yourself, honey. You're on Brandon's team." Noah turned toward the field, missing the looks passing between Jayce and Rory, and the fleeting expression of disappointment that crossed Savannah's face.

Brandon started after Noah, ready to call him out, but Vanna caught his hand.

"Leave it." She shook her head. "Don't make it worse."

"Vanna …"

"It's fine," she whispered, wrapping an arm around his neck and stretching to plant a kiss on his lips.

"Quit making out and get your ass on the field." Noah's voice cut into their pleasant distraction.

Brandon chuckled at the determined look on his girlfriend's face. "Ready to kick his butt?"

"Hell, yes."

Within a few minutes of play, Savannah had clearly sorted out the rules and dove into the game. Even when she displayed a certain ineptitude in passing or catching the ball, she laughed it off, admitting that organized sports weren't her forte.

By the end of two hours of rough play, Noah still regarded her with a touch of suspicion, but even this seemed tempered with grudging admiration.

"I need a swim." Savannah peeled off her top and shorts, revealing her sky-blue bikini. Without hesitation, she waded in and dove neatly into the water a few feet from shore before taking up a strong and steady front crawl.

Brandon discarded his shirt and shoes, enjoying the cool water as he swam toward the diving platform. He arrived only moments behind and flopped onto the wooden planks beside her. "You're fast."

"I may be a failure at football, but I can swim." A contented smile appeared as she stretched out her legs. "Did I redeem myself?"

"You were amazing."

Mia heaved herself onto the platform, shaking the water from her hair, the droplets spraying over Brandon.

"Monkey." He cupped a hand, scooping a handful of cool lake water to splash his sister.

"Brandon." She ducked behind Savannah, tucking her long legs up.

The next to arrive was Rory. "Ahh, I needed that. I have orders to inform you they're firing up the barbecue."

"That means we have to head back?" Savannah sighed.

Brandon rose, extending a hand to pull her to her feet. "Sorry, but I'm starving."

Savannah snickered. "Tell me something new."

Once they arrived at the shore, Savannah slipped on a beach cover-up and helped organize the food on the picnic table while Brandon distributed drinks.

Nick appeared at his side. "Can I have a soda?"

"Sure." Brandon scooped a can out of the ice. "Good game today."

"Yeah, I suppose." Nick slumped onto the bench as he cracked the tab.

"What's up, bud?" Brandon sat beside him. "Girl trouble?"

"You could say that." His gaze wandered to his big sister who sat at one of the picnic tables slicing buns for the hamburgers sizzling on the grill. "When are you moving home? I miss you."

"I miss you too, but Boston is home now." Brandon squeezed the boy's shoulder.

"Because of her?" A note of bitterness crept into the boy's voice as he motioned toward Savannah.

"My medical residency is in Boston."

"You can be a doctor anywhere." Nick tilted his head. "Is she the marrying kind?"

"What?" A frown creased his brow. "Where'd you get that from?"

The boy shrugged. "Are you marrying her?"

"We've only been dating a few months."

"You could still marry Autumn."

"Sorry, bud, but no."

"Why not? She's great."

"No question that's true, but I'm not ready to get married."

"When you are, choose Autumn." The boy jumped to his feet and scuttled away.

∽

"Can I get you another?" Brandon motioned to Savannah's empty bottle.

"Please." Vanna accepted his kiss, caressing his cheek with her fingertips.

He skirted around the flickering campfire and headed to the cooler.

"She's lovely," Autumn said from behind him as he retrieved two cold bottles from the ice. "Everyone seems to be enamored. A Harvard girl."

He straightened, uncapping the drinks as he followed Autumn's gaze. "She's planning on law school."

"Smart, beautiful … and charming the pants off your friends and your little sister." She waved away the bottle Brandon offered. "How old is she?"

"Old enough." He scoffed at the look coming his way. "Why even ask? You already know."

"I'd hoped Jayce was kidding. Eighteen is awfully young." Autumn perched on the edge of the picnic table, emitting a deep sigh. "She doesn't know we dated, does she?"

"It's been over four years, Autumn." Brandon shrugged. "Ancient history."

"Still, she should know. If someone tells her before you do, it could create issues." She stretched. "I should head home. Nick needs to go to bed. Do you want me to drive Mia? This party could go on for hours."

"Are you sure?" He tilted his head. "You don't want to stay? I could run them both home and come back."

Autumn shook her head and dropped her chin. "I'm happy for you, but I've had enough for tonight. And you should take a break from drinking before you drive that fancy rental car."

"I don't take chances like I used to. Part of growing up and becoming serious about my career. And I won't get behind the wheel if I'm over the limit. I've seen the consequences of that stupidity in the ER. Besides, if the accident didn't kill me, Vanna's dad would."

"You've met her family? This must be serious."

"What, the rumor mill didn't fill you in?" He watched her face, noting the tiny twitch that gave her away. "Ahh, you do know."

"Maybe it's none of my business, but—"

"Damn right, it's not. I'm so glad to be out of this shit hole town. Nobody ever minds their own business. I like her. She's a nice girl. End of story."

"Sorry," she whispered. "I'd just hate to see you throw it all away."

"I'm not."

She held her hands up, palms facing him. "Let me take the kids home. Stay and enjoy the party."

"Hey. Is everything okay at home?" His mind traveled to the odd behavior from her younger brother. "How's Nick handling things?"

"He misses you. It's tough to be a fatherless teenager."

Brandon contemplated the boy who sat to the side of the fire pit, digging at the dirt with a stick. "Have him call me if he ever wants to talk."

"Don't worry about us, Brandon. You're not responsible for Nick." She stepped forward and kissed his cheek. "I'll get Mia home safe."

⌒

It was two a.m. before the group extinguished the flames of their fire and said goodnight.

"That went well." Brandon leaned back, enjoying the cool evening air washing over the convertible as he negotiated the dark road. "You charmed my friends."

"Mmm." She rolled her head toward him, blinking her sleepy eyes. "Autumn seemed nice."

"Mmmhmm, she is."

"Anything you want to share?"

He sighed. "Who ratted?"

"I read the signs. She kept giving me those looks. And she avoided me. She didn't seem pleased to learn you're dating a teenager."

He cursed Jayce for the continuous cradle robbing jokes. It hit too close to be funny.

"I like your friends, but to them, I'm the fun chick to play around with until you come to your senses and find a mature woman." She tapped her pursed lips. "Or am I the high maintenance princess?"

"They don't think that, Savannah."

"Right. I misheard Noah's comment?" She scoffed. "Nick hates me, but he's team Autumn."

"I volunteered at the youth center, so I spent time with him. Taught him to throw a baseball, that kind of stuff." Brandon drummed on the wheel with his fingertips. "Nick was three when his dad died in an industrial accident. Their mom puts in a ton of overtime to keep the lights on, and I don't think he has anyone who takes an interest now I'm gone. The teenage years are tough for a boy with no father in the house." A fact he knew all too well.

"Maybe you were right about this visit. The only person who even remotely likes me is Mia."

"You're wrong. Anyway, it's irrelevant what they think. We agreed not to label this. I'm a resident. You're an undergrad. Can't we just have a relationship without putting all these expectations on it?"

But still, the words *marrying kind* rattled around his brain. Where the boy had heard those words, he didn't know. Brandon often wished he'd met Savannah five years into the future when he was ready to commit, not when he poured all of his time and energy into residency. "Let it be, and grow, and …."

"I'll stop." Vanna wrapped her arms around herself and closed her eyes. "I drank too much. It makes me overly emotional."

Brandon focused on the road, hoping he hadn't given the impression she was crowding him or becoming one of those dreaded needy, clingy girls. She'd been a champ, striving to fit in with his friends and being incredible with Mia.

He pulled up to the curb outside his house. "Savannah?" he whispered. "Are you awake?"

She blinked and nodded, undoing the clasp of her seatbelt as Brandon raised the convertible's top.

He slid from his seat, circling around to help her from the car. "Everything's fine in the trunk until tomorrow." He scooped her up, cradling her against his chest as he carried her into the house.

He set her on her feet and she turned toward Piper's room, but he caught her hand, pulling her toward him. He pressed a finger to her lips then lead her downstairs to his room.

As he cupped her face, he stared into her eyes. "You're not just entertainment, sweetheart," he said softly. "I wouldn't have allowed you to meet my friends and family if this meant nothing." He rested his forehead against hers, letting out a soft breath as she flattened her palms against his chest.

She ran them upwards and curled one hand around his neck to play with the hair at the nape of his neck. "Am I pushing too hard?"

"No. You fit with me, with my life as it is now. I love these guys, but they don't understand how things have changed. How I've changed."

As their gazes locked, Brandon's breath caught in his chest, a deep sense of longing overtaking him. He'd never felt like this about anyone. The overwhelming tide of emotions threatened to pull him under, to crush him with the intensity. Yet she was so young. He knew he shouldn't be feeling this way, but he simply couldn't break their growing bond.

Savannah parted her lips, one hand slipping into his hair in the gentlest of caresses, and he drew her against him, their mouths meeting in that kiss he'd been dreaming about all day.

*Playing with fire. Sinking into this pit of swirling emotions. Too deep. Far too deep.* The thoughts circled and entwined until he lost the train, and he pushed them down as she melted into his arms. He savored the whisper of cotton as he drew the sweater over her head, followed by the light t-shirt, and then the swish of her linen shorts sliding to the floor, leaving her before him in lacy pink panties.

"You're so damn beautiful." He sighed against the crook of her neck as he planted soft kisses on her satiny skin. *And I am hopelessly in love.*

# CHAPTER 6

## Savannah

$_{S}$AVANNAH'S EYES POPPED OPEN, BUT she was unsure what had caused her abrupt return to consciousness. Brandon's arm slung over her slim hip created warmth against her bare skin. His deep breaths tickled her neck as he slept on. She closed her eyes, inhaling the remnants of sunshine, beach, and campfire clinging to his hair and skin.

She shivered in the cool basement bedroom, edging closer to Brandon as she sought the top of the sheet. A pervasive sense of being watched forced her to reopen her eyes. Savannah bolted upright, hauling the covers over her bare breasts. "You scared the life out of me."

"Is that …?" Carol's eyes narrowed as she stared at Savannah's shoulder. "What kind of parents allow tattoos?"

"What the hell?" Brandon's hoarse voice rose from the tangle of sheets. He propped himself on his elbows, peering at his mother. "Doesn't anyone in this family knock?"

"Put some clothes on." His mother snatched Brandon's t-shirt from the floor and whipped it at Savannah's head, glowering over her shoulder while stomping toward the door. "Out of bed. It's almost noon." The door slammed behind her.

Savannah cradled her pounding head. "Sorry. I didn't get back to my room."

"Don't be." He rubbed her back. "I'm a grown man dating a grown woman, so let's quit sneaking around like teenagers. Headache?"

"I was fine until I sat." She groaned and swallowed hard. "Me puking all over you would seal my fate. What do you want to bet she's packing my bag?"

"She wouldn't dare." He handed her the water bottle he'd filled during the night. "Rehydrate."

Several swallows of the lukewarm water eased the dry pasty feeling in her mouth. "Why did I drink so much?" She slid his t-shirt over her head.

"You'll feel better after a hot shower." He planted a kiss on her cheek. "And you should eat."

Savannah's stomach rolled. She pulled a face before tiptoeing upstairs and down the hall to her room, thankful she managed the trip without further confrontation.

After a warm shower, followed up with drops to soothe her gritty, red eyes, she slipped on a pair of shorts and a light tank top. It was sweltering, even in the relative coolness of the house.

"Morning." Jeremy looked up as she entered the kitchen. "Help yourself to coffee."

"Thank you." Savannah poured a steaming cup, fighting her grimace at the bitterness of the first sip.

"Carol went to the market." He studied her over the rim of his mug. "She'll cool off by the time she returns."

She bit back the impulse to apologize for sleeping with Brandon. Should she even be sorry? As her boyfriend pointed out, they were adults. Her mind spun as she sought for something to say.

"Brandon never brings girls home." The man set his coffee on the table. "I suspect he never will again."

The words gave little comfort. From his assessment, he expected she wouldn't be the last woman in his stepson's life. Brandon had made it clear they were too young and their careers too unsettled to promise anything, so she'd better rein in the neediness before she scared the guy away.

"You seem like a nice girl, Savannah, but you're in pretty deep. I like Brandon, but I'd never encourage my teenage daughter to date him. Don't believe this little fling will go anywhere. He needs an adult woman. Allowing him to steal your innocence like he clearly has …" Jeremy cleared his throat. "It's a shame. You should be dating boys your own age. What is your father thinking, permitting this to continue?"

She bit her lip. Anything she said would only make things more difficult for Brandon.

What did this man think? That she'd succumbed to Brandon's smooth seduction techniques like a naive school girl? Heat rose in her cheeks. She clenched her hands around the cup, narrowing her eyes as she stared without blinking. "You don't know me or my dad, so—"

"There you are." Brandon's damp hair was adorably tousled. He pressed a kiss to her temple. "Want something to eat?"

The little appetite she'd had deserted her, so she shook her head.

"What are you two up to today?" Jeremy asked as he returned to reading his paper.

"Maybe a hike?" Brandon looked her way. "Orrrr, maybe not," he said as she wrinkled her nose. "How about the beach?"

Savannah nodded, focusing on him and ignoring Jeremy entirely. "Maybe Mia would like to join us?"

The afternoon passed pleasantly as they swam and lounged on the sand. By the end of the afternoon, Savannah felt refreshed, as she often did after spending the day near the water. Even though Jeremy's words kept surfacing, she refused to acknowledge them.

"Rory invited us to a movie tonight." Brandon brushed his fingertips over the palm of her hand as they lounged on the sand, drying off after one last dip.

"Sounds good."

"What are you up to, Mia?" Brandon asked.

"Shaylynn invited me to a party. Don't tell Mom, she thinks we're bowling." Mia peered at Savannah. "You always look so pretty. Will you help me plan an outfit?"

"I'd love to." She smiled at Mia. All reports from Piper had led her to believe this teenager was the worst monster in the world, but Vanna was growing attached to the girl.

"We should head home. Dinner will be ready soon, and we should make an appearance." He rose to gather their things.

"Yeah, like she could see any more of me than she has," Savannah muttered, earning a look from Brandon.

After a tense and virtually silent dinner, punctuated with scathing looks from Carol, Savannah donned a strapless sundress paired with sandals and applied a light touch of makeup.

She joined Mia in her room and they sorted through the girl's closet and drawers.

"I don't have anything that will work." The girl flopped onto the bed.

"Hmmm." Savannah tapped a finger against her lips. She'd packed extra clothing, intending to be prepared for any activity. An outfit came to mind. She hurried to her room and collected the skirt and top, knowing it would look amazing with the girl's dark hair and creamy complexion. As an afterthought, she gathered her makeup bag and brushes.

"Try this," she said as she laid the outfit on the girl's bed.

The girl's eyes widened. Mia wasted no time shucking her shorts and t-shirt. Once dressed, she turned back and forth in front of the mirror. "Wow."

"Yeah, wow. Now, let's apply some make-up and fix your hair." Savannah opened her palette, considering the choices before setting to work. Once she'd finished her transformation, she asked, "What do you think?"

"Amazing. Who taught you to do makeup?"

"My stepmother, Emily. She's beautiful, and she always looks classy and elegant. When we go shopping, she helps me choose incredible outfits."

"Did she help with this one?" The girl motioned to the one she wore.

"My mother, Tiffany, helped me choose that one when I visited her in Chicago. We bought the dress I'm wearing when we toured Italy."

"Italy?" The girl's eyebrows rose. "You're so lucky. My mom hates shopping and is super strict about what I wear, which is why my clothes suck. And Piper never wants to shop with me. She hates me."

"I'm sorry." *I know the feeling.* "But I understand. My mom, Jayde, was awesome, but she died, and my dad hated shopping."

Mia frowned. "How many moms and dads do you have? Has your dad been married several times, like my mom?"

Savannah shook her head. "It's confusing, but the answer is three of each." She explained about her adoption, and how she now lived with Aiden and Emily, but visited with Tiffany and Stefan, leaving out the dramatic details.

"My father left when I was a baby." Mia shrugged. "I've never met him, but Brandon remembers."

"I'm sorry. Having a mother or father out there somewhere, but not knowing them, leaves a lot of unanswered questions."

"Savannah?" Mia bit her lip. "Are you in love with my brother?"

"We've only dated a few months." Savannah gave the girl a gentle smile.

"He never lets me meet his girlfriends. Except for—" Mia snapped her mouth closed, her cheeks turning a bright pink.

"Autumn. I already know." Vanna guided Mia to her chair. "Let's style your hair, or we'll be late."

Savannah brushed Mia's long hair and created an elegant, half-up, half-down braid that suited the lovely curls in her dark, lustrous locks. "You look amazing." She stepped back.

"You think?" Mia examined herself in the mirror.

A knock sounded on the door. "Can I come in?"

Mia grinned. "Come see, Brandon."

He peered around the door before stepping in and closing it. "Whoa. Don't let Carol see you dressed like that."

"It doesn't look good?" Mia's face crumpled. "Savannah helped me."

"You're gorgeous," Brandon said, "but our mother will flip if she sees you with makeup and that outfit." He gave Savannah a sideways look. "She'll chain you in the basement rather than let you go out in a skirt that short."

"All the girls wear them." Mia folded her arms across her chest, a pout forming.

He held up his hands. "All I said was don't let her see you, not that you shouldn't wear it. You look incredible."

Savannah couldn't agree more. Without the baggy shorts and oversized t-shirt, the girl had transformed. The light touch of makeup emphasized her big gray eyes, and the hairstyle revealed her fine cheekbones. Once she grew out of her awkward teenage phase, this girl would be stunning.

Mia grinned, but it faded. "You're right, Mom will lose it."

"Only if she sees you." He winked. "I'll draw her attention while you get in our car. We'll drop you off at Shaylynn's house on our way to the movie. Just take a baggy sweater and wipe off your makeup before you come home, and she'll never know."

⁓

Mia slid from the backseat and hugged her brother before she bounded toward her friend's house, waving at them as she disappeared inside.

"You made her entire night." Brandon rested their linked hands on his thigh.

"I worried I'd overstepped. I should have known your mother wouldn't appreciate the outfit, but it was fun. My parents weren't as tough as your mother, but after Mom died, I missed having that bond. But I have Emily and Tiffany. Mia seems to have nobody to do girl things with her."

Brandon's grip tightened, a dark look descending over his features. "My mother definitely isn't warm and cuddly. It's the hardest thing about living on the East Coast." He smacked a fist on the wheel. "I'm not delusional, right? Mia's neglected. She'll get herself into trouble."

"Does she talk to you? About boys or anything?"

"She's embarrassed when I mention the word boy. How would I approach dating or sex? She's a good kid, but she's growing up and she's sneaking around because our mother is too batshit crazy half of the time to have a decent conversation."

"When I was Mia's age, I had Emily. My dad offered, but he understood it would be weird for me." She took his hand. "Mia needs someone, Brandon."

"So she should call Emily?"

"I meant me, silly. She might open up, woman to woman."

Brandon grimaced. "My sister is a teenage girl, not a woman."

"Are you sure about that, Dr. Reynolds?"

"You think she's …" He shuddered. "Like how old were you when …" Brandon rubbed his temples. "Never mind."

Savannah held back her laughter. "Do you want me to answer the question?" she asked. "Or is it easier to consider how old you were? And how old was the girl?" At his dark look, she said, "I rest my case, doctor."

"You win. Mia's a woman." His theatrical eye roll made her snicker. "Whether or not she's had sex. I hoped because Piper …" He shot a look at Savannah.

"Waited? Or is still waiting?" Savannah asked. "Mia isn't Piper. She's not as naive, and she might not choose to wait. Talk to her."

"Worth a try." He sighed. "I wish she could visit Boston so we had more time, but I have no place for her to stay, and I don't want to stick her in some cheap motel."

"She could stay at my place."

"Right, because your dad will enjoy not only feeding me but my little sister too."

"How much does one teenage girl eat?" She wrinkled her nose. "Besides, he understands confused, messed up fifteen-year-old girls. He had one of his very own."

Brandon pulled into the lot. "Rory's waiting for us. Thanks, Vanna. I'll keep it in mind."

~

After the movie, they stopped at the local burger joint for a late-night snack.

"So, Rory," Savannah said once they were seated in a booth. "You know all about me. How about you? What do you do?"

"Nothing as prestigious as being a doctor." He rubbed a hand through his scruffy blond hair. "I'm a mechanic. It's decent money, and I get to stay close to the ski hills. We spend a lot of time on the slopes. Or used to, anyway."

"Oh, I love skiing. I've been to Colorado, but I've never skied in Montana."

"You'll have to hit the slopes with us this winter."

"Maybe I will." Vanna twirled a lock of her hair. "Do you have a girlfriend?"

"Not at present. Small towns, you know?" He shrugged. "There's a girl I like, but I'm not sure she's available or interested."

Brandon lifted a brow. "You never mentioned this secret crush."

Rory shook his head. "Not tonight."

Savannah grinned. "Oh, come on."

Brandon peered at his phone as it buzzed. "It's Mia." He rose and stepped a few paces from the table.

"You are quite a surprise, Savannah," Rory said, glancing toward Brandon.

"Why is that, Rory?"

"Brandon never brings girls to Montana or lets us meet them. They never last long enough."

"Is that supposed to scare me off? Send me running so he can find someone his own age?" Savannah folded her arms across her chest. "Save him the aggravation of dumping me when his friends remind him I'm too young?"

"Nope. I like you." Rory winked. "A strong woman might be just what he needs to get over his fear of relationships."

"Right." Savannah rolled her eyes. "He seems terrified."

"You scoff, but his mother's a piece of work. If anyone will make you run, it's her." He lowered his voice. "You've been staying in that house but haven't noticed how dysfunctional Carol and Jeremy are?"

The guy had a point. And it was Carol's fifth marriage. "She doesn't scare me. I wish she liked me because it would make it easier for Brandon, but I refuse to cower in a corner or give her the satisfaction of driving me off. That would make her believe she's right when she's dead wrong." Savannah tilted her head. "Everyone needs to accept he's a grown man who is capable of making his own decisions."

"Good luck with that. Carol holds the power." Rory leaned closer, his voice dropping to barely a whisper. "Want to hear the secret?"

Despite her doubt, she nodded, interested in learning more about the man who seemed to hold everyone at a safe distance.

"Brandon craves a woman strong enough to handle his family situation while being soft enough to avoid being domineering. That's a fine balance. Can you be that woman?"

"I guess we'll find out, won't we?" She met his gaze without flinching.

"You two look serious." Brandon held out his hand to Vanna. "Sorry. We have to go. Mia's been busted, and Carol is livid. Mia begged me to come home and run interference."

Savannah collected her sweater and purse from the bench beside her. "I'm ready. The movie was fun. Thanks, Rory." She accepted his hug.

"Stay strong," Rory whispered against her hair. "He needs you."

⌒

Brandon drummed his fingers on the wheel, focusing on the road for most of the drive. "This won't be pretty. I didn't get the whole story through the tears and the yelling in the background, but the cops busted up the house party, and Mia got caught drinking."

"It's fine. I'll go to my room if you need privacy. Maybe I should have stayed with Rory."

"I should have thought of that. Not because I don't want you to hear, but because Carol is raging, and when she gets like that," he said as he pulled up in front of the house, "she turns extra nasty. This trip hasn't given you a wonderful impression of my family, and I'd understand if you don't want to deal with it."

"Do what you need to do for Mia." Savannah took a deep breath as they approached the house.

Carol's strident voice carried through an open window as she berated Mia.

Brandon drew in his own deep breath, closing his eyes and letting it out in a long slow stream of air before he opened the door.

"There you are." Carol's bloodshot eyes locked onto Brandon the moment he appeared, shifting her focus onto Savannah a split-second later. "I welcomed you into my home. This is how you repay me? By dressing my daughter like a streetwalker and encouraging her to party and get drunk?"

"Savannah has nothing to do with this, Mother." Brandon crossed his arms and planted his feet. "Mia is a teenager, and that's what teenagers do. They go to parties. They drink." He moved across the kitchen and kneeled in front of his sister. "You okay?"

Mia gave a tiny negative twitch of her head as if she were too frightened to move an inch.

"Come here." Brandon wrapped his sister in his arms, pulling her head against his shoulder.

"This isn't okay." Carol glowered at Savannah. "Get out. You aren't welcome in my home."

Savannah narrowed her eyes. "I'll leave." She clenched her jaw, keeping her voice low and calm. "But don't you ever tell me how to live my life." She allowed her tone to soften. "Brandon, I'll gather my things and wait in the car." She spun and walked down the hall with measured, unhurried steps. The moment she arrived in the bedroom, she began tossing her belongings into her suitcase.

"That's how you want this, Mother?" Brandon's voice rose, carrying clearly to Savannah's ears. "How dare you. You've been horrible to Savannah from the moment we arrived. This morning was my fault. I wanted her with me. But if you insist, we'll leave."

Savannah zipped her bag and scooped up her coat before heading toward the front door.

"I bet Jeremy is lurking somewhere, cowering like a little girl. Great parenting skills you both have. Come on, munchkin."

Brandon arrived in the foyer at the same time as Savannah with his little sister clinging to him. "Hold the door," he muttered. "Keep walking and don't look back." Brandon tucked his sister into the back seat of the car, ushering Savannah in while he deposited her suitcase in the trunk.

Savannah crawled into the back, fastening her own seatbelt before wrapping an arm around the sobbing girl's shoulders.

Brandon glanced into the rear view mirror as they pulled away from the curb. "Motel?"

"Somewhere clean with comfy beds. I have my credit card, so pick something good." She met his gaze in the mirror.

"Sorry." Mia sniffled. "Now you're in trouble too. She kicked you out."

"Don't worry, I'm fine." She patted the girl's shoulder.

Within half an hour, they were checked into a comfortable room with two queen beds. Savannah walked to the small drugstore down the block, leaving Brandon to have a quiet talk with the distressed Mia. She returned forty-five minutes later with a few toiletries and items for Mia and Brandon, as neither had packed a bag.

"Shh, Mia's asleep." Brandon wrapped his arms around Savannah, cuddling her against his bare chest. "I am so sorry you got caught in the crossfire."

"It's not your fault. So now what?"

"By tomorrow my mother will have cooled off, and I'll take Mia home. I don't really have any other choice." He pulled her to sit with him on the small couch under the window. "She has nowhere else to go, and I have to return to Boston. If I miss my shifts, Kavanagh's reaction will make Carol's look mild in comparison."

"He'd understand if you needed an extra day or two, but … what about Mia?"

"It's not the first time, Vanna. We all know the drill. Carol will take Mia back and be apologetic. It'll be fine for a while, but then it'll explode again. And Jeremy will continue to be weak and spineless, hiding in the bedroom while the woman blows like a geyser over the slightest provocation."

"I doubt I'll get the same forgiveness, so I'll stay out of the way and let you handle it?"

"Probably best. I'll drive Mia home in the morning and pick up my things." He pressed a kiss to her temple. "Where does this leave us?"

"I'm fine, Brandon. Nobody's family is perfect, so don't give it a second thought. We should probably get some sleep."

# CHAPTER 7

## *Brandon*

M IA'S PALE FACE TURNED HIS way as she hunched in the passenger seat. "I don't want to go home," she whispered. "Please don't leave me here, Brandon." Her shimmering eyes filled with distress.

"Sorry, munchkin." He reached over to squeeze her hand. "If I took you with me, Carol would have the cops all over my ass. She'd probably accuse me of kidnapping and have me arrested. And," he said, "I have nowhere for you to stay. I share a tiny apartment with three grown men, not to mention my sixteen-hour shifts and eighty-hour work weeks."

"I hate living with Mom and Jeremy. You're lucky. You get to leave." She blinked at him with sad eyes. "Mom was mean to Vanna because of me."

"Our mother was mean because she's a sad, bitter woman. Allowing Savannah to meet her was stupid." A twinge of regret surfaced. Not only for the turmoil and stress he'd caused his girlfriend, but because he couldn't help Mia. "Can you hang in there? It's only another two years until you graduate. You could apply to an eastern college so you could live closer to me."

"My grades aren't good." She picked at a nail. "Billy promised me more hours at the diner after I graduate. As soon as I'm eighteen, I'll get my own place."

"Oh, Mia." Brandon emitted a long sigh. "Don't do that. You need to get out of this town. Get an education. Promise me you'll bring your grades up and apply for financial assistance for tuition, as I did."

"I'm not you. I'm dumb when it comes to school."

"I refuse to believe that. How about hiring a tutor?"

"With what money? I earn minimum wage, and the tips suck."

"I'll pay for the tutor if you promise to work hard." It would mean rejigging his already impossibly tight budget, but he'd find a way. He pulled to the curb in front of the house and turned in his seat. "Do you want to be stuck in this town for the rest of your life?"

"No." She shot a look toward the house. "Okay. You're right. Maybe I could even go to Harvard like Savannah."

"I bet you could." He ruffled her hair and smiled, but it quickly faded. "We'd better get this over with. I have to pick up Vanna and head to the airport. Ready, munchkin?"

She rolled her eyes. "I'll be sixteen soon. You need to stop calling me that baby name."

"Sorry." A soft laugh escaped. "You've grown up while I've been busy in medical school."

They both headed toward the house, Mia taking the slow steps of one being dragged to her doom. "You don't have to come in."

"No, I really do." He opened the door and ushered her inside. Brandon gave his sister another hug. "Get some rest."

Jeremy sat in his usual spot at the table, flipping through screens on his tablet. "Carol's ready to call the police."

"Where is she?"

"Out back. She's none too pleased about you running off."

"Whatever. I'll get my things and be gone. You can thank Piper for making this an amazing and unforgettable visit."

He bounded down the stairs and packed his bag, taking a moment to ensure he'd gathered all his belongings. This might be the last time he stayed in this bedroom.

Not that he'd miss it. He couldn't remember many happy memories associated with this house aside from those built during those precious few hours with Savannah in this very room.

Now he had to face another encounter with his mother. He couldn't leave without making sure Mia would be okay.

Carol sat on a lounger in the back. "About time you came home."

"Promise you'll let this go. Don't take it out on Mia." He crossed his arms. "You're too hard on her."

"We were just fine until you brought that girl to visit. She put ideas in Mia's head."

"Just promise, Mother. Take care of your daughter. Before you know it, she'll leave just like I did."

His mother tipped her head, her brows rising as she glowered at him. "Like I'd take orders from you."

Brandon scoffed and shook his head. This woman would argue for hours, and they'd get nowhere. He returned to the kitchen. "Can you at least try to talk some sense into that crazy-ass woman? And maybe look out for Mia? Please?" Brandon scrubbed his hands through his hair. "I can't be worrying about her while I try to get through residency."

"I'll do my best." Jeremy rose from his seat. "How's Savannah?"

"Like you care?" Brandon glared at the man. "She never had a chance, did she? Now I have to try to make all this shit up to her. Nobody fucking cares that this might end us."

"I do care, but she's too young for you. You have a bright future. That girl could ruin it."

"I'll take my chances on *that girl*." A short harsh laugh escaped. "Save the advice, Jeremy. I don't have a father, and I never will. Just try to do something useful for Mia." He went down the hallway and tapped on Mia's door.

She opened the door a crack, peering up at him before beckoning him inside.

"I have to go. You take care of yourself and remember, two years and you're out of here." He held out his arms.

"I'll miss you." Mia leaned against his chest and sniffled.

"Call if you need anything, but don't let Carol know you have Vanna's number," he muttered.

"I won't. Come back and see me soon."

"I won't forget about you, I promise." He pressed a kiss to her hair and left her room.

The screen door banged behind him as he trudged down the concrete walkway to the car. This trip had been a complete disaster. He hoped Savannah would forgive him for putting her in the line of fire.

One final stop, and he'd put this town in his rear view mirror.

⌒

"Brandon." Rory looked up from the engine he was hunkered over. "You on your way out of town? Where's Savannah?"

"She stayed at the hotel while I took Mia home. It got ugly last night."

Rory wiped his hands on a rag. "Let's go outside. I could use some air." The moment they'd exited through the bay doors, he asked, "Mia got busted?"

"It's my fault. I knew where she was going, and I encouraged Mia to wear the outfit even though I knew Carol would be pissed. She looked so pretty, and nobody at home pays much attention. Vanna spent an hour helping her get ready and lent Mia clothes, which Carol hated."

Rory grimaced. "Carol took it out on Savannah?"

"She demanded Vanna get out of her house." Brandon rubbed a hand through his hair. "Savannah packed and we stayed at a hotel."

"Now what?"

"Now I return to Boston and get my ass to work." He sighed. "I can't care for a teenager. My living situation is lousy, and I have no money. Can I ask you a huge favor?"

"You want me to keep an eye on Mia?" Rory nodded. "Consider it done."

"Thanks, man. You have no idea what a load that takes off my mind. She's headed for trouble. It's like watching one of those slow-motion scenes where you know the crash is about to happen, but there's nothing you can do to prevent it. I feel so damn powerless."

Rory nodded. "I'll do what I can. In the meantime, work hard. Take care of your girl. This one is something special."

"I'll do my best. Sometimes I wonder who is taking care of who in this relationship." A rueful grin appeared.

"Maybe that's a good thing." Rory gripped his shoulder. "Hold on to her, Brandon. Let her in."

~

September swept by in a flurry of activity. Savannah returned to classes at Harvard and Brandon dug in at work. The hours were long, but at least the work was rewarding.

It seemed he lived at the hospital. When not on shift, he collapsed into bed or studied procedures and read journals to sharpen his skills.

"Someone's here to see you," Dr. Kavanagh said when he caught up to Brandon at the admissions desk. "Give me an update on your patients, and then take an hour for lunch. You look exhausted, and you've worked hard this week."

"Life of an intern." He filled Will in on the series of lab results he was waiting for before he peeked into the lounge. "Vanna."

"I thought I'd visit before you forgot what I looked like." She slid her arms around his neck. "Do you have time to escape for lunch? It's nice outside, so we could enjoy those last rays of sunshine."

"You're on." He kissed her soft lips, thinking about how much he missed these moments. There were nights when he still went to her place, but often he was so exhausted he passed out on her bed.

After hanging up his lab coat, he pulled on a light sweatshirt and followed her into the unseasonably warm afternoon. "Oh, I miss daylight." He flopped onto the grass with a sigh. "I don't know if I want to eat or nap."

"You should eat." She handed him the bag she'd been carrying.

"Did you make this?" He grinned as he discovered the ciabatta bun loaded with his favorite fixings, along with an apple, a large bottle of juice, and a container of chocolate chip cookies.

"I even baked the cookies." She unwrapped her own sandwich and took a dainty bite.

"How did you know I needed this?" He patted her knee.

"You're an intern. I've heard all the stories. I do live with two doctors, both of whom were chief resident in a level one trauma center. You're lucky you matched in Boston, rather than Chicago."

"Perhaps." He tucked into his meal, enjoying the light breeze and fresh air. He'd been on since ten the previous evening, and the last few hours of the shift were always a challenge, especially when he worked almost every day.

Once he finished, Savannah put the empty containers into the bag and pulled him down to rest his head in her lap.

His eyelids grew heavier by the second, the light strokes of her fingers across his hair lulling him. "Make sure I don't fall asleep. Will said an hour, so I'd better be back on time."

"Relax. You scarfed down your lunch in less than ten minutes," she said softly. "Surprised you didn't choke on it."

"Resident rules. If you don't eat fast, you never eat." Brandon yawned, letting his thoughts drift as his eyelids sank closed.

"Hey. Wake up." Savannah's breath tickled his cheek.

His eyes snapped open. "Damn. I fell asleep." He forced himself upright. "How long?"

"You have ten before you have to be back. I kept track of the time, don't worry."

"Sorry, sweetie." He frowned. "We barely said five words to each other. Now I have to go."

She leaned in for a hug. "Having a relationship with someone in residency isn't easy, but I'm not sitting around home doing nothing."

"Ahhh, living the good life."

"If you call interning for Tom, lectures, and study sessions the good life, you bet I am." She patted his cheek. "Why don't you come over after your shift? Aiden's cooking."

"Ooo, that's tempting, but I might—"

"Be late." Her lips twitched. "Text when you escape. Now go." She gave him a gentle push. "No slacking off if you want to earn chief."

～

Nate smothered a yawn and rested his head against the side of his locker. "Want to grab food?"

"I'm seeing Vanna tonight."

"I don't know how you have the energy for a date after the shift from hell." Nate slid on his coat. "I'd be asleep in my dessert."

"I'm a lucky man." Brandon retrieved his wallet. "They feed me dinner and then we hang out, but if I fall asleep, she covers me with a blanket and leaves me."

"So you're going to Dr. Hamilton's place to be spoiled with some fantastic meal and lounge around on his couch?" Nate snickered, but a wistful look appeared in his eyes.

Medical residents seldom found a partner who understood the demands of their career, making it virtually impossible to keep a relationship together. Nate, like Brandon, had moved several states away from where he'd grown up, and they never had much time to cultivate a social life outside of their circle of residents. Out of that group, a third were on shift, another third was ready to go home, shovel food into their mouths, and crash, and the final third was studying or getting ready for their next shift. Partners rarely enjoyed navigating the never ending circle.

"Do you want to join us for dinner?" Brandon asked as he changed his shoes.

"Dude. You can't invite me to someone's house. Especially if that someone is an ER attending."

"We won't show up unannounced." Brandon pulled out his phone and scrolled through his numbers.

"She might not like her date being interrupted. I'll be one of those third wheels."

"It's not like that. It's a family dinner where she's outnumbered by doctors, so what's one more?" Brandon hit dial.

"Hey, Brandon. Are you on your way?" Aiden asked.

"I'm escaping on time." He drew in a breath, hoping he wasn't overstepping. "Nate's finishing his shift and wanted to grab dinner. I don't think he wants to hang around the apartment."

"You're either asking me to put my life on the line by informing Vanna you're not coming, or you want to invite Nate."

"Even asking you to relay such a message would be wrong on every imaginable level."

"Damn right." Aiden laughed. "There's tons of food. I imagine it's been a while since Nate's had a meal that wasn't from a vending machine."

"You really don't mind?" Brandon nodded toward Nate.

"Dinner will be ready in forty-five minutes."

"We're on our way." Brandon hung up. "Let's go."

"She doesn't mind? What about Aiden?"

"That was Aiden. Do you think I would invite another intern to his home without asking him directly? Not a chance in hell."

They exited through the sliding glass doors and headed toward the commons.

"Dylan's hating life right now," Nate said. "You haven't been around much, but he's complaining about being in another ER."

"At least he got half of what he wanted. Wonder how he'll feel when we both move out?"

Nate shrugged. "I don't know, but do you still plan to move with me? You're never around. Half the time you stay with Savannah." His friend tilted his head. "She met your family. That's huge."

"And a complete disaster. I'm surprised Vanna didn't tell me to go to hell after that." Brandon sighed. "We're a long way from being ready to live together. I can't make any big commitments, and she's buried in lectures, term papers, and interning."

"She lives at home." Nate snickered. "I could just see you moving in."

"Not happening." He waved at the doorman as they entered the lobby. "Hey, Jarrod."

The doorman smiled and raised a hand before pressing the door release to allow them elevator access.

Brandon swept a hand through his hair, leaning against the side of the elevator as it rose to the top floor, thankful he had the next day off.

"Damn." Nate muttered as the stepped into the foyer. "No wonder you're never home." He inhaled deeply. "That smells amazing."

"That would be dinner." Savannah appeared, gracing both men with a lovely smile and a warm hug. "Hi, Nate. Come on in."

"Sorry for interrupting your precious free time with Brandon."

"You're not. Rochelle dropped by to work on an assignment, so she's joining us for dinner." Savannah led them into the kitchen. "Can I get you a beverage? Wine? Beer? Something stronger after sixteen hours of ER fun?"

"A beer would be perfect," Nate said.

Brandon waved at Rochelle as Vanna retrieved two bottles from the fridge. "This is Nate. He's my roommate and an intern in the ER." He caught a glimpse of the look on his friend's face and nudged him with an elbow.

"Hi Rochelle." Nate smiled as he accepted his icy cold beer.

Rochelle's wave was unenthusiastic as was her distant smile. "Nate."

"Braaaannnnndonnn." Kellan raced into the kitchen, crashing into the man's legs.

"Hey, bud." Brandon scooped up the boy and tickled him.

Kellan giggled, tucking his chin down as he observed Nate with wide brown eyes.

"Say hi to Nate."

The boy fluttered his fingers and hid his face against Brandon's shoulder.

"Wash your hands, hijo mio. Time for dinner," Emily said as she entered the kitchen. "Perfect timing. Cierra's napping."

"Come on, Kellan. I have to wash my hands too." Brandon carried the boy to the sink and turned on the water, helping the boy wash before buckling him in his booster seat.

Emily squeezed Brandon's arm. "Thank you." She set a small plate in front of Kellan.

Brandon seated himself beside Savannah, allowing Nate to sit by Rochelle.

Nate stared at the plate of prime rib, roasted potatoes, and sautéed vegetables in front of him. "This looks better than any restaurant meal I've ever eaten." He sliced into the tender beef and popped it into his mouth, a smile appearing as he chewed. "Tastes better too."

Emily squeezed Aiden's hand. "When I cook, the dishes are served family style. But this one," she said, rubbing her husband's arm, "presents every meal like it's artwork."

"How do you find the time and energy?" Nate said before scooping another forkful of potato.

"Cooking relaxes me," Aiden said, "and I enjoy a good meal."

Brandon sipped his wine, sending a look at Nate with a shrug. He loved being in this apartment, especially at meal times. Not only because the food was always amazing, but the conversation was never stilted or bitter like it tended to be with his family.

He bit back a laugh at the attention Nate lavished on Rochelle. But, the young woman, though polite, seemed unwilling to encourage the attention. Brandon reached under the table, squeezing Savannah's knee and rolling his eyes towards the couple as he raised a brow.

Savannah's eyes widened almost imperceptibly, accompanied by a subtle shake of her head.

"When do you leave for New Haven?" Rochelle asked.

"New Haven?" Brandon's brows drew together. "What's …?" His heart sank. He knew exactly what and, in particular, *who* would draw her to New Haven.

"Rochelle." Savannah glared at her friend. "Last time I tell you anything."

"I thought he knew."

"I just arranged the trip. He's been working."

"I am right here, you know." Brandon sighed. "I hate it when people talk about me in third person."

"I'll tell you later." Savannah slipped her soft hand into his under the table.

"Brandon," Aiden said, "you ski, right?"

"I've skied most of the hills in Montana, and my friends and I drove to Jackson Hole a few times."

"We were thinking about a trip at the beginning of December if the weather cooperates and gives us some decent snow. If you can book holiday time, you should join us."

"Where are you going?" Brandon asked.

"Canada. Right, Dad?" Savannah grinned. "Tom found a huge private chalet, so there's room for the whole group."

"Other than work, my calendar is pretty open." Brandon laughed. "Send me the dates so I can ask Dr. Kavanagh. And I'll dig out my passport."

"Oh, he already has the dates." Aiden grinned. "He's joining us this trip. There will be thirteen adults including Iona, and five kids."

"Flights?" Brandon raised an eyebrow.

"Jet?" Aiden laughed. "And Tom, Joel, Ryan, Will, and I will split the cost of the chalet, which includes catered meals. You only need your ski equipment."

"Can I line up rentals? I sold my equipment before I left Montana." The thought of a trip into the mountains made him smile, even if it would eat into his budget.

"Or since we know we're the same size"—Aiden threw a look at Savannah—"we'll see if my boots fit. I have several sets of ski equipment."

Brandon bit back his grin. "Thanks, Aiden. Now I only need to beg for some days off."

"We can't have you miss out, so if Dr. Kavanagh gives you a hard time, I'll cover some hours." Nate shrugged. "Maybe you'll return the favor at some point?"

"Deal." Brandon nodded.

Brandon sank onto Savannah's bed, picking up the sketchpad. The soft humming and occasional sweet note of her voice told him she was performing her usual nighttime routine.

His eyes widened as he inspected the first picture then turned the page. "Damn." He flipped through the sketchbook, studying each picture.

"Hey." Savannah snatched the book from his hands. "You aren't supposed to look at that."

"Then you shouldn't leave it on the bed." He looped an arm around her waist, drawing her to stand between his knees and resting his hands on her hips. "They're phenomenal sketches. I don't understand why you decided on law. It's not like you ..." Given the narrowed eyes and firm set of her lips, he suspected it would be wise to leave it alone. "New Haven, huh?"

"It's only three days." She flattened her palms against his chest. "I haven't seen Justin for months, and he's planning a visit to Yale. He'll transfer next fall if he's accepted. With his GPA, he could qualify for financial assistance."

"I figured it had something to do with him." He sighed. "I wish you'd told me before Rochelle blurted it out at the dinner table. Nice intervention by your dad before that heated up."

"Dad's a pro at redirecting conversation. He used to attend swanky benefits and parties with the Chicago elite, so it's second nature." She smiled. "His grandfather knew everyone."

"Why does that not surprise me?" Brandon narrowed his eyes. "Damn, you're good. Aiden's skills are rubbing off on you."

She shrugged. "Are you upset that I'm spending three days with Justin?" She placed her hands on either side of his face, stroking his cheeks with her thumbs. "You have nothing to worry about. He has a girlfriend."

Brandon closed his eyes, letting out a long slow breath. Her words did nothing to soothe the flutter of anxiety in his belly.

"Don't you trust me?" she asked softly.

"It has nothing to do with trusting you." He lifted his chin. "Is his girlfriend joining him in New Haven? Or is she staying in California?"

"This has everything to do with trust. I didn't get all psycho about the flight attendant or about Autumn kissing you at the cookout."

His stomach lurched. "That was nothing. She wished me well and kissed my cheek."

"You've been to Montana without me, and she was there. I see how she looks at you."

"Oh, how's that? We broke up years ago." He frowned. "There's nothing going on."

"Nothing on your side," she muttered. "Anyway, Justin and I had a serious discussion over a year ago. We agreed to explore other relationships and that we wouldn't work as a couple. Did you have that sort of conversation with Autumn?"

"Well …" His frown deepened as he struggled to recall exactly what had been said between them. "She chose to stay in Montana. We ended our relationship about the same time as she realized I'd been accepted at a university on the opposite side of the country. She knew I'd be gone for years."

"Gone for years." Savannah pressed her forehead to his. "That sounds like you plan on returning to Montana someday."

"Everything in my life has changed since then. I ended the relationship with good intentions. I told her I didn't know where I'd end up." He tipped up his chin. "We were kids when we dated. She's a great girl, but … we only dated for ten months. I care about her, but it was never that one relationship."

"And I care about Justin, but we were kids when we dated, and … it was never that one relationship," she whispered against his lips. "I'm not *in love* with him."

He nodded, pulling her onto his knee and wrapping her into a warm embrace. "I'll miss you."

"And I'll miss you, but you'll be so busy at work, you'll barely know I'm gone." She placed a tender kiss on his lips. "After I come home, we'll have an entire week together. You have to book that time off. You don't want to miss this trip. It will be amazing."

# CHAPTER 8

## *Savannah*

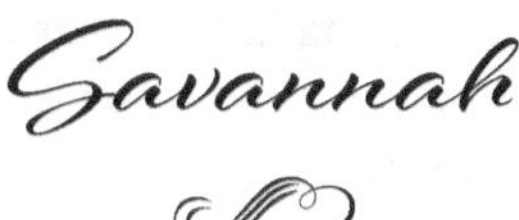

ROCHELLE WAVED FROM HER SEAT in the study area, giving Jackson a poke in the ribs. "Now you can ask her."

"Ask me what?" Vanna slid into the chair next to Rochelle, placing her backpack on the floor at her feet.

"That," Jackson muttered, with a subtle twitch of his head to the left. "Don't look."

Savannah scrunched her nose. "How can I comment if I have no idea what you're asking?"

"Just don't be obvious." Rochelle giggled.

Vanna turned in her chair and then bent to dig for the laptop stowed in her bag, raising her eyes enough to spot Piper. And Gray. Holding hands? She observed as Piper leaned in and captured Gray's lips. Her own lip curled as the guy's fingers tangled in the girl's hair.

She straightened and set her laptop on the table. "I see." Vanna shrugged. "Hadn't heard anything about that. I'm not on speaking terms with either of them, remember?"

"She didn't tell her brother?"

"Stepbrother. Nope. He's not talking to her either." She signed in and connected to the Wi-Fi. "Let's finish this project."

Rochelle tilted her head. "It doesn't bother you that Piper is with Gray? Shouldn't someone warn her he can get ugly?"

"By someone you mean me?" Savannah flattened her lips into a grim line. "Piper can do whatever she wants. I told her why I broke up with that asshole, so if she still chooses to date him, that's her problem. Anyway, she'd never take advice from a little tramp like me." Anger flared at the thought of how things had transpired on their visit to Montana. She knew it had a great deal to do with Piper revealing private details to Jeremy. Brandon was still apologizing for the debacle.

"He's a creep who hurt you."

Savannah squinted at her friend. "What Piper does is none of my business. Leave it, Rochelle. Quit meddling in my relationships."

"Sorry." Rochelle's face flushed as she bowed her head. "Was Brandon mad about New Haven?"

"We talked and smoothed things over. Fortunately I'm dating a grown man, not a juvenile teenage boy."

"Hey." Jackson poked her in the ribs. "I'm a teenage boy."

"I didn't mean you, honey." Vanna laughed and patted his cheek. "You'd be a great catch for some lucky woman. Wouldn't he, Ro?"

Rochelle widened her eyes at Savannah even as Jackson looked away.

Savannah studied Rochelle for a moment before her gaze traveled to Jackson, who'd ducked his head, concentrating on the screen of his laptop. Rochelle had commented on occasion about Jackson, so her expression wasn't totally unexpected, but Jackson's reaction was plain weird.

She shrugged off the feeling that there was more going on here. "Nate sure seemed to be interested, Ro. He's cute."

"Ohhh, no." Her friend shook her head. "Don't even suggest I go out with another one of Brandon's sucky friends. I had to block Dylan el-creepo from my social media and give him his own ring tone. The idiot expects I'll come running when he beckons."

Savannah peeked from the corner of her eye, noting how Jackson stiffened at the mention of Dylan. He seemed immersed in his task, but she sensed he was absorbing every single word. "Dylan isn't Brandon's friend, he's a roommate, which is driven by the exorbitant Boston rental market. Besides, Nate's kind of sweet."

"Ha." Rochelle made a face. "Nate acts all cute and adorable, and he's on his way to a great career, but he's living in a strange city. He's lonely. He sees Brandon living the good life while dating a gorgeous and sweet girl, so he's seeking someone similar to keep him warm at night."

"I suppose dating Nate could put you in the same position I'm in," Savannah said.

"And what position is that?" Jackson straightened.

"In danger of falling in love with someone who, despite his insistence that our age difference doesn't matter, has no intention of allowing this relationship to continue long-term." Savannah twirled a lock of hair around her finger. "Aside from his adorable little sister, his family hates me. He has a beautiful ex-girlfriend rooting for us to break up, and most of his friends think I'm the fun-time girl he'll dump."

"I don't know about that." Rochelle's brows drew together. "It's in the way he looks at you. He totally loves you."

Vanna bit her lip, wishing this were true. "No, Ro. He doesn't. We've known each other for close to a year, but he's never said he loves me."

"Never?" Her brows lifted.

"Time to cut him loose." Jackson drummed his fingers on the table. "I haven't spent much time around him, but the case against continuing the relationship is mounting. When the family is against you, it leads to misery. My mom's family hated my dad, and now they're divorced."

Rochelle shook her head. "Hang in there. He defended you and chose you when his mother went psycho. He's a good one. Be patient."

"How about you, Jackson? How are things going with that girl you were dating?" Savannah asked. "Camille?"

"It's not. We went out a few times, but I wasn't feeling it." Jackson looked away, but then sent a covert look at Rochelle. A flush of red crept into his face as he caught Savannah's gaze for a split second, then bowed his head.

"Next time Brandon has an evening off, you two should join us for a movie," Savannah said.

"Sounds like fun." Rochelle nodded. "Jackson?"

"We'll see." A grin crept onto his face, and when Rochelle leaned down to search for something in her bag, he shot Vanna a guilty, but grateful smile.

～

Two weeks later, Savannah borrowed the SUV and made the drive to New Haven after a difficult goodbye to a quiet but resigned Brandon.

She unpacked her bag and settled at the small table in her hotel room just as a light knock sounded, and she bounded from her chair and flung the door open.

"Savannah." Justin grinned, wrapping her in his arms and lifting her from her feet, planting a kiss on her cheek. "It been forever. I can't believe you drove here, but I'm so glad you did."

"New Haven isn't far from Boston. Dad lets me borrow the SUV whenever I need it. I hope you transfer." She tugged him inside, the door clicking closed behind him.

"I don't know. I might miss the California sunshine."

"If you're here, you can visit Boston and sail with me. Besides, Yale is an amazing school."

"Sold." Justin slipped an arm around her waist. "It's too bad Leanne doesn't want to make the move. She's settled on the West Coast."

The grin faded from Savannah's lips. "She's busy with school and new friends. We used to be close, but this past year has been tough."

"She's buried in lectures, coursework, and all the fun stuff that comes with undergrad. Don't take it personally."

"On top of the same stuff, I'm still interning for Tom, and there are some big cases developing. I haven't forgotten my friends."

"And you're managing the new man in your life. How's Brandon?" Justin rested his hands on her shoulders. "Was he upset about this trip?"

She peered at him, lifting one eyebrow.

"It's like that, is it? I'll have to meet this man of yours so he can cross me off his impending threat list." Justin glanced at his watch. "Are you ready? The tour starts in half an hour."

"Let me grab my bag. I'm excited to visit the campus." She slung her pack over her shoulder. "Let's go."

Three hours later, they were finished with the organized portion of the tour and stopped to purchase cold drinks.

"So?" Savannah asked.

"This place is amazing. It feels right, you know? More me than Stanford. How about you?"

"Tom warned me I'd fall in love with Yale." She bounced on her toes. "He's so right. This visit almost convinced me to transfer."

"Now that would be amazing." Justin poked a finger into her side. "Could you imagine how fantastic that would be? We made a great study team during our Mediterranean sailing voyage, here we'd be unstoppable."

"The undefeatable duo." Her smile faded. "I've thought about Yale. Tom thinks it would be a better fit for me than Harvard, but that means leaving Boston and my family."

"And Brandon?" Justin looped his arm around her shoulders.

She bit her lip, anticipating the next words from her friend's mouth.

"Please don't decide your future based on some guy. As you pointed out, Boston isn't far. You could drive there, and Brandon could visit."

"You're right. I'll be nineteen soon, so living away from home isn't out of the question."

"You're always saying how Brandon works insane hours so you're filling your time with other things."

"Living in a different state wouldn't do much for the relationship."

"This is your entire future. Are you ready to sacrifice your dreams for a guy you've dated for a few months?"

"Studying law at Harvard hardly qualifies as a major sacrifice. Both schools have a lot to offer. And it's not just about Brandon, but leaving Dad, Emily, Kellan, and Cierra."

Justin tugged her toward the offices. "I'm talking to an admissions officer while I'm here. Why don't you do the same? Even if they offer you a spot, you don't have to take it, but it opens up your options. You wouldn't have to make any decisions until spring, and who knows how you'll feel by then?"

Savannah sat in the small waiting area. "Complete your application. I'll wait." She tucked her bag onto her lap, waving as he disappeared.

She twirled a lock of her hair around her finger. So much of what Justin said made sense. Part of her wanted to hold on and see where things went with Brandon, but she feared he'd never love her as deeply as she'd fallen in love with him.

Another part of her wrestled with how right this campus felt. The classes were smaller, and she could picture herself here, finishing undergrad and graduating from law school. Her grades were respectable, so she had a decent chance of acceptance, especially with a recommendation letter from Tom.

She stared through the windows before tugging her laptop free from her bag. Linking into the visitor Wi-Fi, she searched for the Yale website and located the *new students* tab. What would it hurt to try?

⌒

"You're quiet." Justin took her hand in his as they wandered down the main street the next afternoon. "Missing home?"

"A little, but I have amazing company."

Justin squeezed her fingers. "Back at you. How about I treat you to a hot chocolate? It's chilly out here."

"Ha, try surviving winter in Boston," she said. "But yes please."

They found a table in a small coffee shop, Savannah unwinding her scarf and peeling off her gloves as Justin approached the counter to order drinks.

"What's on your mind?" Justin asked as he set a steaming cup in front of her minutes later.

Savannah dipped a fingertip into the swirl of whipped cream on top. "Yum," she said as she licked it, savoring the chocolate sprinkles.

"Avoiding the question. Hmmm." He tilted his head. "Does that mean you're giving serious consideration to my suggestion?"

She wrapped her icy fingers around her cup. "I already submitted my application."

A grin spread across Justin's face.

"Don't gloat." Savannah squinted at her friend. "It doesn't mean I'll be accepted."

"Ha, right. You have a higher GPA than I do. Add that to an alumni recommendation from your big shot Boston lawyer," he said, snickering, "and you're in."

"Maybe," she said with a shrug. "How does Cassidy feel about you leaving Stanford?" Savannah sipped her hot chocolate and licked the remnants of whipped cream from her lips.

"Missed a spot." Justin leaned forward and ran his thumb over her top lip, catching the stray dab of cream.

She tilted her head, widening her eyes to show him she recognized his game.

"I'm not sure it matters. She's a few months younger than I am, and neither of us are ready for a serious relationship." He leveled his gaze at her over the rim of his cup.

Savannah wrinkled her nose. "Subtle."

He fiddled with the napkin, tearing tiny shreds from the edges. "You've heard my viewpoint. We broke up for many of the same reasons. That was absolutely the right decision."

She stared into beautiful eyes framed with gorgeous thick lashes, on the receiving end of one of his heart-stopping smiles once again. Vanna remembered the days when the sight of this guy made her weak in the knees. Now Brandon caused that delicious feeling in her belly.

"It was." She nodded, content in the knowledge the love they shared had evolved into a deep friendship, the romantic feelings fading after their final summer of romance.

"I can see you're in love with him. Will it be enough?"

This guy understood her on a level few people did. They'd shared experiences that no one could take away, giving them insights into each other's thoughts and feelings. "I honestly don't know. I'm not sure he'll ever feel that way about me. He's an amazing guy. I love every minute we're together, but …" She emitted a soft sigh. "He's not ready. Maybe I'm not either, but I have this feeling. Like he's the one. I can't shake it."

Justin reached across the table and caught her hand. "Damn, you have it bad for this guy. Can I say something?"

"What? Am I acting like a lovesick teenager living in fantasyland? A man like him could never fall in love with me."

"Except he could. Your maturity level is far beyond the average undergrad. It makes sense you're attracted to an older man. That you'd attract someone who's mature, driven, and successful. You deserve more than some immature jerk."

"But? I know there's one lurking."

"If he's the one, he'll make it work and encourage you every step of the way. It's a finite time, living a short drive away, with the benefit of a phenomenal education. Meanwhile, he's immersed in a medical residency, which takes up a huge portion of his time. It took him years of intense study and hard work to win a position in Boston. Any man worth earning your love will want you to reach your full potential and be his equal."

"You're sweet. Don't ever change," she said with a tender smile. This adorable man would make some girl happy one day, of that she was sure. She half-wished it could be her, but that would never be. "If he doesn't want a long-distance relationship?"

"Then cut him loose. Don't compromise or cling to something that isn't there. You're not even nineteen."

Savannah rounded the table, leaning down to hug Justin. "Thank you," she whispered. "You always believe in me. I love you so much."

"I love you, sweetie." He held her tight, kissing her temple.

She kissed his cheek before returning to her seat. "Best we not mention this love thing to anyone, though."

"Probably a solid plan." He laughed softly. "Cassidy gets upset about our texting. I see her point, but I can't picture my life without you in it."

"Brandon has commented as have other boyfriends in the past. I don't know how to explain our friendship without people getting uptight. It is possible to get on with life and accept the situation. Emily's fine with Tiffany in the picture. Dad will always love my mother on some level. I bet Emily understands."

"They were married. Maintaining a civil connection with your ex-wife is mandatory when you have a kid."

"It's very similar. You were my first crush, my first boyfriend, and my first lover. I've known you my entire life. A lot of firsts are tied up in there."

"Does Brandon know that?"

"Does Cassidy know I was your first?"

"Touché." A tiny, guilty grin appeared. "If you were my girlfriend, I wouldn't love the idea of you visiting an ex for three days. Hotel rooms involved … yeah, not so thrilling for a guy to hear."

"He'll have to trust me."

"It's not just about trust. We're close friends, but remember when things blew up between your dad and Joel over your Aunt Alex? Even if nothing happened romantically, they have an unusually close friendship, which created insecurity. Brandon might not understand why an ex-boyfriend should be trusted."

"It's not me he mistrusts, but you?"

"It's natural to fear the unknown. Do you want him to be close friends with his ex-girlfriends? He's almost twenty-four, so I assume he's had more than a few."

Savannah pictured the perky, dark-haired Autumn and shuddered. "I met one of his exes. I hated her, even though she seems like a nice person."

"Exactly. When you get back to Boston, be gentle with him. I don't want to lose our friendship, but don't forget the cost of overstepping boundaries."

"I've missed you so much."

"I'm only a phone call away." He rewarded her with a crooked grin before he became serious. "I respect Brandon for not rushing your relationship. Those three little words are deceptively simple, but they're loaded and dangerous. The moment they leave your mouth, everything changes."

Savannah gave him a small nod to show she understood. By saying those simple, yet devastating words first and far too early, she'd delivered the balance of power to Brandon. Those three words, even when meant to be reassuring and express positive emotions, left one vulnerable. Even assuring Brandon she wasn't in love with Justin implied there was someone she loved, which left her in danger of heartbreak.

Justin smiled and lifted his cup. "Here's to us and getting into Yale."

"To us." Savannah clinked her cup with his. "And to Yale."

The grin widened as he extracted a paper from his pocket. "Up for a party? One of the tour guides from yesterday invited me. Could be a good time. We can grab dinner, change, and celebrate our last night in New Haven."

"Sounds like fun to me."

∼

Savannah giggled, fumbling with her room key. She grasped Justin's arm, which was looped around her waist. "Don' lemme fall over, 'kay?"

A low laugh rumbled from his throat as he propped a shoulder against the wall, retrieving the key from her fingers. "Not sure I can hold myself up."

The lock clicked and Vanna pressed her weight against the heavy door. She tugged at Justin's hand, dragging him into the room. "Bathroom." She wobbled inside, pushing the door closed.

Moments later, the chatter of conversation from some TV show carried through the air, along with rattling of the mini-bar.

"Vanna." Justin tapped on the door. "Can we order room service? I'm starving."

"Yes. Get me a burger with yam fries." She splashed water on her face. "Damn," she mumbled as water soaked through her top. She hauled the blouse over her head, hanging it over the edge of the tub before she stumbled into the main room.

"I ordered extra pickles on your burger." Justin lounged against the pillows of her queen-sized bed, his shoes abandoned on the floor halfway across the room. He held up a glass. "Want one?"

"Uh-huh." She nodded as she located Brandon's soft over-sized t-shirt, which she'd shoved in her bag. Turning her back, she unhooked her lacy bra, slinging it over her bag before donning the shirt, and slipping off her skirt. She crawled onto the bed, accepting her drink.

Justin joined her, sitting cross-legged in front of her. "Think of all the fun parties when we move here."

Vanna gave him a gentle shove. "Who says I'm movin'?"

"You know you want to. Admit it. You had fun."

"Course I did, but ..." She shrugged.

Justin bounded from the bed to answer the knock. "Hold that thought." He opened the door and stepped back to allow room for the cart, shoving a generous tip in the man's hands before ushering him into the hallway.

Savannah sighed after swallowing her first bite. "This is yummy." She popped a fry into her mouth.

"This entire hotel is nice."

"Tom recommended it. Y'know, he owns a place here, but it's rented. He lived in New Haven for several years while he finished law school." She took another bite from her burger, her buzz easing as the food hit her belly.

"Let me know if it becomes available before I move. But then, it's probably swanky and expensive."

"And it's two or three bedrooms, but it's walking distance to campus."

"You could be my roommate." Justin snickered.

"You're not giving up on this idea." She giggled. "Wouldn't my boyfriend just love me shacking up with my ex?"

"Being roommates is hardly shacking up."

"Still, not sure he'd be thrilled. It would take some serious sweet talk." She set aside her plate, patting her belly. "I'm stuffed. We should watch a movie."

Justin cleared the dishes and wheeled the cart into the hall as she found the remote and snuggled under the covers, propping herself up on pillows against the headboard. He joined her on the bed, sliding an arm around her shoulder. "This," he said as he plucked at her cotton shirt, "smells like aftershave."

"It's Brandon's. The scent comforts me."

"I figured." He leaned back, settling in as the movie started.

Savannah sank against his chest, her eyelids growing heavy.

"Vanna." The soft low voice in her ear was accompanied by a gentle shake. "Wake up, sweetie."

"Hmmm?" She blinked, the room coming into focus. The first thing she noticed was the daylight filtering through a crack in the drapes.

"Let me up. I have a flight, and I need to shower." Justin wiggled his arm out from under her. "We crashed. I don't even remember the end of the movie."

"Me either." She propped up on one elbow, puffing out a burst of air to blow the strands of hair from her face.

Justin handed her a water bottle before heading toward the door. "Good thing my room is just down the hall."

"I'll shower and we can grab breakfast before I drop you at the airport."

"Thanks, hon. See you in thirty." He waved and bounded out the door.

Savannah leaned against the wall of the elevator, closing her eyes. The entire trip back she'd spent mulling over Justin's words, feeling conflicted. So many of the points he'd made were solid, but her heart wasn't sure.

How could she keep it together with Brandon if she moved to attend Yale? Was Justin right about being patient, or had Brandon already slotted her into a short-term spot, someone to be remembered fondly in later years while he went about his life with his wife and kids? Would that wife be Autumn?

As she stepped into the foyer, familiar voices carried from the kitchen. Her smile brightened as she set her bag by the coat rack and headed into the kitchen.

"Brandon." She jumped into his arms, sighing as his well-known scent enveloped her. Seeing him swept away her fears about the future, being held in his arms calmed her racing thoughts.

He held her tight, kissing her long and hard. "I hoped you'd be home soon," he murmured against her lips before capturing them again.

Savannah buried her head in the crook of his neck and closed her eyes. "What are you doing here?"

"The gang had pizza and beer after basketball. Your dad invited me to hang out until you got home. How was New Haven?"

"Fun. We toured and asked a lot of questions. Justin spent some time with an admissions officer, and then we explored the area. It went well. He applied to transfer from Stanford."

"Good." He nodded and smiled.

Savannah tilted her head, studying his face for any sign of jealousy, but he seemed level and calm. She kissed him again before rounding the counter to give her dad and Kellan hugs.

"It went well?" Aiden's brows rose.

She gave a tiny nod. The questions he wanted to ask, but wouldn't, sat between them. They'd agreed nothing would be discussed until she'd made her own decisions about leaving Harvard for Yale.

"How was the trip?" Rochelle set her bag on the floor beside her seat. "Did you get any studying done?"

"Nada. The trip was fantastic. Justin is a lot of fun. It was like old times."

"Old times, huh?" Rochelle's brows shot up.

"Not those kind." Savannah elbowed her friend. "None of that. We're friends."

"Friends with benefits." The other girl snickered.

"Not anymore. I wouldn't do that to Brandon."

"No hugging or kissing or other extracurriculars?"

"Nope. Well, I kissed his cheek and hugged him once or twice, but that's it …" *Except for him falling asleep in my room. But nothing happened. It didn't count.*

"Why the guilty look?"

Savannah glanced around and lowered her voice. "We went to a party, and when we came back, we fell asleep in my bed, but nothing happened," she whispered. "He has a girlfriend, and I'm dating Brandon."

"He stayed in your room?" she asked. "Did you tell Brandon?"

"Shh. Don't announce it. And no, are you insane? He was upset I even went to New Haven, so stirring up a pile of trouble would be stupid."

"I see your point. I won't tell, I promise." She zipped a fingertip across her lips. "How about a study session on Saturday? We have finals coming up."

"Sounds good. Brandon got the time off for the ski trip so that should be fun."

"Lucky girl." Rochelle turned to the front as their professor began their lecture.

# CHAPTER 9

BRANDON PACKED THE LAST OF the items in his bag, thankful to be escaping for an entire week. He smothered a yawn and rubbed his eyes, longing for an extra-strong cup of coffee to combat the long hours he'd worked to justify this time off.

Dylan leaned against the door frame, watching every move. "Damn. I should've picked up Savannah and let you have Rochelle."

"Like she'd date a disgusting pig like you," he muttered under his breath.

"Canada for a week of skiing and sucking up to three ER attending physicians?" His roommate snorted. "Damn. You hit the big time."

"Shut the hell up." Brandon zipped his bag. "No sleeping in my bed and stay out of my clothes."

Dylan snickered. "You mean the fancy designer stuff your sugar mamma is always buying you?"

"Spend your time wisely. Like"—Brandon narrowed gritty tired eyes—"looking for new roommates." His phone buzzed and a text appeared:

*Car's here!*

After a quick reply to say he was on his way down, he shoved his laptop into his bag and patted down his pockets for his wallet, keys, and passport. He pushed past Dylan, not even bothering to say goodbye as he exited, letting the door slam behind him. He hoped he and Nate would have time to visit some of the listings they'd been accumulating once he got back.

A sleek black sedan waited at the curb in front of his building. The driver stepped forward and opened the door before depositing Brandon's bag in the trunk.

Savannah took his hand as he slipped into his seat. "Ready for a week of fun?"

"More than ready." He brushed her lips with his, lingering before he settled in and accepted the cup she offered as they pulled into traffic. "I'm beat. Last night was crazy. I barely managed to get home and shower."

She caressed his cheek. "Close your eyes and relax until we get to the airport."

He sighed and sank into the plush leather, zoning out until Savannah's light squeeze to his knee alerted him they'd arrived at the hangar.

They exited the car as their bags were transferred from the trunk to the baggage compartment of the jet. Savannah led him up the steps and into the interior of the Gulfstream.

He smiled and waved at Emily, who cuddled Cierra. Kellan sat on the sofa beside them, engrossed in the antics of colorful animated characters on the screen.

"Let me do that, sweetie." Brandon stowed their carry-on bags before they settled into seats.

Kellan crawled into Brandon's lap, leaning his head against his chest.

"You have a fan." Emily laughed. "You arrived just in time. Cierra needs a change. Keep an eye on your brother, Vanna? Don't let him get underfoot while Aiden completes preflight."

"We'll keep him contained," Vanna said.

A few minutes later, Savannah jumped to her feet as Alex arrived, struggling with a crying Devon in a carrier and a whining Daniel clinging to her hand.

"Teddy, Mommy." Daniel sank onto the floor and wrapped his arms around Alex's calves.

"I'll take Devon and Daniel while you organize for the flight," Vanna said to Alex, kneeling to unbuckle the fussing baby boy from his carrier.

"Thank you. Joel is supervising the baggage and both of these boys are cranky. Can you find Daniel's bear?" Alex's face scrunched and she blinked hard, emitting a sniffle.

"Here." Savannah took the diaper bag.

Brandon set Kellan on the seat beside him. "Stay here, bud. I'll be right back." He made his way to the front, crouching in front of Daniel as Savannah searched the diaper bag. "We're watching a movie, and maybe it would be okay with Mommy if we made snacks." He smiled as Vanna handed Daniel his teddy bear.

"Cocoa bear." Daniel clutched the stuffed toy, releasing Alex.

"Thank you," Alex said softly.

Brandon hauled Daniel to his feet, leading him to the sofa and settling him beside Kellan. He reached over to straighten Devon's blanket as Savannah rested the baby against her shoulder. "I'll get these two guys some juice. Want anything?"

"Shh, Devon." She shook her head as she rubbed the baby's back. "I'll get this little guy calmed down."

Brandon moved to the small galley, checking the supply of snacks. Minutes later he returned to the sofa, laden with spill-proof toddler cups and a small tray of crackers, cheese, and sliced fruit for the two boys to share.

Jenna arrived soon afterward, bouncing Adrianna on her hip, followed by Will and his guest for the trip, Andre, and Iona.

"Preflight exterior check is done and the baggage is loaded," Aiden said to Tom as they appeared in the doorway. "All passengers are on-board."

"Thanks for managing all of that. Sorry we're late. We had a toddler emergency." Tom closed the exterior door, and they both disappeared into the cockpit.

"Go." Savannah motioned to the front as Iona joined her on the couch. "You missed out during the New York trip. I know you want to."

"You don't mind?"

"You have about five seconds before we leave the hangar. Go."

Brandon made the short trip to the front and tapped on the cockpit door.

"Enter," Tom said. He glanced over his shoulder. "Ahh, looking for the best view for takeoff?"

"Is the jump seat available?"

"You bet. Sit down and fasten your belt." Aiden flipped a switch and the engines whirred to life. "We're next in line for the runway."

Brandon buckled in, fascinated as Tom and Aiden talked on their headsets and checked various gauges, listening to the chatter back and forth from the tower.

Soon they were taxiing from the hangar and rolling onto the runway. Aiden responded to air traffic control and drew the control back smoothly, the jet increasing speed and lifting off.

Brandon's stomach performed a tiny flip, the one that hit him for that split second when the sense of weightlessness took over.

Once they reached cruising altitude, Aiden flipped another switch. "Autopilot on." He stretched and glanced over his shoulder. "Get some sleep, Brandon. You look like hell."

"Thanks for noticing, but it was a long shift."

"I imagine. It'll be nothing but clouds for a while, and we set up the stateroom."

"Sleep sounds amazing." Brandon made his way through the cabin to where Vanna chatted with Jenna.

Vanna rose, taking his hand and leading him to the rear of the plane into the small, but adequate stateroom. "You're ready to crash."

"I'm so tired, I can barely move." He stripped off his sweatshirt and jeans and crawled between the covers, enjoying the soft scent of her as she brushed his lips with hers, stroking his hair with her fingertips.

"Get some rest," she whispered as he sank into darkness.

Sunshine glinted off the fresh powder as their group gazed down the slope. They'd risen early, determined to take advantage of the fresh snowfall on this quiet weekday morning and get in a few runs before the powder was disturbed by other skiers. Light, fluffy flakes of snow had fallen most of the night, but ceased in the early hours, the clouds miraculously opening up to reveal a bright sun in a blue sky, even though the air remained cold and crisp.

Aiden adjusted his goggles and grinned before pushing off, followed by Tom and Alex seconds later.

Brandon glanced at Savannah, who waited until Ryan, Joel, and Jenna started on their descent. "What are you waiting for?"

She snickered. "Are you kidding? I'd get run over. Unless I'm skiing with just one of them, I let the pros go first. Look." She pointed.

The group was flying down the steep grade, showing no hesitation even considering the difficulty of the slope.

Savannah pushed off, followed by Emily, Will, Kaari, and Andre. Brandon brought up the rear, attacking the run, catching sight of the bright pink trim on Savannah's ski helmet as she executed a graceful descent. Her wide turns kept her speed under tight control, allowing him to catch up easily.

By the time they reached the bottom, most of the group was already on the chairs on the way toward the summit.

Vanna smiled as they joined the lift line. "You don't have to wait for me. Aside from Emily, I'm the slowest skier in the group."

"I don't mind." He shrugged, sliding into place for the chair to scoop them up. He gazed at the mountains, sucking in a long breath of crisp air. "This is amazing. And that chalet … wow." From first sight, he'd been overwhelmed by the private lodge, with its luxurious bedroom suites, gym, current pool, and massage room.

"We've gone on an amazing vacation every year since I met Aiden. The first year, he took me to Maui. I learned to surf and snorkel and took scuba lessons. Other years it's been ski trips, the Vineyard, and New York."

"He's generous. I've never met anyone quite like him. He doesn't make a deal about me staying over, the meals they feed me, or this trip. Aiden allowing me to use his expensive ski equipment was unexpected." He pointed at the performance boots and skis on his feet. "It's so opposite to how my family treated you, it's embarrassing."

"Stop beating yourself up over Montana. It's like Aiden feeling responsible for James or Thomas Hamilton, or Tiffany being apologetic because David Baxter is … was … a horrible man. You think your mother's the worst I've dealt with? Not by a long shot."

"You are so much like your dad."

"Learned from the best." She snickered as she lifted the safety bar, holding her poles in one hand as she slid down the exit ramp. A huge grin appeared. "Race you to the bottom."

After several hours on the slopes, they headed to the chalet, stowing all the gear in the locker room on the main floor.

"Wow," Brandon took in the snacks laid out for them. "This catering thing is amazing."

"It's a nice break," Emily said as she selected items from the buffet. "Aiden works hard, so when Tom told me we had the option of hiring chefs for aprés-ski snacks and dinners, I told him to book it."

"Tired of his cooking?" Brandon grinned.

"Completely." She rolled her eyes. "My husband deserves to spend our precious vacation time with his kids without worrying about everyone else."

"He is a caretaker."

"I love that about him, but occasionally, he's the one who needs to be taken care of. That doesn't come easily for Aiden, believe me." She popped a canapé into her mouth. "He and Tom are planning to take Kellan and Adrianna out on the slopes tomorrow."

"They're not even three."

"They walk, therefore they ski." She gave a light laugh. "Good thing Aiden convinced me, because Kellan can't stop talking about Daddy teaching him."

"He's a great dad." Brandon shot a look over his shoulder to where Aiden sat with Cierra cuddled in one arm, picking at his plate of snacks while talking to Ryan and Kaari.

"He's amazing. All the guys in this group are exceptional with the kids, and everyone helps. We have a well-established village. If only we all had such fantastic role models. I sure didn't, and neither did Aiden. We strive to be as opposite to our fathers as possible."

"I hear that." Brandon observed as Savannah appeared and stopped to chat with Tom.

"Everything okay with you two?" Emily asked.

"More than okay, though I feel awful about how my mother treated Savannah. And when she left for New Haven, I was less than supportive about the trip, but it appears she's forgiven me for being an ass about Justin."

Emily smiled softly. "Dealing with exes can be tough, but try to let her know how you feel without getting hostile, and talk things out. It's a whole new skill set."

"Experience talking?"

"Tiffany?" Emily raised a brow. "Not to mention another woman who tried to rekindle her relationship with Aiden during one of our mini break-ups."

"Damn." Brandon winced. "How did you handle that?"

"Not well on any level. It almost destroyed our wedding. Having the supermodel appearing in the mix was disastrous."

Brandon smirked. "Attractive was she."

"All of his exes are, but this was literally a supermodel. Yet he chose me and forgave me on the grounds of temporary insanity. I got over his past and learned to trust him. Without trust, there is nothing. Absolutely nothing."

～

Brandon peered through the windows as dusk settled over the mountain. "Do you think we could manage a dip in that hot tub? I overdid it on the slopes today."

"Too much time in the hospital and not enough time working out?" Vanna came up behind him to rub his shoulders with her flattened palms.

"That feels amazing." He sighed, relaxing under her gentle touch.

"After a soak in the tub, maybe I'll give you a massage." She wrapped her arms around his waist from behind, pressing against his back.

"How are you so good to me?" He folded his arms over hers, holding her hands, before turning within the comforting circle of her embrace. "Vanna? I'm sorry for being a jerk about New Haven. I admit I'm jealous about Justin."

"I get jealous when ex-girlfriends kiss you." She slid her hands up his back, looping one around the nape of his neck. "Justin wants to meet you so you can set your fears to rest."

"You told him?"

"I didn't have to. He's a smart guy, so he understood the situation without explanations. I've known him a long time, but you don't need to be worried about me and Justin. We're not getting back together."

He nodded, considering the advice he'd received not only from Aiden while Vanna was away, but from Emily. Time to put the jealousy aside or risk pushing her away. It would be difficult to accept the friendship, but he either trusted or he didn't. "I'd love to meet Justin."

"Good." She patted his cheek. "How are things with Mia? She's been texting, and I'm not sure how to take some of her comments."

"Like what?"

"Carol and Jeremy always seem to be fighting."

"Damn. I knew it." He scrubbed at his face. "While you were in New Haven, I asked Aiden if he knows how to locate my father. Maybe the guy won't give a damn. Hell, he might be dead, but I have to try. My mother isn't close to any of her family, and I don't know any of my father's family. I have to get Mia out of that house."

"What did Dad say?"

"He put me in touch with an investigator Tom uses at the law firm, and he's working on it."

"It's worth a try, for Mia. So before you fall asleep, let's have some hot tub time." She dug into her suitcase, pulling out one of her bikinis, dangling it from her fingertips. "This one?"

Brandon nodded his approval at the deep pink he knew would look amazing against her creamy skin and blonde hair. He shucked his own clothes and pulled on swim trunks while she fastened her top.

Savannah turned, swiftly creating an elegant side braid to keep her hair out of the water.

"I'm not sure we're making it out of this bedroom." His gaze lingered on the swell of her breasts peeking from the top of the triangles of fabric, over her taught belly and the soft flare of her hips, down to her shapely legs.

A soft smile tugged at the corners of her mouth. She fiddled with the end of her braid as she performed her own inspection, taking small slow steps toward him.

Brandon caught her around the waist, tossing her lightly on the bed and hovering over her. "Damn. You get more beautiful every time I look at you." The delicate flush of her cheeks and bright sparkling eyes captivated him. He leaned in, capturing her bottom lip as he caressed the breasts that seemed fuller and more voluptuous each and every day. The softness of her skin and full round hips enticed him.

He buried his face in the crook of her neck, inhaling. "You smell so damn good." A deep sigh escaped as he allowed those now-familiar emotions to carry him away. *Was this how it felt to be in love?*

～⌣

"We still haven't been to the hot tub." Vanna trickled her fingers down his chest, rousing him from the dream like state he'd fallen into.

Life at this moment felt perfect. An incredible woman in his arms, in a luxurious retreat with a group of people who had become like family. A convoluted set of relationships, no doubt, as three of the people in this house were key to his future as a doctor, but he couldn't think about that. All he could think about was how to make this work with Savannah.

He pressed his lips to the top of her head as he gave her a light squeeze. "Surprised nobody sent a search party. We've been in here for over an hour."

Savannah peeked at him. "Everyone is respectful of privacy on these trips, and there's no set schedule. We could sleep all day and nobody would say a word." She giggled. "Though we'd better be on time for dinner as we both know you can't miss a meal."

"Haha, funny girl. I doubt we'd starve. Have you seen the load of snacks in the guest kitchen? But you're right. We should have our soak so we can shower before dinner, though … I'm pretty relaxed at this moment."

Another light laugh issued from her lips. "Up, then. We only have an hour before dinner." She rose from the bed in a sinuous move, tossing his swim trunks at him as she located her bikini.

Brandon admired her as she adjusted her top.

"What? Got to tuck in the girls. I swear this bikini used to fit better."

"Fits pretty well from where I'm sitting," he said with a playful leer. "All this fresh air and skiing has given you a lovely glow."

"Quit flirting." She winked as she slid on a pair of flip-flops and a light beach cover up.

"Nothing but the truth." He followed her through the house and onto the stone patio.

The outdoor fireplace crackled merrily, and it seemed all of the men had migrated to the hot tub.

"Drinks?" Ryan motioned to a bucket of bottles. "Or I can mix you something sweet and fruity." A cheeky grin appeared as he winked at Vanna.

"I'll try one of those craft beers, Uncle Ryan," Savannah said.

"Same for me." Brandon accepted the bottle and they both slid into the hot water, joining in on the conversation.

After five minutes, Savannah lifted herself out, perching on the edge and setting her barely-touched beer aside.

"You okay, honey?" Aiden asked, eyeing his daughter.

Savannah's face paled, her eyes watering as she pressed the back of her hand over her mouth.

Aiden's eyes widened. He hauled himself out of the tub, grabbing for one of the empty buckets on the deck as Savannah lunged to the side of the patio, leaned over the railing, and vomited into the bank of snow.

Her dad grabbed a towel from the pile, wrapping it around her trembling body and rubbing her back.

Brandon dragged himself out of the water and crossed the icy flagstones with her flip-flops in hand, helping her slip them on. "Where did that come from?"

"I don't know." She rubbed her eyes. "I felt dizzy, and then nauseous, and now, I want to sleep. I'm so embarrassed."

Aiden hugged her. "Don't be. If you heard some of the stories about everyone else on this patio …"

This brought a faint smile to her lips. "I bet they'd appreciate that."

"I bet they wouldn't." Aiden smirked. "Why don't you take a nap before dinner? You're probably jet-lagged and dehydrated." He wrapped an arm around his daughter. "I've got it, Brandon. Enjoy a soak before dinner. I should check on Emily while I'm inside. She went in to feed Cierra."

After Savannah and Aiden were inside, Brandon rejoined the men in the tub. "Is this a guy's only thing?" He motioned around the circle.

Tom laughed. "No, but Jenna's expecting our second child next summer. The skiing and fresh air did her in."

"Congrats." Brandon raised his beer.

Aiden appeared and lowered himself in the tub with a fresh icy bottle in his hand. "I tucked Savannah into bed. She was out cold in seconds."

"That was sudden," Tom said. "You sure she's okay?"

"Nothing sleep won't fix." Aiden tipped back his beer.

Brandon closed his eyes, content in knowing Vanna was resting, but he reopened them at the click of a lighter.

Aiden and Will both gave Brandon a look as Ryan hauled himself onto the edge of the tub, taking the slim white object from Tom.

The unmistakable aroma brought a half-grin to Brandon's face. "Don't we have to worry about work?"

Aiden accepted the joint from Ryan. "We're not on duty or in danger of being called in. It's a vacation tradition." The man closed his eyes, letting out a stream of smoke, his hand extended toward Andre who passed the joint to Will.

Will took a hit and held it out to Brandon. "It's quality."

Brandon tipped his head, looking toward Aiden, who cracked one eye open as if he sensed Brandon's stare.

"It's up to you. Not your thing, that's fine. But if it is, enjoy. You won't endanger your career. What happens on vacation never really happened at all."

"Kind of like Vegas, huh?" Brandon took it between his fingertips, studying it for a moment before taking a drag. "Damn." His grin widened. "The good stuff." He rested his head against the side, enjoying the few stars peeking out from between the clouds as a calmness settled over him. The only sounds were the bubbles in the hot tub and the occasional clink of a bottle.

"I bought a ring," Ryan said as the joint began its second round.

Brandon opened his eyes, rolling his head toward the man who had earned the attention of everyone in the hot tub.

"It's in my bag. I thought I'd ask her this week, but"—the man raked his fingers through his hair—"I'm so damn nervous. I want to share it with everyone, so maybe one night after dinner?"

"Noooooooooo." Aiden shook his head. "Don't even think it. Private, romantic, special, and memorable."

"I second that," Tom said. "I asked Jenna in the Vineyard because of all our happy memories there."

"I asked Alex on our beach in the Vineyard," Joel said, "on a romantic sunset walk. One knee, the whole deal."

"Aiden?" Ryan grinned. "Never heard either of your stories."

"Do I have to?" Aiden's lips twisted. "Em was a tough one, but she said yes in Boston at that perfect moment, unplanned as it was."

"How about Sharkie?"

"Fuck, Ryan, you need to stop with that." Aiden saluted Ryan with his middle finger. "I'm not telling."

Tom smirked. "A romantic interlude in the mausoleum with a special heirloom ring. Tiffany scored major vintage rock."

"You proposed in a mausoleum?" Brandon frowned.

A round of laughter burst out.

"That's our nickname for Gramma Grace's mega-mansion," Tom said. "Our boy Aiden scaled trellises and sneaked through bedroom windows like a pro, so smuggling her in presented no challenge."

Aiden squinted at Tom, raising his middle finger. "Watch it. I could tell some stories about you, Tommy."

"I have even better ones about you." Tom quirked a brow. "Remember the time—"

"Settle down, you two." Ryan made a timeout motion. "So your advice is wait until we're in California?"

"Hell no." Aiden shook his head. "But pulling out a ring in front of a room full of people is not the right kind of memorable. I can't wait to see it, though."

"I visited your jeweler and he delivered. It's spectacular, though maybe not quite as amazing as Emily's."

"I'm sure she'll love it," Tom said. "It's not a competition, though we all agree Aiden should stop showering his wife with expensive jewelry."

"Right?" Joel rolled his eyes. "Alex about fainted when she saw Emily's engagement ring. I appeased my wife with a big-ass diamond for our tenth anniversary."

"Is this pick on Aiden night?" Aiden took a long drag from the joint. "Ryan, ask the girl already. We'll crack one of those bottles of champagne."

Tom lifted his beer. "Here's to a successful proposal. Kaari's great. We were beginning to wonder what was taking you so long."

"Fear." A sheepish grin appeared. "What if she says no?"

"You've talked about it, right?" Aiden lifted a shoulder. "She seems ready. Why would she say no?" He tapped his bottle against Ryan's. "She's a catch. Better make it official."

Brandon joined in the round of toasts, glad he'd been able to join in on the trip. Savannah really did have the best family ever.

# CHAPTER 10

## *Savannah*

AVANNAH FELT GROGGY, HER MOUTH dry and pasty. She wished she'd brushed her teeth instead of allowing a rinse with water to suffice. After her dad tucked her in, she'd fallen into a deep sleep, barely surfacing to use the bathroom before crawling back into bed, her eyelids sinking closed right away.

Her dad seemed convinced she'd been pushing herself too hard, with too many late-night study sessions. Working at the law firm while managing a social life around Brandon's hectic schedule as an intern added to the stress.

She sucked in a breath as she adjusted her position, ignoring the discomfort of her tender breasts. She feared the heightened color in her cheeks had nothing to do with fresh crisp mountain air.

How, she didn't know. They'd been careful. *Most of the time.* And she'd been diligent with her pills. *Almost always.* She closed her eyes, picturing her reunion with Brandon after the New Haven trip. The sweetness of his apology. The tenderness of his lips against her heated flesh. Kisses, growing deeper, more passionate, and urgent as she caressed his hot smooth skin.

She rose from the bed, stopping in front of the full-length mirror on the closet door on her way to the bathroom, lifting her t-shirt to examine her profile, cupping a hand over her flat belly.

The symptoms had stolen over her, unnoticed. *Until now.* The aching fullness of her breasts, the rosy color in her cheeks, the recent bouts of nausea.

Even her multiple trips to the bathroom during the flight signaled significant changes in her body.

The door handle turned and she straightened her shirt, smoothing it down. This would be a delicate conversation.

"You're up." Brandon crossed the wood floor and wrapped his arms around her. "Feeling better?"

"Much. The sleep helped." Her belly rumbled. "I could probably eat."

"So I hear." He grinned as he patted her stomach.

Savannah cupped his face and stared into his red-rimmed eyes. "Are you … high?" She stretched to sniff his hair. "You smell like weed." Her eyes widened. "You are."

"Am I in trouble?" His mouth twitched into a goofy grin. "I'll join the club."

"Let me guess." A snicker escaped. "Tom?"

He shrugged.

"You smoked pot with my dad."

"Everyone did, except Andre, so … it's like Vegas, baby." Confusion clouded his eyes. "Is Kavanagh …?" His frown deepened. "Is Andre his … boyfriend?"

The peel of laughter broke free. She'd seen Brandon drink, but this presented a new side. "You didn't know?" She patted his cheek. "You've been accepted into the family. Vacation habits are top secret."

"You're not mad?" He spanned her waist with his hands.

She shook her head. "My dad wouldn't have allowed you to join them if he thought I'd freak."

"He's a chill dude." He snickered. "Funny, when you said your dad checked on you, I pictured a white-haired middle-aged man. You have the best family, ever."

"That I do." She leaned in, resting her head against his chest. The levity distracted her from the fears she longed to share with Brandon, but the guy wasn't in control of his emotions or words, so she'd keep them to herself. "Let's eat dinner."

His eyes lit up. "I'm starving."

Savannah held out her hand. "Come on. Let's join the best-ever family."

⌒〜

The next morning came too early. Even though they'd retired not long after dinnertime, her eyelids felt heavy. She burrowed into her pillow, squirming closer to the warm body beside her, comforted by his presence.

He mumbled something she couldn't make out, but he curled an arm over her waist, not even waking.

Her thoughts drifted as she dozed, until the pressure became too much. She lifted his hand, but he only wrapped her tighter against him.

"Don't go."

"I'm about to explode." Vanna tugged at the arm pinning her. "Let me up." Her stomach lurched and she pressed the back of her hand over her mouth.

The gagging sound alerted him and he released his hold, propping himself on one elbow as she scrambled from bed.

Vanna dashed into the bathroom, sinking to her knees as her mouth watered and a sour taste rose. She clutched her blonde locks in one hand as she heaved her stomach contents into the shiny white porcelain.

Brandon brushed the strands of hair from her face, gathering the curls and tying them back with one of the bands on the counter. He draped one of the fluffy robes around her shoulders. "I thought I'd be the one hanging over the toilet. How much did you drink?"

"I didn't drink." She'd refused the wine at dinner and stuck to water all night. Hungover, she wasn't.

He tipped her chin toward him, wiping her face with a warm wash cloth. "You're pale." After setting the cloth aside, he pressed two fingers against her wrist. "Pulse is strong, but you're shaking. Rinse." He passed her a glass of water.

She swished it around her mouth and spat before taking ginger sips.

"All done?" At her nod, Brandon scooped her into his arms, carrying her to bed and tucking her under the covers. He crawled in beside her. "You should rest." He pressed the back of his hand to her forehead. "You don't seem warm. Sore throat? Headache?"

She shook her head. "It's not the flu," she said.

Brandon sucked in a breath. "What's going on?" He closed his eyes. "Please tell me you're not."

Savannah bit her lip, blinking up at him. "I'm late," she whispered.

"Fuck." Brandon sat, burying his face in his hands. "How late? Have you taken a test?"

"I thought it was stress, but now I feel sick."

"Your skin is flushed, which means increased blood flow, and your body is changing." His gaze seemed drawn to her chest. "We need to find out for sure. Until then, no drinking or hot tub, and you should take it easy on the slopes."

"You're angry, aren't you?" She dragged a hand through her mass of hair. "What if I am?"

"I'm upset I wasn't more careful," he said in a level voice. "But your dad will bust my ass. He could too. I've seen those kick-boxing moves on that poor defenseless heavy-bag in the gym."

"Maybe I'm not." She exhaled, long and slow. "There must be a pharmacy nearby."

"I'm sure there is. It's Canada, not the Outback." Brandon scrubbed his hands through his hair. "How will we manage a trip to town without tipping anyone off?"

"I don't feel great, so you stay to keep me company. We'll ask the chalet's driver to take us. We'd be back before anyone notices."

"Do you feel well enough?"

"I'll shower, and we'll see." She shrugged. "Tell my dad I'm taking a day's rest from skiing."

He pressed a kiss to her forehead. "I'll start the shower so it's warm."

She took her time sliding from the bed, crossing the room as the sound of water pattered in the shower.

"You good?" He helped her remove her shirt and step into the stall.

"I'm not an invalid." She patted his cheek, grateful for his concern. "Let everyone know so they're not waiting for us."

She rested a palm against the tile as he left, savoring the soothing warm spray washing over her. By the time she finished, she felt much better. Her stomach settled and her anxiety was easing now that Brandon shared her secret.

She brushed out her hair, selecting a fresh pair of leggings and topping them with a bulky sweater, forgoing the pain-inducing bra. Then she made her way to the kitchen. "Everyone gone?"

"Iona is with the babies, but everyone else left. I assured your dad you needed extra sleep and said we might join them later if you felt up to it."

"Good." She selected one of the blueberry muffins from under the glass dome, breaking off a chunk and popping it in her mouth. "Did you ask about the car?"

"We'll leave whenever you're ready." He linked their fingers. "This is my fault. I've been going over the timing in my head, and that night you came home from New Haven"—he kissed the back of her hand—"I slipped up?"

She picked at a nail. "I missed my pill that morning. I didn't think about it at the time." She bowed her head. "I messed up. It's not all on you."

"No matter. It leaves us in the same spot. It's bad timing all around. How can we take care of a baby? I barely manage my own life without being responsible for one."

Savannah set her half-eaten muffin on a plate. "What are you saying?"

"I have no idea." He covered his face with his hands. "Let's talk about something else until we know for sure."

For the duration of the ride into town they were saved from talking. The driver pointed out local landmarks and chatted amiably.

"I'll wait in the coffee shop." The man offered Brandon a card. "Text me when you're ready to go home."

"Thanks." Brandon adjusted Savannah's scarf around her neck. "Don't get chilled." He took her gloved hand in his. "There is a serious amount of snow here. I heard about the amazing skiing but, even living in Montana, we never crossed the border."

"It's my first time too." Her breath formed a white puff. "It's a bit like Boston. Cold in the winter with lots of snow. The mountains here are enormous and it's pretty. I'd love to visit in the summer."

Brandon hesitated before opening the door of the drugstore and ushering Savannah inside. The warmth surrounded them, and they both unwrapped their scarves and removed their gloves.

Savannah spotted the sign above the aisle. "There." She pointed, taking careful steps toward the middle of the store. She picked up a box, scanning the label before setting it on the shelf and examining another. "Which is best?" she whispered, shooting a look at her boyfriend. "You're a doctor. Pick one."

"Ummm." He selected a box. "Accurate results one week after missed period in five minutes. Nothing fancy, but there are three tests." He tapped the package against his hand. "Anything else?"

"Chocolate," Savannah said. "Or something salty. I'm hungry."

"And it begins." He stopped in the snack aisle. "Pick what you'd like. I spotted a café down the street. We could eat before we head back. Meet me up front."

Savannah chose two of her favorite chocolate bars and a small bag of chips, setting them on the counter. "I have to pee," she mumbled.

"Hold that thought." Brandon paid, took the bag, and they exited onto the street. "The diner is down the block. Looks like you can order breakfast. Maybe you could …" He lifted the bag. "I can't wait another hour or however long it takes to eat and drive back."

They entered the café and chose a booth near the window overlooking the picturesque street.

Savannah accepted the box, searching for the bathroom sign. "Order me eggs and hash browns with bacon or sausage." Her mouth watered at the savory smells. "And peppermint tea."

Savannah read the directions three times before mustering the courage to pee on the stick. She returned the completed test to the plastic wrapper without looking, tucking the unused ones in her purse.

At least the color was returning to her cheeks. She could pretend nothing was different. *Almost.* The outline of the stick in her pocket reminded her nothing would ever be the same. Even with a negative result, this moment would define a new chapter in their relationship.

A small ceramic pot of hot water with a teabag on the side had arrived at her spot during her absence. "Thanks." She slid into the booth.

"What does it say?"

"I'm too scared to look." She bit her lip.

His small nod and audible inhale told her she wasn't alone. "Pass it over."

She shook her head. "Together?"

Brandon joined her on her bench. "Let's do this. The results must be showing by now."

Savannah slid the stick from her pocket, the pink letters on the wrapper blurring. "Just … here." She pushed it into his hand. "I can't even …" Her stomach twisted.

He removed the stick from the wrapper and turned it. His eyes met hers for a second before his chin tipped down again. "What now?"

"Should I take another?"

"False positives are rare." He returned to his side of the table as the waitress appeared with their food.

Savannah picked at her meal, sending frequent glances in Brandon's direction.

"Eat, sweetie," he said before retrieving a container from the bag. "Take two of these." Brandon placed it in front of her.

"When did you buy these?" Savannah studied the prenatal vitamins.

"While you were choosing chocolate."

"You knew it would be positive."

He lifted a shoulder. "I suspected."

Savannah tipped two tablets into her palm and tossed them into her mouth, chasing them down with a mouthful of water. "You want to have the baby?"

"I have no idea what I want."

She stared into those deep gray eyes, her heart breaking, even if only a little. The lost and sad look on his face made her want to weep. Maybe she mirrored his devastated look on her own face. She had no idea what to do or how to make this easier.

"I'm sorry, Vanna. I'm sure you want more from me right now, but I just don't know. My life is a mess. Damn. I want to be what you need, but I'm not ready for any of this."

She lowered her gaze, staring sightlessly at her half-finished meal. Here it was, the moment everything ended. The moment she'd feared. "I'm tired." She pulled out her wallet and tucked some bills under the edge of her cup before she slid from the seat and donned her coat and scarf.

"Vanna." Brandon reached for her hand, but she shook her head.

"I'll wait outside." She strode through the door and sucked in gulps of crisp air, tipping her chin and closing her eyes as light flakes of snow drifted onto her cheeks. Then she walked, focused on reaching the van.

"Hey." Brandon caught her arm, forcing her to turn. "Don't run away."

She dropped her chin to her chest, the lump in her throat preventing her from speaking.

He wrapped an arm around her shoulders. "We'll figure it out."

She shrugged but allowed him to keep his arm tucked around her as they arrived at the van. The driver had seen them coming and appeared to open the door. Savannah settled into her seat, leaning her forehead against the cool glass of the window.

# Chapter 11

## Brandon

The return ride to the chalet seemed tense, though if the driver noticed, he didn't show it. The man made light conversation with Brandon while Savannah pretended to be asleep.

Brandon allowed her this bit of peace, certain a storm was about to break.

"Thanks for the ride." Brandon smiled, struggling to keep the facade in place as Savannah disappeared inside without a word. Instead of following, he circled around back and trudged to the flagstone patio. The outdoor fireplace lit up at the simple flick of a switch, and he hunched in front of it.

Brandon's head swam and his whole body shook, but he couldn't control it. His twenty-fourth birthday was next week, but he'd only begun some of the toughest years of his life. Residency was hell with long hours and crappy pay, topped off by repayment of student loans. Savannah had years before she was even close to completing law school.

How could they raise a child? Marriage and babies were something he wanted, someday. But not now. Not like this. Maybe the answer wasn't so difficult. Or was it?

He leaned forward, propping his head in his hands and letting his thoughts drift with only a vague awareness of the passage of time.

The light touch to his shoulder forced him to look up.

Ryan offered him a cup. "You look frozen." The man sat in the chair beside him. "This fireplace is nice. It's warmer than I thought."

Brandon wrapped his fingers around his mug. "I figured everyone would be on the slopes for hours."

"I'm getting ready. I've arranged a private and romantic evening in town with Kaari." Ryan grinned. "Crazy, right?"

"How long have you been dating Kaari?"

"Over two years. It's about time this old man made things official. My friends are married with kids, yet I'm still dating." Ryan rubbed his hands together.

"You're what, thirty-four?"

Ryan nodded. "We're all roughly the same age. Will is the oldest at thirty-six."

"You're hardly an old man." Brandon considered him. "Nothing wrong with taking your time and establishing a career before committing to marriage … and kids."

"I'd love to have a couple of little ones to chase around. I adore my nieces and nephews. But I had to find the right woman. Thought I'd beat Aiden. He was gun-shy for the longest time. Don't tell him I said that."

"Why did you?"

"I've seen less destructive bomb blasts than the ending of his first marriage. Complete train wreck. I thought those two would kill each other. She's pulled insane shit over the years, so I'm surprised he's forgiven her. There were many reasons they should never have married, but did he listen?" Ryan's expression appeared rueful as he shook his head. "I love that man like a brother, but he is a stubborn one."

"Hadn't noticed." Brandon allowed a faint smile. "Are you trying to tell me something?"

"Be gentle with Vanna's heart." Ryan shrugged. "She's my darling niece. I fear she's in over her head."

*You have no idea.* "I care about Savannah. I'll do my best not to hurt her." He scrubbed his hands across his face. "How well do you know her? I mean, I know the story, so …"

"Ahh. Tom was the first to have the honor of meeting her, but I've spent a fair amount of time with Vanna. What is it you want to know?"

"I'm in a difficult spot. She's incredibly mature, so I constantly remind myself of her actual age. She'll be in law school when I'm finished residency, and I wonder about the wisdom of this entire relationship. If I'd known her age when I met her, I wouldn't have gotten involved, but I did, and she's amazing, but now, I don't know where to take it."

"What's the rush?" Ryan narrowed his eyes. "There's something happening here. I can tell when my girl is upset, and you're all moody and asking questions. Trouble in paradise?"

Brandon lifted a shoulder, avoiding Ryan's gaze.

"You'd better resolve the issue, because Aiden will spot it. Nothing gets by that man when it involves his family."

Brandon shot a look at Ryan. "Does anything ever get by him?" he muttered.

"Spill it. What did you do?" Ryan's expression softened. "Maybe I can help."

Maybe he should be more scared of Ryan's reaction than Aiden's. The man had given him the evil eye that night in the bar and told Vanna to date someone her own age. Ryan might seem like a gentle giant, and Brandon wasn't small himself, but he suspected the man could annihilate him. Especially if he felt his precious niece was being disrespected.

A mad dash for the airport seemed the smart option if the goal was self-preservation. Each and every member of the uncle posse could kick his ass. But what kind of man would that make him? The worst kind. The kind that didn't deserve her love.

"That bad, huh. I'm dead serious. If she needs something, or you need something, now is the time to ask. Don't let whatever this is blow up."

"No matter what, crap will fly." Brandon pinched the bridge of his nose.

"Oh, shit." Ryan leaned forward. "Please tell me she's not! Bloody hell. It's written all over your face."

Brandon dared a covert glance toward the man.

Ryan leaned back, his hands splayed over his face. "This is bad."

"How worried should I be that you're about to end me?"

"That would solve what, exactly? Engaging in ridiculous macho shit would destroy Savannah." Ryan scrubbed a hand through his hair. "What's the plan? Maybe that door looks damn good, but if you even think it, you'll have more than me to worry about."

Brandon held back the bitter laugh. Was he that transparent? "We only found out, so she's upset. Vanna needed space." *And so do you,* his inner voice screamed. Brandon clenched his jaw. "Please don't tell Aiden."

Ryan rested his forearms on his knees, leaning forward as he sent Brandon a sideways look. "You two will lay this on Aiden when you're ready. My job is to support my niece in whatever decision she makes."

A sigh of relief escaped him. "I appreciate your discretion."

"Don't sound so surprised. And definitely don't underestimate Aiden. He's handled far worse, at a much younger age."

"He won't beat the crap out of me?"

"What you must imagine about this family." Ryan leveled his gaze at Brandon. "This will define you. Act like a man, own it, and you'll gain the respect of everyone in this house."

Brandon slouched lower in his seat, unsure he could tackle the challenge. He dropped his head in his hands, rubbing at his temples.

Ryan rose and rested a hand on Brandon's shoulder. "If you can't support her decision one-hundred-percent," he said, "walk away and never look back. Don't play games, or pretend, or any of that shit. She deserves better." The man squeezed before he retreated, followed by the soft click of a closing door.

Brandon closed his eyes, sorting through the mixed message. He still had no idea what to do. Ask her to terminate? Insist on putting the baby up for adoption? Try to raise a child and face the consequences to his career? To hers? Whatever he chose, something had to give.

The issue wouldn't resolve itself. He pushed out of his seat and entered the house, taking slow measured steps toward the bedroom he shared with Savannah.

The lump in the bed didn't move as he crawled onto it, draping an arm over her still form. He closed his eyes, not wanting to wake her.

The muffled sniffle alerted him.

"I'm sorry, Vanna." Brandon rubbed her arm through the covers.

"I thought you left," she whispered.

"I figured you needed space." Brandon peeled back the sheet, her blotchy red cheeks coming into view. "Come here." He wrapped his arms around her, wiggling closer and allowing her to burrow against his chest. "We'll figure it out."

"My dad will flip. He'll give me that disappointed expression. How will I tell him? He's always cautioned me and told me to be responsible. I promised."

Brandon knew that look. The residents earned it when they didn't treat a patient as instructed or failed to consult an attending physician. Some of the doctors yelled when errors were made, but Aiden's look had proven far more effective.

He kissed her hair. "He won't be disappointed, sweetheart. He'll understand."

"We should tell my dad?"

"Maybe we should have a plan first? Discuss our options?"

"You don't want a baby," she said. "You said you're not ready to be a father."

"It's not the right time. It changes everything."

"You think I don't know that?" She sat, curling her arms around her knees. "What would you have me do?"

He bit his lip, unsure of what to say. No matter what they chose, there were consequences. Things between them would be altered. The perfectly planned path of his life would veer off track.

"There's one thing I can't do." She stared at him, red-eyed and weepy. "What if they'd gotten rid of me?"

Brandon's chest constricted. *What if?* "So … you want to have it?"

"Terminating scares me more than being a mother."

"How do you see this going?" There were things he should say, but Ryan's words clung to him. This woman deserved the truth. "I'm not ready to get married."

"I get it." Vanna dipped her head, hiding her face. "You don't want this. Any of it. If you want out, go. Leave now."

"I can't." His own answer surprised him. "I won't abandon you."

"Are you sure?"

"Positive. I won't run away. If you're having the baby, we need to tell your family."

"Not yet. Let's pretend for a little longer that nothing's changed."

Brandon gave her a little nod. What would that hurt? Soon everything would change.

~

Brandon adjusted his boots, standing to add a wool hat to his head.

Aiden held out an electronic device to Brandon.

"Locater beacon?"

"You've used one, right?" Aiden waited for Brandon's nod. "We all carry one when we ski back country. Wear this." Aiden handed him a pack. "Avalanche gear. If you get hit, pull the side cord right away, that's the airbag. There's a water bottle and high-energy snacks, a flashlight, whistle … all the good stuff."

"Don't look so worried." Tom laughed. "The snow pack is stable, conditions are reported as good, but we take extra precautions as things quickly change."

Brandon had never been heli-skiing before, and the offer was too good to pass up, but a part of him worried, given his new status in life. Impending fatherhood. The very thought made his head spin.

Aiden drew him aside. "You don't have to do this," he said in a low voice. "Nobody would condemn you for backing out. We ski as a team, and if someone isn't in top form or fully committed, they don't go. It puts everyone in danger."

"I'm good. It's first time nerves, though I'm not sure why. I love being on the mountain."

"Nerves are good, they keep you from getting cocky. You have the skills, so keep your head in the game and it'll be amazing." Aiden squeezed his shoulder. "You read the emergency rescue plan, and the company we booked with has an excellent safety rating."

"I'm ready."

"Okay, then. You can ride in the first helicopter with me, Alex, and Joel."

They met the chopper on the pad outside the house and loaded the gear. Brandon peered out the window, admiring the breath-taking vista below as they rose over the mountains, heading toward the summit. It only took a few minutes, and the helicopter touched down, they unloaded, and the pilot took off. The second helicopter carrying Tom, Ryan, Will, and Andre landed minutes later.

Aiden dug in his bag. "Group pic." He offered his camera to one of the guides, who snapped a few photos before handing it back.

"Let's rock." Ryan adjusted his goggles. "You good, Brandon?"

Brandon nodded, adjusting his own gear before following Aiden down the slope.

⌣

That day they managed several runs and Brandon was hooked. The sheer thrill and rush of adrenaline skyrocketed his heart rate, and the enthusiasm from the rest of the group infected him. He loved this extreme sport.

"We returned your boy safe and sound, Vanna." Ryan leaned in to kiss his niece's cheek. "You feeling better, honey?"

"I'm good. Emily and I had a great day skiing." Savannah hugged Ryan.

"You sure skiing is a good idea?" Ryan's brows rose.

Savannah's eyes widened. "What do you mean?"

Ryan patted her shoulder before locating his seat at the dinner table.

Savannah dragged Brandon aside. "You told my Uncle Ryan?" she asked, her voice barely a whisper.

Brandon cringed. "He guessed."

"Are you crazy?" Savannah cupped both hands over her mouth. "What if he tells my dad?"

"He won't. Sit. Everyone is staring at us."

Vanna narrowed her eyes, but pasted on a smile before she took her seat.

Aiden hadn't missed the show, his stare a laser beam, sussing out the guilt rampaging through Brandon's soul.

All through dinner Brandon received looks, both from Aiden and Ryan, accompanied by a stony silence from Vanna.

"It's time for a celebration." Will stood. "Brandon's twenty-fourth birthday is next week. As he won't be allowed out of the hospital for a month after he gets home, we thought we'd end our meal with a birthday cake."

Brandon couldn't help the smile. Aside from a call from Mia, and texts from his friends who were all thousands of miles away, nobody noticed his birthdays. He was lucky to get a card in the mail from his mother.

Emily appeared with an amazing chocolate double layer cake, complete with buttercream frosting and candles. "Happy Birthday, Brandon."

He obliged and blew them out, feeling even worse about what would go down within the next few days. "Thank you, Emily. This looks amazing."

Emily sliced and distributed pieces of cake before setting a box beside his plate. "This is from me and Aiden."

"You didn't have to do that. You've been so generous already with this trip and the skiing. I don't even know what to say. Thank-you. This has been one of the best birthdays, and it's not even my birthday until next Tuesday."

Ryan passed another gift box down the table. "Hope you like it."

Soon a pile of gifts had appeared on the table. He rubbed his jaw, unable to fathom how people he barely knew treated him more like family than his own ever had.

As Vanna set her gift beside the rest he caught her hand. "Am I forgiven?" he whispered as she settled in the chair beside him. "We'll talk to your dad tomorrow. Hiding it from your family is too hard."

A faint smile appeared as she leaned in to kiss him. "Tomorrow. For now, enjoy your early birthday."

After he'd opened his presents, everyone settled in the living room, sipping cocktails or coffee. Aiden appeared with two bottles, followed by Tom with champagne flutes.

"More news to share." Aiden popped the cork from the first bottle, pouring champagne for everyone. He lifted his glass. "A toast to Ryan and Kaari. Congratulations on your engagement. May you have many wonderful years together. Welcome to the family, Kaari."

Savannah joined the toast, taking a tiny sip of champagne. "It's one sip," she muttered at Brandon's raised brow. She shoved the glass into his hands before heading toward the group inspecting Kaari's glittering diamond ring.

Brandon stared at the flute of golden liquid. He hadn't meant anything by the look, and he understood her wanting everything to seem normal, but the woman had become touchy about everything. It didn't bode well for the next few months.

He sighed and downed the champagne before approaching Ryan. "Congrats, man," he said. "Beautiful ring." He glanced at Savannah's smiling face as she hugged Kaari.

"Thank you." Ryan's eyes cut toward Vanna, who moved to the couch. "Everything good?" The man squeezed his shoulder before responding to something said by Tom.

Brandon returned to the sofa and sat beside Vanna, entwining his fingers with hers, giving her a reassuring smile as Kellan crawled onto his lap. "Hey, bud." He leaned around the small boy to kiss her. "Thanks again for the watch. It's perfect for work."

"Glad you like it. It's similar to the one Dad wears."

"Now you can stop complaining about my beat-up wallet. I should empty my old one and toss it. I think I left it in my coat pocket."

"I get it!" Kellan slid from Brandon's knee, his feet pounding across the floor as he charged toward the entrance.

Brandon grinned. "He's pretty darn cute."

"Found it!" Kellan skipped toward them with the wallet clutched in his little hand. "Here." He placed it on the coffee table beside Vanna's empty glass, a proud smile appearing.

Brandon's heart lurched. A slim white package sat on top, its bright pink lettering shining like a beacon. The end of the stick peeked out, announcing not only what it was, but that it had been used.

"Crap," Savannah muttered as they reached for it simultaneously, knocking it under the table.

Brandon snatched it from the floor and shoved it into the pocket of his hoodie, hoping nobody had noticed.

Aiden sat frozen, his glass suspended partway to his mouth, a frown wrinkling his brow as he fixed his gaze on Brandon's pocket.

Brandon dared a look at Ryan whose eyebrows had risen, the tilt and small motion of his head toward Aiden saying one thing; *that crap is all over the place.*

Savannah pressed her hand to her mouth. "Why did you keep that?" she mumbled, shooting a glance at her dad. She sprang to her feet, practically sprinting from the room.

Aiden rose, narrowing his eyes at Brandon as he placed the crystal flute on the coffee table with remarkable calm and strode from the room.

Emily paused mid-conversation with Alex as she tracked her husband's exit, her lips pursing. "Excuse me," she said, setting her glass aside and hurrying after Aiden.

Alex tilted her head as she stared at the archway. "What was that about?"

Tom tore his gaze away from Brandon, an eyebrow lifting in Ryan's direction, some form of silent communication flowing between the two men. He tipped back his glass, emptying it in one long swallow. "Can I pour anyone a refill?"

The low buzz of conversation resumed, allowing Brandon to escape without further comment. He leaned a hand against the wall, nausea rising.

*Time's up.* Aiden had discovered their secret.

He trudged toward the bedroom, finding the door closed, but the murmur of voices alerted him they were inside. He tapped on the frame before opening the door.

Savannah sat on the small couch clinging to Aiden, her shoulders shaking as Emily rubbed her back. "I'm sorry, Daddy. I really screwed up."

"Shhh, sweetie. It'll be okay." Aiden closed his eyes, resting his cheek against his daughter's hair.

"Come in and shut the door, Brandon," Emily said in a low voice. "Take a seat."

Brandon complied, perching on the edge of the chair opposite and dropping his head into his hands.

"So Ryan knows. Who else?" Aiden asked.

"Nobody … well, maybe Tom, judging from the look he just gave me." Brandon ducked his head.

"How long have you known?" Emily continued to rub Vanna's back.

"Two days."

"How far along?" Aiden asked.

"Six weeks, based on the dates." Brandon dragged his hand through his hair. "We planned to tell you after we discussed our options."

"What are the initial thoughts?" Emily rose and filled a glass with water, then pressed it into Savannah's hands along with a tissue.

"That we have the baby, but from there, I don't know."

Savannah's chest hitched, and Aiden pressed a kiss to her temple, keeping his arm around her.

"Neither of us are in a position to raise a child," Brandon said. "I admit, I am nowhere near ready for this. Maybe we should consider adoption."

A troubled look settled on Aiden's face. "Adoption seems like the magic solution. It's wonderful to believe you're giving someone a child, creating a family, all of that. For some, it's the right choice, but it's a difficult one. For the rest of your life, you'll know this child is out there."

"What about open adoption?" Brandon asked.

"The adoptive parents can agree, but legally, they never have to allow actual visitation."

"So, what? We get married and struggle along as I complete my residency? Vanna drops out of school? What kind of life can we provide?"

Vanna straightened, brushing at her tears. "Adoption is a hard no," she said. "My parents were amazing, but I can't." She swept a trembling hand through her hair. "I'm not marrying you."

"Vanna won't be dropping out of school," Emily said, meeting her husband's gaze. "This is our grandchild. Aiden and I will help with the baby."

The smile Aiden directed at his wife was so full of love, it made Brandon's heart ache.

"We can make this work." Aiden looked at Brandon. "You don't have to give up your career, Vanna can continue her undergrad, and there's no need to rush into marriage or endure financial hardship. Vanna has access to excellent prenatal care through the hospital."

Brandon nodded and stared at his hands. This hadn't turned out anything like he expected. All the decisions had been removed from his hands, yet he was the father of this child. It left him more confused.

"Daddy?" Savannah said. "Can Brandon and I have a minute?"

"You know where we are if you need us. Remember, you aren't alone. You have an entire extended family. We'll figure out logistics once you two have talked." He gave her another hug, followed by one from Emily before they left the room.

"I have no idea what you're thinking," Savannah said.

Brandon drew his brows together. "I've just been run over by a damn truck. It's all decided, and I barely opened my mouth. This is my kid, and I have no say in what happens?"

"They offered their help."

"But that's not …" Brandon clenched his jaw. "I don't even know what I want, Savannah. Except for things to go back to how they were, but now it's all messed up."

"You're right. We screwed up, and it'll never be what it was. Where does that leave us?"

"In a battle? Who's going to win that, do ya think?" He glowered in her direction. "It's bullshit."

"You know what's bullshit? You being perfectly fine about signing your child over to complete strangers but getting pissy when my dad and Emily make an offer that saves your ass. You could walk out that door and never look back. Get on with your career. Why don't you just do that, Brandon? You don't want this baby, you don't want me, so"—she pointed—"there's the door."

"We didn't have a chance to discuss this."

"Let's discuss it. What do you want?"

He rubbed his hands over his face. "I don't know."

"You're an asshole, just like the rest of them. You promised I could trust you. That we'd work it out. What happened to that man?" The door slammed behind her as she stomped from the room.

Brandon dropped his head into his hands, wondering the same thing. This had become far too real, far too fast. He flopped onto the bed, trying to silence the tumultuous cacophony of thoughts racing through his head. What next? How could he be what she wanted and needed, without playing a role? Without playing house.

Silence eventually fell within the chalet, with no sign of Savannah returning to the room. Maybe she really meant for him to go. She didn't want marriage, but she also wasn't giving up this child.

Ryan's words preyed on his mind; "if you aren't in this one-hundred-percent, walk away right now. Never look back."

Could he give the one-hundred-percent she deserved? He yanked at the neckline of the hoodie, fighting the tightness building in his throat and chest. Without further thought, he tossed his belongings into his bag, glancing around the room before he cracked open the door. The house remained dark and silent as he crept upstairs and located his coat.

"Where are you going?" Tom asked in a low voice.

Brandon pressed a hand to his chest. "I didn't think anyone was up."

"Clearly." Tom scanned the bag slung over Brandon's shoulder.

Brandon hung his head, unable to look the man in the eye. "I'm the biggest asshole in the world, right?" he said in a low voice. "I need some space, and …" His shoulders sagged.

Tom propped himself against the wall. "We can be an overwhelming group. Where you headed?"

Brandon closed his eyes, giving his head a small shake.

"Anywhere but here, huh?" Tom grabbed his coat and a set of keys from the hall table. "I'll give you a lift. It's a long walk to any sort of transportation."

"Thanks, Tom." Brandon followed the man to the SUV. "Can you tell her I'm sorry, but …?" A lump formed in his throat. *Coward.* Sneaking away in the night.

"Call her once you get your head straight, okay?"

Brandon nodded and leaned his forehead against the cool glass. She'd never forgive him for this, but he didn't know what else to do.

# CHAPTER 12

## Savannah

IT WAS MIRACULOUS SHE'D SLEPT at all, but the familiar comfort of cuddling into bed between her dad and Emily soothed her. Even after Kellan crawled into the bed and proceeded to squirm and kick in his sleep, she still managed to get some rest.

"Urgh." She removed Kellan's foot from the middle of her back, trying not to disturb her little brother.

"You okay?" Emily whispered.

"Sorry for waking you," Savannah said softly. "You must be tired of me getting between you and Dad."

"I've kind of missed it." Her stepmother gave her a sleepy smile. "I love family co-sleeping. Sounds crazy, but I enjoy our special bonding time. Kellan and Cierra share our bed quite often, but you rarely do now you're grown."

She pondered Emily's response. "Hard to imagine missing an extra fully grown person taking up your space. Remember Portland? It must have been weird when your boyfriend's long-lost teenage daughter crawled into bed with you."

"It never bothered me. I'd already gotten to know you. Plus, you'd lost Ross. Anyone could see the comfort it provided. It allowed you to build a stronger connection with your dad," Emily said. "It made me love him even more."

"Tell me why."

"He was completely unapologetic about your presence. I'm a sucker for a strong man who's not afraid to put it all on the line for their child. I'd never pictured him as a father … but then, I did."

Savannah silently willed her to continue.

"I realized I knew him, but I also didn't. Maybe that's why I found it impossible to lower my defenses. It became overwhelmingly real. A potential future I could almost taste, but one that terrified me. Total commitment, to one person, for a lifetime. I kept asking myself how people managed fifty years of marriage. And now, if I'm lucky, I've learned the secret."

Savannah wondered if she might find that with Brandon. It seemed a long shot. Not many people found the connection or love on the level Emily enjoyed with Aiden.

"Our life together is more than I ever dreamed possible. *Una vida hermosa con mi media naranja.*"

"How do you know when you've found that beautiful life with your soulmate?"

"It might not be obvious at first," Emily said with a soft smile. "You might doubt yourself. You might doubt him. For me," she said, brushing a hand over her son's hair, "someone turned my life upside down. It became clear who I needed beside me on the journey."

Vanna leaned over to kiss Emily's cheek. "Thank you," she whispered before crawling off the end of the bed. She paused in the doorway, glancing over her shoulder, viewing what her future could be; a complete, blissful family.

"*Te amo con todo mi corazón, mi cielo,*" Aiden whispered as he reached for his wife's hand.

A smile tugged at Vanna's lips as she closed the door behind her. Those two truly were two halves making a whole.

She pressed a hand to her belly as she shuffled around the corner in the hallway. Her heart sank. The bedroom door hung open. A brief inspection of the closet confirmed her worst fear. He'd broken his promise. She flopped onto the bed and hugged his pillow, wishing it were him. Deep sadness crept over her, the pain crushing her heart.

She should be angry, but what was the point? It wouldn't change a single thing. It wouldn't magically bring him running or make him love her. It wouldn't turn him into what she craved. It would only create pity.

She should have anticipated this outcome. Brandon had been honest. He wasn't ready. He didn't want to be a father. He didn't want marriage.

Not now? Or not with her? Not that the distinction mattered. It all added up to the same thing. Her choices hadn't meshed with his. It might appear she had multiple options, that she could make a different choice, but her head and heart told her no, she didn't, and couldn't. No matter what, she'd lose something. Maybe everything.

No. Not everything. Just one important person. She'd lost Brandon.

Another choice that wasn't even a choice. She'd let him go because she couldn't bear being an encumbrance. An obligation. The clingy, needful, too-young-by-far hindrance he'd eventually regard with resentment, if he didn't already.

Her family would be there. Supporting her. Loving her. Brandon had broken every promise he'd made, but her dad would never break his.

Savannah wandered to the window. The heavy gray clouds perfectly reflected her state of mind. A glance at her phone showed no messages, and she wished for the hundredth time that Justin would respond. She both dreaded and longed to hear what he'd say about her news.

"Here, sweetie." Aiden handed her a steaming cup of tea, looping an arm around her waist. "Nothing?"

She shook her head, resting against his chest, grateful for the silent house. Everyone else had left, keeping themselves busy with various activities, giving her much-needed time and space to digest the events of the past few days.

"I don't know what I expected." Her chin trembled. "He said he didn't want any of this, and I told him to go. Now I know where I rank in his life."

"You can't assume that. It's understandable he'd crack, surrounded by so many people. I've been there, and it's not easy."

Vanna tipped her chin to study her dad. "How did you keep it together?"

"I have no idea. A complete fog hit my brain, and it was autopilot from there on in."

"But you didn't run," she said in a flat voice.

"Your mother didn't have what you have. If I had left, she would have dealt with it alone. We didn't know who to trust. Our friends are amazing, but one wrong word overheard by a parent or teacher would have been disastrous."

She knew what he meant, given everything she'd learned about his family. "He's never coming back."

"I'd be surprised if he doesn't resurface in Boston."

"Right, because his precious career is there."

"He's not a bad guy, Vanna. Give him time to think things through." Her dad gave her a squeeze. "And never discount his career. An MD is precious, taking years of dedicated study and hard work."

"Sorry." She bowed her head. "It hasn't been easy for him."

"His home life was certainly less than ideal," Aiden said. "Yet look at what he's accomplished." He dropped a kiss on her hair. "Don't push or pressure.

Allow him time to process and accept this change of direction. It's not a small thing. I'm sure you're also overwhelmed."

She could only nod, her mind wandering to her visit with his friends in Montana. "Rory said something interesting," she said. "Brandon's afraid of relationships. That should have clued me in, but nope, I stuck around anyway." Maybe Jackson had it right. There were too many strikes against her with his mother's clear hatred and his friends' opinions on everything from her age to her princess status.

"I was deathly afraid of relationships. Completely terrified." He sat on the arm of the couch. "Then an incredible woman came into my life and changed everything. Fear of one relationship doesn't mean he'll never commit. It simply means he's been hurt in the past."

How could she discount history? Aiden had been strong, keeping her world level and steady after Ross had died. Yet there had been so much more lurking beneath the surface. Vulnerability, sadness, and the deep pain of his own losses, although she hadn't been mature enough to identify it at the time. "You think I'm Brandon's Emily?"

"The only one who can know that is Brandon."

"Better not to get my hopes up, right?" She contemplated her dad. There were many parallels between Brandon and her dad, even if Aiden grew up privileged and her boyfriend hadn't. Both had been fatherless. *Like my own child might be.*

Her dad must recognize the striking similarities and understand her boyfriend in a way she didn't. *Ex-boyfriend.* She had to shut down her feelings. Prevent them from getting the upper hand.

"Honey." Aiden placed his palms on her cheeks, forcing her to look at him. "Don't drive yourself crazy speculating. He's only been gone a few hours. I'm certain you'll have the chance to talk to him soon. And remember, you're never alone." He embraced her in a warm and familiar hug.

"I know, Daddy."

He pulled her onto the couch beside him. "I want to say something, but understand, I'm not taking sides."

Savannah nodded.

"Remember in the Vineyard, right after Emily left? That was a difficult time. I wanted to be what you needed, but I had no clue how to be your dad."

"You never showed it." Vanna took his hand. "You've been amazing." But a memory surfaced; Aiden had failed to respond to his phone one night. It had thrown her into panic mode, and she called the only people she knew could help. Alex and Joel had responded immediately, taking her to their home and reassuring her everything was fine.

She hadn't seen her dad until the next day. He'd apologized, she'd melted down, but she'd lacked the courage to ask why he'd disappeared. "That's when I met Jenna."

He nodded. "I had my own crisis when the responsibility overwhelmed me. I didn't have any idea how to be a single father to a teenage girl. It took us time to figure it out, right?"

She'd been a challenge with her bundle of insecurities and pain over the loss of her parents and her life in Portland. "But we did eventually."

Now she understood why her dad wasn't freaking out on her behalf. He must believe Brandon would find his way back. That this messy situation would resolve itself.

Her phone buzzed, pulling her from her thoughts. "It's Justin."

Aiden patted her knee and rose, exiting the room as she answered her phone.

"Sweetie." Justin's cheerful voice carried down the line, causing a tearful smile. "Sorry, there were issues with my flight, but I've arrived in Portland for the break."

"I'm in Canada." She flopped onto the bed. "We fly back to Boston on Sunday, and then get ready for the holidays."

"Chicago this year?"

"It's Christmas in Boston. Dad promised to cover some shifts as he's taken a lot of time off." She didn't want to travel anyhow.

The joy of early pregnancy. Fatigue, queasiness, and smells that turned her stomach.

"Wish you could have Christmas in Portland sometime. Leanne's home. Have you talked to her?"

"No." Her heart sank. "I've left a couple of messages, but she hasn't bothered to call or text me for days. I hear she's dating some new guy."

"That's right. Ahh, the blush of first love where you barely come up for air." A low laugh rumbled down the line. "How's the fabulous Brandon? Did he pass the dad test and get invited on the trip?"

"He was here. It's gotten complicated. He left."

"Oh, honey, I'm sorry. What happened?"

"Are you sitting down?" She rested a hand on her belly. Saying it out loud, telling her friends, these were things making her reality more substantial by the minute.

"Now you have me dying to know. What did he do? Are you okay?"

"Depends on your definition of okay," she said. "I'm ..." After a long breath, she said, "I'm having a baby."

The long, stunned silence spoke volumes.

"Say something," she whispered.

"Damn. Wow. I'm … speechless," Justin said. "But, wait. Brandon walked out on you? This time I am coming out there and beating his ass. What? The? Fuck?"

A rueful grin appeared. "Easy, tough guy. No damaging the father of my unborn child."

"No?" His voice rose a touch. "Damn. I want to ask how you're doing, but it's a lame ass question. I wish I was there to give you a hug."

"I'm hanging in there, and my family has been amazing and super supportive. I worried they'd be disappointed." She caught a strand of her hair between her fingers. "Are you disappointed?"

"No way. Add me to your list of supporters. Now I have to get into Yale, so I can live nearby and be a good uncle."

"I feel better already." Her heart lightened. "As for Brandon, try not to get too riled up."

"Why not? What guy does that? I'd never have ditched you like a coward."

"His family life is completely different from mine, or yours. I promised I'd be patient and give Brandon a chance to make it right."

"Promised who? Who in the hell would give you that advice? Are they crazy?"

"My dad isn't the least bit crazy," she said. "He has specific insight into the situation, considering, and he knows Brandon pretty well."

"Still, I'm pissed that he's not more upset at the guy."

"Dad reminded me how rough those first few months were after Ross passed. I never realized how hard it was for him. He seemed in control of everything." And she'd been mired in her own misery, unable to see it. "Imagine being responsible for a messed-up teenager without any warning."

"That's interesting advice from your dad. I wonder how mine would be? Probably he'd beat my ass if I did something so callous."

"He'd be wonderful and supportive. Your parents were always so nice to me."

"They love you. They always did, right from the first day we met the adorable blonde sweetheart with the ringlets at preschool. Remember how you'd come over to play on my swings?"

"And all the birthday parties? We had a lot of fun as kids."

"Friends forever, right?"

"How could we not be?" she asked. "Can I ask a huge favor? Will you keep this to yourself for now? I want to be the one to tell Leanne, but I have things to sort out first."

"It'll be tough, but you got it, hon. I won't say a word until you're ready. And remember, I'm here, so call if you need anything."

After they'd talked for another half-hour, Savannah catching up on the news about her friends in Portland, she hung up and wandered into the massive living room. The whole group had gathered around the flickering, crackling flames of the stone fireplace for the customary après-ski drinks and snacks.

"There's my darlin'." Ryan wrapped her into a hug. "We're here for you. Don't you worry about a thing." He pressed a kiss to her cheek. "What can I get you to drink? The usual, minus the shot of rum?"

Jenna was next in line. "Oh, sweetie. How are you feeling?"

"I'm good." The absolute truth. Her talk with Justin made her feel loads better. "Not a fan of morning sickness, though."

"Who is?" Her aunt hugged her.

"Can I have a minute with my niece?" Tom tucked an arm around Vanna, guiding her into the adjoining room. The man motioned for her to sit, sinking onto the couch beside her. "I'm sorry." Tom rubbed his hands over his face. "I didn't stop him."

Vanna frowned. "Brandon?"

"I aided and abetted the escape. Complete stupidity on my part. I should have talked him into staying, but instead, I drove him to the damn airport."

She studied her uncle, noting the dark circles under his eyes, the down turn of his lips, and the guilt reflected in his expression. "Leaving was his decision. He needs to be here because he wants to be, not because he's scared of the repercussions." Savannah rested her head against Tom's shoulder. "You did the right thing by letting him go." She forced a smile even as she blinked back the tears. "I'm not mad."

"You don't have to put on a brave face, love," he whispered. "Sometimes we're not okay, and it's healthier to let it out. To be angry, to be hurt, to cry."

His gentle words broke her, and she sobbed, scalding, angry tears to spilling down her cheeks.

Tom encircled her in his arms, rocking her gently "We've got you, sweetie. Everything will be all right.

# CHAPTER 13

## Brandon

RORY GRINNED AT THE SIGHT of Brandon. "Hey. Back so soon? You missed us that much?" His friend gave him a light punch on the shoulder. "I'm almost done. We could grab a beer if you have time."

"That would be great." He adjusted the bag slung over his shoulder. "Could I crash on your couch? I can't deal with Carol and Jeremy."

"It's lumpy, but sure." Rory eyed him. "You look like shit. When was the last time you ate or slept?"

Brandon couldn't remember. He'd dozed fitfully on the plane, but with the short flight, all he'd been offered was a small cup of soda and package of crackers. No first-class flights or highballs on his meager budget. He shrugged.

"I see. Let me clock out."

Rory disappeared into the office while Brandon inspected the car his friend had been working on.

"Nice old GTO," he said as his friend reappeared.

"We get the classics now and then." Rory motioned to the door. "Let's get out of here. I'll buy you dinner."

After a quick stop to deposit Brandon's bag in the trunk of Rory's car, they headed to the pub. The last time he'd been in the establishment, the world seemed full of possibilities with Savannah due back from Paris. Now a dark cloud hung over him, making him question everything.

"What's up?" Rory set a pint in front of Brandon. "How's your lovely lady?"

Brandon took a sip and swallowed hard. "Pregnant."

"No shit." Rory's brows drew together. "No wonder you look like hell. Retreating to the wilds of Montana to escape the wrath of her father?"

Brandon shook his head. "It's crazy. I expected at least one of her uncles to take a shot at me, but … nothing. It's scarier than having one of them beat me down then and there."

"Why's that?" Rory cocked his head.

"It was like having a huge target on my back. It was coming, but it would hit like a stealth missile." He sighed. "There I was, surrounded by a posse of large men who consider Savannah their darling niece. I freaked out."

"She's having the kid?"

"Yup." He chugged half of the ale, then set it onto the table with a thump. "Time to kiss my career goodbye. I'm such a dumbass. My supervisor is a close family friend, and her dad and stepmother work in the ER." Brandon groaned, dropping his head onto his forearms.

"Dude, you're a mess." Rory scoffed. "Unplanned babies happen daily, and you're a grown-ass man. Pull it together, or you'll end up like your old deadbeat."

"And how's that? I haven't seen him in years." Brandon lifted his head.

"Exactly. Do you want your kid to look up at Mommy one day and ask; *where's my daddy? why didn't he want me?*" Rory glowered. "You're the last one I expected this dumbass bullshit behavior from."

"She ordered me to leave. Her family is amazing, so they'll—"

"Clean up your mess? I should beat the shit out of you myself. Even if you don't see a future with Savannah, which would make you the stupidest man on the planet, you should want your kid." Rory shook his head slowly. "You failed her first test. How pitiful."

Brandon tipped back his head and closed his eyes. This guy had just slammed him with the unapologetic and unvarnished truth. "Damn." Considering Savannah's history, it must be difficult for her to imagine how he could suggest signing away their rights to parent this baby. His innocent unborn child. What if "there's the door" really meant "will you bother to stick around?"

"You're so wrapped up in your head, you're missing the obvious. Do you love her?"

Brandon stared at Rory.

"It's an easy question. Do. You. Love. Her?"

"I don't know what I want. She's an amazing girl, with an amazing family, but love …" Brandon fought the ache in his chest. "It's only been a few months."

"You are way gone and don't even see it. My advice is to haul your ass onto a plane and go home to your girl. Get down on your knees and beg forgiveness for being a complete idiot. Be a proper father to your kid."

After a restless night on Rory's lumpy sofa, Brandon waved his friend off to work and packed his bag, killing some time before lunch. He arrived at the high school as the kids were pouring through the doors.

"Brandon." Mia waved at her friends before she scurried across the crowded parking lot, dodging the rush of cars and students. "What are you doing here?"

"Making a quick trip through town, so I had to see you. How have things been?"

"Awful. Mom and Jeremy are fighting nonstop. Piper came for a visit, which made it even worse. She called Vanna nasty names, and Mom went batshit crazy, ranting about you making a huge mistake." Mia shrugged. "And she talked about some guy she's dating with a weird name. Gray. Like the color."

"She's … dating Gray?" Brandon frowned. "For how long?"

Mia shrugged. "You know him, right? He's in some of Piper's classes, so he must know Vanna."

"Yeah." His stomach turned at the thought of the guy, and how he'd treated Vanna that night at the club. As much as he didn't want to, he'd have to warn Jeremy about the guy's dark side.

"I'd better stop at home before I head to the airport."

"You're not staying?" She peered around. "Where's Vanna?"

"She's in Canada, skiing with her family." *And making plans to have me murdered.* His stomach felt queasy, as it had since he'd walked out the door of the chalet. Even with Tom's assurances that he'd have a quiet word with Aiden, the feared lingered. *I've made the worst mistake a man could ever make.*

"You sound sad." Mia's expression made his stomach tighten into a knot. "Did you break up with Vanna?"

Brandon didn't know how to answer the little sister who was no longer so little. The truth would come out sooner or later, though he trusted Rory to use discretion and keep it secret.

"Is that a yes or no? Did you do something bad?"

The tiny scoff escaped.

"You did." Mia crossed her arms. "Did you sleep with someone else?"

"Mia." A frisson of shock ran through him.

"What? Why else would Vanna dump you?"

"She didn't dump me," he said softly. *Or was I deluding myself?* He blew out a long slow stream of air. "It's complicated mun—Mia." So much for his promise to stop calling her that babyish name.

*Baby.* The blood drained from his face, his head swimming, a lightheadedness sweeping over him as he swayed on his feet. He stepped from the sidewalk to lean against one of the trees lining the street. He bent his head, taking long steady breaths, forcing himself to control the panic building inside, fighting back the spots dancing before his eyes.

"Brandon?" Mia's pale face came into view. "What's wrong? Are you ill?"

He scrunched his eyes closed, shaking it off. "Nothing. I've been working long hours with far too little sleep."

"Why aren't you skiing with Vanna?" She fell into step beside him, throwing the occasional glance his way. "What's complicated?"

"Can you leave it alone?"

"Uh-uh."

Brandon sighed as the house came into sight. "Don't you have a class or something?"

"I'm done till after New Year's."

Brandon planted a palm across his face with a groan. "Christmas." He'd been so immersed in his own life, he'd neglected to buy something for his sister, or anyone else for that matter.

Mia gave him a knowing look. "So no presents under the tree from you?"

"I'll make it up to you," he said as they arrived on the front steps. "I need to talk to Jeremy. Can you give us a few minutes?"

"I'm not a child to be banished to my room." Her eyes blazed.

"I never said you were, but he'll talk if you aren't there."

"Fine." She extended a fist. "Then you tell me what's happening with Vanna."

"Deal." He bumped her clenched hand with his.

Jeremy was ensconced in his lounger. "Look what the cat dragged in." The man barely glanced up. "Your mother is out."

"I'm not here to see her." He slid into the chair across from the man. "Are you and Carol fighting?"

"Hardly any of your business, is it, son?" Jeremy flicked a finger across the screen of his tablet.

"I'm not your son." He leaned back, crossing his arms. "You promised to watch out for Mia."

"Carol told me to butt out." The man finally looked up. "I can't take much more of this dysfunctional mess. Don't lay your responsibilities or issues on me. I have enough with Piper and dealing with your mother."

Brandon closed his eyes for a moment, silently cursing this weak man. "Do me a favor and call before you move. That's all I ask."

A bitter half-smile appeared. "End of the week and I'll be gone."

"Damn."

They stared at each other for several seconds.

"Piper shouldn't be dating Gray. He's abusive if he doesn't get what he wants."

"You know him?" Jeremy straightened, his full attention now on Brandon.

"Piper won't listen to me, so talk some sense into her before she gets hurt." He rose, unsure what else to say to this man who'd been so briefly in their lives. Even if he'd lasted longer than most, the end result was the same. Another useless guy exiting through the revolving door.

"Brandon?" Jeremy grabbed his wrist. "Carol's drinking heavily. I've stayed longer than I should because I worry about Mia's safety."

Brandon acknowledged the man's confirmation of his worst fears with a brief nod before proceeding down the hallway to Mia's room. "Mia?" He slipped inside and closed the door.

Mia lounged across the bed, but she sat, patting the mattress beside her. "What's happening with Vanna?"

He took her hand. "How's Mom been? Is she …?" His brows went up.

"Coming home so pissed she can barely stand and turning into a raving lunatic?" Her head bobbed. "I'm keeping my head down. Most of the time, Jeremy runs interference."

"He's splitting." Brandon scrubbed his jaw. "Is there anywhere you can stay? A friend's house?"

She twisted a lock of her hair. "Shaylynn's not allowed to hang out with me after we got busted. Small town, word travels fast. So … no?"

"I have to work over the holidays." His stomach twisted as he mentally calculated the dwindling balance in his bank account. His next pay check wouldn't be deposited for two weeks, and he'd spent his tiny buffer on a plane ticket and the drugstore items for Savannah. "How much money do you have?"

"Less than one-hundred. I've been buying meals, though Billy lets me eat dinner before my shift on the days I work."

"Mom's not buying groceries?"

His sister shook her head. "She lost her job."

"When?" he asked. "Never mind." He slumped onto her bed. His vague hope that Jeremy would hold Carol together vanished. "Pack a bag. You can't stay once Jeremy leaves."

Another drill he knew all too well. A cycle on repeat. Binge drinking. Verbal abuse directed at anyone within range. The current man rushing for the door. More drinking. Escalating neglect and verbal onslaughts. The vicious circle could last weeks or even months until his mother found some unsuspecting victim and lured him home. The men were often unstable alcoholics, which created more issues. Jeremy had been a rare semi-respectable specimen.

"Where are we going?"

"Boston." Brandon covered the few steps to her closet. "Take anything you value, because when—"

"Our mother goes crazy"—Mia yanked open her dresser drawer—"nothing is safe."

Brandon dragged a section of clothing from the rod in the closet. Stark memories raced through his mind. The vivid and unforgettable picture of the night his father left scorched into his brain. The cold draft from the open back door washing over him as he crouched on his hard bedroom floor with his hands clamped over his ears. His baby sister's wail. His mother hauling the few items Darien had left behind into the backyard. Her gleeful half-maddened cries—*a bonfire, honey*—as she danced around the smoldering pile. The stench of burning gasoline as she fed the fire from the small red container used to fuel the lawnmower.

He'd never shared this memory with Mia. He'd never told anyone, too frightened by the grim tales of kids abandoned to foster care. Instead, he learned to read the signs and kept Mia out of Carol's way when she spiraled.

But only so much could remain hidden. His sister witnessed the aftermath of enough of their mother's breakups to absorb the harsh realities when it came to the dark side of the human psyche. Carol's mind often grew pitch black, shrouding their lives.

"How are we getting there?"

"Excellent question." Brandon inspected her pile of belongings. "We can't take all that on a plane, and I can't afford tickets for both of us. Maybe … a rental car?" He estimated how many hours the drive would take. Coast to coast, or pretty darn close. "Pack the essentials in your suitcase, and make sure your ID is in your purse. I have to make a call."

Brandon stepped outside onto the deck, dreading his next unavoidable move. He stared at his phone for several seconds before dialing.

"Brandon?" Will said in a low voice. "Where are you?"

"Montana." He leaned on the railing, kicking a boot into the pile of snow that had slid from the roof. "How's …" He sighed. "Never mind."

"Ballsy, calling me for information. If you want to inquire, you'd best call Vanna."

"I can't face that discussion," he muttered. "Yes, I'm an idiot. An idiot with a situation. I'm driving my sister to Boston, but it'll take several days."

"That's why they invented airplanes," Will said. "Why drive?"

"She has too much luggage, and …" He heaved another long sigh.

"You're broke?"

"I'm an intern." Brandon rubbed his jaw. "I didn't expect to pay for flights."

"What's up with your sister?" Will's voice softened. "Where will she stay?"

"On my sofa?"

"Ahh. I'll call you back in five. Don't rush to rent a car."

The line went dead before Brandon could respond. He returned inside, finding Jeremy planted in front of the television. "Do you have a couple of extra boxes and packing tape?"

"In your old room." The man barely looked up.

Brandon bounded down the stairs and selected two solid boxes and the tape gun, then halting as his phone rang. He cringed at the name on the display. "Crap." Brandon tapped his phone against his forehead until it stopped ringing. *Kavanagh ratted me out.* He hit redial. "How mad are you?" Brandon sat on the bottom step. "How's Vanna?"

"Let's not talk about that," Aiden said. "Why are you bringing your sister to Boston?"

"My stepfather is splitting, and it won't be pretty. Mia has nowhere else to go over Christmas."

"Does your mother know?"

Brandon closed his eyes. As humbling as it was, he owed Aiden an honest answer. "It could be days before her drunken ass notices." A lump formed in his throat. "I don't know what else …" He sucked in a harsh breath.

"We'll get you and Mia safely to Boston," Aiden said in a level voice. "Driving from Montana to Boston in the winter is pure insanity. Pack your sister one suitcase. If she needs more for longer term, box and label it for shipping to my Boston address. How much time do you need?"

"About an hour." That might allow him to disappear with Mia before Carol dragged herself home.

"Collect Mia's birth certificate, passport, and any other ID you can locate. I'll send an itinerary with flights and instructions for the boxes, and order you a car for the airport. We'll book a hotel in Boston. You can't stay in that dump with your little sister."

He shuddered as he pictured the pigsty with the beer-drinking slob ensconced on the sofa. "Agreed." Considering how Dylan treated women, Brandon would worry about Mia being alone with the guy. "What then?"

"The resident apartments will be available mid-January, so that might be an option."

"I don't have any idea how long she'll stay," he said. "Why are you helping me? You should be ripping my face off or beating the crap out of me."

"Would it make you feel better if I did?"

Brandon leaned forward, rubbing a hand in his hair, before sweeping it through. "It might. I screwed up, and I'm sorry for freaking out."

"Don't look for me to assuage your guilt." Aiden sighed. "Besides, it seems like you're doing a fine job of beating yourself up. Once you've dealt with your family situation, talk to Vanna. Be honest about how you feel, and what role you want to play, if any."

"You'd allow me to walk away?" Brandon tried to reconcile his actions with this reaction. The man seemed too calm by far.

"Grown men make their own decisions, including what involvement they want in their children's lives. Nobody in my family will force you, or threaten you, or whatever you're expecting. A child should bring joy, not fear and misery."

"You surprise the hell out of me on a continual basis. You don't act like the typical dad."

"Probably not, but how would I know?" Aiden said. "My father was never around and he lacked noticeable parenting skills. I make it up as I go and hope I don't screw up my kids too badly."

"I had my mother, a bunch of flaky stepdads, and her messed up boyfriends. Carol never won mother of the year."

"I got that impression. Must be something about that name … Carol … Caroline…."

To Brandon, the similarity in both the names and the lack of maternal concern evident in these women was eerie. "Thanks Aiden." He had no idea how to be a parent, but maybe he too could make it up and muddle through. "Can you tell Savannah I'll call her when I get home? I don't want her to think …."

"Take care of your sister, and don't stress. Do what you think is right, and the rest will sort itself out."

After they hung up, Brandon grabbed the boxes and returned to Mia's room. "Pack one suitcase with a week's worth of essentials, and we'll box up the rest. We need to be done in an hour."

His sister nodded and began the task of tucking articles into the boxes. "Am I ever coming back?"

"How would you feel about living in Boston? It means leaving your friends, but you'd be with me."

"I hate it here." She threw her arms around him. "I'm so sad, all the time, and Mom is impossible, and my best friend is no longer my best friend because her parents blame me for the drinking."

Brandon peered into her shiny tear-filled eyes. "I'm so sorry I haven't done more for you. Mom might fight it, but pack everything, and I'll do my best to keep you in Boston."

They worked for the next half an hour, double checking the various rooms of the house, including the front closet and the pile of dirty laundry.

"The sum of my life." Mia stared at the suitcase and four boxes stacked by the front door. "Not much."

"You're really doing this?" Jeremy roused himself from his seat. "Carol won't be happy."

"When is she ever? Who knows? Maybe she'll be thrilled to be childless and responsibility free." He peered through the curtains. "The car's waiting, Mia. Put on your coat."

"How did you manage that?" Jeremy lifted a brow.

"You'll answer the door for the delivery driver? He'll be here soon." Brandon slid on his coat as Jeremy nodded. "I guess this is goodbye."

Jeremy hugged Mia. "Listen to your brother, and study hard so you can go to Harvard."

"Thanks, Jeremy."

"Get in the car, Mia."

His sister scampered down the front walk towing her suitcase. She appeared pleased as the driver opened the door of the sleek sedan and stowed her luggage in the trunk.

"Take care of her, Brandon. I'm sorry I didn't do a better job, but ..."

"She's not your kid." Brandon slung his bag over his shoulder. "You don't owe us anything, Jeremy. I hope things work out for you and Piper."

"You're still Piper's brother. Can you keep an eye on her with this guy, Gray?"

"I can't promise." Brandon fixed his gaze on his stepfather. The pure audacity of this man, asking him to babysit Piper after how she'd treated Savannah irked him. "I have Mia, and"—he sucked in a breath—"I'll have my own kid to worry about."

Jeremy frowned. "Savannah's pregnant?"

"Pretty great, right?" Brandon's lips twitched. A baby wasn't such a tragedy. Maybe he'd beat the odds, be like Aiden, and do the complete opposite of everything his parents had done. Be the father he'd never had himself. "Mia doesn't know yet, but I bet she'll be happier in Boston. She'll be near her niece or nephew."

"It's tragic you've been brainwashed to believe an unplanned baby is a great thing. Savannah's a child, having your child. Don't wreck your life like you've ruined hers. Babies are a huge responsibility." Jeremy shook his head. "Mia is one thing. She'll be off to university in a couple of years, but tying yourself down to a girl like that? That's insanity."

"It's a shock to the system, but I don't see it as a bad thing. Maybe it's what I need." He wished Jeremy could be supportive, but it was another thing that simply didn't matter. Brandon couldn't see them keeping in touch, considering how little his stepfather had done for him over the past few years.

"You're bailing before you tell Carol? Expect me to do it so you don't have to face her wrath?"

"Why should I care what she thinks? Tell her or don't, doesn't much matter. She's formed her opinion of Savannah, thanks to Piper. I won't bring Vanna or an innocent helpless baby here. I may never be back." He shrugged. "I wish you well, but don't worry about us. We've managed without parents until now. We'll be fine."

⁓

"This is cool." Mia settled into the wide first class seat and fastened her belt. "How did you pay for this?"

"I've made good friends in Boston, and you will too." He squeezed her hand. "Wave goodbye to Montana. If our luck holds, it'll be a long time before we're back."

His sister lifted her middle finger and pressed it against the window.

"Mia." A laugh escaped. Maybe he should be chastising his sister, but he didn't have the heart to bring her down. The next few months would be hard enough with her entire life being uprooted.

"I'm exercising my freedom to express an opinion. I can't wait to get to Boston. I've never been anywhere."

"It's different from Nowheresville, Montana." He snickered as he borrowed Piper's term for their home town. "Boston has amazing schools."

"And Vanna?" Her brows lifted. "Will I get to see her?"

"Vanna would love to see you." He didn't doubt it. Savannah would never take his failings out on Mia. "She'll be home in a few days."

"You promised you'd share, but you're avoiding telling me."

He gulped a mouthful of his drink. "You have to keep it to yourself. I told Jeremy, but don't get into it with our mother, please?"

A furrow appeared between her brows, but she nodded.

"I did something stupid."

Her eyes widened. "Tell me already."

"I'm going to be a dad. But I screwed up with Vanna, and I'm not sure how it will affect our relationship."

"Savannah's having a baby? Or," she said, pressing a fingertip to her lips, "you cheated and got someone else pregnant?"

"I wasn't quite that stupid." He shot a sideways look at her. "It's the way I left that makes it stupid. I made her a promise, and I broke it."

"You'd better apologize." His sister wagged a finger in his face. "And never do it again." Even as she scolded him, her smile widened. "I'll be an aunt. I definitely want to live in Boston. I can babysit."

"You can." Brandon adjusted his seat. "I'm ready for a nap. Get yourself something to eat and then rest." He closed his eyes. Hopefully, he'd manage to make amends and come out of this unscathed.

# Chapter 14

## Savannah

THE SMELL WAFTING UNDER SAVANNAH'S door was oddly enticing, yet at the same time it made her stomach turn in the most unpleasant way. She reached for the package of crackers on her bedside table, nibbling on one before she eased into an upright position. After several deep breaths, she sipped from her glass of water and pressed a hand to her belly.

Now she understood how poor Emily felt during her pregnancies with Kellan and Cierra. Morning sickness never seemed to contain itself to the morning. It hit without warning, brought to life by smells she loved but couldn't tolerate.

This morning, she managed a shower and the short trek to the kitchen without issue.

"Can I have some of that?" Vanna eyed the plate her dad set on the counter.

"It's all yours." Aiden pushed his breakfast in front of her before he poured steaming water into a cup. "You can have this too." He set the tea beside her breakfast.

"Thanks, Daddy." She took a dainty bite of a toast triangle, before reaching for the jar of peanut butter.

"You're welcome, cariño. What are your plans for the day?" he asked as he prepared a plate for himself.

"I'm meeting Rochelle for shopping this afternoon. Time to break the news to more friends."

"Let me know if you need money for clothes. Or do you want to shop with Emily?"

"She offered to take me, but I'll need to pick up a few things today." Her pants fit, but her tops were straining across her voluptuous chest. "I have plenty of money, Daddy."

"I'll still transfer extra funds for you. Get whatever you need." Aiden set another plate onto the counter and sat beside her.

"Brandon texted. He wants to meet later." Savannah twirled a strand of hair around her finger as she ate another bite. "I'm scared to hear what he has to say."

Aiden rubbed her back. "Don't be. I always find not knowing is the worst."

"Not knowing means you can still hope." She leaned against his shoulder and closed her eyes. "This might be the end."

"Stay positive, sweetheart. It's far from over."

Savannah kept her dad's words in mind as she dressed and headed to the mall to meet Rochelle. Despite the crowd jostling through the stores, a simple shopping trip with a favorite friend brought some normalcy to her life.

"This is cute," Rochelle held up a top. "It would look amazing on you."

"It's pretty, but I doubt it'll fit." She glanced around before covertly adjusting her bra. The next stop would be for new undergarments to contain her chest. "I have big news."

Her friend's eyebrows arched. "Did something awesome happen with Brandon?"

"I wouldn't say awesome."

"Sounds serious," Rochelle said. "What's going on?"

Savannah nibbled on her lip. "I'm pregnant."

Her friend tilted her head as her eyes widened. "Whhhatttt? Did you tell him?" she whispered.

"Uh-huh. He freaked out and split."

"What a jerk. I'm sorry." Her friend hugged her. "What about your family?"

"They've been amazing. When we're done shopping, I'm meeting Brandon. After he left, he ended up in Montana and moved his sister to Boston. Piper's dad left and is divorcing their mother."

Rochelle's eyes narrowed. "Does Piper know?"

"No idea. It's not like she'd confide in me. Especially now she's doing whatever it is she'd doing with Gray."

"True." Her friend wrapped her in a warm embrace. "You can count on me. Let me know what I can do to help. And don't worry, I'm sure Brandon will realize he's being a dumbass."

"Thank you for being a good friend." Savannah's heart lightened a touch. Each and every person she added to her support system made this easier. Her true friends were stepping up, and she appreciated it more than she could say.

Butterflies flitted in Savannah's belly as she trudged down the snowy street later that afternoon. Aside from the text, she hadn't heard from Brandon in several days, only garnering bits of information from her dad about the situation in Montana.

She paused in front of the coffee shop, closing her eyes and lifting her chin, the light fluffy snowflakes dancing around her, settling on her cheeks and clinging to the exposed ends of the hair poking out from under her beanie.

A feeling of being watched made her open her eyes, her gaze meeting that of the dark-haired man standing only a few feet away.

Brandon shoved his hands into his pockets, dropping his head for moment, those thick dark lashes fluttering as he peered at her. A sad smile crossed his face as he approached, one slow step at a time.

Savannah froze, but the tiniest smile twitched at the corners of her mouth at the sight of him, red-eyed and scruffy, looking as devastated as she felt. Even the way his hair stuck out as he rubbed a hand through it endeared him. She emitted a small sniffle as the tears burned behind her eyes.

He inched forward, hesitating briefly before pulling her into an embrace. The warmth of his arms and familiarity of his scent made it feel like they'd never been apart.

Savannah wrapped her arms around him, pressing her face against the softness of his coat. She lifted her chin, staring into his beautiful gray eyes, a sense of hope blossoming and lifting her from her sadness. *He's come back to me.*

He cupped her face in his palms, caressing her cheeks with his thumbs before he captured her lips, each kiss deeper, but gentle, making her long for more. "I've come to my senses," he whispered against her cheek. "Can you forgive me?"

A lump formed in her throat. She nodded, stretching for another kiss before pressing her forehead against his. A tear escaped and trickled down her face.

"I'm sorry, sweetheart," he murmured. "I won't run again. I promise." Brandon stroked her cheek, mopping away the dampness.

"I'm happy you're here," she said softly.

"Me too." He linked his fingers with hers. "Let's go inside. It's freezing."

Once they'd settled in a booth with hot drinks, he took her hand again. "I'm a complete idiot for leaving. It was overwhelming, everything spinning out of control."

"And now?"

"It's still overwhelming, but the initial shock has passed. I'd like to be a proper dad for him … or her." He ran a finger around the rim of his cup. "My father leaving affected me." He lifted his gaze to meet hers. "Obviously not in a good way. Will you let me be involved?"

She nodded, containing her sigh of relief. With the history of parental neglect within her own family, she hoped to avoid the same fate for her child. Brandon returning as a willing participant made all the difference.

"I don't know how to do this." Brandon bowed his head. "Maybe I'll be a complete failure, but I have to try."

"You're amazing with kids. I see how you are with Kellan and Cierra. And you're terrific with Mia." She circled the table to slide in beside him. "If we do this together, we'll manage."

He looped an arm around her, cuddling her against him. "How do *we* move forward? I don't want to assume everything is perfect and rosy after what's happened, but do we still have a chance as a couple?"

Savannah had spent hours debating this very question. "We shouldn't rush. I'm not looking for marriage."

"I'm clear on your marriage view. But where does that leave us? Our relationship was good, but everything's changed."

"You can be a part of the baby's life without us being together." Her heart broke a little at the idea. This might end them as a couple. "If you don't want—"

"What if I do want?" Brandon heaved a sigh. "I'm not ready for marriage, but it doesn't mean we should break up. Can we still be together?" He drew his brows together. "That sounds just bad, right? What I mean is—"

"I understand." Savannah placed a hand over his. "Do you want to resume the relationship and see how it goes? Take our time, live each day, and deal with issues as they come?"

"Would you be okay with that?"

She nodded. "If the baby hadn't happened, I assume we'd be dating, with me studying and you in residency. Why can't we define how we want it to be without the pressure of a wedding or living together? We have to make this work on our own terms."

"Sounds like we have a plan. Will it upset your family?"

"My family will support my decision. How about yours?"

"Mia's thrilled about the baby. She's the only one in my family who matters, though she is pushing the marriage idea." Brandon shrugged. "Everyone else will have to just deal with it."

"I'm sorry about your mother and Jeremy. How's Mia?"

"Excited to be in Boston. Doubly excited now she'll have a niece or nephew."

"We should pick her up. It's time she met my family. You can both join us for dinner."

"Yeah." He gazed at her. "Nobody will mind? I'm sure your family will have a few choice words for me. Especially your dad."

"It's like ripping off a bandaid. Get it over with." She kept her tone low and gentle. "If I forgive you, so will they."

An hour later, Savannah ushered Mia into the apartment foyer. "We're home."

The girl's eyes grew round as she clutched her hands in front of her, following Savannah and Brandon into the kitchen.

"Brandon. Brandon's here." Kellan raced over, jumping up and down in front of the young doctor.

"Hey, Kellan." Brandon scooped him up and draped him over his shoulder, the boy emitting a volley of giggles. "Say hi to my little sister, Mia."

The boy fluttered his hand as Brandon set him onto his feet.

"Hi, Kellan." Mia waved back.

Savannah gave a soft smile and gentle nod toward her dad and Emily, signifying it had all been worked out.

Aiden rounded the counter. "Welcome, Mia. We've heard a lot about you."

"Thanks." She peered at Brandon from the corner of her eye.

"This is my sister, Cierra." Vanna drew Mia's attention to the baby girl, allowing Brandon a moment to say a few quiet words to her dad and Emily. Her boyfriend had been nervous and unsure of his reception, despite her reassurances.

He relaxed visibly once the initial awkwardness passed, and everyone was settled in with cold drinks.

"Smells delicious." Mia peered over the counter. "What are you making?"

"Ravioli." Aiden looked up from his task. "Did you want to try?" He set Kellan on a stool in front of the counter, giving him a spoon to stir the filling.

"I'm not much of a cook." Mia's cheeks took on a delicate flush. "I wish I could make stuff like that."

"Come around, and I'll show you."

Mia's eyes lit up, but she hesitated, glancing at Savannah.

"My dad is acknowledged as one of the best chefs in the family. I've always cooked, but he's taught me amazing recipes." Vanna steered the girl around the counter.

In a matter of minutes, Aiden had the girl feeding the dough through the roller assembly and proceeded to show her how to create the savory pasta pockets.

Brandon followed Savannah to her room. "He's damn great with kids." He wrapped an arm around Vanna's waist from behind, pressing his cheek against her hair. "And so are you. Thanks for being so kind to my sister."

"She's sweet." She turned within his embrace. "I'm proud of you. Taking on a teenage girl isn't easy, but if you run into issues, talk to my dad. He's been through it all."

"I don't know where to start. Those apartments won't be ready for almost a month, and I don't trust Dylan around my sister. Maybe your dad will have some ideas."

"We have an empty guest room." Savannah tipped her chin. "She should stay until you figure out housing. You spend a lot of time here, and I'm off until after the holidays."

"I can't dump my sister onto your family."

"I'm inviting her. It'll be fun. She can join in on the traditional holiday activities, and I'll show her around Boston. She won't be alone in a hotel room or getting into trouble. She's not even sixteen. You work long hours. It makes sense."

"Are you sure?" A hopeful look appeared on his face.

"Positive. We can keep her so busy, she won't miss home."

Brandon snorted. "Yeah, cause that will happen." A frown knit his brow. "She was miserable and begged me not to leave her when we visited. I feel like the worst brother in the world for not seeing how bad it had gotten."

"It wasn't pleasant but it wasn't terrible."

"This last visit it was. No food in the house, laundry stacking up, and Jeremy ready to vault through the exit. But now what? I work insane hours. Next year will be worse. I must be out of my freakin' mind to take on a teenager, but what else can I do?" He sank onto the edge of her bed. "I don't even know how to feed us both."

"Relax." She stood between his knees, rubbing his shoulders.

Brandon rested his hands on her hips, his head tipping down as he stared at her navel. "We're having a baby." He flattened his palm against her belly. "It's surreal. And I took in my teenage sister?" He leaned forward, resting his forehead against her, dragging in long breaths.

"Shhh." She pressed a kiss to his temple, wrapping her arms around his shoulders. "You know you did the right thing getting her out of that house."

His hand rose, and he pinched the bridge of his nose. "I can't ..." he whispered, the words squeezing out in a harsh sob, his body trembling as he choked back the brewing turmoil.

She knew these moments all too well. The sharp edge of emotion, that dark moment right before the floor collapsed underneath you and the blackened sky obscured you with a hazy veil, making it impossible to breathe, or even think. Your entire world about to end. The panic attack had crept over him almost unnoticed, but she sensed it in his tense shoulders, clenched jaw, and dragging breaths.

"You're not carrying the burden alone." She pulled him closer. "Long deep breaths. Don't think. Just breathe." Savannah closed her eyes, rubbing his back in slow smooth strokes. "Breathe."

He finally looked up, his eyes reflecting complete exhaustion. "I'm falling apart. Maybe I'm not strong enough."

"You are." Savannah brushed a hand over his hair, placing a kiss on his forehead before she reached down, taking hold of the bottom of his sweater. "Lift."

He complied without question, closing his eyes as she plumped up the pillows and drew back the covers.

"Rest. You're so tired you can barely string a sentence together."

He nodded and helped her remove his jeans. "Stay until I fall asleep?"

She crawled onto the bed, curling up with her head on his chest, running her fingers down his firm abdomen. *I love you.* She wanted to say it, but things were complicated enough without adding those three deceptively simple little words.

～

She crept from her room, closing the door behind her with a gentle click. All seemed quiet, but as she wandered through the apartment, she spotted a flicker of light from the media room. She slipped through the door, closing it behind her.

Mia grinned and fluttered her fingers, looking cozy in pajamas with a throw tucked around her. Her attention returned to the big screen mounted to the wall.

Kellan, curled up beside Mia, dipped a small hand into a bowl of popcorn, his eyes wide as he followed the action on TV.

Emily had claimed her favorite arm chair and cuddled Cierra against her.

Aiden lounged beside Kellan with his feet propped on an ottoman. "Just wake up?" he whispered as she sat next to him.

She nodded. "Brandon crashed and shows no signs of regaining consciousness anytime soon."

"We saved you dinner." Aiden patted her knee. "Can I heat it for you?"

"Thanks, Daddy. I'll help." She followed him to the kitchen. "Mia looks happy."

"She's a nice kid."

"You sound so surprised. But why? You had disinterested parents who fled the state yet you turned out pretty okay." She nudged him with her elbow.

"Thanks, honey." He rolled his eyes. "Your discussion with Brandon went well? He seems suitably contrite for being a jackass."

"His words were 'a complete idiot.'"

"It's good he recognizes it. What's next?"

"The biggest win is he wants to be involved with the baby. Be a proper dad." Vanna twirled a lock of hair. "We'll continue to see each other without committing further. It's too soon."

Aiden stirred the sauce and cranked the heat under a pot of water. "Sounds like an excellent start. You plan to live at home? Or have you thought more about Yale?"

"How would I manage Yale with a baby?"

"Don't rule it out. A childcare plan is something we'll discuss as a family. You can count on me, Emily, Iona … your mother, and some help from Brandon. In a pinch, we have all the aunts and uncles."

"I haven't been accepted."

Aiden motioned to the built-in desk at the side of the kitchen. "You received a letter today."

"Already? Must be bad news. A *no way in hell, honey,* notification of rejection."

"Open it and find out."

She shuffled over to pick up the envelope, her palms growing damp as she stared at it. The urge to rip into it grew, but she was too scared to give in.

"Daddy?" She fiddled with the envelope. "Can Mia stay with us for a while? Brandon works crazy hours. I'll be home over the holidays, so I can help out. Do you think Emily would mind?"

"No, Em's on board," he said. "Brandon's heart overruled his head. A broke intern managing a teenage girl is near impossible."

"Do you think he was wrong to bring her to Boston?"

He shook his head. "I would have done the same in his situation, but it creates a dilemma. It's no problem for us to host Mia until Brandon makes appropriate arrangements. They can join us for the holidays. Brandon and I are both working Christmas, but you and Em are here, so Mia will have plenty of company."

"You saw this coming."

"Hard to miss. I've been there," he said.

Savannah hugged him. "I love you all so much. Everyone has been incredible with their support. Thank you, Daddy." She straightened. Some of the hardest days were yet to come. "Now, I have to break our news to Tiffany."

# Chapter 15

## Brandon

At eleven, Brandon had awoken to find the bed beside him empty. The moment Savannah had tucked him into bed and cuddled against him, he'd relaxed, exhaustion forcing him into a deep sleep. He'd slept for a solid sixteen hours.

After a steamy shower, he padded to the kitchen and helped himself to a coffee. The apartment seemed peaceful and quiet. He wondered where everyone had gone.

"You're up." Aiden appeared and filled his own cup.

"Off to work?"

Aiden nodded. "You're back tonight?"

"I start at six." He met Aiden's gaze. "I haven't thanked you properly. I'll find a way to pay you back for the tickets and the car."

"Not necessary. The emergency fund covers these types of situations."

"It does?" Brandon's suspected this wasn't the entire story. "The fund provides broke interns and their sister's first class tickets?"

"You caught me." Aiden laughed. "I upgraded using travel miles, but the majority was paid from the fund. Kavanagh put you and Nate on the list for the subsidized rentals, so you two can move out of that hellhole you call an apartment."

"Dylan?"

"Our residents get first dibs, so he's out of luck. There's already a waiting list." He shrugged. "Give notice to your landlord for the end of January, and tell Dylan you're moving."

"Can Mia live with me?"

"We set provisions for residents with dependents." Aiden's steady gaze piqued Brandon's curiosity.

"But?"

"There are better options for Mia."

"I'm not sending her back to Montana."

"I would never suggest it."

"I might not have a choice. It's premature to worry about living arrangements. Damn. I'll need a lawyer I can't afford."

"Tom offered pro bono for you. He thinks you have a great case to win guardianship."

"He knows?"

"Sorry." Aiden lifted a shoulder. "It's impossible to keep secrets in this family. Especially with how it all unfolded."

"My own fault. I appreciate everything you're doing." He rubbed a hand through his hair as the impossibility of the task overwhelmed him. The legal side was only a tiny piece. "I need to support Mia and find her a school for January."

"How about a boarding school? They offer a great education, proper supervision, scheduled meals, and she'll be nearby for visits."

"Just ship her off?" Brandon scoffed. "Thanks for your confidence in my abilities. And I have no money. Those places aren't free."

"It's not meant to be a judgment or to discount how much you love your sister." The man propped himself against the counter. "It's your reality. Sixteen-hour days. Eighty-hour weeks. An unpredictable and demanding schedule. Add that to a teenage girl left unattended for hours daily to wander the streets of Boston? This isn't small town Montana."

"I'm aware." He planted his hands on the counter and bowed his head. "You managed with Vanna."

"I had a regular work schedule as an attending and sufficient income." The man's lifted brow conveyed the clear message; Brandon had none of that. "Just wait until after the baby is born."

"How would I pay for it?"

"Financial assistance and scholarships. Find a school nearby with a space they want filled for January term."

"It sounds perfect." Brandon mulled this over in his mind. Savannah hadn't been shy about her experience in private school in Boston, and she'd improved her grades enough to warrant Harvard. "How do I find one of these amazing schools mid-term?"

Aiden gave him a sideways glance. "It's about knowing the right person."

"I hardly know anyone in Boston."

"There's a difference between hardly anyone and the right one."

Brandon opened his mouth to object, but something about Aiden's expression made him hesitate. He contemplated the man. "You'd do that?"

"Why the tone of surprise?" Aiden's soft laugh brought a smile to Brandon's face. "I'll contact a few people and see what surfaces."

"That would be amazing. You've been great about everything. I don't know what to say."

"You've already said it. Making the difference for one person is enough, and I get to help many. You, your sister, and the countless patients you'll treat as a doctor." He glanced at the clock. "I have a shift, but we'll talk later. Vanna took Mia shopping. They'll be back in a couple of hours. And you're both welcome to stay here over the holidays."

Brandon nodded, unable to say a word. To have someone take an avid interest in their well-being seemed miraculous. It had been years since anyone had cared enough to even try, aside from a few weak attempts from Jeremy.

After Aiden left, he located his phone and texted Vanna to let her know he'd check out of the hotel and visit his apartment. Within two hours, he'd transferred both his and Mia's belongings to the penthouse. He then headed home.

Nate looked up from the kitchen sink as he entered. "Thought you'd gotten lost in the wilds of Canada. Weren't you back on Sunday?"

"Long story. Dylan not here?" He looked around. "It's unusually clean and quiet."

"He's on shift. Did Kavanagh tell you? We can vacate this dump after the holidays."

"Aiden told me. If I had to live here much longer …" He shook his head.

"You're hardly ever home. Not that I blame you for enjoying the luxury of a Back Bay penthouse, gourmet meals, and cushy vacations." Nate smirked. "How was it?"

"Incredible. Amazing chalet, meals, and the best skiing ever." Brandon perched on the arm of the couch. "Even did a full day of heli-skiing."

"Lucky bastard. So are you interested in sharing one of the two-bedroom units?"

"Might have to make it a three bedroom." Brandon sighed. "My mother managed to screw up another relationship. Mia's moving to Boston."

"Sorry, man. She'll live with you?"

"I don't know yet. There's something else, but you can't say anything to anyone, especially Dylan."

"What's up?"

"Damn." He stared at his ringing phone. "I have to get this. If I ignore her, she'll only get worse."

"Mia's gone." Carol's slurred voice greeted him. "As is my husband."

"I didn't take him." He wandered across to the window. "But Mia's staying with me."

"Celebrating the holidays with that trampy girlfriend of yours?" The words came down the line as a snarl. "You knocked her up? I won't support you, Brandon. Get that girl to a clinic and take care of the brat before it costs you."

"Support me." He couldn't quell the derisive snort. "I earned the scholarships, saved money, sold my car, and took out loans. As for Savannah, get over it." He shot a glance toward Nate. "We're keeping the baby," he said in a low voice.

The other man tilted his head, his brows rising as his eyes widened. "Oh, shit," he mouthed at Brandon.

"And you know what? Mia wants to move to Boston."

"You expect to get money out of me that way?"

"Whether you choose to provide support for Mia or not, she's staying in Boston. My lawyer says we have a strong case to keep her here." He crossed his fingers, hoping Aiden's assessment was correct. His next call would be Tom. "The easy way is you assign me guardianship. The hard way is court."

"You can't manage a teenage girl. And no judge would agree."

"Mia's almost sixteen. A judge will listen to her wishes. Think about it and call with your decision." He hung up and rubbed a hand through his hair, taking a few breaths before he turned.

"Damn. You're having a kid? Congratulations?"

"I haven't wrapped my mind around it, but I guess I am. Life's complicated but strangely good." Intermingling with the confusion, there were small flashes of joy. He'd never expected the happiness to creep up on him or for his panic to fade so quickly.

⌒

"Are you sure you want to be there?" Savannah asked him from the comfort of her bed.

"I'm in this, sweetie." He fastened the strap of his new watch and located his wallet. "That means doctor's appointments, shopping for baby clothes, choosing names, and being in the delivery room."

"And the nasty diapers and two a.m. feedings?" She smothered a yawn.

"All of that," he said with a brief nod. "It's early. Go back to sleep."

"Don't be late for the appointment."

"Kavanagh already approved my time off for this afternoon." He leaned in and kissed her. "I have to run."

He tiptoed through the apartment and poured a coffee, then grabbed a muffin and his lunch on the way out the door. *Stay focused on the ultimate goal. Manage this first year, and things will get …* He shook his head. No way would his residency get easier. Adding in a baby would make it even more interesting.

$\sim$

"Look at you. Early again." Nate poured a fresh cup of coffee.

"So are you." Brandon smirked.

"Someone has to battle you for chief. Halle has been early every shift too." Nate glanced at the clock. "Haven't see you much. It seems like you've moved in with Vanna."

"Mia's there, so Emily and Aiden invited me to stay over the holidays. You traveling to Wyoming?"

"Nope. I'm working. My family is off to New Zealand but I can't afford airfare." Nate shrugged. "Besides, it's a good time to get in some procedures. Lots of people requested time off."

"True." A smile twitched at his lips. "We have our first doctor's appointment today."

"You're really into this baby thing." Nate grinned.

"I'm nervous as hell, but what else can I do?"

"Nothing, man." His friend patted his shoulder. "Enjoy it. A couple of my high school buddies have kids. They love being dads."

They both exited onto the floor, retrieved tablets, and signed up for the next patients in the queue.

By early afternoon, Brandon was ready to drop. It had been non-stop, with several messy traumas and a packed waiting room of people with minor complaints.

"Why don't you take a break? Have lunch and get some fresh air." Will glanced around and lowered his voice. "Prenatal this afternoon, right?"

"Yup. Is it still good? I don't know how long it'll take."

"I have it covered. It's important you attend the appointments. I'll monitor your patients and watch for their lab results."

Brandon hurried to the lounge, managing to eat and grab a coffee before he headed upstairs to the clinic.

Vanna looked up from her magazine as he sat in the chair beside her. "You made it." She leaned in for a kiss.

"Told you I would. How are you feeling?"

"Nervous." She reached for his hand.

"Savannah?" A familiar looking nurse beckoned to his girlfriend. "Come in. I'm Joelle." She eyed Brandon's ID tag. "You work in the ER."

"That's right." Brandon hoped Joelle was a nurse who took her confidentiality seriously. The baby news would travel at lightning speed once it was out, and he wanted to keep it private for as long as possible.

The nurse weighed Vanna and ushered them into an exam room, instructing her to don a gown.

She changed and sat on the table, swinging her legs. "I haven't told Tiffany yet."

"I assumed the entire family knew."

"No. Everyone understands why I'd like to tell her in person, so it's been kept in strict confidence." She blinked at him. "You'll come with me, right?"

"Being in includes breaking the news to your mother. You have my schedule."

The doctor tapped on the door and peeked in. "Savannah. Lovely to see you. Is this Dad?"

Brandon almost protested, but at Vanna's nod, he realized the doctor referred to him being *Dad* to the tiny being developing inside her. Such a strange reality.

"Brandon is an intern in the ER."

"You'll be well taken care of."

"Of course. I'm living at home while I attend Harvard, so it makes it easier to eat properly."

"We started prenatal vitamins right away." Brandon said.

"Excellent." The doctor launched into a string of health questions, noting the responses on the chart. "I'll perform a full exam today. Did you want Brandon to stay?" She smiled warmly. "Not everyone is comfortable with an extra body in the room."

"Stay." Savannah reached for his hand. "Is that okay?"

He moved to the head of the bed, entwining his fingers with hers, determined to stick by her side. To be there. To be what she needed. To make up for every moment he'd failed her.

The exam was routine, and over within a few minutes. The doctor jotted some notes and filled out a lab request. "Get these tests done, and I'll contact you if there are any concerns, but you appear perfectly healthy. Any questions?"

Savannah squeezed Brandon's hand as she shook her head.

"We'll see you in four weeks." The doctor smiled and left the room.

With her pregnancy progressing normally, Savannah decided they should tell her mother. Brandon's next days off involved a flight to Chicago.

Brandon smoothed his hair. "What do you think she'll say?"

"I have no idea." She tugged his arm down as his fingers wandered through his hair yet again. "Quit fussing."

Nerves. They wouldn't allow him to stay still. He'd met Tiffany, but he hadn't spent much time with her. The need to make a good impression hovered over him, but how could he overcome the situation? This series of awkward moments with Vanna's extensive family would culminate with the moment he told her mother he'd been careless. He'd put her daughter into this position.

"She likes you. It'll be fine." She stretched, her fingers lingering, brushing in a gentle sweep against his temple before she kissed him.

He closed his eyes, savoring the light taste of mint on her breath and the softness of her lips. It relaxed him, but only until the swish of the elevator door brought him back to the present. He straightened and captured her hand, pressing her fingers to his lips.

Tiffany greeted them with a huge smile and immediately pulled Vanna into an embrace, rocking on her feet. "I haven't seen you for so long." She took her daughter's hands in hers. "You look amazing." The woman drew Brandon in for a hug and kissed his cheek. "Wonderful to see you again. Come in."

"Savannah." Stefan hugged her and kissed her cheek before holding out a hand to Brandon. "Welcome."

"This place is great." Savannah wandered to the window, taking a look out over the lake. "Much bigger than your old apartment."

"Let me give you a tour." Tiffany smiled. "Maybe next time you visit, you'll stay with us."

Brandon trailed the two women, half-listening to Tiffany as she made comments about the home she shared with Stefan.

"Mom will be here in an hour and we'll go for dinner." Tiffany ushered them into the spacious living room. "I wanted to share our news. Stefan asked me to marry him."

"That's amazing." Savannah rounded the coffee table to give her mother a hug before she moved on to Stefan.

Brandon offered his congratulations to the couple and they admired the ring; a sparkling diamond and emerald gemstone combination.

"Beautiful. When is the wedding?"

"I'm not sure yet. Your dad mentioned Ryan finally took the leap and asked his girlfriend to marry him. You'll want to attend both, plus you have a busy school schedule."

"You told Dad about your engagement?" Savannah's brows rose.

"We do talk, Savannah."

"You didn't before he ga—"

"What can I get you to drink?" Tiffany stood and headed toward the bar.

Brandon bit his lip as Ryan's comment in the hot tub popped into his mind. *Sharkie.* The woman's tight smile almost suited that nickname, even though Tiffany's interactions with her daughter and her ex-husband generally seemed lovely and sweet. He wiped his damp palms across his pants.

"Tell me all your news. I hear you toured Yale."

"I went to see Justin. He applied for a transfer." Savannah's reached for Brandon's hand. "I don't even know how to say this."

"What?" Tiffany's surreptitious look at Vanna's left hand seemed involuntary, as was the relief written across her face.

Brandon figured she might be less relieved when she heard the actual news and learned she'd be a grandmother at the ripe age of thirty-five.

"Are you leaving Harvard?"

"No." Savannah tipped her head. "I liked Yale, but ..." She heaved a sigh as her grip tightened on Brandon's fingers. "You'll be disappointed."

Tiffany moved to sit beside her daughter. "Why would you ever think ..." She pressed trembling fingertips to her pursed lips. "Ohh, honey. Are you ...?" Tiffany studied her daughter's glistening eyes. "How far along?"

"Eight weeks."

"You've told your dad?"

Savannah nodded.

"Come with me." Tiffany rose, tugging her daughter down the hallway, followed by the sound of a closing door.

Brandon scrubbed a hand through his hair, unsure of what to do. He leaned forward, putting his palms over his face and avoiding Stefan's gaze.

The other man rose and crossed the room, followed by the clink of a bottle, and a touch on Brandon's shoulder. "You look in dire need of this."

Brandon accepted the glass with the portion of amber liquid, taking a long swallow. It burned its way down but left a pleasant aftertaste in his mouth. The expensive stuff. The same brand Aiden drank.

He leaned back, tipping his head against the leather. "What are they doing?"

"My guess is talking with Aiden." Stefan sighed. "What's the plan?"

"We're keeping the baby." Brandon took another swallow of his drink and glanced down the hall. "I wonder if I should ..." He motioned with one hand.

"Nope." Stefan lifted his glass. "Best you stay out of it."

"How does that work? This involves me, or so you'd think."

"Yes and no. Learn to live with it, if you plan to stick around."

"Live with what? Everyone making decisions about my kid without any input from me?"

Stefan shrugged. "This is an emotionally charged issue for most families. For Tiffany and Aiden, it's far more. You've heard the story, haven't you?"

"Bits and pieces." Brandon rested his hands on his knees with the glass cupped his glass in his hands. "But this isn't them. It's me, Vanna, and our child. These decisions have nothing to do with them." *At least Aiden and Emily allowed me to be in the room while they decided my fate.*

"Ahhh, that's where you're wrong." Stefan wandered to the bar and retrieved the decanter, bringing it over to refill their drinks. "You have to accept her family's involvement, but on the plus side, your child will never go without anything."

"It doesn't make it any easier when you're sitting on the outside and being told how it's going to be. I promised her I was in, but this doesn't feel in."

"Patience, young man, patience."

"How do you deal with it?" Brandon muttered.

Stefan set aside his empty glass. "It's natural to be frustrated, Brandon, but Savannah is Aiden's daughter, not mine. It may sound crazy to support their constant contact, but I'm actually relieved that those two are able to peacefully co-parent their child. That hasn't always been the case, and it took a toll on everybody involved."

Brandon couldn't bring himself to look up as the two women returned. How could bear the disappointment and condemnation in Tiffany's eyes? He'd failed to protect her daughter.

"Everything okay?" Stefan asked softly.

"We're good. Thank you for allowing us a few minutes." Tiffany squeezed Brandon's shoulder on her way by.

Savannah sat beside Brandon and trickled her fingers down his back. Her gentle touch reassured him, and he dared to lift his head.

Tiffany looked at Stefan, waiting for his nod before focusing on Brandon and Savannah. "Aiden and I have strong feelings about what happens with our grandchild. We want this to end differently than it did when Savannah was born. Please let us do what our families didn't for us."

"We appreciate it." Brandon took Savannah's hand. "Everyone has been incredible and supportive."

Tiffany gave him a sad smile and small nod as Stefan wrapped an arm around her.

None of this would be easy, especially for Savannah's mother. History repeated itself with her daughter, but Brandon was determined this would all work out. Their child would know the love of both parents and an extended family.

⌒〰

They'd only returned from Chicago, when Aiden handed him an envelope.

Brandon noted the insignia and address of one of the boarding schools he'd applied to on Mia's behalf. "That was fast."

"It's only a couple of weeks until second term begins. The fat envelope looks promising."

Brandon ripped it open and extracted the paperwork. A sense of relief flooded him as he realized Mia had been accepted and the majority of her school fees and tuition would be covered by scholarships and various financial aid packages. "She's in. Now I just have to swing the difference. Two thousand. I wonder if I can pick up some extra shifts."

Aiden shook his head. "You already work the maximum eighty on a regular basis, but there are other options. You can apply for emergency money through the new fund, or I'll lend it to you interest free until you finish your residency."

"I can't take money from you." The man had been incredibly generous and already Brandon owed more than he could ever repay. "I can't ask it of you."

"I said lend, not take. Pay me back when you can."

Brandon longed for the day when he had a spare two grand sitting in his bank account. "Then, thank you. I guess it's time to break the news." He'd mentioned the possibility to his sister, and boarding school was in her best interest, but he still felt like he was wiggling out of his responsibility to care for Mia.

He tapped on Mia's door.

"Come in." Her cheerful voice made him feel that much worse.

"Can we talk?" He stepped inside, closing the door behind him.

"Oh-oh. You look serious." A crease formed in her forehead as her eyes widened. "Did Carol win the battle?"

"No. That's ongoing, but Tom says not to worry." He sat on the edge of her bed, holding out the acceptance letter. "We found a school."

"January?" She stared at the paper.

He reached for her hand. "I promised you'd be with me, but with my hours it's not practical. Aiden and Emily have been kind to host us over the holidays, but we can't live here forever."

A smile crept over Mia's face. "This will keep me nearby?" She threw her arms around her brother, planting a huge kiss on his cheek. "Thank you, thank you, thank you."

"You're not upset?"

"No. I love it here. I'll do whatever you need to make this work."

He blew out a puff of air. "I was worried. But Tom believes this will nail down our case for guardianship."

Mia jumped to her feet, swinging her arms and swaying her hips. "I'm free, free, free." The smile slid from her face as she pointed at the letter. "Wait. How are you paying for this? You already owe so much for medical school."

"Financial assistance and scholarships." He met her gaze. "Aiden offered to lend me the shortfall."

"He did that?" Mia's eyes shimmered. "I'll repay it one day, I promise. Why couldn't our parents be like Vanna's?"

"Don't worry about the money." He hugged her. "I'm sorry for not getting you out of there sooner."

She shook her head. "It's not your fault. You always came back. I know that was for me."

"That's what brothers are for. Now, make me proud and get your butt into Harvard."

"You make me proud and be the best doctor ever. I bet you'll be the best Dad. And the best husband."

"Don't plan the wedding. We haven't been together even a year."

"But you love her, right? Why don't you marry her? She's amazing. And her family too."

"It's complicated. Vanna isn't ready, and I'm not sure I am either. Having a baby is enough for now."

The holidays passed in a rush, with Brandon spending countless hours on shift. With Mia happy and well taken care of, he'd regained his focus. Now he looked forward to his first New Year's celebration with Savannah.

He squinted in the mirror, grimacing as he made a third attempt at the bow tie. "Why do I need a monkey suit for New Year's?" He dropped his arms to his side, tilting his head at the slightly mangled result. "Doesn't your dad own clip-ons?" He caught her eye in his reflection and winked.

Vanna laughed. "It's inappropriate to wear cheap ties with Brioni. Do me up?" She draped her hair over her shoulder, clearing it from the tiny hooks on the halter of the dress.

Brandon's body reacted to the soft floral scent tickling his nostrils as he moved closer. He skimmed his fingertips over the smooth bare skin of her back, placing a kiss on the nape of her neck as he brushed away the stray wisps of hair. "You smell so damn good," he murmured.

"None of that. Everyone is waiting." As soon as her top was fastened, she sat on the edge of her bed, adding silver heels to her ensemble.

"You look amazing." He scanned her from head to toe as she rose, taking in the form-fitted chiffon skirt with a side slit that ran up her thigh, revealing smooth legs and a well-toned thigh.

"You look pretty good yourself." She fiddled with his bow tie. "Except for this. Ask my dad to resuscitate that thing."

He stepped into the hallway. His eyes widened at this sight of his little sister. "You look … Wow."

"You like? Vanna helped me choose it." Mia spun, the skirt flaring out. "Emily did my makeup."

Aiden appeared at the end of the hall. "Lovely, Mia." As he approached, a frown crossed his face. "Yikes. What happened to that poor thing?" He tugged at Brandon's tie, retying and straightening it within seconds. "Much better. Em is saying goodnight to the kids, and then we'll go." He smiled as Savannah appeared. "Beautiful, cariño." He brushed her cheek with a gentle kiss. His eyes lit up as Emily appeared, looking stunning and elegant in a coral-colored silk dress.

Vanna hugged her stepmother. "You look amazing."

"Gorgeous." Aiden looped an arm around his wife, leaning in to murmur something indistinguishable in her ear before ushering everyone toward the door. "The limo will be waiting."

Mia's eyes widened, a joyous smile on her face.

Though he didn't understand the fuss over a New Year's celebration, Brandon would go along with it. It had been forever since he'd seen his sister this happy.

# Chapter 16

## Savannah

FAIRY LIGHTS TWINKLED AMONG THE decorations, creating a magical atmosphere aboard the yacht. Savannah gazed around the room, a smile tugging at her lips as she spotted Tiffany, who immediately excused herself from her conversation and hurried toward her.

"Sweetie. You made it." Tiffany wrapped her in a hug.

"And so did you." Savannah sank into the embrace.

"I'm so excited to see you. Brandon got the night off?"

"He traded to work tomorrow, as did Dad."

"Crazy hours those men keep." Her mother shook her head.

"How did you handle it? When you were with Dad?"

"Not very well. I don't know how anyone deals with their spouse being a doctor, except other doctors." Tiffany's gaze wandered to Emily, who'd joined Alex and Jenna at one of the tables. "When we married, he was in medical school, putting in long hours of study. What can I say? It was stressful and incredibly lonely at times."

"I understand. Brandon's hours are crazy but living with Dad, I expected it." Savannah followed her mother's look, which had traveled to Aiden and Brandon who were ordering drinks at the bar.

"They get along. That's a good sign." Tiffany sipped her drink. "Makes sense as the age gap is only ten years." A thoughtful look appeared. "Brandon reminds me of Aiden at that age."

Over the past few weeks, Savannah had thought the same thing many times. The similarities between the two men's lives struck her often but she hoped her relationship with Brandon fared better than her parents' marriage. Perhaps she was better prepared for the realities of a doctor's life.

"How are you feeling?" Tiffany reached a tentative hand toward Savannah's belly.

Vanna pressed her mother's palm against her flat stomach. "Not much to feel yet. It seems unreal."

"I felt that way when I was pregnant with you," her mother said softly. "This time is special. Enjoy it. How's Brandon coping?"

"So far, he's good. He got the freak out over with early." She allowed a faint smile.

"I'm sorry I wasn't there for you, but it sounds like he had a natural reaction. You should have seen your dad when we found out about you. I will never forget that day."

"Why?"

"The pacing. The terror that David or Thomas would murder him. All the normal thoughts for a teenage boy, I guess." Tiffany took Savannah's hand. "The part that sticks in my mind was his concern for me. How he let go of his own fears. He put them aside to be my support."

"Like he did for me when my dad died … and numerous times since." Savannah knew she was lucky. Not everyone had an Aiden in their lives.

"He's one of a kind. The entire experience cemented the bond between us. One that will never break. Even after the struggles we've endured, I consider him the most amazing man I've ever met. He's always there for me in a way nobody else ever has been, and I love him for it."

"He offered to take the baby if I can't manage."

"My offer to help is open too, Savannah, but I get he's the better choice. He's a great dad, and he has Emily."

Savannah squeezed her mother's hand. "Thank you, but Brandon and I need to raise our child. Not to say I won't gladly accept babysitting once in a while."

"I'd love that." Her eyes shimmered as she drew Savannah in for a hug. "I failed you, in so many ways, but now …" She dabbed at the corners of her eyes.

"It's okay, Mom. You're here now, and that's what matters most." Vanna rested her head on her mother's shoulder, enjoying the closeness.

"You called me Mom," Tiffany whispered in a choked-up voice.

The familiar term seemed to fit now. Savannah's heart ached for the time they'd lost. The memories they'd never have.

⁓

"Five … Four … Three … Two … One … Happy New Year!"

The cheers and voices surrounded her even as she sank into Brandon's embrace, the delicious warm kiss sending a quiver down her spine.

Savannah turned in his arms, snuggling against his chest as she looked skyward at the first crackle, captivated by the blossoming bright sparkles of silver and gold twinkling in the sky, suspended for a moment before cascading and crackling toward earth, followed by a pop and a magnificent show of red.

A hush fell over the viewing deck as the entire group gazed up at the display, swaying to the strains of the music floating over the harbor.

"Best seats in the house," Brandon murmured in her ear. "Amazing. An incredible night."

Savannah leaned her head back against his chest as bright colors lit the sky. Her feet ached from dancing and her cheeks were frozen into a permanent smile, but she wouldn't change anything about this moment. Locked in the arms of the man she loved, surrounded by her family, the world seemed perfect.

She sighed as the finale lit up the sky, the crowd disbursing as the last of the fireworks faded in the expanse of black.

"We should go inside. It's chilly." Vanna entwined their fingers, leading him down the stairs.

"Your dad is incredible with my little sister." He motioned to where Aiden was dancing with Mia, spinning the giggling girl as music reverberated through the room. "Your entire family has welcomed her."

"She's a sweet girl." She tugged him onto the floor as the song ended and a slower selection floated through the air. "Let's have our last dance before we arrive at the dock."

Brandon held out his arms, welcoming her into his embrace. "I never thanked you for what you've done for Mia. Whatever you said to her worked, because she's excited about boarding school."

A smile touched her lips. "It's been fun getting to know her."

"How lucky am I? You just get it. You've forgiven me for so much."

She moved closer, resting her head against his chest. *How lucky am I?* This man kept surprising her in the best of ways. If he was this good with his sister, he'd be a terrific father. "Forgiveness works both ways, Brandon."

She enjoyed the last few minutes in his arms, wishing the evening weren't ending. Too soon, everyone was saying goodnight with plenty of hugs, kisses, and New Year's wishes.

⌒

"Sweetheart. We're home." Brandon assisted her from the limo, scooped her into his arms, and carried her straight through the lobby into the elevator.

"Mmm. I'm so tired." She yawned as she rested her head against his chest.

"It's two in the morning. Surprised you lasted this long," Emily said as they rode upward.

"Night, sweetie." Aiden pressed a kiss to her cheek once they reached the foyer. "Sleep well."

"Night." She allowed Brandon to carry her to her room, where he set her onto the bed.

"Let's get these off." He kneeled to remove her shoes, giving each foot a short massage before unzipping her dress and slipping one of his oversized t-shirts over her head.

"Bathroom. Then sleep," she murmured as she padded across the room. She took a moment to clean the makeup from her face before she returned to the dimly lit bedroom.

Brandon lounged against the pillows, one arm tucked behind his head.

"You look comfy." She slid under the covers. "Ahh, and you're snuggly warm." Vanna wiggled closer.

"You smell good." He nuzzled against her neck, curling a hand around her back. The other hand crept under her t-shirt, working it upward to expose her belly. He stroked his fingers over her skin, causing goosebumps to rise along her arms before he flattened his palm. "You can't even tell our baby is in there."

Savannah rested a hand over his. "Soon we won't be able to hide it. Are you ready for that?"

He slid down, pushing aside the covers and pressing kisses onto her exposed belly. "We don't need to hide our baby. I'll love him or her just like I love you." He lingered over her navel for a moment before working his way up to her lips. "I'm in love with you, Savannah," he whispered.

Her heart rate sped up at the sweet words she'd craved hearing from this man for so long.

"I needed to be sure. It's been such a short time, yet," he said before he brushed his lips against hers. "I love you. I love you. I love you."

Savannah blinked, hoping she wasn't dreaming this entire fantastic moment. Suddenly, she was wide awake. "And I love you."

Only a few days after they celebrated New Year's in Boston, the family, including Brandon, flew to Chicago. Almost everyone had heard the news, but Aiden insisted Gramma Grace be told in person.

Savannah clutched Brandon's hand, cringing at the displeased moue displayed by Caroline Hamilton.

Gramma Grace, however, sported a wide smile. "Oh, my dear. I'll be a great-great-grandmother." She stood, opening her arms to her great-granddaughter.

Relief flooded Vanna. Breaking the news became easier each time she was faced with it. Even her Abuela Nina surprised her with the warm reception at the news of the unexpected arrival in the family when she'd visited over the holidays.

"Great-grandmother," Caroline muttered, shooting a scathing look at her son. "How did you allow this to happen? I thought you'd learned." Her gaze drifted to Brandon. "Perhaps you haven't taught your daughter appropriate behavior befitting a young lady."

"Shut up, Caroline," Aiden said under his breath. "Or get the hell out."

"How dare you." Caroline's lips set in a grim line. "I demand you show me respect."

"Respect is earned, not given." Aiden narrowed his eyes at his mother. "You disrespect everyone."

"Enough." Grace's gentle admonishment accompanied the stern look in her grandson's direction. "Today is about Savannah and Brandon and their wonderful news."

"Wonderful?" Caroline scoffed.

Grace frowned at her daughter-in-law, but extended a hand to Brandon, drawing him in for a hug. "Promise you'll take good care of our Savannah."

"You have my word." He kissed Grace's cheek.

Grace gave a satisfied nod. "After all the excitement, I need to rest before dinner. Aiden? I left some paperwork on the desk in the office for you to review. James had stored the box in my attic. There are two envelopes for Tom, and one for my bank, if you wouldn't mind delivering them?"

"I'll take care of everything." He rose, offering her his arm to lean on, their low tones carrying down the hall as they retreated.

Emily headed for the door. "I should check on the kids."

Savannah linked hands with Brandon, leading him from the room and toward the kitchen, leaving Caroline alone in the library.

"That went better than expected. Except for Caroline." He frowned. "She's ..."

"A piece of work?"

Brandon nodded. "Equally as bad as my mother, even if in a different way."

Savannah understood his meaning. Carol was outright hostile. Caroline leaned toward passive-aggressive. Both had a history of causing damage to those around them, especially their sons.

Emily appeared moments later with Kellan and Cierra.

"Where's Dad?" Savannah asked.

"He's sorting through the files for Grace. He wanted to get it done, and then we can enjoy the afternoon." She cradled a fussing Cierra, while Brandon helped Kellan locate a coloring book. "Could you take your dad a drink? I need to deal with this grouch."

"Sure." Savannah went through to the kitchen and poured a glass of lemonade. She carried it down the hallway toward the office, but stopped short as she heard raised voices.

"Why would she leave it for you? I'm his wife."

"Ex-wife. I dealt with the estate, not you. Most of this is Gramma's personal paperwork."

"You've seen her financials?" Caroline's voice rose.

"I've been managing her accounts ever since Grandfather passed away. If you don't mind, I'd like to finish so I can spend the afternoon with my family."

Savannah tapped on the door, not wanting Caroline to catch her loitering in the hallway, eavesdropping on the conversation. "I brought some lemonade, Dad." She set the glass on the desk.

"Thanks, sweetie." Aiden removed the top from a file box.

Caroline froze in place, her eyes tracking every move as he lifted a stack of papers from the carton. Her eyes widened as Aiden turned an envelope and she took a large step forward. "I'll go through that one." She snatched at it.

"Uh-uh." He held it out of her reach, inspecting the small logo on the top corner of the envelope. "Gramma asked me to deal with it, not you."

"I'd like to help." A saccharine smile appeared. "It's not like his medical records are a secret from me."

"How do you know these are medical records?" His brows rose.

"The logo. That's the medical group we used. Some of that is mine."

"If it is, I'll give it to you. After I've sorted it."

"It would be quicker if I do it." Caroline made another attempt to grab the envelope from Aiden's hands.

Aiden stepped back, his head tilting as he studied Caroline. He narrowed his eyes, keeping his gaze trained on her as he opened the flap and extracted the paperwork from inside. "Now I am curious."

"Why?" Caroline's knuckles whitened as she clutched the edge of the desk.

"You're fixated on this specific envelope. Why is that, *Mother*?" He perused the top paper and he removed the paper clip from the top corner. "Hmm." His eyes lifted toward Caroline's pale face before he flipped to the next form.

Savannah couldn't move, riveted on this small piece of drama unfolding between her father and grandmother. Maybe they'd forgotten she was even in the room. She held her breath as he turned to the next paper.

"What the …?" He rubbed a hand through his hair.

Caroline craned her neck, her eyes widening.

"Your blood type is O positive?" Aiden stared at his mother.

Caroline's shoulders sagged, some of the tension leaving her, along with a slight exhale. "Oh, yes, that's right." She smiled.

"So was James?"

Caroline nodded. "I believe so."

Savannah's mouth grew dry. Even if her grandmother hadn't picked up on the significance of Aiden's comment, she had. A conversation crept into her mind; one from that long-ago day in Portland. The day they'd met for the DNA testing.

"Sweetie, could you give us a minute?" Her dad looked her way.

Vanna nodded, heading out of the room with a small glance over her shoulder. She pulled the door almost closed and halted in the hallway. This wouldn't be good, but her curiosity was piqued. She strained her ears to hear the conversation.

"What's the issue with some old blood test results?" Caroline asked.

"I'm A positive," he said in a low voice.

"Okay." Caroline's reply sounded forced and overly bright. "I don't see the issue."

Vanna leaned against the wall and closed her eyes, feeling guilty about eavesdropping but unable to move. A heavy silence lingered for the longest time in the office.

"There are pictures of you, so …"

"Aiden," Caroline's whisper carried clearly to Vanna's ears.

Savannah sucked in a breath, wishing she had listened to her instinct to leave at once.

"That's why he never wanted me around. Why he couldn't wait to dump me into boarding school."

She could picture her dad, waiting it out, hoping to get her grandmother to fill the space left by the silence. It almost always worked, today being the exception.

"You have nothing to say?" Aiden asked finally. "If not James, then who?"

"I can't."

"Can't what? Be honest? Yeah, that's impossible for you, right? You owe me the truth."

Savannah tiptoed away, creeping along the tile, hoping to remain undetected.

"There you are." Emily appeared in the doorway. "What's the matter, sweetie?" Her expression morphed into concern.

"I'm … just hungry."

Her stepmother perked up, alerted by raised voices carrying down the hallway. "Go eat, cariño." Emily strode past, entering the office and closing the door behind her.

"How was Chicago?" Rochelle asked as Savannah set her pack on the floor by their favorite table.

"Eventful." She dug out her small packet of trail mix and sipped her peppermint tea. "My Gramma Grace accepted the news and even hugged Brandon."

"The royal seal of approval." Her friend snickered. "I guess her name is Grace for a reason."

She couldn't argue. Her great-grandmother was elegant with infinite composure. The person she worried about was her dad. Caroline had left minutes after Emily had joined them in the office and nothing further had been said, but she could tell from Aiden's moodiness, and his wife's extra-gentle attentiveness, that the result of the conversation hadn't been good.

Her stomach clenched. She wasn't sure if it was morning sickness, or the after effects of a tense weekend. Worse, she couldn't even discuss her fears with anyone.

"Still nauseous?" Rochelle set her laptop to the side.

"Mornings are the worst, but snacking helps. I'll be fat." Savannah sipped her tea.

"Nah. You'll look cute with a belly. How far along now?"

"Ten weeks." Savannah tossed a small handful of nuts into her mouth, hoping the starchy snack would settle her stomach. "My dad has a Doppler unit, so we heard the heartbeat."

At the sound of someone clearing their throat, Savannah looked up.

Piper loomed over the table, her arms crossed. "Unbelievable." She sneered at Rochelle before returning her attention to Savannah. "That's one way to get the guy to stick around."

Savannah pushed back her chair and rose to her feet in one smooth motion, folding her own arms across her chest. "My relationship with Brandon isn't your concern."

"He'll always be my brother, even if our parents divorce." Her eyes narrowed. "No matter. Once he gets what he wants from your rich family, he'll leave you." She smirked. "Like father, like son."

"Go back to Gray." Rochelle stood. "You two deserve each other."

"You insist our relationship will end soon. Yet, he's still with me." Vanna lifted her chin. "Worry about your own boyfriend."

Piper took a large step forward. "Like I'd take"—she jabbed her index finger at Savannah's chest—"your advice."

"Back off, Piper." Jackson appeared, sliding an arm around Savannah's waist. "Brandon wouldn't enjoy you threatening his girlfriend."

"Thanks for sharing our private details with Jeremy." Savannah quirked a brow. "And good luck with keeping Gray out of everyone's panties." She fluttered her fingers dismissively.

Piper squinted at her before spinning and stalking toward the exit.

Jackson furrowed his brow. "What was that about?" His looked at Savannah and then to Rochelle.

"Thanks, Jackson." Savannah gave her friend a hug, planting a resounding kiss on his cheek. "It's a long story. Have a seat."

Savannah hated keeping secrets from Brandon, but she figured there was nothing to be gained by bringing up the incident with Piper. She pasted on a smile, hid her worries, and busied herself unpacking dishes in Brandon and Nate's new apartment.

Savannah placed the last plate in the cupboard, slashing the packing tape with a knife and folding the box, adding it to the stack.

"Take it easy." Brandon passed her a bottle of water. "Stay hydrated and don't strain yourself."

"I didn't lift any furniture. You barely let me carry anything. And my doctor said—"

"Normal activities. I know, I was at your appointment." Brandon patted her belly. "But you have enough stress with school."

"Putting a few dishes into cupboards is hardly major stress." Savannah wandered into the living room and plumped a pillow on the couch. "This is much nicer than your other place. So clean." She smirked. "So Dylan free."

Nate appeared from his bedroom with another empty box. "I can't believe we lucked out and snagged one of the best apartments. There's already a waiting list. Kavanagh said it'll be months before the next building is ready."

"Guess working in the ER has its benefits."

"Ha." Nate snorted. "Or maybe hanging out on ski holidays with the attending doctors magically elevated our names to the top of the list, oh golden boy."

"It's not favoritism. All of the ER residents were offered apartments before they opened it up to other departments."

"Dylan was some pissed. Wonder how our ER drew the long straw."

Savannah turned toward the window, hiding her expression as the two guys bantered back and forth. Tom had worked on the paperwork for the LaRousseau Foundation, and Vanna had seen the signatures. Aiden Hamilton and William Kavanagh shared the duties as co-chairs.

All Nate and Brandon had to do was look at the Foundation's paperwork, and they'd know why their ER had the funding when others didn't. It hadn't taken Vanna long to tally the amounts—which were stunning—and connect the recent sale of James Hamilton's luxurious New York apartment and the transfer of funds from his massive estate into the coffers of the Foundation.

From there, a few Google searches and she'd pieced together the story. Matthias LaRousseau, medical student, University of Pennsylvania, deceased. Cause of death; suicide by hanging. Found in his apartment by two members of his study group. Her stomach had turned as she realized what had never been said. Aiden and her Uncle Will were members of the study group.

She couldn't tell Brandon. One day, it would all be revealed. Until then, she'd been sworn to secrecy.

Brandon wrapped an arm around her waist, rubbing her belly with his palm. "How are you feeling?"

"I'm a little tired." She leaned back against his chest. "And I'm starving."

"We were discussing dinner." He pressed his cheek against hers. "You zoned out."

"I'm good." She gave him a reassuring smile. "Let's eat."

# CHAPTER 17

## *Brandon*

BRANDON EXAMINED THE PHOTO ON his phone. "One more." He pointed it at Savannah again, assessing her profile. A tiny rounded belly had developed over the past two weeks. One easily hidden under her flowing tops, but it reminded him of the ticking clock. "I'll air drop the copies."

Savannah nodded as she lowered her blouse. "Perfect." Her phone chimed and she focused on her screen.

"Posting time?"

"Just keeping my friends in the loop."

Brandon smothered a yawn as his phone notified him of her new post. He fought the surge of annoyance. The first comment was from Justin. And he'd bet anything the furious text she was typing at this moment was in response to the very same guy. Like the dude had nothing better to do than message his ex-girlfriend.

She eyed him as he covered his mouth, hiding a second yawn.

"Sorry, honey. Long day. What are you reading?" He picked up the book she'd left on his coffee table. "Heavy stuff." He examined the page about pregnancy and childbirth that she'd marked. "Don't freak yourself out with this stuff."

"It was on the bookshelf in Dad's office." She rested a hand on her belly. "Do you want to know if we're having a boy or a girl?"

He leaned close and kissed her belly. "What do you think?"

"I don't know. We have an ultrasound soon and if we find out, we could pick names." She grinned. "But no peeking."

Brandon laughed. "Ultrasounds are designed exactly for peeking at babies."

"But if you see the sex, you have to share. Aiden saw when Emily was pregnant with Kellan, but he didn't admit it until months later."

"Sneaky." He tucked an arm around her shoulders. "I vote for wait." He tugged at the corner of the envelope tucked between the pages. "A letter from Yale?"

A guilty smile appeared. "It's nothing."

He fished out the letter, his eyes widening. "An invitation from Yale to interview with the admissions office is hardly nothing." His heart sank. "Are you considering it?"

"There's no guarantee I'll get in."

He turned, cupping her face in his hands. "Are you transferring to Yale?"

"I haven't even been accepted."

"Huh. So Justin knew, right?" *The damn ex-boyfriend who never stopped texting.*

"He was with me," she said. "I planned to discuss it with you, but I needed space to think. I loved the campus. It's so different from Harvard."

"What happens with us." He curved a hand over the firm roundness under her top. "And our baby?"

"My dad and Emily will help, and it's only a couple of hours from Boston to New Haven. It's my education, so it makes sense to entertain every option."

"You could have told me you applied."

"I didn't want to stir things up. You were already pissed about the trip, and I didn't know where our relationship was headed." She patted the hand he had on her belly. "A lot has changed since November."

"Have you told your dad?"

She nodded. "If it bothers you, I won't go."

He tipped his head back, exhaling a long breath. Another foot forward, balancing on the tightrope. One misstep and their entire relationship might topple. "Go for the interview. I refuse to stand in the way of your career."

"You're angry."

"I'm upset you didn't share this earlier. If we have any hope of making us work, you need to be honest. No more secrets."

She bit her lip, blinking those doe eyes that melted him every single time. "I'm sorry."

"Come here." He softened his tone as he wrapped her in his arms. "I have something to share with you. I decided to visit my father."

"You did?"

"Yeah. It's too late for him to do anything for me, but maybe he'll see Mia. Albany is only a few hours from here."

"Do you want me to go with you?"

"It's something I should do alone." Brandon smiled, hoping to reassure her. "I'll go on my next days off."

It was just after one in the afternoon when Brandon pulled up at the curb and stared at the average, middle-class suburban home. He'd been on the East Coast for years, but never imagined his father lived so close.

Until recently, he hadn't wasted his time or thoughts on the man, but his little sister's sad comments about not knowing her father spurred him into action.

This visit might give them more than just each other. Or perhaps it would allow some closure. Or maybe it would simply reopen old wounds. He had no way of knowing.

An bike lay abandoned across the walkway, its shiny red paint glinting in the sunlight. Brandon skirted it and mounted the concrete steps, pausing for a moment before rapping on the weathered blue door. After several moments of silence, he knocked again.

The door opened a crack, and a teenage boy peered at him. "Who are you?"

"Is Darien Reynolds here?"

"Dad!" The boy tilted his head, his eyes narrowing as he stared at Brandon.

"Who is it?" The door swung open, the man's gray eyes widening a touch. "Finish your homework, Tristan." Darien ruffled the boy's hair before he stepped onto the front porch, closing the door behind him.

"How old is he?" Brandon asked, even though he already knew from the notes the investigator had provided. Replacement son, Tristan Darien Reynolds—thirteen. Replacement daughter, Amber Sophia Reynolds—twelve. Replacement wife, Madeline Janelle Reynolds—forty-two.

"Thirteen," Darien said. "How are you?"

Brandon shrugged. *How am I?* Disappointed? Angry? Sad? Resigned to the fact his father never wanted him or Mia and replaced them with ease?

Darien studied him. "You look good."

*No thanks to you.*

"Man of few words." His father tilted his head, the resemblance to Tristan striking. "What brings you here?"

"I have no idea," Brandon muttered. He stepped back, examining the middle-aged man, seeing nothing but a complete stranger. The dark hair and steel-gray eyes were vaguely familiar, but Brandon had no idea who he was. This man who'd left him and his sister without a second thought.

"Wait." Darien grabbed his arm. "What do you need? Money?"

"You're not dead, or incapacitated, or ..." He furrowed his brow. "You have a family." With a sharp tug, he freed his arm from Darien's grasp and spun, loping down the stairs and striding toward the sidewalk. What had he expected? His family had lived in the same small town his entire life. Yet this man had never visited or bothered to send a single birthday card.

"Brandon." Footsteps clunked against the front steps.

Brandon dug for the keys to the SUV, refusing to look back.

Darien grabbed his arm. "You came for a reason. Why, after all this time?"

Brandon shrugged off the man's hand. "Just needed to know."

"Let me buy you a drink. There's a pub down the block. Please?"

"Does your family know about us?"

"You're here, so let's talk. I'll answer your questions."

Brandon contemplated the man and nodded. He'd driven a long way, and one question burned at the top of his mind. Spending a few minutes in discomfort in order to get it answered might be worth the pain.

A few minutes later they were seated in a booth in the small local pub, each with a beer in front of them.

"It's good to see you. Tell me ... what are you doing? Your car has Massachusetts plates."

Brandon tipped back his beer, letting the icy liquid soothe his throat. "I'm a doctor in Boston."

"Damn, son. Good for you." Darien's brows lifted. "Explains the fancy ride."

"It's borrowed, so don't be too impressed." Brandon glowered across the table at the man. "And don't patronize me."

Darien held up a hand. "No need to take offense. I'm proud my kid earned an MD." He smirked. "Please tell me you aren't one of those head shrinkers that specialize in psycho babble."

"Would it matter?"

Darien narrowed his eyes, but shook his index finger at Brandon. "Ha, you almost had me. What's your specialty?"

Brandon took a leisurely swallow of beer. "Emergency medicine."

"You work ..."

"Level one trauma in an ER. The majority of my day is spent dealing with major accidents, gunshots, on-scene for major incidents."

"Impressive. Not everyone could stomach it."

Brandon shrugged. The pride in the man's eyes failed to move him. The man had no right to be proud of anything he'd accomplished.

"You have questions. That's why you're here?"

"Why did you leave?"

Darien focused on his drink. "You were born around my twentieth birthday. I hung in as long as I could, but Carol's a difficult woman."

"You walked out on two kids. How do you live with that?"

"Mia's not mine." Darien's lips twisted into a sneer. "Your mother had issues with fidelity. I refused to raise another man's kid."

"I'm not your kid?"

Darien blew out a breath. "I wasn't equipped to be a single father. You were better off with Carol."

*Wrong.* He picked at the label on his bottle. This man had no idea what he'd done.

"How is Carol?"

Brandon ripped a strip from the paper. "I imagine she's as crazy as when you left."

"And Mia?"

"Don't concern yourself. She's not your kid. Therefore, she's not your responsibility."

"Who's …?" Darien studied his face. "Ahhh. That's why you're really here. I can't help you."

"Didn't ask you to. I don't want your money, or your bullshit, or your excuses. Coming here was a huge mistake." Brandon peeled some bills from his wallet and tossed them onto the table. "One more question, and you can go back to your happy little family. If you're not Mia's father, who is?"

The man shrugged. "There were several candidates. I'm not convinced even Carol knows the answer." Darien stared at Brandon's phone as the screen lit up, a small green bar appearing at the top with a text message. He motioned to the screen saver. "She's a pretty one." He squinted at the picture, examining the latest belly shot of Savannah. "Damn. Is she …?"

Brandon scooped up his phone.

"You're too young, Brandon. A baby is a huge commitment. Though by the looks of it, it's too late."

"Skip the advice. You're not my dad." He leveled his gaze at Darien. "Unlike you, I refuse to abandon my child." Brandon rose and shoved his arms into his coat. He headed straight out the door, never looking back.

~

"How did it go?" Savannah asked as Brandon stepped from the elevator.

Brandon wrapped his arms around her and closed his burning eyes, grateful to be home. "He didn't have much to say aside from some sad excuse about being young and immature." He scoffed. "He was twenty-eight when he walked out that door. It took him two whole years to be mature enough to have an entirely new family. He hasn't given us a second thought. He even gave his replacement son my middle name."

"Oh, Brandon." Savannah sniffled. "I'm so sorry."

"It was stupid to bother. If he cared, he would have attempted to visit." He scrubbed at his jaw. "He's not Mia's father."

"Did you ask who was?"

"A number of candidates, he said. That would kill Mia. How would I say that to my little sister?"

"You should leave it alone, at least for now." Savannah sighed. "You suspected it."

"Yes." Visions floated before his eyes. He'd seen far more than he should have at a young age. Men coming and going while his father was at work. Being told to play outside. The empty bottles littering the coffee table. "I remember my mother being happy when she was pregnant with Mia. But she and my father fought constantly, and then he left. Her moods got worse over time. As long as she had some guy, she was okay, but men never stayed long. How did they not see it?"

"Who?"

"All the men she dated. Did they just not care?" His eyes burned. "Or maybe I should be grateful they never paid us any attention." *Maybe we escaped a fate far worse than neglect.* "It surprises me that Mia survived her childhood years."

"You're tired."

"I'm fine," he whispered. *Nope. Not fine.* He'd slammed headfirst into the invisible wall he'd been warned about at the beginning of his intern year. "I should head home." He held out the keys. "Thank Aiden for lending me the SUV."

"Stay. Please? You're exhausted after being on the road all day. You know Aiden and Emily don't mind."

"I just want to sleep." He allowed her to lead him to her room.

Savannah flipped back the covers while he stripped off his clothes and settled between the cool sheets. Moments later she joined him, snuggling against his chest. "Close your eyes."

Brandon tipped his head, gazing into her eyes as he combed her hair back with his fingertips. "I won't do what he did." He slid his hand downward, placing it over the tiny firm bump pressing into his side. "I love you. Both of you."

"We love you." She accepted his kiss as she brushed soft fingers over his.

A smile crept over his face at the flutter against his palm.

"Did you feel it?" she whispered. "That's your son or daughter."

"I can't wait to meet them." Even as he said it, he vowed to be worthy of Savannah and of this child.

"Other foot." Brandon leaned back, grasping her right foot and slathering it with peppermint lotion, taking his time as he massaged upward from her big toe. He pressed his thumbs into the flesh, eliciting a contented sigh as her eyelids fluttered closed.

"That feels like heaven."

"Thank you for letting me win," Brandon said softly. "It means a lot."

"Win?" She cracked an eyelid.

"The boy or girl issue." Brandon moved up her foot, using his knuckle to dig into the pad of her foot. "Things have seemed …" *So out of control.* He couldn't say it out loud, but many decisions had been made with so little input from him. Having his voice heard on this matter seemed a victory.

"It's important to you." She rubbed his leg, which was propped up on the couch beside her. "We counted fingers and toes. The baby's healthy. That's what matters." She glanced toward the ultrasound picture tacked to the front of his fridge. "We have our first baby picture."

"That was amazing." The appointment had driven home the fact he'd soon be a dad. Seeing their baby moving and listening to the strong heartbeat strengthened his resolve to be a better father than his own. "It's unreal. We'll be parents. Totally responsible for a little being."

Vanna graced him with a faint smile. "It's freaky. Not looking forward to labor, especially after watching Emily give birth to Cierra."

"You could change your mind about the drugs. Lots of women use—"

"Emily didn't. She's managed two babies. Women give birth every day without epidurals or heavy pain medications in countries with great health care systems. When it comes time, stick to our plan. Please, Brandon?"

"I'll honor your choice." He had no reasonable basis to veto her decision, aside from his aversion to seeing her suffer. Vanna had done the research. They'd discussed the issue, not only with the midwife overseeing their care at the hospital, but with Emily and Aiden. "But I reserve the right to override if it becomes medically necessary."

"That's part of our birth plan. And if in doubt—"

"Call your dad. I've got it, Vanna. We're not married, so it's his right to make medical decisions if you can't. I know all this."

"Then stop bitching."

He lifted his brows.

"Sorry." Savannah bit her lip. "My hormones are running rampant."

"No, I'm sorry. This is my baby," he said, rubbing her rounded belly, "but you're Aiden's baby. I trust his medical judgment." He smiled to lighten the heavy atmosphere. "Promise you'll call the minute labor begins. I don't want to miss a single moment." He'd refused to be one of those panicked fathers showing up too late, saddened by the fact they'd missed the most important moment of their lives. "Will said he'll let me leave right away."

"You have it all sorted?" Her brows rose. "It's months away."

"Less than four. And you should talk." Brandon eyed the shopping bags piled on the floor near the couch. "You've bought a ridiculous amount of clothing and toys."

"Can't have our child running around naked." She grinned. "And it's impossible to resist all the adorable baby outfits."

"Running is at least a year away." Brandon patted her calf and rose to wash the lotion from his hands. On his way back, he scooped up a bag. "I can't wait to see what you bought." He tugged the tiny sleeper free from the bag. He rubbed the soft bunny ears on the matching hat between his thumb and forefinger before he held it up. "Hard to believe anyone could be small enough to fit this." He rubbed her tummy. "But you're tiny, so maybe it's possible."

Savannah splayed her hands over her belly. "I understand how my dad and Tiffany hid it for so long. He says I'm carrying like she did, barely showing even at twenty weeks. No one at school has even noticed."

"How's it been with Piper and Gray?"

"They keep their distance, but I tend to hang around Rochelle and Jackson, so she wouldn't dare get in my face."

"He's protective." The tiniest frisson of jealousy hit him.

Savannah rolled her eyes. "Sure, but he's got a thing for Rochelle, even if he won't own up. It's crazy how they eye each other. On your next day off, we should invite them to a movie and see if we can get them together."

"Matchmaker? Nooooooo." Brandon laughed at the expression on his girlfriend's face. "Bad idea. Rochelle resents me for the Dylan debacle."

"She doesn't—" Savannah bit her lip to smother the laugh. "Well, only a little, now she realizes you aren't friends with that Neanderthal. But let's go out with them one evening. You barely see daylight."

"Not like I have much free time." He smothered a yawn. "Time for a nap before I head into work. These long hours are killing me."

Savannah nodded. "I'll head home. I have class in the morning." She twirled a lock of her hair around her finger.

"What? You've had something brewing all afternoon."

"I have an interview in New Haven with the admissions team." She rubbed his knee. "Do you think we can make it through if I transfer?"

His heart sank. Having her living so far away would make things that much harder. Inevitably, there was only one answer he could give. "It's not ideal, but I want you to be happy, and I'm busy with my residency. We'll make it work."

"Thank you." Savannah placed a kiss on his lips. "That makes my decision easier."

# Chapter 18

## *Savannah*

AVANNAH LEANED BACK AGAINST THE pillows on her bed, staring at the envelope. After a few moments, she extracted the paper and skimmed through it, even though she knew each and every word by heart.

She folded it and tucked it inside her book as the soft tap sounded on her door.

Aiden peeked into the room. "Can I come in?"

"Sure." She wiggled to the side of the bed.

"How did your exam go?"

"Good." She tucked back a stray lock of hair. "I'm happy school is almost done for another year."

"Feel up for a drive? I want to show you something."

She didn't have the heart to say no. He looked so hopeful, a smile twitching at the corners of his mouth. Something was up. Both her dad and Emily had been whispering and plotting, so she anticipated big news. She nodded.

"Grab a sweater, and we'll go."

Fifteen minutes later they were in the car, heading out of town on I-90.

Savannah leaned back in her seat. "Where's Emily?"

"A job interview. She's on the third round. It'll mean a change of workplace, but it's a great promotion for her."

"I hope she gets it." She closed her eyes, letting her thoughts drift as they sped along.

"We're here." Aiden slowed and turned through a set of wrought iron gates. They rounded the circular drive, and he stopped in front of a large house with a wide veranda. It seemed elegant and modern, yet homey and well set into the landscape

"Whose house is this?"

Aiden simply slid from his seat and rounded the car to open her door. He held out a hand to assist her before leading her to the front door. A key appeared in his hand, and he ushered her inside.

Savannah followed as Aiden led her through the main floor of the house. "Why are we here? Are you …?" She gazed around. Even given the spaciousness, the main level felt more welcoming and cozier than Gramma Grace's mansion.

"Em and I are considering this place, but we wanted your opinion before we finalize the purchase. It's close to Boston, we'll have more bedrooms, and a huge yard." He motioned to the kitchen. "It needs a few renovations, but overall it fits our requirements." Aiden grinned. "Want a tour?"

Savannah nodded.

Her dad showed her the bedrooms, each of which had its own en-suite bathroom. "One level up is a huge space we plan to convert into a nanny suite."

Savannah inspected the master bedroom before stepping onto the spacious deck overlooking the back yard. "Wow, a pool? And I love the stone patio."

"It has an outdoor kitchen and fireplace." He tugged her into the hall. "Want to see your room?"

She preceded him into a large airy room at the opposite end of the upstairs. "This is beautiful." She peered into the walk-in closet and the well-appointed en-suite. The set of French doors captured her eyes, and she found they led onto a spacious private deck. "It's amazing, Dad." A grin sneaked onto her face. "Unexpected. I pictured a waterfront home."

"Have to keep you guessing. Waterfront has drawbacks, so Em and I compromised."

*Compromise.* Her catch phrase these days. Savannah rested a hand on her belly, feeling content even with the changes coming in her life.

Her dad tucked an arm around her waist, covering her hand with his. "Sometimes unexpected ends up as incredible."

Savannah leaned into his chest. "You're incredible, buying a new house to make room for my child."

"My grandchild." He kissed her temple. "This move is good for everyone. Em loves the idea of the house and yard." Aiden looked around the room. "We'll have room for the kids to play outdoors without it being a huge production to take them to the park."

"It's great, Dad."

"There's a great room for the baby next door."

She followed him into the smaller room, which adjoined her suite. "This is perfect." Savannah closed her eyes, picturing the room painted with a mural, soft flowing drapes on the windows, and a crib against one wall. "So how does everyone feel about you moving?"

"Tom and Jenn made an offer on a house down the road."

"And Joel and Alex aren't far behind." Savannah smiled at his nod. An image of happy children running free across the expanse of lawn sprang into her mind. Soon, her own child would be one of them. "What if I transfer to New Haven?"

"We'll work it out. No matter if you're living in New Haven or Boston, you'll always have a home with us."

"Thank you, Dad." She wrapped an arm around him, absorbing the quiet comfort he offered. With the continuing support of her family, she could achieve her goals, even with the challenges of being a mother. Of that she was certain.

～

Savannah reached across the console and rested her hand on the back of Brandon's neck, rubbing gently. "Thanks for coming."

He caught her hand, bringing it to rest on his thigh. "I've never been to New Haven. And, I figured it was time to meet the infamous Justin."

She straightened as she caught the edge to his voice. "Give him a chance, please?"

"I'll be good, I promise." He squeezed her fingers. "And I want to support you through the interview."

"Thanks for the interview tutoring." She smiled.

"Happy to help. With the number of applicants the interviewer has to choose from, we need to make you memorable."

"Somehow, I doubt that'll be an issue." She cupped her belly. "How many people will waddle in there looking like they're about to pop out a kid?"

"You don't waddle." He smirked. "Not yet, anyway."

Savannah swatted his arm but laughed. Over the past week, her belly had expanded at an unbelievable rate. Though everyone said she looked tiny, she felt huge and ungainly.

Brandon maneuvered the car into the valet lane in front of the hotel and cut the engine. "You look amazing." He planted a kiss on her lips before he slid from behind the wheel.

Savannah waited until he opened her door and held out his hand to assist her from the passenger seat while the bell boy retrieved their bags from the back of the SUV.

"There she is."

The familiar voice made her turn. "Leanne." Tears rushed to her eyes as her friend embraced her. "What are you doing here?"

"Justin invited me. It's been forever since I've seen you." Leanne grasped her shoulders and stepped back, scanning downward. She rested her hands on Vanna's belly. "You're so tiny. Hard to believe there's a whole person in there."

"I assure you, there is." Savannah guided one of her friend's hands to the side.

"I felt that." Leanne's eyes grew round. "Amazing." She turned to Brandon, inspecting him from head to toe. "I finally get to meet the man who stole my friend's heart."

"And I finally meet the best friend." Brandon smiled but seemed preoccupied, focusing over Leanne's right shoulder.

"Justin." Savannah waved and dodged around Leanne, meeting the man half-way.

Justin swept her up, spinning her around. "You look beautiful," he whispered in her ear as he set her to her feet. His head tilted as he surveyed her, splaying a hand over her belly. "Are you eating enough? You need to grow junior big and strong."

"I eat more than you'd believe." Savannah patted his hand. "The baby is perfectly healthy. I'll point out fingers and toes over dinner."

"I can't wait to see the pictures." Justin offered one of his adorable grins before guiding her toward the group. He extended a hand. "Nice to meet you, Brandon. You're taking care of our girl?"

Brandon's brow rose, but he shook the offered hand, meeting Justin's steady gaze without blinking. "Justin." He jutted his chin toward the other man.

The two men sized each other up, their grips on each other's hand tightening, neither breaking eye contact.

"Testosterone alert," Leanne whispered in Vanna's ear.

Justin's eyes narrowed a touch as he let go of Brandon's hand. "You should check in. I made dinner reservations for six-thirty."

Savannah dragged Leanne toward reception, wishing she had a clue to what the two men were thinking. Maybe her greeting to Justin was too friendly?

"What was that?" Leanne giggled as she cast a glance over her shoulder.

"Justin is pushing Brandon's buttons," Savannah muttered, replaying her friend's comments in her head. "But why?"

"Justin being Justin. He worries about his girl."

"Except when he says it like that to my boyfriend, he sounds like he's planting his flag."

Leanne burst into laughter. "Well, it wouldn't be the first time."

Savannah reddened. "I didn't mean ..." She glared at her friend, but it was impossible to stay mad. The expression on her friend's face reminded her of the absurdity of the situation. Brandon agreeing to meet her ex-boyfriend was a significant step forward, so she'd remember to be grateful for his effort. "They'd better learn to get along." She rested a hand on her belly. "Brandon's gonna be sticking around."

"He'd better stick by his baby momma."

"Don't ever use those words again." Savannah shuddered at the term that flowed so easily from her friend's lips. The off-handed comment reduced her relationship with Brandon; like the only reason he would stay was because of a sense of duty to the baby.

Her friend ignored her discomfort, peering over her shoulder to where the two men were conversing. "That man is a mighty fine specimen. Maybe it's"— Leanne wiggled her brows—"envy on Justin's part."

"Do you suggest they whip 'em out and measure?" Savannah snorted as she accepted her room keys. "Not that either of them are lacking in that department."

"Do tell." Leanne brought one hand up to smother a giggle. "One thing for certain, this bambino will be the most adorable kid on the planet. Brandon's a scorching hot daddy."

"Enough ogling my man." Savannah grasped Leanne's arm, turning her away from the two men. "Tell me about yours."

"Not much to tell," Leanne said. "You know that feeling you get in your stomach, where your knees about give out every time you're near him?"

Savannah motioned with her chin toward Brandon, smirking at her friend.

Leanne followed her gaze. "Right. Well, I don't have it with my current boyfriend. We've agreed to date other people over the summer."

"It's like that, huh?"

"It's no biggie. I'm happy to regain my freedom. Reconnect with someone who makes me feel the rush." Her friend dropped her chin. "Don't freak."

"Why would I … no … are you and Justin involved?" Her heart flipped. "Is that why he invited you?"

"Oh. No, no." Leanne's eyes widened as her head swung from side to side. "I'd never. Not with Justin." Her lips twitched into a coy smile. "You're not the only one who's capable of reigniting an old flame."

"Tony?" Relief washed over her at her friend's nod, followed by a twinge to her heart. How had she not known? "For how long?"

"Off and on since graduation," she said. "We've hung out with Justin and his various girlfriends on occasion. It's casual, but it might develop into something."

"I hope it works out." Savannah forced a bright smile, despite the sadness in her heart. There'd been a time when she shared everything with her friend, yet Leanne had chosen to keep the relationship with Tony secret, at least from her. Maybe this visit would rekindle their friendship and recapture some of the closeness from their high school years.

$\sim$

Savannah tipped her chin, studying the man beside her as they strolled hand in hand across the campus. The day had turned warm and many of the students were relaxing in the sunshine. She could picture herself here, lounging on the lush green lawns with her classmates.

"Where's the sidekick?" Brandon asked.

"Leanne? She went with Justin to be his moral support." She glanced at her watch. "His interview should be done soon."

"You sound sad. Is there something going on between Justin and Leanne?"

"Definitely not. She dated Tony, who's one of Justin's closest friends." She bit her lip. "Or she's dating Tony. Off and on since high school. Which she never told me."

"Ahh." Brandon nodded, giving her hand a squeeze.

"The four of us used to hang around together, but when my dad died ..." Her brow furrowed. "I'm rambling and I'm getting weepy. Damn hormones."

He tugged her to a halt. "I don't think this is about hormones, sweetie," he said as he held her hands in his. "At least not entirely. It's natural to be sad when friendships change, but it's inevitable. You moved to the opposite side of the country at fifteen. Five years is forever for teenagers."

"I'm being ridiculous. She's made new friends, as have I, but still." She couldn't pin down what part bothered her. Her initial idea that Leanne had become involved with Justin panicked her, followed by a deep sense of relief at the mention of Tony. Then sadness had emerged and lingered.

She loved Brandon, and the relationship between her and Justin was firmly in the friend zone. Jealousy hadn't been a factor with any of Justin's girlfriends since the sailing trip. So why had even a vague thought of Leanne and Justin together threatened to bring her down?

"It's not ridiculous, sweetheart. It's nostalgic. My high school friends have mostly moved on with their lives. None of us are the same people, and aside from Rory, we've drifted apart. It became evident during my last visits."

"And I admit, for a split second, Leanne having a relationship with Justin crossed my mind. And I hated her for it. What does that say about me as her friend? Or Justin's. He dates all the time, and it's never bothered me."

"Then I wasn't the only one who picked up a proprietary vibe from Leanne." He nodded. "She's grown closer with Justin than she is with you. You're marking your territory. Justin marked his yesterday."

She widened her eyes.

"Don't pretend you didn't notice that *our girl* comment." Brandon contemplated her. "But he understands I have no intention of sharing you."

"Now who's territorial?"

"Damn right. I don't need Justin to remind me of my responsibilities to you, or to our baby."

Tears pricked her eyes. "We're a responsibility? A burden?"

"You're not a burden." He cradled her against his chest. "My responsibilities are to love you, support you in your career, to treasure you, and take care of you and our baby in the way you deserve."

"Does that mean you've finished your pissing match with Justin?" She looped her arms around his neck.

"I'm controlling my jealous streak, but I told him to back off. He's your friend, but I demand respect for our relationship. I may not be your husband, but I am the father of this baby." Brandon placed his hands on either side of her bump. "You're my family."

"And you're mine." She buried her face against the soft cotton of his sweater, savoring his distinctive earthy smell.

"Now, dry your tears. Time to kick ass and claim your spot in the future graduating class of Yale law."

She'd never loved this man more than at this moment. At the entrance of the admissions offices, she gave him a long kiss, aware of the stares they received.

Brandon paid no attention. He cupped her cheeks and gazed into her eyes. "You've worked hard to get here. You deserve this. Walk in there, and show them the amazing, confident woman I know and love."

"Love you. See you soon."

"I'll be waiting."

# CHAPTER 19

## *Brandon*

A WEEKEND IN NEW HAVEN PROVIDED a welcome opportunity to discover the past of the woman he loved, even if it meant contending with the infamous Justin.

He liked Leanne, but he was grateful she lived on the opposite coast. She reminded him of Piper. Not the disgruntled nasty Piper who'd emerged over the past year with her mile-high grudge, but the immature woman-child from Montana. Leanne wasn't as innocent as his stepsister when it came to men, but her outlook seemed naive.

The clear distinction between Savannah and Leanne stunned him. He'd expected her friend to be entirely different. As the weekend wore on, he further understood their growing distance. Leanne floated along without evident purpose or direction. Or maybe she just had indiscernible goals, other than securing a man to provide her a meal ticket.

In contrast, Savannah navigated her world with assurance. Fiercely independent. Laser focused on a finish line that might take years to reach, but Brandon never doubted she'd achieve every one of her goals and become an amazing lawyer.

"I bet you killed it." Justin tapped his glass against Savannah's and patted her belly. "Junior will be very proud of Mommy."

Brandon gritted his teeth. *Stay calm. It means nothing. Soon, we'll be home.* He forced down a swallow of beer. Until she moved to New Haven. Justin would be there, because Yale would never pass him by. The man had a natural and obvious intelligence and a hunger for success.

"I'm sure you rocked it." A brilliant smile lit up Vanna's entire face.

Leanne's lip twitched, curling ever-so-slightly before she focused on her phone. "Tony's returning to Portland for the summer." A smile flitted across her features as her thumbs flew over the screen.

Brandon bit back a frustrated retort. With Leanne in the picture, apparently no conversation was complete without a mention of Tony.

"He says congratulations."

"Tell him thanks." Vanna stared at her friend, who never even bothered to glance up.

Justin shot a look at Savannah, a wry expression on his face as his eyes cut to Leanne and back.

Vanna's nose wrinkled in return, annoyance fleeting across her face.

Irritation rose on his girlfriend's behalf. Vanna had made numerous attempts to reconnect with Leanne, but her friend seemed oblivious. This pushed Savannah toward Justin, which wasn't ideal in Brandon's view. Though he admitted if Justin hadn't been the perfect ex-boyfriend who tracked his every move, the two of them might have become friends.

"How about a game of pool?" Justin asked, his gaze resting on Brandon. "Would you like to play?" He squeezed Savannah's hand.

"You know me. I welcome every opportunity to whoop your ass." Vanna grinned. "Let me out? Time for another trip to the ladies'." She wiggled out of the booth and accepted Brandon's hand, allowing him to help her to her feet.

Leanne continued her text conversation, giving no sign she'd heard.

"Leanne?" Vanna rested a hand on her belly, her gaze fixed on her friend. "Get off your phone." She snatched the offending object out of the girl's hands. "You flew here, so why don't you join the party?" Her fingers flew as she typed. "Tony," she said, her movements firm and purposeful. "Have to go. I'm being an obnoxious ho to my friends. Talk later."

"You did not." Leanne sprang from her seat, lunging at Vanna with her arms flailing as she grabbed for the phone.

"Easy." Brandon inserted an arm between the two, catching Leanne around the waist to block her advance.

"You deserve it." Savannah tipped the phone into Leanne's hands. "Payback's a bitch."

"That's ancient history. Besides, you told him it was me."

"Then tell Tony it was me. But it doesn't make it any less true. You've been ignoring everyone, spending all your time texting. Stop it. You'll see Tony all summer. You haven't seen me in months, but I guess you don't care." Vanna spun, heading with remarkable speed towards the bathrooms at the rear of the pub.

"Wow. Those hormones are out of control," Leanne muttered. "How do you stand her?"

Justin snorted. "She's not hormonal. She's right. You flew across the country to see your best friend, yet you've spent the entire time gushing about Tony. It's making me nauseous."

"Let's play pool," Brandon turned away, hoping to hide his irritation.

Justin followed. "Sorry," he muttered as Brandon handed him a cue. "It's crazy when those two get together. I feel for Savannah. Leanne's ignoring her."

"Just like high school. Can't say I love bitchy teenage girl drama." He racked the balls.

"Vanna's not into it, but lately, Leanne's pushing her over the edge. Leanne seemed excited about this reunion, but maybe it was a mistake to invite her."

He motioned for Justin to break. "Kudos for trying, but I'm happy Leanne decided to stay at Stanford. She reminds me of my immature stepsister."

"I heard about the Piper drama." Justin lined up his shot, the balls scattering across the table, one solid rolling into a pocket. The man surveyed the table before sinking another solid. "I had hope. Leanne and Vanna were so close until the big move to Boston." He missed his next shot.

Brandon leaned over the table, casting a glance toward the back of the pub before he sank a stripe. He straightened, searching for the sight of either woman.

"Relax. Leanne won't hurt her." Justin's gaze was direct. "Oh, yeah. That protective instinct's really kicked in."

"The girl needs to calm the fuck down," he muttered. "Doesn't she get that her friend can't fight back? Roughhousing is dangerous for both Vanna and the baby."

"Awww, the concerned Daddy act," Leanne said as she appeared beside Justin.

Vanna arrived seconds later. "I need a nap." She leaned against Brandon's chest. "You can stay, though."

He hadn't missed the downturn of her lips or the slump of her shoulders. "I'll walk you to the hotel." He handed Leanne his cue. "Knock yourself out." *Please.*

"I'll get the bill." Justin's eyes narrowed slightly, as if he'd read Brandon's uncharitable thought. "Have a good rest. I'll call you later." He gripped Vanna's hand for a moment.

"Thanks, Justin." Savannah offered him a faint smile, dropping a quick peck on his cheek.

"What was that about?" Brandon asked as they emerged on the street.

The corners of her mouth tugged downward. "I don't know why she bothered." A sniffle escaped. "And it's not raging hormones."

"Nope. Not at all." He forced his lips into a straight line.

"Not you too." She pulled free of his grasp, wrapping her arms around herself. "Her comments are getting old."

"No argument from me. My concern is not an act." He curled an arm around her. "She doesn't understand."

"No, she doesn't give a crap," she muttered. "She told me I picked a good one to be my baby daddy."

"I'm not a good one?" His brows rose.

"*Picked.* And baby daddy?" Her lip curled in disgust. "It's the way she said it. Her main goal in life may be to hunt down a man to support her, but this"— she rubbed her belly—"isn't a ploy. It's not a joke, or a game, or a way to get the guy to stick around. It's a little human I'm responsible for."

"*We* are responsible." He pulled her to halt. "So she thinks …?"

"You'll be a rich successful doctor, so I'm set for life. It's ridiculous." She shook her head. "Not the successful part, but her implication about me trapping you."

Brandon smirked. "Shouldn't she be concerned it's the other way around? She has met your dad, hasn't she?"

"It's her view on appearances. I've achieved her definition of the gold-standard. The older man. The hot doctor. It's shallow, immature, and archaic."

"Never considered achieving status as a trophy husband." Brandon held back the laugh. "Ignore her, Vanna."

"But it hurts. She's acting all crazy and jealous, but she knows better. Even when she learned my dad was a wealthy doctor, she was envious."

"She was fifteen. You can't reasonably hold it against her. Anyway, the visit is almost over. Stress isn't good for you or the baby." He rubbed her back.

"It's not your friend who's turned into a bitchy shrew," she muttered. "She's spoiling our trip with her crap attitude and mean comments."

He slid his hands up to massage her shoulders. "Don't let her spoil it."

"That feels good." The tension drained from her petite frame as she rolled her neck. "I'm sorry about Leanne."

"I owed you one." Brandon's thoughts strayed to the treatment she'd received at the hands of his family and the judgmental comments from his friends, especially Noah. "Hey, Justin isn't so bad, even if Leanne's a little … *Piper-ish* for my liking."

Savannah turned in his arms. "Thank you for making the effort." She sighed. "Maybe we should just go home. This hasn't been much fun."

"It's late and traffic will be bad, sweetie. But we can make an early exit after dinner. Have some cuddle time in our room? And we'll leave first thing in the morning. Deal?"

Her head bobbed followed by her pressing her head against his chest, her eyes sinking closed. "Thanks for understanding."

After a tense ending to their New Haven trip, returning to the ER was a relief. The rules were simple. Work hard. When in doubt, ask your senior resident or attending for assistance. Even patients were easier to deal with as the connection was more professional and less personal.

Toward the end of his shift, Will Kavanagh beckoned him into the office.

"Just the intern I wanted to see," Will said.

"Everything okay?" He cast an involuntary glance at his watch. He'd promised Savannah he'd leave on time, as they'd planned dinner and a movie with Rochelle and Jackson.

"Hot date?" Will's brows rose. "Don't worry, this will only take five minutes." He held out a thick envelope. "An amazing opportunity opened up." His supervisor leaned on the edge of the desk, his gaze intent as Brandon peeked inside.

The moment his eyes hit the top line, he knew this was more than amazing. A successful application would be life-altering. "Do I have a chance?"

"I wouldn't have offered this otherwise. The competition is open to residents country wide, but your overall performance and ranking in your graduating class warrants our recommendation."

Brandon scanned the top paper. "It's five years."

"Four, technically. You've completed almost a full year." A thoughtful look appeared on his supervisor's face. "Why the hesitation?"

"Vanna interviewed at Yale."

"Why would that affect your application? Unless you're entertaining the crazy notion of quitting."

"No, but she's brilliant. They'll admit her."

"No doubt." Will nodded. "But, this is your career. She's taking care of hers."

This twist of events gave Brandon even more to consider. If this offer had been handed to him six months ago, he'd have jumped at it. Now, his crowded mind struggled to sort the pros and cons. "I'll consider it."

"No. The paperwork is due on my desk Friday morning. Nine a.m. sharp." Will straightened, his gaze direct and steady. "I've seen the spark, and the way you function in the trauma room. This is an exceptional opportunity. Don't let it pass you by." Will motioned to the door. "Don't keep Vanna waiting."

"Thanks, Will." He stowed the papers in his pack, turning to leave.

"Friday morning, Brandon."

The words echoed in his ears. *Friday.* Scant time to make a huge decision.

Savannah linked their fingers as they walked toward his apartment after the movie had concluded. "Sorry you didn't enjoy the evening. After New Haven, I should know better than to force my friends on you."

"What?" He shook himself from his thoughts.

"You've been distracted all night."

"Just tired."

"What did you think of the ending?"

"It was great." He squeezed her hand.

"It's great when one of the main characters meets a horrible demise?"

"Well, that was sad, obviously."

Savannah snorted. "I bet you don't even remember the name of the movie. Nobody died. They lived happily-ever-until-the-credits-rolled."

His lips twisted into a rueful grin. "You caught me." He heaved a sigh. "But it wasn't the company. Rochelle and Jackson are a fun couple. Wait. Are they a couple?"

"I don't think they even know." She shrugged. "Given time, I'd bet on yes. But we're off topic. What's bugging you?"

"You won't like it," he said under his breath. At her quizzical look, he decided to get it over with. "Will offered me an application for the Trauma Fellowship."

A grin spread across her face as she threw her arms around him. "That's amazing."

He held her close, rocking them slightly on their feet. "It means another full year in Boston."

She tipped her head upward. "And?"

"This." He rubbed her belly. "I can't do everything just because I want to. I have to think of you and the baby."

"Not applying would be a mistake of epic proportions. A career killer. It's a huge honor to be offered a Fellowship." She shook her head. "I don't want that on my conscience."

"It's another full year."

"And one step closer to being my trophy." Savannah wiggled her brows and grinned.

He rolled his eyes. "Thanks."

"Anytime," she said before her lips flattened into a thin line. "Brandon," she said, pressing her palms against his cheeks, "it's scary that you'd give up something you've dreamed about for me."

"Why? I'm thinking of you and our child."

"I appreciate it, but what if you wake up one day, look at me, and think *if only it wasn't for her*? All the *what ifs* preying on you? A big pile of regrets, caused by me?"

"That will never happen."

"In fantasyland." Her eyes grew misty. "I've wrestled with *what ifs* every single day. I couldn't handle being your *what if*. You have to apply. And if you win the spot, you'll take it, because in here," she said, flattening her palm against his chest, "it's what you want."

"There's another *what if*, Savannah." His heart broke even considering the possibility. "Three years is forever. Four is eternity. *What if* our relationship doesn't survive the separation?"

"We'll do our best to make the distance work." She offered a sad smile. "Choosing between not having you, or making you miserable for eternity, well, that's not even a real choice." Her helpless shrug did nothing to calm his fears.

"Vanna—"

She pressed a fingertip to his lips. "Promise you'll hand in the application before the deadline. I'm not accepted to Yale, and you haven't been offered the Fellowship until those confirmation letters arrive. Let's focus on our goals, and the future will work itself out."

"In return, you promise if you're accepted to Yale, you'll go. I don't want that disappointment on me."

"I promise," she said softly.

He nodded as they headed for home, their hands tightly linked. The opportunity presented to him was truly amazing, but also a risk. High achievement in his career could mean losing the woman he loved. The years of education and residency were hard on any relationship. How would this one be any different?

⁓

Three weeks later, the inevitable happened. A thick acceptance package addressed to Savannah arrived. And now, Brandon was in the last place he expected; New Haven. Viewing houses. *Houses.* The activity felt foreign, domesticated, and more than a little scary. *Welcome to your new life.*

"This is a lovely family home," Sylvie, their real estate agent, glanced at Savannah's protruding belly, a joyful smile on her face.

*Planning on how to spend her commission, no doubt.*

The woman's excitement displayed openly in her expression when they appeared in the shiny SUV and doubled at the sight of Savannah's pregnant belly. *Guaranteed sale* must have flashed through her brain.

"Four bright, spacious bedrooms, and a roomy office. Wait until you lay eyes on the master suite."

"Love the kitchen," Savannah whispered as Sylvie darted ahead. "And it's a great neighborhood. Close to Yale and a beautiful park."

Brandon forced himself to nod and smile before he dragged his eyes to the feature sheet. The listed price of the home caused heart palpitations.

His girlfriend sported a huge grin as she peered through the bank of windows overlooking the backyard. The patch of lawn hosted a pool with a safety cover, a solid wooden play structure with swings and a slide, and an expanse of flagstone patio. Mature trees dotted the landscape, providing splashes of shade.

"Shall we?" Sylvie asked, motioning to the staircase.

Savannah bounced up the stairs … or would have if her rounded belly allowed for it.

Every step upward made Brandon's gut clench. It didn't take a psychic to see Savannah loved this place. With its gourmet kitchen, airy rooms, and gleaming hardwood floors, it was a dream home. How would they afford the mortgage? *Forget that.* Where would they scrounge the down payment? Only one logical answer came to mind.

Sylvie showed them each bedroom and the office. "Now the best part." She ushered Savannah toward the end of the hallway.

Brandon sucked for air as he stepped into the enormous master bedroom that ran the expanse of one side of the house, back to front. He met Vanna's delighted expression with his own pasted on smile.

"Walk-in closet, full en-suite, fireplace, and a sitting area." The woman lit up as her gaze dropped to the belly. "And plenty of room to tuck in that crib."

Savannah wandered through the room, asking astute questions and taking notes, as she had on each of the five previous houses.

"I saved the best for last. This one is the *crème de la crème*." The agent added extra details, extolling the virtues of this home over the others. "Any questions, Brandon? You've been quiet."

He glanced at the listing, the numbers blurring together. *Can you call an ambulance?* "No. Vanna's thorough."

"Thank you, Sylvie. We'll discuss the options," Savannah said with a smile. "I'll call you this evening."

Brandon took a last look as they exited. Ten years down the road, he could picture this as home. Right now it seemed the impossible dream. He opened Vanna's door, assisting her into her seat. "You look tired." He noted how she sank into the plush leather, closing her eyes. "I hope you didn't overdo it."

"I'm fine." The smile she bestowed was tender. "You worry too much. I could murder a burger, though."

He laughed. "Done." He drummed on the steering wheel as he pulled away from the curb and headed toward their hotel.

"What do you think?" she asked as they stopped at a red light.

He glanced her way before focusing on the traffic. "I think I'm having a coronary."

A snort of laughter burst from the woman beside him, amusement dancing in her eyes. "Oh, there." She pointed to the right. "Tom said that place has the best burgers in town."

"Glad my heart attack is a laughing matter." A grin crept across his face, delighted at the way she lit up when she laughed. "Love you too, baby cakes." He blew her a kiss.

"Quit stressing." She patted his thigh.

His grin faded. Already he drove one of Aiden's cars and spent numerous nights at their dinner table. Both he and his sister had been adopted for holidays and often slept under the man's roof. Not to mention the tuition loan for Mia's boarding school. "It's generous of your dad to offer, but no. I owe your dad too much." He guided the vehicle into a vacant spot near the restaurant.

"Who said my dad offered anything?"

"Do you have it lurking around your sock drawer? I'd barely eat if your family didn't feed me, so …" The complete silence from her direction had his pulse rate climbing. "Savannah?"

She clutched her bag, eyes focused on her hands as her teeth clamped onto her lower lip.

"Wait. You do have it?" His brows rose. "You're kidding, right?"

She shook her head. "When my dad passed away, the sale proceeds from our house in Portland and his life insurance payout were deposited into my trust account. Plus he had pensions and savings. I inherited it all, but never had to spend even a penny."

He emitted a puff of air, unable to release his grip on the steering wheel. "I can't allow you to use it all on a down payment. And we'd have to make payments, and there are taxes, and utilities, and upkeep."

She folded her arms across her chest. "You won't allow me?" Her eyes flashed. "Who made you boss? Don't you dare tell me how to manage my finances."

"I said can't, but if you're making a stupid decision, I'll tell you. Saddling yourself with debt? Do you plan to run to Daddy every month for money? Why did you look at houses you can't afford?"

"I can afford them." She closed her eyes, taking deep calming breaths before she wiggled in her seat, angling toward him. "I'll live here for at least eight months of the year until I finish law school," she said in a low voice as she pressed her hands against her rounded belly, "with our child. That's a lot of rent, Brandon. Assuming I can find a suitable rental with a baby."

His mind whirred to life, calculating expenses on an apartment. The dorms were out of the question.

"With a house, the baby will have space to grow and a back yard to play in. The extra bedrooms means everyone can visit without the hassle of hotels. A family neighborhood is perfect."

"I'm a broke-ass medical intern."

"It's fair I manage my own expenses and buy the house. You rent in Boston, and you have medical loans to repay." She shrugged. "My financial advisor agreed to the purchase. I can afford a house."

"Your dad, you mean?"

"He would have been capable, but no. Uncle Ryan is my financial wizard."

"And the mortgage? Just how are you swinging it?"

"I have money," she said softly. "Don't worry about my finances. My dad, Ryan, Tom, Emily … they all agree it makes sense for me to buy. They've seen the listings. They know how much I intend to spend."

"Why am I here?" He quirked a brow.

"To help me choose. I want you to be comfortable there," she said. "I value your opinion."

"I give. Bring your file." He rounded the car to open her door. "Come on, Mommy. Let's get you that burger."

Once the hostess had seated them and they'd ordered, Savannah pulled out the sheaf of papers.

"The way you handled Sylvie made you look like a professional home buyer."

"I helped Aiden pick the Boston condo. I'm a quick study."

"And he's allow—" He cleared his throat as her brows shot upward. "You're nineteen, buying your first house, and not taking advantage of Aiden's apparent expertise in real estate?"

"Now you're talking crazy." She nudged him with her elbow. "Once we've picked our favorite, Tom offered to view it and give us a second opinion. It makes sense as Tom lived here, and he's a lawyer."

"Pulling out the big guns for the negotiations?" He winked. "But won't Aiden be upset if you ask your uncle?"

"No way. He trusts Tom implicitly, as do I," she said. "I'm not sure who is my favorite uncle—Tom or Ryan."

Brandon cringed as he remembered the first time he met Ryan, and how brutally honest the man had been ever since. "Not Joel, though. Why is that? There's a tension in the air with Joel."

Savannah smiled faintly as the waitress delivered their meals. She took a bite of her burger, sighing in contentment.

"Avoiding that one, are we?"

"It's complicated. And it's between Aiden and Joel. It's not mine to share."

"But you aren't close to Joel. Why?"

She brushed her fingers over her napkin. "Remember when I told you I almost lost Aiden?" Her mouth set in a grim line. "Joel caused the sailing accident." A mixture of pain and sadness etched her features.

"Damn."

"It'll never be the same between them. Joel broke a major rule. He got loaded while we were sailing, and he was angry, and if I hadn't been with them …" She blinked hard. "Kellan was only two weeks old. He'll never know how close he came to being fatherless."

"I'm sorry, sweetheart." From the expression on her face, he wished he hadn't been so insistent. It wouldn't have only been Kellan left without a father.

Her sad smile made his heart ache, but she took another bite of her burger. "Sylvie did a great job in picking houses."

"As she mentally counted the stack of commission cash." He smirked.

"Brandon." She wagged a finger at him. "I like her. She's a successful, strong, and motivated woman. Does she intimidate you?"

"Oh yeah. I never see *any* strong successful women in my profession."

"Get that away." She prodded at the pickle on the side of her plate, averting her head. "I can't stomach seeing it."

He snagged it, crunching into the salty sweetness. "Mmmm. Delicious." At her unamused glare, he finished it in two quick bites. "You know, my girl is a strong, independent, successful woman." He gazed straight into her eyes. "She's incredibly sexy."

Her pupils dilated as she sucked in her lower lip. "Next, you'll say you love big bellies."

"On my girl? Definitely beautiful and sexier than she'd believe." He held her gaze, refusing to blink. "I love my girl."

"And she loves you," she whispered. "We'll manage the distance, won't we?"

"Living so far away from you and the baby won't be easy, but we'll make it work."

"Everything okay?" The waitress appeared beside the table, eyeing their plates.

"It's good, thanks." Brandon silently cursed the woman's timing.

Savannah blinked, picking up her fork to dig into her salad. "Which house was your favorite?"

"They were all great, but the last one. Having the coach house over the garage is a bonus. You could rent it to another student."

She ate the last bite of her burger, dabbing at her lips.

"Missed a spot."

"Still think I'm sexy?" She licked at the corner of her mouth.

Brandon brushed away the dab of sauce with his thumb. "Always. Your turn. Which house do you want?"

"The last one. It's perfect. I'll call Tom."

Brandon finished the last of his fries as she conversed with her uncle, adding details.

"He's on his way," she said as she disconnected the call.

"Just like that? He dropped everything?" The tiny lift of her one shoulder had him shaking his head. "Insane."

"He's family. He'll view the house this evening so he can return home tomorrow. Jenna will have her baby soon." She tapped a text into her phone. "And now Sylvie will book the appointment. You done eating?"

He motioned to the waitress for the bill. "Hotel for your afternoon nap?"

The sight of those perfect white teeth nibbling at her lip caused another spike in his heart rate.

"Definitely." Her sparkling brown eyes scanned over him. "We have at least a couple of hours."

〜

Two days later, Brandon's head still spun from the whirlwind of events. After a second intensive inspection of the home with Tom, Savannah had written an offer. After a short period of negotiation, her final acceptance had been signed with a flourish.

The next afternoon, he'd driven to Boston with a deliriously happy Savannah in the passenger seat. Thirty days, and she'd be a proud homeowner.

Nate appeared beside him at the counter, a deep frown on his face as he peered at his tablet. "This makes no sense." He propped his head on a hand, scrolling through the chart.

"Hey. Haven't seen you for days."

"I was on-call, so I slept here. If you can call it sleep. What do you make of this?"

Brandon scanned the test results. "Let me …" He reviewed the patient history, comparing them to the new series of tests. "Wait. I worked a case similar to this on my first rotation." He pointed at the line before flipping back to the previous results. "Look at the anomalies."

"Crap. Is that what I think?" His friend's lips tugged into a frown at Brandon's nod. "This kid is ten. Better get another scan and a consult before I worry the parents." Nate entered some information onto the chart. "How did it go in New Haven?"

"She bought a house."

"Damn. She's doing this, huh? Hang in there, bud."

"Trying to." He added a note to his patient's information before searching the queue for his next case. "It's a rogue wave."

"Drinks tonight? You can tell me about it. My resident is giving me a move-your-ass look, so I gotta go."

"Can't. Doctor's appointment, and I'm covering a shift to repay my time off. Tomorrow?"

"I'm working. Rain check." Nate gave him a fist bump before striding toward the exam rooms.

Brandon rubbed at his forehead with his fingertips, a headache setting in. They were closing in on the finish line, the birth of their child merely weeks away. Details were piling up in his brain.

"Tough case?" Will logged into the computer on the desk.

"Just a headache."

Will eyed him with concern. "Your appointment is in forty-five minutes. Take a break, eat, and while you're at it, read this." His supervisor extended an envelope. "It arrived this morning."

Brandon scanned the front, his palms sweating as he realized what was enclosed. "Thanks, Dr. Kavanagh. I'll make up the extra time at the end of my shift."

"I appreciate it. Good luck with that." He motioned to the envelope with his chin before he strode toward one of the exam rooms.

Brandon entered the lounge, glancing at his watch. He'd have to hurry to get to the deli and back before he ran upstairs for their prenatal appointment.

Aiden glanced up from his spot, half of a turkey baguette in his hand. "You look like you need this." He pushed the deli wrapper containing the untouched half of his meal across the table, along with a large takeout cup. "Em caught a tough case. Drink it before it gets cold."

"She'll love you for feeding me her lunch." Brandon grinned as he settled into a chair, taking a sip followed by a large bite of sandwich.

"When she enjoys a hot latte, she'll love me even more." He flipped a page of paperwork, skimming down the side with his pen as he read the document.

Brandon helped himself to a carrot from the container near Aiden. "I got this." He held up the envelope.

"And?"

"I'm not sure I made the right choice." He lowered his voice. "It's another full year."

"Open it before you drive yourself mental." Aiden set aside his sandwich, brushing crumbs from his hands.

Brandon's hands trembled under the scrutiny of the doctor across from him, but he broke the seal with his index finger. The words danced in front of his eyes. "That didn't help at all," he whispered.

"Congratulations, Dr. Reynolds. That," he said, pointing to the letter, "is an honor, and a huge career booster. You'll add a year of residency, but the upside is every ER in the country will want to hire you."

"But Savannah—"

"No." Aiden held up a hand. "Don't you dare."

Brandon stared at the man across from him. "I don't get you. You're the first one to jump in front of the bus for your family. You walked away from a chief resident position for your daughter." He narrowed his eyes. "And for Emily."

Aiden's return gaze contained equal intensity. "I love my career," his said in a low voice, "but I can risk walking away. You, Brandon, cannot."

"You mean financially?" he muttered. "What does that say to Vanna if I commit to another full year in Boston, when she's in New Haven? What about her and this baby?"

"You want to go there?" Aiden didn't even blink. "What did she say when you applied?"

Brandon sucked in a breath. The woman had encouraged him and supported his application, like she had with everything career related.

"And you hate the idea of her living in New Haven, yet you agreed. Why is that, Brandon?"

"I'm afraid she'll resent me for standing in the way of her career," he said softly. "And if I refuse this, she worries I'll regret it."

"And there you have it." Aiden lifted a shoulder. "Work through the issues, make the hard sacrifices now, and your relationship will be stronger for the struggle."

Brandon tilted his head, pondering the man's words, shaking his head as he sought for understanding.

"I'd tell any resident the same thing," Aiden said in a level voice. "Take the damn fellowship."

"Is this is my ER mentor advising me?"

"Yes and no. It's difficult for me to separate the personal from professional when it's you," he said. "And I won't pretend the extra year will be easy, but the reward is worth it. I want you to reach your full potential as a doctor as much as I want Savannah happy and fulfilled with her career."

"And if it ruins us?"

"What if you refuse the position?" Aiden asked. "Are you saying it won't affect your relationship? How will you handle watching the runner-up for the fellowship enjoy the position you passed on?"

Brandon rubbed his jaw. "Who is it?"

"Irrelevant line of questioning."

"Damn. You knew before I opened the envelope."

"Again, irrelevant." Aiden didn't allow even a flicker of emotion in his expression to confirm if Brandon was correct. "Are you planning to let fortune pass you by? If you want the relationship to work, deep down in here"—he tapped his chest with a finger—"it will."

Brandon exhaled a stream of air. The man's logic couldn't be denied.

"Eat or you'll miss your appointment." Aiden tossed his trash into the garbage. "Better get Em her latte, or there will be hell to pay." The man grinned as he left the lounge.

Brandon glanced at his watch, practically inhaling his half of the baguette and washing it down with the latte. He was due upstairs.

As he entered the clinic, Savannah's gaze rose, and she set aside her magazine.

"Hi, sweetie." Brandon pecked her lips and rubbed her belly.

"I'm a magic genie," she whispered as she placed a hand over his. "Everyone rubs my belly."

"Should I quit?"

"Nope." She linked their fingers. "It's okay when it's you. It's the strangers. Some lady accosted me in the park, practically chasing me down."

"Maybe I should get you a t-shirt." He snickered. "Hands off the belly."

She rolled her eyes but didn't comment further as the nurse called her name, ushering them down the hallway.

"Usual drill, Savannah." Pat motioned to the scale. "Slip off your shoes."

"Go." Vanna shooed Brandon toward the exam room. "You don't want to see the number."

He complied, dropping into his usual chair and flipping through a magazine while he waited.

"What's this?" Savannah stood in the doorway, holding up an envelope. "It fell out of your pocket." She tapped it against her hand as she closed the door.

"Let's talk about it later." He reached for the envelope.

"Uh-uh. You can tell me about it while I change into a gown." Her eyes widened. "Is it about the Fellowship?" A grin spread across her face. "It is. You got it." At his nod she slid onto his lap, wrapping her arms around him and planting a resounding kiss on his lips. "I'm proud of you."

"You're not upset? It extends my commitment by another year."

"It's a huge deal for your career. You've supported my Yale dream. I want to support you."

"I'm not sure I should take it."

"Are you insane?" She cupped his cheeks, forcing him to look at her. "You promised. It's your future as a doctor. What's one more year after the investment you've put in already?"

"Thank you." He kissed her long and hard. "How do I deserve you? Most women would freak out."

She gave him a saucy grin. "Haven't you figured it out? I'm not most women."

"No, my love, you most certainly aren't."

# CHAPTER 20

## Savannah

THE FINAL WEEKS OF PREGNANCY passed in a blur of appointments and final preparations for the baby's arrival, including a move to the new house outside of Boston and furnishing her home in New Haven. Now, at thirty-seven weeks, all Savannah could do was wait and hope she hadn't forgotten anything.

Savannah shifted, trying to find a comfortable position. It had been harder and harder to sleep, and now everything ached. She hauled in a long breath before wiggling off the edge of the bed, her feet touching the mercifully cool wooden floor.

She ambled to the bathroom, rubbing her back while avoiding looking at herself in the mirror. These past weeks, she'd ballooned beyond recognition. It amazed her that anyone could find her attractive. Being inside this ungainly and awkward body felt strange and foreign, yet her boyfriend frequently told her she was beautiful and sexy, backing up his words with extra cuddling and affection.

Part way across the floor, the twinge and tight feeling across her belly made her hesitate. She turned and crept into the hallway, trailing a hand against the wall as she padded toward the far end, tapping on the door before pushing it ajar. "Daddy?" she whispered, crossing the short distance to the king-sized bed. "Dad, wake up." She prodded at Aiden's shoulder.

He blinked at her. "What's wrong, honey?"

"It's time."

He sat, rubbing a hand through his hair. "The baby?"

"I think so." Vanna grimaced as another pain squeezed her belly. "Brandon isn't here."

He smiled as he swung his feet to the floor. "Sit." He patted the bed. "How are you feeling?"

She nibbled her lower lip. "I'm scared."

"Perfectly normal." Aiden slid an arm around her shoulders. "We'll do this together, okay?"

"What's happening?" Emily whispered from somewhere under the covers.

"Savannah's in early labor. You can sleep for a while longer, if you like."

"No way. I'm up." Emily emerged and kneeled beside Vanna. "How far apart?"

"It just started."

"We have time." Her stepmother plumped the pillows, and they settled Savannah on the bed. "I'll dress and make tea." She disappeared into the bathroom.

Vanna closed her eyes and drew in a deep breath, fighting the panic inside. This was it. The moment she'd been waiting for, yet dreading. "I have no idea what to do."

"Overwhelming, isn't it?" Aiden rubbed her back. "Have you called Brandon?"

She shook her head. "I wanted to make sure it was really happening. He's on shift, and there's no point in him rushing if it's a false alarm." Vanna sucked in another breath as her belly tightened. "Oohhh."

Aiden picked up his watch from the nightstand and peered at it as Vanna rubbed her belly. He handed her his phone. "Call Brandon. False alarm or not, he'll want to be here."

Savannah hit the speed dial, but it went through to voicemail. "He's not answering," she whispered.

"Leave a message, and I'll contact Will in case Brandon is with a patient."

"Will you call Tiffany?" she asked Aiden once she'd left the message. Even if she didn't intend to have her mother in the room, she'd promised she'd let her know.

"You bet." Aiden dialed, giving Vanna a reassuring smile as he waited for Tiffany to answer. "It's happening. Can you get here today?" He nodded at Savannah. "Let me know …" After disconnecting the call he said, "She'll book the next flight."

"What if she can't make it today?"

"I'll send Tom to Chicago to get her."

She laughed despite her lingering fear. "I bet you would, too."

"You know it. Tom would do anything for you." He took her hand. "Close your eyes and rest. It'll be a long day." Aiden covered her with a light blanket as she snuggled into the pillows.

⁓

Savannah rubbed at her tight belly and opened her eyes, savoring the fresh air wafting through the open patio doors. The calm low voices carried inside, Aiden and Emily having retreated to their private oasis, allowing her to rest.

She slid from the bed and ambled across the room, one hand on her hip. Both Aiden and Emily looked up as she padded onto the sun-warmed flagstone, lifting her face to the morning rays.

Aiden rose and moved to her side. "What can we get you?"

"Juice?" She glanced at the tray on the small wicker side table.

Emily poured a glass of fresh-squeezed orange juice from the pitcher and offered it.

Vanna rested one hand on her belly as it tightened and a twinge ran through her. "Where's Brandon."

"He's on his way," Aiden said. "He'll be here soon, but he stopped at his apartment to pick up his bag."

Vanna let out a slow breath, a smile touching her lips. She longed to have Brandon with her sharing this special day. "Time for a few laps." All the advice she'd read or received had told her it was best to keep moving. She paced the expansive patio, stopping now and then to take deep breaths and allow either Aiden or Emily to rub her back.

"Where is he?" Savannah closed her eyes, leaning on the stone railing. "It'll be time to go to the hospital."

"You have plenty of time. How about a warm shower to help you relax?" Emily motioned Savannah into the plush master bath, flicking on the water and testing it with one hand. "It may feel intense, but it's still early labor."

Savannah stripped off her pajamas, stepping under the soothing spray and shutting her eyes as Emily closed the glass door.

"I'll be right back." Emily's soft voice carried over the patter of water.

"Thank you," she said, leaning a hand against the stone wall, scrunching up her nose as the ripple of pain ran through her. Vanna fought the urge to hold her breath, which would only tense her muscles further. *Breathe.* She'd become well practiced in the art of calming, given her history of panic attacks.

Emily tapped on the glass. "Need anything?"

"I'm good."

"Call out if you need me."

Vanna squeezed a dollop of Emily's luxurious body scrub onto her washcloth, inhaling the lavender scent. This shower idea had merits. Already, she felt calmer and more in control. After shampooing her hair, she stepped out, wrapping herself in an oversized fluffy towel.

Her stepmother peeked in. "Smells lovely in here. The lavender is my favorite." Emily handed Vanna a container of lotion. "I left fresh clothes on our bed."

"Thanks, Emily." Savannah slathered the soothing cream over her body before returning to the master bedroom.

Brandon appeared in the doorway. "How are you?" He strode across the room as she pulled her light sundress over her head. His arms wrapped around her. "This is it."

She stared up at him. "Are you ready?"

"Don't have a choice, do I? This baby is coming."

She closed her eyes, a frown tugging at her lips as disappointment flooded her. This wasn't what she hoped to hear at this pivotal moment in their lives.

"I'm ready," he said softly, cupping her face between his palms. "I love you."

She rested her forehead against his chest as the baby kicked. "Feel this." Vanna pressed his hand against the small bulge created by the baby's limb. "Oh." She clenched her jaw as her muscles tightened.

"Another one?" Brandon massaged her back in gentle swirls. "Tell me what you need."

"That helps." Savannah drew in a long breath, concentrating on relaxing her body. "Just don't leave me. I need you."

"I won't." He combed his fingers through her damp, tangled locks. "How about we fix this hair? Sit." He patted the small bench at the end of the bed.

Tears sprung to her eyes as he teased a brush through the ends, working upwards in sections.

"Am I pulling too hard?"

She shook her head, sweeping the back of her hand over her cheek. "My mom brushed my hair like this when I was little. She was so patient and gentle even when I cried." A lump formed in her throat. "They'll never meet their grandchild," she whispered. Days like today, the big moments in her life, created an intense longing for her parents.

"I'm sorry." Brandon rubbed her shoulders, a sad smile on his face. "I wish I could have known them." A far away look appeared in his eyes.

"What are you thinking?"

"It's funny how the smallest moments often leave the strongest imprint." He worked on the next tangle. "My mother would pass out after a late night at the bar, so I'd get Mia ready for school, brushing her hair just like this. It's such a vivid memory for me. I wonder if Mia remembers."

"It seems like a small thing, but I'm sure she does." Vanna caught his hand, giving it a gentle squeeze. "Even if she never says it, she adores you. You'll be an amazing dad." She could picture him brushing his own child's hair for the first day of school. Playing ball in the back yard. Taking them to the park and the zoo. All of the things Ross had done with her.

"I hope so." He swept her hair back over her shoulders. "Much better. Let's go downstairs."

Savannah allowed everyone to pamper her for the next hour, enjoying a light breakfast on the sunny patio and taking short strolls down the expanse of lawn. Brandon remained attentive, rubbing her back through each contraction.

He glanced at his watch as they turned toward the house after one such foray across the lush grass. "You're doing great."

Emily tilted her head as they reached the bottom of the steps of the stone patio. "We should check the position of the baby." She managed three steps forward before the flash of pain hit Vanna.

Savannah gasped and doubled over at the force of the massive contraction. A gush of warmth flowed down her leg. "Ohhh, that hurts. Is that blood?"

Emily dashed across the flagstones as Brandon helped her to the closest lounger. She cupped Savannah's face between her palms. "Your water broke. It's not blood. Take a few deep breaths."

Brandon rubbed her back and glanced at his watch as another pain rolled through her. "You went from zero to sixty."

"You're in active labor." Emily looked up as Aiden appeared. "Breathe, sweetie. We'll take care of you."

She squeezed her eyes closed, struggling for air as her belly cramped.

Brandon crouched beside the lounger and took her hand. "I'm right here. Focus on me."

Vanna forced her gaze to her boyfriend, his reassuring smile and low voice calming her fears.

"Good. Now, inhale. With me," he squeezed her hand as they each drew in air. "Exhale."

"Help her inside while I get my bag." Aiden disappeared into the house, leaving the French doors ajar.

"What's happening?" Panic rolled through Vanna, the pain gripping her as they settled her on the sofa in the sitting room. "It hurts."

"I'll take a look. Relax." Emily peered under her sundress. "It's transition, Vanna. It's normal, even if quicker than usual. There's no bleeding, but this baby is ready to join us."

"We're not going to the hospital?"

"I doubt we have time," Emily said.

Aiden reappeared, handing Emily his medical kit and setting aside a pile of fresh towels.

Emily retrieved the Doppler from the bag and adjusted it. "Let's listen to the baby." She pressed the device to Vanna's belly, moving it until she picked up the whoosh of the baby's heartbeat. "Even and strong and within normal range."

Brandon wrapped an arm around Savannah. "The baby's fine," he said in a trembling voice, his grip tightening on her hand. "It'll be okay."

Savannah's shaky laugh was cut short by another pain. Once she caught her breath, she forced a smile to her lips. "Who are you trying to convince? Me? Or yourself?"

Brandon shook his head, an answering smile touching his lips.

"Either way, he's right, sweetie." Aiden set another small pile on the far arm of the sofa before he positioned himself beside Savannah. "We're ready. Brandon, you're catching the baby."

"I get to …" Brandon's eyes widened.

"Delivering your own child is an experience not to be missed," Aiden said. "Everything you need is in my kit. You're in charge."

Brandon tugged gloves from the package in Aiden's medical bag. "I can't believe I'm doing this."

Savannah sucked in a breath. "Hurry up. This kid wants out." She let out a groan, the urge to push almost unbearable.

Her dad took her hand, assisting her into a semi-sitting position. "You're doing great."

"I'll ruin the sofa." Her laugh sounded half-hysterical, even to her own ears.

"Concentrate on delivering this baby." Aiden brushed back her damp hair. "That's your job now."

Savannah nodded, scrunching her eyes closed against the pain, her free hand extended toward Brandon. A sense of calm descended over her at his warm and reassuring touch. It meant everything to have him here, sharing the birth of their child.

"Next contraction, you can push," Brandon said.

She nodded, tears flooding her eyes as she dragged in air, and her body took over. A long low moan left her lips.

"The baby has dark hair." Brandon's breathless voice washed over her. "Take a few breaths … and …" His eyes shimmered as their gazes locked on each other. "I'm ready," he said softly, a smile touching his lips. "One more push."

Vanna focused on the top of his head, pressing her chin to her chest. She clutched her dad's hand and wished for the agony to end, groaning with the effort. And then the pain faded out, followed by a hush before an indignant piercing cry cut through the air.

Brandon tilted his head as he blinked hard. "She's ... a girl." A rueful grin appeared as he gave his head a little shake and held her up. "We have a daughter." The grin widened as the baby emitted a loud squawk. "Cold, sunshine?" He grabbed a towel from the pile and rubbed her dry before he placed the baby in Savannah's arms.

"She's tiny." Vanna cradled the baby against her, a jumble of emotions flooding through her. "Oh, look at you." She brushed a fingertip over the downy patch of dark hair on the baby's scalp.

"She's beautiful." Aiden kissed Vanna's temple. "You did great," he whispered.

Emily squeezed Brandon's shoulder. "Take a minute with your baby girl."

Savannah leaned into Brandon's chest as he curled an arm around her shoulders. The rush of emotion was replaced by complete contentment at being held in the arms of the man she loved, holding their daughter. With the arrival of their precious baby girl, they'd suddenly become a family.

# Chapter 21

## Brandon

THIS FELT LIKE THE STRANGEST, yet most wonderful dream. He'd delivered his own child. Become a father. Pride flowed through him at the sight of his daughter's sweet face and at Savannah's remarkable calm, bravery, and grace.

He pressed a kiss to his girlfriend's damp brow. "You were a rock star." Brandon's eyes burned as he stared at the tiny red infant. A tiny pout formed on her lips as she stared at him. "She's beautiful." He tightened his embrace, meeting Vanna's shimmering eyes with his own. "I don't even …" Nothing had prepared him for the overwhelming of emotions, the awe, or the pure love he felt for this little person.

He accepted the small silver instrument extended by Emily and snipped between the clamps, grateful for a moment to gather his thoughts.

Aiden transferred the baby onto a soft cotton blanket, rubbing the metal end of his stethoscope before listening to the baby's chest. "Strong heartbeat." He supported the infant as he checked her back. "Lungs are clear. She looks great." With practiced, economical moves, Aiden diapered the baby and placed a small knit cap on her head, bundling her in a blanket and tucking her into Savannah's arms.

Brandon brushed at his eyes with the back of his hand, rendered speechless as he looped an arm around his girlfriend's shoulders.

"She's so little," Savannah whispered. "And so serious."

He cleared his throat. "She looks like her mommy." Brandon traced a fingertip over the baby's cheek. "Shouldn't we take them to the hospital?"

"No point," Aiden said. "Savannah and the baby are both in good health. She'll recover better here."

"I feel good, considering." Savannah turned her flushed face toward Brandon. "I don't need the hospital. Besides, we have our own medical team."

Aiden transferred the baby to Brandon and scooped up Savannah. "Let's move you upstairs. You'll be more comfortable in bed."

Brandon followed and sank onto the rocking chair with his newborn daughter cradled in his arms while Emily helped Savannah freshen up and then tucked her under a light sheet.

"This isn't as hard as I expected." Vanna peered at the baby girl nestled against her breast. "She's hungry."

"She's doing great." Brandon tucked a pillow under Savannah's arm before joining her on the bed. He emitted a happy sigh as he propped another pillow under his head. "So weird. I'm a dad."

He took a tiny hand in his. This little girl had captured his heart the moment he set eyes on her. *Like mother, like daughter.* How could he express everything in his heart to this amazing woman who'd given him so much? She'd permitted him a chance to be part of his daughter's life.

He moved closer, lifting his gaze to her face. This woman seemed especially beautiful at this moment, peering at their daughter with love and tenderness in her eyes. His heart skipped a beat. She often looked at him the same way.

Aiden appeared with two large glasses of ice water and set them on the side table. "Tiffany just arrived. She'll be up in a minute."

"Perfect. Thanks, Dad." Savannah sipped her water as her dad smiled and left the room.

Brandon yawned, exhaustion washing over him. "Sorry." He pressed the back of his hand over his mouth. "It's all catching up to me. I need a nap."

"So did someone else," Vanna whispered. She adjusted her clothing as a tap sounded on the door.

"Can I come in?" Tiffany asked.

Savannah beckoned to her mother, who crossed the room, leaning in to hug her daughter around the baby.

"She's sweet. Can I hold her?"

Vanna nodded and transferred the precious bundle into her mother's arms.

Tiffany cuddled the baby, her eyes glistening with tears. "Hi, little girl. I'm your grandma." A small laugh escaped her lips as she dropped a gentle kiss on her granddaughter's forehead. "That sounds so weird. But kind of wonderful."

Brandon squeezed Vanna's hand, giving her a tender smile before he looked at the woman holding their daughter.

Tiffany's expression contained joy, but the shiny eyes made her appear ready to burst into tears. "You look amazing, Savannah. Is there anything you need?"

Vanna shook her head. "I'm good. Sorry for the long drive out here."

"Don't worry, honey. Emily offered us a guest room." Her mother rocked on her feet, riveted on her granddaughter.

Brandon couldn't help the twinge of surprise. From everything he knew, the relationship between Emily and Tiffany had been adversarial until recent times.

Stefan tapped softly on the door frame. "Hi, sweetheart. You look great." He approached the bed, bending to give Savannah a warm hug. "Congratulations." The man shook Brandon's hand before peering over Tiffany's shoulder. "She's a beauty."

Aiden and Emily appeared moments later, Aiden with a camera. He took a few quick snapshots of a beaming Tiffany and proud-looking Stefan with the baby.

"Does our little girl have a name?" Tiffany asked.

Brandon glanced at Vanna, who smiled and nodded. They'd discussed names in depth, and one had consistently risen to the top of the favorite list. "London Gabrielle," he said.

Tiffany blinked hard before a tear trickled down her face. "That's beautiful." She pressed a hand to her chest. "I'm honored. She has the same middle name as me."

Stefan slid an arm around Tiffany, placing a kiss on the top of her hair.

"How are you doing? Need anything?" Aiden asked Brandon in a low voice, as Tiffany finally allowed Stefan a turn at holding the baby.

"A massive cup of coffee? This visit might last for hours." Brandon scrubbed his jaw.

"Everyone will clear out in the next ten minutes so you and Vanna can enjoy quiet time with your daughter and get some rest."

"You have ESP." Brandon laughed.

"Nope, but we've had two babies. Just tell me what you need, and it's done. We'll keep everyone occupied until you're ready to socialize."

"Surprised you're not in there." Brandon motioned toward where his baby girl was being cuddled and fussed over by doting grandparents.

"I got to be there for her birth." A far away look appeared. "Tiffany needs uninterrupted time with her daughter and granddaughter. They've had so little time to bond."

Brandon noted the misty eyes of the woman holding the baby. He remembered Aiden's comment about not having the opportunity to be with Tiffany for Savannah's birth. How their daughter had been taken from her mother's arms within moments after her arrival. "You were right about catching the baby. I'll never forget that moment."

"There's nothing more incredible. Just wait until you see the pictures."

Brandon wrinkled his brow. He'd been concentrating on Vanna and the baby and blocked out everything else. "We have pictures?"

"Are you two ready for lunch?" Emily looked at Tiffany and Stefan. "We should let Brandon and Vanna rest."

Reluctance reflected on Tiffany's face, but she nodded and tucked the baby into her daughter's arms. A wistful expression appeared, her gaze lingering on London. "I won't be far if you need me."

Emily and Stefan exited, their voices carrying down the hallway as they headed toward the stairs.

But Tiffany seemed frozen in place.

"Tiff." Aiden place a hand on the small of her back, ushering her toward the door, but not before Brandon caught the shimmer of a tear trickling down her face.

Savannah hadn't missed it either. Her intent gaze followed her parents, and she clamped her teeth onto her bottom lip. After a moment, she closed her eyes and inhaled, as if fighting her own emotions.

"I've never figured out their dynamic." Brandon sat on the edge of the bed, taking her hand in his.

"What's to figure out?" Savannah lifted a shoulder as she adjusted the baby's blanket. "They're conflicted."

"Your dad's chill."

"My dad is a pro at concealing his true emotions. Sometimes, I imagine he's screaming on the inside. I would be," she said. "But there's one person who pushes him over the edge."

He considered her words. The man exhibited a level of control he'd rarely experienced, especially at home. Brandon's family ranked high on the volatility scale. But Aiden and Emily, and the people surrounding them, tended to stay level. "Who is his weakness? It can't be Emily."

"Two guesses."

"Huh. But I could see it."

"She's happy with Stefan, but," Savannah said, "it's complicated. And the baby thing doesn't help."

"She wants a baby?" Brandon scrubbed a hand through his hair. "Does Stefan not want kids?"

"He does, but it's not happening," she said in a low voice. "Tiffany was crazy emotional the day we told her and offered to take the baby if we decided not to."

"Our girl won't lack willing parties to help raise her, and I'm grateful, but we'll manage. We need to do this." He held out his arms. "Quit hogging our daughter."

Vanna smiled. "Okay, Daddy. Your turn."

"Come here, my sunshine." He cradled London in his arms. Having these precious moments made him thankful he'd stayed.

Hours later, Brandon awoke, finding himself alone in the big bed, but he heard the patter of water from the shower combined with the fussing coming from the bassinet by the bed. "Shh," he said softly as he lifted the baby, soothing her with soft humming as he rocked on his feet.

"You're a natural." Savannah appeared in the doorway of the bathroom, wrapped in a towel. "Sorry, she woke you."

"My stomach did that." He inhaled the succulent aroma wafting in through the open French doors, still rocking London. "The barbecue's amazing." He cuddled the little girl against his chest. "Come on, sunshine. Let's check your diaper while Mommy dresses." He wrinkled his nose at the mess, but it wasn't new to him. He'd changed his first diaper when Mia was a baby, not to mention the pediatric rotations. He'd gained plenty of experience handling infants.

"Why don't you shower before we join the party? I'll feed London while I wait."

"Are you up to visiting?" He fastened the onesie, still amazed that this tiny person was his daughter.

"I had a good sleep. Not being in the hospital has its benefits." She stepped into the walk-in closet, reappearing in a sundress. "Remember how Aiden took care of Emily after Cierra was born? I doubt we'll be expected to do much aside from eat and hold the baby."

"Silly me." Brandon grinned. The man had pampered his wife, ensuring she had plenty of time to sleep and recover. He wasn't sure they'd even have an opportunity to hold the baby with the excited grandparents in the house.

"Wait until all the aunts and uncles and great-grandparents arrive over this week." She laughed at his expression. "It'll be great, I promise. Everyone will stay a few days, *Abuela* will cook amazing Spanish feasts, and then we'll escape to the Vineyard until September."

"I can't believe I get time off for having a baby when you did all the work."

"You did your part." She winked. "But parental leave is important. Emily and Aiden will help, but the person I want is you. Let's make the most of our time with London."

The words reminded him things would change come September. "I want you to go to school, but I don't. Are you sure about attending classes so soon?"

"I need to, Brandon. This is my career. We'll make this work, four months at a time."

"Stick to the plan." There was no way to win this battle. If he pushed the issue, she'd believe he wasn't supportive of her career goals, when she'd been so accommodating of his. How could he expect her to give up her education to stay home and raise a child while he took the Fellowship? "It'll be fine." He pressed a kiss to her temple, inhaling her soft scent, along with the fresh baby smell. "I'll be quick in the shower."

"What's this. No phone call? I had to find out from Vanna's social media account?" Rory's voice ripped down the line. "You're a dad."

"Crazy, right?" Brandon wandered down the lush lawn, peeking over his shoulder at the gathering on the patio. The group had grown while he and Vanna rested. Tom and Jenna brought Mia home, and Joel and Alex had appeared. Along with the group, the pile of baby gifts seemed to have expanded and several bright colorful bouquets with foil balloons had been delivered. "Sorry, it's been insane delivering the news and dealing with the influx of relatives."

"When can I visit the new family?" Rory asked.

"You want to come here?" Brandon furrowed his brow. None of his friends had ever visited. "We're leaving for the Vineyard at the end of the week. There's plenty of room."

"Sweet," he said, the pleasure evident in his voice. "Man, you really hit it. A sweet, beautiful girlfriend with an incredible family. I can't wait to get out there. Love the pics, by the way."

Brandon chuckled. "How Emily caught those, I'll never know. I didn't even know she had the camera." He closed his eyes, recalling those first precious moments with his daughter. The raw emotion captured on film for eternity.

"Congrats, man. London's adorable. I can't wait to see you."

Rory promised to text once he'd figured out travel arrangements, and they signed off.

"Just in time. Everyone's anxious for the gift opening." Savannah entwined their fingers as he settled into the seat beside her. Her cheeks displayed a delicate pink tone and her eyes sparkled. "Dad has something big, I can tell."

Brandon's eyes wandered to the rather small gift box on the table beside Aiden. He wasn't sure he wanted to know, though he supposed now Savannah had purchased a home in New Haven, they wouldn't be offered house keys.

His gaze traveled to the next sofa, where Tiffany snuggled London. The woman had a blissful look on her face and had barely let the baby out of her sight since they'd arrived on the patio. The rest of the group seemed content to let her enjoy uninterrupted time with her granddaughter.

"I'll start." Alex offered a gift basket stuffed to the brim with baby products and clothes, followed by a second large basket of items to pamper the new parents.

Present after present followed. Brandon wondered where they'd put all the amazing gifts when Savannah had the nursery so well stocked already.

Once the pile had dwindled, Aiden rose and held out a hand to Savannah. "Now, you get to unwrap your gift from Em and me."

Her eyes lit up as she took his hand, reaching for Brandon to tug him along. "Where are we going?"

Brandon wondered the same thing, but the trip from the back patio through to the front door only took a few moments. He glanced at the entourage surrounding them, his heart thudding.

Emily beamed and Alex practically hopped up and down as Savannah accepted the gift box from Aiden.

"Noooooo." Savannah tipped the box so Brandon could view to contents as Aiden opened the front door.

The new BMW SUV sat in the driveway, the large red satin ribbon and bow across the hood fluttering in the breeze. The bright sun glinted off the sleek paint.

"Holy shit," he muttered as Vanna's grip on his hand tightened.

"A car?" Savannah pressed a hand to her mouth before throwing her arms around her dad. "You're the best Dad ever." She turned to Emily, tears glistening in her eyes. "Thank you."

"That's incredible." Brandon hesitated only for a moment before he hugged Emily. "Thank you."

The woman kissed his cheek, her warm smile saying it all.

He turned to Aiden, hesitating for a moment before he accepted a hug. The warm embrace surprised him, bringing a rush of unfamiliar feelings to the surface. He simply couldn't recall the last time he'd been hugged by anyone close to being a parental figure.

His mother never hugged anyone aside from her latest man. Brandon wasn't even sure he'd allow Carol that close if she tried. "The car is amazing. Thank you," he said, clearing his throat. This simple display of affection brought him to the edge of tears.

"You're welcome." Aiden squeezed his shoulder.

This man was the closest he'd come to having a father figure since his own father had left. Despite the relatively small age gap, it felt comfortable. Perhaps because Aiden understood him in a way he wasn't sure he understood himself. Or maybe it was the close bond forged over the many hours working in the ER.

No matter, he decided. Aiden's easy acceptance of him into their tight-knit family provided something indefinable that Brandon had been missing.

# Chapter 22

## Savannah

THE NEXT FEW DAYS CHALLENGED Savannah in unexpected ways. Logically she knew how to care for a baby. She'd seen Emily, Aiden, and the family surrounding her manage newborns, but being the responsible party was an entirely new experience.

Fortunately, Brandon kept his promise of being all in, and they settled into a routine. Or as much of one as they could, considering the constant influx of visitors. And the lack of sleep. And the unpredictable and frequent feedings. Not to mention numerous diaper changes.

"You have everything?" Brandon fastened London into her car seat, adjusting the straps with care.

"Yes." Savannah balanced the bag, which overflowed with baby needs. She pushed aside the outfit on top, taking a last inventory "Diapers, wipes, changing pad, fresh clothes, and ..." *Too many items to list.*

"That thing is about to burst." Brandon glanced at his watch. "We'd better go or we'll be late for our first pediatrician's visit." His eyes widened as London began to fuss. "Getting impatient, sunshine?" He leaned in checking straps, giving a little sniff. "Man. I just changed her."

"Welcome to life with a baby." She laughed as he unbuckled the tiny girl, undoing all the work he'd only completed.

"Ahh, London." He shook his head as he unfastened the onesie, turning his head aside and wrinkling his nose in mock disgust at the soiled diaper. "Whew, baby girl. What have you been eating?"

"Big tough man can't handle a little baby poop?" Savannah giggled as she handed him several wipes, followed by a fresh diaper.

"After what I see at work?" A grin appeared as he packaged the used wipes into the diaper and wrapped it into a self-contained parcel in two efficient moves. "That's so much better, isn't it, sunshine?"

"Look at that teamwork," Savannah said as she disposed of the neat little package. "Daddy did a great job."

Brandon glanced up from his task of redressing London. "Good thing, or we'd never leave the house." He squinted at her. "She's not the only one who needs a change."

"Not again." Vanna brushed at the damp patches on her blouse. Whenever London made the slightest sound, her breasts sprang a leak. She waved a hand. "Get her into the car. I'll be right down."

He slung the diaper bag over his shoulder, hoisting the car seat with the opposite hand. "I'll pull up to the front door."

Savannah changed, making a final inspection of her clothing before grabbing her small purse and dashing downstairs.

"Cariño." Nina met her at the bottom, presenting two travel mugs and two bags. "Don't forget these. Please deliver this to your papa for his lunch. The other is for you and Brandon."

"Gracias, Abuela." She kissed her grandmother's cheek, grateful for the extra sustenance. With the constant demands of a baby, she always felt starved.

Brandon already had the car's passenger door open. "Nina's been at it again," he said, a grin spreading across his face. "I love your Abuela." He relieved her of one of the cups, taking a sip as she settled into her seat.

"Is London okay?" She glanced over her shoulder, squinting at her daughter's reflection in the small mirror mounted above the car seat.

"She's asleep. Let's go before she wakes up or loads another diaper." The engine purred to life, and Brandon guided the car down the driveway and through the iron gates. Once they'd merged into the Boston bound traffic, he reached for her hand. "Relax, sweetie. It's a short trip."

Savannah sagged into the buttery leather, exhausted by the rush and extra work of leaving the house. "I need a nap."

"I hear you." He took another sip from his mug, eyeing the bag she held on her lap. "What did Abuela make?"

"Oh. I forgot I even had it." Vanna peeked inside. "Fresh muffins." She broke off a piece, tucking it into her mouth. "Mmm. So good."

"What about me?"

"You want some?" She snickered as she popped in another morsel. Swayed by his imploring look, she fed him a bite-sized chunk. "Good, right?"

He nodded as he chewed. "Nina's an amazing cook. I see why Aiden loves her visits."

She fed him another bite. "Nina spoils Dad. She must see how happy he makes Emily."

"He does spoil his wife. But, Nina's a caretaker. The true Spanish Abuela," he said. "Caroline is more reserved. Odd how Nina and Michelle are relaxed with Aiden, where his own mother's so uptight."

Savannah laughed out loud. "Doesn't surprise me in the least. Grandmother Caroline walks on eggshells. She's terrified of opening her mouth. There's a zero-tolerance policy in effect, especially after she was so nasty during our last Chicago trip."

"Huh. Maybe your dad and I do have a lot in common. He gets along with his mother about as well as I do with mine."

"What do you expect? Caroline allowed James to dump my dad into a boarding school. Dad rarely spent time with his parents. They were always jetting all over the globe or in New York." She twirled a lock of hair around her finger, staring out the window. Brandon still didn't know the full story of what happened in Chicago. It would feel like a betrayal to share what she'd overheard with anyone.

A small sound from the back seat had her craning her neck to check on London. The angelic, peaceful face of their daughter reflected in the mirror. "Still asleep." She sighed. "Not sure we'll see Caroline again anytime soon. She barely acknowledged my existence before, and now I've shamed the family by taking after my mother, she'll visit even less."

Brandon heaved a sigh, shaking his head. "There's nothing shameful in having a child, married or not. But, I guess anyone who allows their husband to give away their grandchild ..." His lip curled.

"Well, if you believe her story, she didn't know about me." Savannah smothered a snort as she contemplated Caroline's hypocrisy, given the new information. Cheating on a cheater and getting pregnant must not count in her grandmother's mind. "Imagine being that disconnected from your son."

Brandon's sideways look had her reaching for his hand.

"Sorry, I'm being stupid," she muttered. "You don't have to imagine. You already know how it feels."

"I'm over it."

Savannah didn't believe his words for a second. In her experience, parental rejection caused permanent and incalculable damage. But she'd let it go. For now. She rested a hand on his knee, rubbing slightly and leaving it there for the remainder of the trip.

Brandon guided the BMW into a parking spot in the doctor's lot at the hospital and glanced at the dashboard display. "Right on time. Let's check in for our appointment."

After both Savannah and London had been examined and pronounced in excellent health, they rode the elevator to the ER.

Nate waved as they appeared, striding over to greet them. "You look amazing." He leaned in for a hug.

"You're sweet, but I look like hell." Savannah laughed lightly, sure that her hair was a mess, her eyes red, and she felt puffy and lumpy in her leggings and flowing blouse.

The young doctor shook his head. "Nope. You're gorgeous as always. And congratulations. Let's see the little miss." He claimed London from Brandon, snuggling her in the crook of his arm.

"Look at you. The professional baby cuddler," Savannah said as Nate folded the edge of the blanket, peering at the tiny infant.

"I've had practice with my nieces and nephews." The man rocked London before dropping a gentle kiss on her nose. "What a sweet girl you are," he murmured. "Are you a good sleeper for Mommy and Daddy?"

Brandon grinned. "I think we found another babysitter."

"Perhaps." Nate dodged a nurse's attempt to steal the baby from his arms. "Wait your turn."

Savannah was surprised at the attention their appearance garnered. A steady stream of Brandon's coworkers came by, congratulating them on the new arrival and claiming a cuddle with the baby.

"There's something for you in the lounge," Halle transferred London into Brandon's arm. "We're about to get slammed with a major accident, but congratulations, in case I don't see you before you leave."

"Thank you," he said as the other resident hurried toward the ambulance bay.

"Damn," Nate whispered, gazing over Savannah's shoulder toward the entrance. "I forgot to warn you." He motioned with his chin.

Brandon frowned in the same direction, a hand rising to sweep through his hair. "What in the hell is he doing here?"

Vanna's breath caught at the sight of the solidly built man in the doorway. He needed no introduction to her. The touch of frost at his temples added a distinguished look to familiar features, the distinctive gray eyes making him instantly recognizable. She sidled closer to Brandon and slid an arm around him, as if her presence could shield him from the unpleasantness to come.

Darien took slow steps towards them, his gaze scanning her in a dismissive way, before traveling to his son, then dropping to the bundle in his arms.

"You good?" Nate asked, a hand resting on Brandon's shoulder. "Sorry, incoming. I have to …" He dashed across the ER to meet the paramedics who were wheeling a gurney through the door.

"Wow, I can make everyone scatter," Darien said with a wry grin.

"Unless you caused the accident, you can hardly take credit." Brandon planted his feet as the man advanced. "Why are you here?"

"I can't visit my son?"

"I'm not your son."

Savannah noted the covert glances coming their way from the ER staff, even as busy as they were with the influx of patients. "This isn't the place," she said under her breath as she pressed a hand on Brandon's back, propelling him toward the lounge with a gentle push.

With a curt nod, Brandon strode across the floor, disappearing through the door before either Savannah or Darien could move. They glanced at each other before following in his footsteps.

"Wait here," Darien said as they reached the door. "This doesn't concern you."

She lifted a brow, throwing him the darkest look she could muster before she shoved past. No way would she abandon Brandon the moment he needed her unwavering allegiance. Nor would she allow this imperious man to order her around like she meant nothing.

Brandon tucked London into her arms, looping an arm around them. "What are you doing in Boston?"

"Boy or girl?" Darien motioned to the baby.

"Why do you care?" Brandon's face remained a blank mask.

"You think I haven't been a good father, but that"—he pointed his index finger at London—"is my grandchild. I deserve a chance."

Brandon's embrace tightened. "Deserve?" His lip curled despite his obvious attempt to keep his mouth set in a grim line. Slight creases appeared at the corners of his eyes. All sure signs of his thinly veiled contempt and deep well of anger begging to be unleashed upon his unwelcome visitor.

Her man had played it off, insisting he was over it. Pretended the absence of his father didn't burn. That he didn't carry a burden of pain and resentment after learning about the entire family—*the son*—who had somehow earned a father's love and devotion when Brandon himself had been abandoned.

"She doesn't need to hear this," Darien said, eyeing Savannah. "This is a family matter."

"What do you know about family?" Brandon asked in a curt tone. "Oh, I forgot. You have an entire new one. So, go home to them. You're not welcome in mine."

"You opened this door by showing up in Albany."

"Did I?" Brandon shrugged. "I don't think so."

The man drew in a long breath, letting it out slowly. "I get it, you know." He bowed his head. "I never meant to disappear, but once I left, it was impossible to return. Carol dragged me down, and it took a long time to recover. By the time I did, I figured you were better off without me."

"How would you know? You never bothered to find out. Not once in sixteen years. Now you show up, expecting what? For me to welcome you with open arms? Life doesn't work that way."

"You've done fine. Look at where you are."

"Done fine … without you. Why would I need you now?" Brandon motioned toward the exit. "Let's go, sweetie."

Darien covered the space between them in two strides, latching onto Brandon's arm. "Don't walk away. You're my son."

Brandon shook it off, a dark look appearing on his face as he spun to face Darien. "No." He used a flattened palm to hold the man back. "I'm not. If I was, you never would have left me."

The lounge door opened behind them, and her dad appeared by Vanna's side. "Everything okay?" Aiden asked, his eyes narrowing as he took in the tense stance of the two men in the middle of the room.

"This isn't your concern." Darien squinted in their direction.

"Actually, it is. You're in my ER." Aiden planted his feet and folded his arms over his chest. "Brandon?"

"I'd like you to leave," Brandon said, lifting his chin and staring down Darien. "There's nothing more to say." He stepped aside, motioning for his father to exit.

Darien tilted his head, his gaze traveling from Brandon, to Aiden, to Savannah, then back to his son. He gave a small nod, taking slow steps toward the door. He hesitated, taking another look at Aiden. "I know you from somewhere." A hand rose, and he pointed his index finger, wagging it slightly. "Yeah, I'm certain of it. You look really familiar."

Aiden shrugged. "Sorry, I don't recall meeting you."

"Hmm. Have you ever been to New York?"

"Many times." Her dad barely blinked, but lifted his arm, motioning for Darien to precede him from the room. "I'll walk you out." He opened the door, clearly refusing to take no for an answer.

Darien cast another glance at Savannah and Brandon before he heaved a sigh and allowed himself to be ushered from the room.

Brandon sank onto the sofa once the door closed. He covered his face with his hands, hunching forward.

Vanna moved closer, wrapping her free arm around him. "Want to talk about it?"

"I'm fine." He shrugged off her embrace and pushed up from his seat. "Let's get out of here. We have to pack for our trip to the Vineyard."

"You're not," she said softly. "It's okay to not be fine. To not have it all figured out. To be hurt, or sad, or angry."

Brandon scoffed. "You sound like a shrink. Don't. Please. Just let it go." He pushed through the door, heading toward the exit.

She trailed after him, holding their daughter close as he strode toward the car. "Don't worry, mi angelito," she whispered. "Daddy won't leave you alone. We both love you so much." She pressed a kiss to the tiny nose.

One day, Brandon would realize maybe he wasn't okay. That those deep gashes in his soul could heal. It always left a scar, but those scars could be beautiful in their own way, illuminating a new level of love, acceptance, and compassion.

When that realization arrived, he'd need her, and she'd be there to support him. Like Aiden had been for her. And Tom had been for Aiden. And … that was the beauty of her family. They all understood and would be there to break the fall.

# Chapter 23

## Brandon

The late afternoon sun glinted off the water, the occasional clank of dishes from the kitchen giving it the homey feel Brandon had become accustomed to. Only two weeks into their vacation, and things had settled into a blissful routine.

"This is insane." Rory, who'd arrived two days earlier, sat across from him on the flagstone patio. His friend tipped back his beer, staring at the two sailboats moored to the dock. "Do you think we'll get out on the water again before I leave?"

"I'll check with Vanna."

"Ha. That girl has you wrapped around her little finger." Rory snickered. "You're finally in love."

Brandon sipped his own drink, lifting one shoulder in what he hoped was a casual gesture. "I'm a whipped idiot," he said in a light tone. "But we have a three-week-old baby. I don't get to—"

"Dude." Rory held up a hand. "I respect your commitment. And," he said, wagging a finger, "never apologize for being a devoted father."

Brandon stretched his legs, enjoying the warmth of the bright sun. Best not to encourage his friend, even if he was one-hundred percent correct. Those three little words had crept out, and he'd meant them.

"Lucky bastard." Rory lowered his voice. "It's a sweet life you've built."

He allowed a small smile to acknowledge his friend's words.

"When you planning to marry the girl?"

"Whoa." Brandon straightened. "We're not ready for that."

"Hmmm." Rory picked at the label on his bottle. "You can't imagine a lifetime with her? With all this?" He swung his hand in a loop mid-air. "Are you insane?"

"I'm not sure I believe in big white weddings. Commitment? Love?" Brandon shrugged it off. Marriage, with all its legal and emotional entanglements, was an entirely different matter from love.

"The kid isn't for a lifetime?"

"It's different." Or was it? Savannah had a permanent hold on him, one way or another. He shook off the thoughts. His girlfriend had been pretty clear about her view on marriage. "What about you? Anyone special?"

Rory stood and stretched before wandering to the bin and dropping in his empty bottle. He grabbed two more from the ice bucket, offering one to Brandon as he returned to his seat.

"Who is this mystery girl?" Brandon studied his friend, curious at his quiet avoidance of the question. "Do I know her?"

Rory huffed out a breath, hanging his head. "Promise you won't be upset?" The guy seemed focused on the flagstones.

"Why would I be …?" Brandon's mouth went dry. Eligible women their age were in short supply in that small town. "No."

His friend shot him a guilt-ridden look.

"Didn't see that one coming." He swept his hand through his hair, rubbing at the back of his neck to ease the sudden ache.

"Are you mad?" Rory leaned forward, resting his elbows on his thighs, keeping his head down.

"I'm speechless, is what I am," he said, buying time on the loaded question. His best friend and his ex-girlfriend? Brandon sucked in a breath. "How long?"

"Not long. A few months." Rory sighed. "It happened not long after you told me about the baby situation."

"You told Autumn? What the fuck, dude? Why would you share my private information with my ex-girlfriend?"

"Between Jeremy's loose lips and viper Piper, it didn't remain private for long. You know how news travels in a small town." Rory shrugged. "What's the big deal?"

"The big deal is you screwing my ex-girlfriend." Brandon emitted a small snort.

"Were you planning on coming back and marrying her? I don't think so. You've moved on, so why is it a problem if she does too?"

"It isn't." Brandon dragged in a long breath, rubbing his clammy palms along his shorts. Now he understood why Savannah was uptight over the thought of Leanne hooking up with Justin. Except that situation had only been her imagination in overdrive. This was real. "She's sweet. I hope it works out."

"Do you mean that? You look pissed."

"I mean it. Go forth and be happy." He waved a hand.

"Thanks." Rory's jaw clenched, and he swiped at the beads of sweat on his brow. He glanced at Brandon. "What?" His knee bounced as he shifted in the deck chair.

Brandon eyed his friend, who appeared ready to bolt. Another truth lurked behind his confession about Autumn. "Spill it."

Rory straightened. "How'd you know?"

"I've know you since grade school."

"Right." His friend wiped a palm across his t-shirt, the rate of bounce in his knee increasing exponentially.

One thing Brandon knew about Rory. The guy might take forever to reveal his innermost feelings. He reclined in his chair, raising his bottle to his lips.

"Will-you-be-my-best-man?" Rory mumbled.

Brandon sucked in a lungful of air, choking and coughing on his mouthful of beer. "What?" He bolted upright, thumping at his chest and clearing his throat. "You're getting married? To Autumn?" Now the man's fascination over his relationship with Savannah made sense. The fixation on marriage, the questions about the baby ... "Is she pregnant?"

"Hell no." His friend's violent head shake almost made Brandon laugh.

*Almost. But not quite.* "You asked her?" This seemed like a strange dream. Or maybe more like a nightmare.

"Not yet." Rory dug into his pocket with trembling fingers, glancing down before he shoved a black velvet box at Brandon.

He stared, unsure of what to say, but opened it, holding the gold ring up to the light. Brandon tilted his head, squinting at the tiny diamond inset in the center.

Rory frowned. "It's too small."

"No." He cleared his throat again, handing the jeweler's box to Rory. "I don't know what to say is all."

His friend sighed as he stared at the ring. "It's crap, but not everyone can spend fifty grand on a ring."

Brandon searched for the right words. "It suits her low-key lifestyle."

"Low-key? Code for what us poor folk can afford?" Rory rolled his eyes as his voice dropped to barely a whisper. "Wait until you're faced with buying a ring. Be sure to include a magnifying glass so daddy's little princess can compare her minuscule diamond to her stepmother's million-dollar skating rink." His friend snorted. "Never mind. You'll be a rich doctor, marrying into a wealthy family. It won't be an issue."

Brandon's brow knit into a frown.

"It's a sweet ride you're on. Ski trips. Summer homes. Fancy sports cars. Oh, and let's not forget the private jet. Tell me you don't love the fancy-ass lifestyle as much as the girl. Makes your angst about having a kid seem a touch melodramatic. It cemented your standing as far as I can tell."

"It's never been about money," Brandon said softly, wondering where this previously hidden anger stemmed from. "And you know what? You should stop obsessing about the damn ring. I'll tell you right now, if a girl says no to a proposal because you can't afford a massive rock, she's not the one." He leveled his gaze at this man who suddenly seemed a stranger. "Quit making this about something it's not."

Rory rested his bottle on his thigh, staring at it as if it would give him the answers he sought. "Even when we were teenagers, everyone knew you'd end up somewhere. Live a big life with a bright shiny future. This whole"—Rory waved his free hand in a circle above his head—"package suits you."

Brandon fixed his gaze on the dock, uncertain how to respond. This package wasn't his. The lifestyle could disappear without notice. A borrowed existence he wasn't sure he deserved. The space between him and Rory widened, creating a gaping chasm.

"Now you're doubly pissed off."

"Damn right I'm pissed. You have this misguided notion that my life is so damn perfect. You don't have the first clue."

"Then tell me. We all have problems, Brandon. You left town, barely looking back at what you left behind."

"And what's that? My alcoholic, verbally abusive mother? My shitty memories of how that asshole Darien abandoned me? The small-minded finger-pointers who whispered about my family? The people who blackballed Mia and blamed her for that stupid house party fiasco?" He clenched his fists, wishing he had something to punch, to take out his anger on. "The only reason I ever visited was to see you guys and my little sister. Now, almost everyone is gone, and Mia's here. Why would I ever look back?"

"Sounds pretty together to me." His friend scoffed. "I'm a mechanic in a dead-end town I can't leave."

"Nobody forced you to stay." Brandon tilted his head. "Why not leave?" He read the truth in his friend's eyes. "Autumn?"

"Until her brother graduates, she won't budge. She tried to get her mother to relocate, but it'll never happen." Rory clenched a hand around his drink.

"You had the opportunity right after our graduation. If you'd taken it then …" A picture began to form in Brandon's mind. "How is it you're so ready to propose to a woman you've dated for less than ten months?"

His friend's chin dipped, the man avoiding even the tiniest glance his way.

"How long has it been going on?" He clenched his hands together. "Long before I started seeing Vanna, I'd bet."

Rory dropped his head into his hands, peering at Brandon from between his fingers.

"Maybe you could pry that knife out of my back before you leave." Brandon pushed out of his chair. He had so few people he trusted, which made this betrayal even harder to bear.

"It's not like that. I promise." Rory lurched from his seat. "Yeah, I fell in love with your ex-girlfriend and took over your spot with Nick, but nothing happened until after you were with Savannah."

Brandon folded his arms across his chest. "That's not the whole truth. I see it in your eyes."

"You don't want to hear this." Rory heaved a sigh when Brandon didn't move or relax his stance. "Okay," he mumbled. "I've loved Autumn forever. Yes, even when you were dating her. I hurt for her when you left to move to Philly. Yes, I'm a disloyal idiot who coveted everything you had." He allowed a hesitant half-smile. "Except for your crazy-ass mother and bitch stepsister."

"Wow, you're making jokes? Right now. While you're standing there like the asshole you are, telling me how much you resent the tiny bit of happiness I found in that shit hole of a town? How you were there to console my girl the minute I left?" The entire idea shook him. It changed everything he knew about a man who'd been his friend through many ups and downs. It also put a new spin on all the wisdom his friend had doled out over the years. "All your sage advice had only one purpose. To keep me away from Autumn?"

"No. You never loved her. She was your bit of fun before you got the hell out and lived your dream."

Brandon shook his head. "I'm going for a walk. It would be awesome if you weren't here when I get back." He turned, heading toward the beach, his footsteps leaden, but he kept going. Listening to another second of excuses seemed impossible after the afternoon's confessions.

# Chapter 24

## Savannah

T HE FRESH BREEZE BLEW IN from the ocean, lulling Savannah as she watched Brandon and Mia cavorting in the water. London napped under the beach shade nearby, her fingers and lips twitching. "Sweet dreams?" she murmured as she skimmed a hand over the little girl's belly, entranced with the expressions fleeting across the baby's face. She looked back to the water.

A smile touched her lips as her man sloshed through the waves onto the beach, slicking back his hair with splayed fingers, the droplets of water clinging to his golden skin, glistening in the sunlight. Moments like this felt like a scene from a movie with the buff and sexy lifeguard emerging from the water after heroically rescuing the drowning victim. Except this man would only be saving her if she had any say in the matter.

"How are my girls?" He dabbed the water from his face with the edge of a beach towel before he peeked at London. "What do babies dream about?" Brandon ran a fingertip over his daughter's tiny hand.

"I'm wondering the same thing."

Brandon spread a towel over a lounge chair, stretching out to soak up the sun. His lips turned down as he scanned the water.

"Care to share?"

He rolled his head toward her as he added sunglasses, hiding the look in his eyes.

"What happened between you and Rory? He barely looked at me when he left, and you've been in a mood since."

"Slithered off like the snake he is. It doesn't matter. He's gone. Leave it at that."

"No." Savannah directed her full attention toward Brandon. "It's something huge, so I want to hear it."

"He's dating Autumn."

Her heart thumped harder. "Oh."

His lips flattened into a thin line. "He bought an engagement ring."

Her mouth went dry, a pang stabbing her chest. "That's serious. How long have they been together?"

"Months? He didn't specify, only that …" Brandon's rubbed his neck as his eyes closed.

"Finish that thought."

"It became clear I wasn't coming back, so he made his move."

She closed her fingers around her heart pendant. "Are you angry that he didn't tell you?" Her fingers tightened, the tiny diamonds pressing into her skin.

Brandon looked away, hunching his shoulders.

"You're upset that he's dating her."

"It's not like that, Savannah. But nobody bothered to mention it. Traitors," he muttered. "I asked him who he was seeing many times." He planted his feet in the sand. "You heard him. The unavailable woman." Brandon scoffed.

Savannah sighed, but rose and then sat beside him, taking one of his hands between hers. "I'm sure the unavailable part was true," she said. "I'm sorry he never shared the details."

He removed his sunglasses. "Why do you agree about the unavailable part?"

"Unavailable is code for pining over the ex-boyfriend." She kept her voice flat and level, even though she wanted to scream. How could he be so clueless? It had been clear to Vanna who Autumn wanted in her life after only one afternoon.

"Not true."

"Then why are you protesting?"

He hung his head, his forearms draped over his knees as he stared at the sand.

"Exactly," she muttered. "Difficult position to be in. I don't blame him for keeping it secret."

"Huh. Rich, coming from the one who ranted about Leanne and her fictional interest in your ex-boyfriend. I don't hear you chatting it up with her since the visit to New Haven."

"Don't start." It annoyed her that the Justin issue never seemed far from his mind, no matter what she said to alleviate his concerns. "She didn't mention Tony. It's different. And we have talked." Vanna shrugged. After Leanne's attitude during the trip, she'd been less inclined to share details of her own life.

Brandon glowered. "Not what I meant."

"Are you jealous Rory is dating Autumn?"

"Don't be ridiculous. We were over years ago." He blew out a breath. "It's the betrayal."

"I feel that." If Leanne *had* been lusting after Justin, her deception and disloyalty might have ended their friendship. "But what do I know?"

"More than you think."

Savannah squeezed his hand in silent support. The man walked a fine line. He could be tempted to interfere. "Be happy for him. Support him no matter what." She pressed a kiss to his lips, luxuriating in the sun-drenched scent of his skin. "It's out of your control," she whispered.

"You're right. Let me be happy, hope it works out, and pretend he didn't harbor a secret crush on my girlfriend the entire time we were dating."

"What?" Her heart lurched as she absorbed the statement.

"He admitted he's loved her for years. Even while she was my girlfriend. And he was there to console her when I left. Who does that?"

Savannah held back a unladylike snort. "Everyone? The game of love is never fair."

"My ex and my best friend. Classic."

"At least nothing happened between them while you were still dating."

Brandon lifted his head. "Who says it didn't?"

"Did he say that?" The guy had some serious issues with trust. But then Rory admitting to an obsession with Autumn hadn't been his finest move.

"He says nothing happened until after you and I were together. But still, all that time he lusted after her? Encouraged me to leave for school? Why? So he could take my place? He admitted to it, so don't say it's untrue."

"I'm sorry." She rubbed his hand between hers.

"Whatever. It's over and done. He's gone, and I probably won't ever see him again. End of story."

"Brandon," she said softly. "If they weren't together until after—"

"Stop right there." He narrowed his eyes. "I'm done talking about Rory, Autumn, my crappy parents, and … everything else. Let me enjoy this holiday at least a little, okay?"

"Fine," she whispered. "Could you at least watch your daughter while I get a cold drink from the house?"

"Vanna." He caught her hand. "I'm sorry. It's just been difficult the past few weeks. Can you let it go?"

She nodded. It would do no good to push the issue anyway. When he was ready, after he'd had time to process, maybe he'd vent his frustration and they could discuss it.

"Go, and I'll keep an eye on London." Brandon moved to the lounger beside the baby.

She hurried across the hot sand and into the house, heading straight for the fridge.

"No, Em, she's still refusing," Aiden's voice carried from the direction of the stairs. "This seems like the only thing to do."

"I guess it couldn't hurt." Emily rounded the corner, stopping short as she spotted Savannah. "Sweetie. I didn't know you were there."

"Sorry. We got thirsty." She held up the pitcher of lemonade. "What's happening?"

"Nothing much." Her stepmother looked at Aiden.

"I think my little eavesdropper already figured it out, Em."

Savannah lifted one shoulder. "I remembered my biology, even if Caroline was clueless. But what will Gramma say if she finds out?"

"She already knew." Aiden retrieved two extra glasses, setting them in front of her. "It felt wrong to keep it from her. We've had enough secrets and lies in this family. But she admitted she's known for years, even though she never intended for me to find the evidence."

Emily slid an arm around her husband. "Her reaction makes sense. She's considered you her grandson ever since you were born. It's not so easy to turn off your love for a child."

"It's like being adopted. Gramma is your family, even if you aren't blood related." Savannah observed her dad. "You don't seem terribly upset or angry."

"I am, but mainly at Caroline because she refuses to disclose a name. It's a relief not to be a blood relation to James. He wasn't a warm or loving person, so learning I'm not his son doesn't break me up. And it explains a hell of a lot. I never understood why he distanced himself. Now it makes complete sense."

"I don't get it," Savannah said. "If he knew, why did he let her stick around?"

"Why not disown me and divorce her?" Aiden's smile carried a hint of sadness. "By the time he learned he couldn't father children, I was five. A messy, public divorce and an admission she'd tricked him would have ruined his image. Even though he cheated constantly, he'd never admit to his wife's infidelity."

"Ahh. The double standard."

"How do you feel about it?" Aiden asked. "You changed your last name to Hamilton, but it's not really who we are. We may never know the entire truth."

"Gramma Grace is my great-grandmother, no matter what." Savannah moved closer, wrapping him in a hug. "Anyway, it doesn't matter to me what my last name is. You'll always be my dad, and I'll love you forever."

The weeks of summer sped by and before she knew it, they were back in Boston. The days after that were consumed with packing for her impending move to New Haven.

With Brandon's reluctant agreement, she'd rented the coach house to Justin. It seemed a good compromise to her; the ex-boyfriend wouldn't be sharing her house, but he'd be nearby to allow them to share transportation and study together as planned.

"I'll miss you." She hugged Brandon tight. "I'll be home next weekend, and the week after that, you'll visit me on your days off."

He cupped her face between his hands. "I have the schedule. This will work. Four months at a time, remember?" After another long embrace, he kissed London, cuddling her against his chest. "Don't grow too much, sunshine. I'll see you soon."

Together, they fastened the seat in the SUV. Now that it was time to go, she wasn't so sure she could make herself drive away. But she'd committed, and she didn't want to delay her education, or waste the significant investment they'd made in tuition. With a last tearful wave, she pointed the car down the driveway, thankful Iona would arrive in New Haven the next day to begin her duties as full-time nanny for London. She wouldn't be entirely alone with a tiny baby in a strange city.

She would have faith in Brandon and their relationship. It would all work out.

# CHAPTER 25

## Brandon

W ITH THEIR VACATION ONLY A distant memory, Savannah busy with college in New Haven, and Mia enrolled in boarding school for another year, Brandon had little else to do but dig in at work. He took on the maximum allowable hours each week, hoping to justify receiving the Fellowship.

"What's up?" he asked Will as he added the final instructions on his patient.

Will motioned for the tablet in Brandon's hands, using it to peruse the chart and add his notes. "Your sister is getting stitches. I thought you'd want to know."

"Mia?" Brandon frowned. "What is she doing in Boston? Is she okay?"

"No, the other one. Piper?" Will lifted a brow.

"Oh. She's not my sister. She's my ex-stepsister." Brandon wasn't sure if it worked that way. When the parents divorced, were the stepchildren no longer related? Not that it mattered. He'd had little to do with Piper for months.

"Complicated. Well, Nate's with her, if you want to check in. Exam 3."

Brandon sighed and glanced at his watch. The shift had been long and busy, but he probably should pop in. He tapped on the door, grimacing as he caught sight of Gray lounging on the chair while Nate closed the deep gash on Piper's hand.

Piper's head popped up. "I thought you might be working."

"When am I not?" He peered over his colleague's shoulder, admiring the neat row of stitches. "You wanted to see me?"

"I figured I'd say congratulations. I saw the pictures of you and Savannah." She wrinkled her nose. "The baby doesn't look much like you, though."

Brandon crossed his arms, averting his gaze from Gray. The guy's smug-assed grin made him grit his teeth. "How's your dad?"

"Fine. I visited him a couple of weeks ago. Ouch." Piper slapped at Nate's hand. "That hurts."

"Almost done," Nate said. "I can give you more local anesthetic if it's not numb enough."

"Never mind. Can we just get it done?" She turned to Brandon. "I heard Savannah transferred to New Haven." Piper twirled her hair. "Figures, since Justin moved there."

"Pretty boy, Justin." Gray's mouth twisted into a sneer. "She hooked up with him in California while we were dating," the guy muttered.

Brandon forced his lips into a flat line as he sorted through this information, but held back the words he longed to unload on the slimy creep. *Don't react. They'll be gone soon.*

"I forgot about California." Piper blinked at Gray, then mumbled, "And she invited him on that sailing trip she wouldn't shut up about. Didn't she say something about that New Haven trip to Rochelle?" The girl's look cut toward Brandon. "Gray?"

"Typical girls being secretive," Gray glance was sly, his grin tight and suggestive. "You might want to inquire about the trip, Brando. It sounded like that hotel room got cozy."

"Are you finished?" Brandon narrowed his eyes. "My relationship with Vanna is none of your business." He stalked from the exam room, a sick feeling growing in the pit of his stomach. *November.* He bowed his head, pushing through the door into the lounge.

"Hey, man," Nate said as he appeared behind Brandon moments later. "Don't mind their shit."

He clenched his eyes shut, leaning flattened palms on the counter.

"They were getting their digs in." Nate handed him a cup of water. "Piper gripes about Savannah, and Gray is her abusive ex-boyfriend."

Brandon gulped down the icy liquid and sucked in a breath. "You're right. Vanna wouldn't do that … would she?" The part about the sailing trip was fact. Piper had fed him tidbits about Savannah when he first learned about the fake ID. Savannah had never denied Justin had joined her, or that Aiden had paid the guy's flights and fees. Or that they were doing more than sailing for those three months.

"She's not the type. Anyway, Aiden would never go along with that sort of bullshit."

"What if he doesn't know? She visited New Haven in November. That's when she got pregnant. I can't even …" He sank into a chair, dropping his head into his hands. "London has blue eyes. She doesn't look like me."

"She's two months old and looks like a baby. Her eye color could change, or maybe it comes from Tiffany's genetics. That's one of the first things I noticed. That woman has the most incredible blue eyes."

Brandon shook off the feeling. "I'm being ridiculous. Savannah wouldn't let me believe …" His phone vibrated. "Incoming trauma."

"Should you be handling trauma patients?" Nate rested a hand on his shoulder. "You seem distracted."

"I'm good. I let Piper and that idiot Gray get to me when I have no reason to believe any of it. Savannah wouldn't lie."

⁓

By the end of the shift, all Brandon wanted to do was crawl into bed. It had been a busy afternoon, keeping him from dwelling on the conversation with Gray and Piper as the team dealt with a major pile-up on the expressway, followed by casualties from an apartment fire.

"Going to Aiden's?" Nate peeled off his scrub top.

"I'm heading to our apartment." Brandon collected his items from the locker. "Figured I'd sleep in my own bed tonight."

Nate looked at him sideways, shaking his head as they exited through the sliding doors.

"What?" Brandon quelled the urge to roll his eyes.

His friend lifted his brows as they turned toward home.

"Shut up," Brandon muttered. It was obvious what Nate thought without the man saying a single word.

"Talk to her. Hear her side."

"You think there's truth to it?"

"Do you even hear yourself?" Nate scowled. "Your stepsister and her boy-toy baited you. They both have issues with Vanna, yet you bought their crap?"

"She's lied before."

"A fib about her name isn't even close to a monumental lie about her kid's father."

"She saw Justin that weekend." Brandon jammed his key into the lock. "Lay off and give me one night's peace." He stalked into his room and slammed the door before flopping onto his bed. He couldn't explain his mood. Maybe life was too good and this was payback for getting comfortable. For letting down his guard. He'd known Rory forever, and look what his so-called best friend had hidden for the past seven years. He hadn't known Savannah for even two.

A text popped up on his phone:

*Sleep well, Daddy. Hugs and kisses. Miss you. Love you. Your sunshine.*

He gazed at the accompanying photo of London's sweet face and toothless grin. A pang of guilt overtook him as he replied:

*Hugs and kisses. Love you, my sunshine.*

Savannah didn't deserve his suspicion or anger. She supported him, never complained about his hours, and had become a doting mother to their daughter. Her gentle inquiry did nothing to relieve his guilt:

*I miss you. See you tomorrow? I'll be there in the afternoon.*

He tucked an arm behind his head as he dialed her number. "Can't wait," he said.

"Long day?" Savannah's soft soothing tone washed over him, punctuated by the baby gurgles in the background.

"The longest." He closed his eyes.

"What's wrong?"

"Nothing. Why?"

"You sound funny."

"Just tired. And wishing to be there and not here." Brandon stared at the empty baby bed positioned against the bedroom wall. "Anything new?"

"She's steadier when she lifts her head. And the book you bought was a hit. She loved the animal sounds." She smothered a yawn. "Sorry. London was up about ten times last night."

"Get some sleep, sweetie. I'll see you tomorrow. Drive safe."

"Love you. Night."

He held the phone against his chest. *Leave it alone. She's the best thing that's ever happened to you.* With those thoughts drifting through his mind, he sank into sleep.

By the next evening, he still didn't feel any better about the situation. He'd endured twenty-four hours in hell. A rough shift. Several inane messages from Rory, who he hadn't spoken to since the guy had left the Vineyard. Then, the flash of anger at the post on Savannah's social media.

Well, not so much the post, but the cutesy reply from Justin. The insipid gushing over an adorable London in her new outfit from her abuelo. Didn't the guy see Savannah enough already? He lived in the coach house, only feet from her place. Did he need to make lovesick comments? And, the man spent more time with London than Brandon did.

"Why are you in such a crap mood?" Savannah's lips turned downward as she pushed her half-empty plate away. "You don't like it?"

He stared at his plate. "It's fine." Normally, he'd devour every scrap on his plate, but at the moment, he couldn't stomach a single bite. Every time he looked at her, he wondered. And she'd shown up with dinner, but no London. Maybe in response to his reluctance to see either of them, caused by the doubts swirling in his brain.

"Oh." She rose to scrape her half-eaten meal into the trash. "You clearly don't want company." Her head tipped downward as she employed her infamous tactic of hiding behind her silky mane of hair. "If I go now, I can be home in time to put London to bed."

"Savannah." He rubbed a hand through his hair. "I'm tired."

"It's fine." She searched through the items on the side table, shaking her head. "You need a maid. Ahh." The keys jingled. "Maybe you'll manage to make time for London before Sunday."

"Wait." He pushed out of his chair, sighing as she lifted her chin, her eyes shimmering. "Don't cry." The words came out with unintended harshness. Brandon cupped his palms over his face and scrubbed at his stubbly cheeks. He softened his next words. "Every time we talk, you get over-the-top emotional."

"I can't help it." A wrinkle appeared in her brow. "You've been in a mood all week. I drove from New Haven so you could spend time with your daughter, but you don't want to see her. Or me."

"Sometimes I'm so exhausted, having company is difficult."

"Taking care of a baby isn't exhausting? I'm up three to four times every night, plus I have classes, assignments, and group study. Not to mention making long drives to Boston."

"All with plenty of help from a full-time nanny, the housekeeper, your dad, and Emily. Did I miss anyone?" Oh, right. *Justin.* Always Justin.

She scoffed, slinging her bag across her shoulder. "Well, I'm glad I invested my time wisely. Don't worry about seeing your daughter. I know how damn tired and busy you are."

"Is she? Is London mine?"

Her eyes widened, her lips parting as she choked back a sob. She stared at him, her pearly teeth clamping onto her bottom lip.

"You can't answer a simple question?" He narrowed his eyes.

"Unbelievable," she muttered. "How can you ask?"

"It's a valid question." He crossed his arms. "One that has a simple yes or no answer. Did you or did you not sleep with Justin?"

"You think …?" Her eyes grew misty and she looked away, heavy silence looming.

"Something went on in New Haven, and then you came home to me. You know the dates. Tell me you didn't spend the night with him."

"We didn't have sex." She jutted out her chin. "He stayed in my room, but nothing happened."

"Why didn't you tell me?" he whispered. "If you had nothing to hide—"

"I knew you'd overreact." She narrowed her eyes. "We went to a party, ordered room service, watched a movie, and fell asleep. That's the entire story."

"You protest too much." He scoffed. "No wonder he's always there. He worries about her and comments non-stop about how adorable she is. Why is that?"

Savannah bowed her head, her hair obscuring her expression.

"Nothing to say?"

Her mouth set into a grim line as she raised her head, her eyes dark and stormy, but now without a trace of tears. "You caught me." The furrow between her brows deepened. "I'm a rotten liar and a dirty tramp." Savannah squinted. "You want out? You're out. Don't you worry, we'll be fine without you." She spun, yanking the door open. The windows rattled as she slammed it on the way out.

He fought the urge to follow, to beg answers to his questions, but the worst version of himself kept him frozen in place. His mind chanted that she'd confirmed his deepest fear. *The kid isn't mine.*

Perhaps the details didn't matter. Letting her go would be best for everyone. Aiden would keep his daughter and granddaughter safe. The child would have everything. Of that he had no doubt.

〜

The next few days passed in a blur with no word from Savannah. The slow burn of anger prevented him from picking up the phone. If she wanted to make amends or answer his damn question, it was on her to do so. Her continued silence meant only one thing; guilty as charged.

Brandon buried himself in his routine, slogging from work to home, and picking up as many hours as Kavanagh would allow, all the while hoping he wouldn't cross paths with Aiden or Emily.

By some stroke of luck, he avoided that hurdle. Still, he kept an eye out, constantly looking over his shoulder. He had no idea how this break up would affect his working relationships.

"Hey."

Brandon jumped, bringing one hand against his chest.

"Nervous?" Nate snickered. "You should see your face."

"You would be too if you'd broken up with an attending's daughter. I keep wondering when the sneak attack is coming." When yet another knife would be thrust into his back, buried to the hilt.

His friend's expression grew serious. "Why you made such a dumbass move, I will never know. Have you tried talking to Vanna?"

Brandon shook his head. "If she wants to talk, she knows my number. It's a relief Aiden hasn't been on any of the same shifts. I can't work with him. It's a *him or me* kind of situation."

"So you've said. I guess you get a reprieve."

"How's that?"

"Something happened with Aiden's grandmother, so he's in Chicago."

"Gramma Grace?" Brandon's heart sank. He'd grown to love the feisty lady. "I hope she's okay. When is he back?"

Nate shrugged. "They have two new attending physicians starting over the weekend to cover for both Aiden and Emily. Will mentioned something about them taking a sabbatical. Emily turned down some major promotion at another hospital, but she's not coming back here either."

A stab of guilt mingled with his immense relief. Maybe this wasn't the end of his career or his life in Boston. He had to face Will, but that wasn't nearly as awkward as avoiding the two doctors who up until now, had been his strongest mentors and supporters.

# CHAPTER 26

## Savannah

S AVANNAH WRAPPED HER ARMS AROUND herself, peering at the image of
Aiden on her laptop screen. "Is Gramma okay?"

"She's fine, sweetie. It was a minor fall. We'll be in Chicago for several weeks while I sort things out." Aiden gave her a half-hearted smile. "Iona will stay with you in New Haven to help with London."

"You're selling Gramma's house?"

He nodded. "She agreed to move into my penthouse so she doesn't have to manage all the stairs. The Lake Forest house was way too big for one person," he said. "How are you holding up?"

"I'm okay, Daddy." She forced a smile, unsure that he bought her false levity. Her own change of circumstances was hard to bear.

The worst part had been Brandon's reaction, or lack of reaction, to her statement he could be out if he wanted out. He'd allowed her to walk away. His mute acceptance confirmed the worst of her fears; he didn't want any of it. Not her. Not London.

If he cared, even a little, he would have … What? Run after her? Begged her to stay? *Declared his undying love?*

Not that his words would mean anything. He'd made a huge deal about only saying those three words when he really meant them, but apparently he was full of crap like every other guy she'd ever dated.

Brandon wanted to be absolved of responsibility. His entire family hated her and wanted her gone. Except for Mia, but even the beloved little sister would turn away once she heard Brandon's side of the story.

At least she could relieve them of the burden. She'd own her choice to raise her daughter, even if it meant being alone for eternity.

"Sweetheart. Do you want me to fly up for the weekend?" The sad expression on her dad's face brought the tears trickling down her face to her attention.

She brushed at her damp cheeks with the back of her hand. "No. Take care of Gramma Grace. Justin's moving into the spare room, and with Iona's help, I can manage London and school."

He blew her a kiss. "Emily sends her love. You call if you need anything. Promise?"

She nodded, the lump forming in her throat preventing her from speaking.

"I love you, Vanna."

"Back at you. Hugs to everyone." She blew a kiss before they signed off.

Savannah took several long cleansing inhales before she brushed the tips of her index fingers under her eyes, clearing away the last of the tears. She'd made her choices, for better or worse. Allowing Brandon freedom was a double-edged sword that cut her life into shreds. A mantra forced its way through her mind:

*I am strong. I don't need him. I can do this without a man. Especially a man who's spent half of our relationship running away. Away from me. Away from his child. Away from commitment.*

Whatever. No matter what he was avoiding, it amounted to the same thing.

There was no way around it or any clear-cut reason to return. There would be no begging from her. No forcing him into a life he didn't want. She blinked hard. *Don't cry, don't cry, don't …*

"Are you okay?" Justin crouched in front of her, concern written on his face. "Vanna?"

A fresh rivulet of tears trickled down her cheeks as reality washed over her. Why had she served up her heart to someone unworthy? Why hadn't she learned the lesson the first time he'd run? Or from the bevy of useless boyfriends who'd preceded him?

Justin, the sole exception to the asshole-boyfriend trend, brushed the salty drops away with his thumbs. Without a word, he drew her in his arms, rubbing her back as she sobbed. "Now can I beat the crap out of him?" he asked softly.

She shook her head. "Why bother? It won't make him love me or want her. I did the best thing for everyone. I let him go."

"It's not the best thing for his daughter."

"The daughter he thinks isn't his? Why drag him kicking and screaming into her life? What happens when she grows attached, but then he leaves her anyway? Isn't that worse than letting him make a quiet exit now when we can contain the damage?"

"I'm not sure it's containable." Justin pressed a kiss to her temple. "But it's your decision, and I'm here, Vanna. Just tell me what you need."

The next few weeks seemed the toughest of her life, but every day was a tiny bit easier. They settled into a revised routine, with Justin keeping her focused on her classes. Her long-time friend even sacrificed an entire weekend to attend her mother's wedding in Chicago.

"Thanks for being my date." She rubbed her eyes as he opened the passenger door of the SUV. "I couldn't have managed that alone."

"Hmm. Hanging out in a fancy hotel for the weekend. First class flight. Gourmet meals. Open bar. Fun party with your family." He tapped a fingertip against his lips. "It was horrifying." He placed a hand on the small of her back, steering her toward the house. "It's freezing out here. Open the door while I get London."

She had no energy to argue. It was a relief to have him here, giving her a shoulder to lean on when it all became too much. By the time she'd unlocked the door, he'd released her fussing daughter from her seat, bouncing her as he carried her and handed her to Vanna. "I owe you."

"No, you don't," he said in a soft voice. "I'll grab our bags. Get London into bed."

"Oh, mi angelito." Savannah kicked off her snowy boots before carrying her squirming daughter upstairs. "You're so grumpy." She lowered her voice and made funny faces at her daughter, hoping it would help cheer her up.

London continued to kick and cry as Vanna changed her daughter into a sleeper. She draped the little girl over her shoulder and paced up and down the hallway, singing London's favorite Spanish lullaby.

Despite the fact the tune always worked like some sort of magical sleep potion when Emily or Aiden sang it, London continued to fuss and whine.

"What's the matter?" Her friend appeared from the direction of the stairs, holding out his arms. "You want Uncle Justin, love?" He took the girl from her. "You look exhausted. Change into your pajamas. I'll take a turn with grumpy miss."

"Thank you. You're a life saver," she said, smothering a yawn. "I'll be quick, I promise."

The next hours seemed endless. The moment she thought London had drifted off, her daughter would erupt into another round of wailing. She sang, paced the floor, and rocked the baby girl, but nothing soothed her. Even Justin took several turns, to no avail.

"Get some sleep." Savannah waved a hand at Justin as she lifted London from her bed yet again, pressing a kiss to the baby's beet-red face. "At least one of us should attend class tomorrow. Shush, baby. Why won't you sleep?" Tears rolled down her cheeks. "Dad and Emily make it look so easy. Why won't you stop crying?" She sank onto the side of the bed, rocking her screaming daughter and sobbing.

"Lie down," he said, taking London from her arms. "I'll hold her while you take a nap, then we'll switch off."

"No rest for me until she's sleeping." She rubbed at her gritty tired eyes, wishing Iona's flight to New Haven hadn't been delayed.

"Don't be stubborn." Justin shook his head, but kept moving until the girl let out a little hiccuping sob, curling her fingers into his sweater, her eyes closing. After several minutes of silence, his eyes traveled to the crib.

Savannah shook her head. "No," she mouthed at him, patting the bed beside her.

Justin sat, holding his breath, but London didn't open her eyes. Slowly, inch by inch, he reclined, resting her on his chest, giving a small nod and thumbs up to Savannah.

She covered them all with a blanket, curling up on the bed, almost asleep before her head hit the pillow.

⁓

"Thanks for last night." Savannah yawned as she set a cup of steaming coffee in front of him.

"I'm happy to keep you company." He cupped his hands around the mug. "I need this by IV."

"You've been doing a lot of keeping me company. Sorry, it's cutting into your love life."

"Ahh." He waved a hand. "It's not a big deal, sweetie. I know it's tough. Thankfully, Iona will be here later." His eyes widened. "She will, right?"

"Yeah, she texted to confirm her arrival time. Go to class. London is sleeping, so I might head back to bed."

"Into the shower for me." Justin hesitated a moment at the bottom of the stairs. "Will you be okay tonight? I have a date."

"That's great. Is it with …?" Her smile widened.

He nodded, grinning in return.

"Have fun. You deserve a night out."

She kept the smile on her face as her friend bounded up the stairs like he hadn't spent the entire night calming a screaming baby. Though she appreciated his help, she felt guilty for taking up so much of his time. These years of undergrad should involve a social life, dates, and parties. He'd been giving up too much of it for her. In the future, she'd demand less.

She sank into one of the chairs in the sunroom and closed her eyes, picturing the happy memories she'd shared with Brandon in this house. It had only been a few days at a time, but still enough to give her a taste of what almost was. But now, she'd raise her daughter alone.

She'd almost drifted to sleep, when her phone rang. "Hello?" she whispered.

"Savannah? It's Rory. Is Brandon there?"

"Why would he be here?" She blinked hard, hoping to clear her mind.

"I've been trying to reach him, but he's ignoring me. He hasn't spoken to me since I left the Vineyard. Did he tell you?"

"No. But, Rory—"

"Maybe he doesn't want to hear it, but I am sorry. He'll be thrilled to hear Autumn dumped me. She doesn't love me. Or not enough to marry me."

"I'm sorry."

"Are you okay? You sound funny."

"Brandon's not here. I haven't spoken to him for weeks either. You'll be thrilled to know he dumped me." She tapped the disconnect button and pressed the phone to her chest.

It was news to her that Rory and Autumn hadn't made it as a couple. She supposed it cleared the way. Brandon could run back to his ex-girlfriend and get his revenge. On her, and on Rory.

She closed her eyes, wishing she could sink into the floor and disappear.

# CHAPTER 27

## Brandon

HIS LIFE SETTLED INTO AN endless routine. Nothing existed aside from the slog to work, home to catch a few hours sleep, and then back to the hospital. The day blurred together.

Christmas decorations and colorful light displays popped up all over the city for the holidays and then disappeared again after New Year's. None of it excited Brandon. He could barely keep his head above water.

At the end of another long shift, Brandon slung his pack over one shoulder, waving at the nursing station as he headed for the exit. He paused outside the doors, shivering in the chill wind.

"Dr. Reynolds." Jill, one of the medical students, stopped in front of him. "Heading home?"

"Mmmhmm." Brandon dug out his black beanie, tugging it onto his head to cover his ears.

"I thought I'd stop for something to eat." She blinked at him. "You could join me, if you like."

"Thanks, but I'm beat."

"You still have to eat." A hopeful smile appeared. "I could make you something. My place isn't far."

Brandon tilted his head, trying to sort out the signals coming from this touch-too-young medical student. Cute? *Yup.* Flirting? *Most definitely.* Good idea? *Nope.* This little flirting cutie had disaster written all over her. Women were trouble. Full stop.

"Brandon?"

"Thanks for the invitation, but it's not a good idea. I'm just going to …" He motioned in the general direction of his own apartment. "Good night." His boots crunched in the layer of fresh snow covering the sidewalk as he began walking. He glanced at the figure loitering by the wall, stopping to take a second look as the teenager advanced. It couldn't be.

"It's you." The boy tilted his head. "You visited my house."

Brandon narrowed his eyes. "What are you doing here?"

"I'm Tristan."

"I know who you are."

"But who are you?" The teenager studied him, his mouth set in a way reminiscent of Darien. "Are you my brother?"

Brandon didn't know what to say to this kid. He blew out a puff of air. "How did you find me?"

"Can we go inside?" Tristan rubbed his hands over his arms and stomped his feet. "It's freezing."

There went his date with leftover pizza, a hot shower, and his pillow. But he couldn't ditch this kid—*his little brother*—on the streets of Boston in the middle of the winter. And despite the annoyance, his curiosity was piqued. "There's a diner down the block. Come on." He motioned for Tristan to follow.

The boy fell into step beside him, peering at Brandon occasionally from under a fringe of dark, untidy hair.

"Quit staring." Brandon hunched his shoulders against the cold, thankful when they reached the small diner.

Once they'd settled into a booth with hot drinks, Brandon surveyed the kid. The resemblance to Darien seemed even more pronounced now he was sitting across the table from the boy.

Tristan rubbed his hands together before wrapping them around the cup. "Are you really my brother?"

"What makes you think that?"

"I overheard my dad talking to Mom about his son. A doctor in Boston, he said. It wasn't hard to find you with an internet search. There was an article about some medical award and it listed this hospital with your name and photo." The kid studied him. "You look like him. And your last name is Reynolds, same as ours."

Brandon sipped from his cup. "Then why ask?"

"Why have I never even heard of you before now?"

"Ask Darien."

"Can't. He doesn't know that I know." The kid shook his head. "Weird. I have a brother." Tristan drummed on the table. "Has Dad been here?"

Brandon smothered a bitter laugh. "That man walked out of my life when I was eight. He's not my dad."

A frown appeared. "For real?"

Brandon shrugged. "Sorry to disappoint, but this is the last place he'd be." He contemplated Tristan, wondering exactly what Darien had said to his wife. "Does anyone know where you are?"

The boy focused on the cup, his head wagging back and forth.

"How did you get here?"

Tristan stuck up his thumb, waggling his hand.

"Dumb-ass." Brandon glanced at his watch and sighed. Too late to stick him on a bus to Albany tonight. "Hungry?"

"I'm a teenager." The boy's lips twitched.

He lifted a hand to signal the waitress. "Where are you sleeping tonight?"

"Dunno."

"You have a phone?"

"Battery's dead."

"Money?" Brandon fought the urge to roll his eyes as the boy shook his head. He dug his mobile from his pocket and slid it across the table. "Call your mother. She must be worried."

"She'll be pissed." Tristan lifted his gaze, but punched in the numbers. After a moment, he sighed and stabbed a finger at the screen. "Voice mail."

"Leave a message."

The teen eyed him, but dialed again. "Where are you?" he asked. "Call me back at this number. My phone's dead." His lips flattened into a thin line as he hung up. "There. Satisfied?"

Brandon glowered at the kid.

"Why are you angry?"

"Gee, I don't know. I'm exhausted, starving, and dying to shower after sixteen horrific hours in an ER. Instead, I'm sitting in a diner with a runaway teenager." His phone rang. *Mia.* "What's up, munchkin?"

"Stop calling me that."

"Sorry. Old habit."

"I'll forgive you, but only because I love you," she said. "Did you call her? It's her birthday."

Brandon closed his eyes. January the fifth. Savannah's twentieth birthday.

"You didn't forget, did you?"

"No, I didn't forget."

"But you didn't call her either," she said in a flat tone.

"What did you need?"

"I just …" Mia's heavy sigh carried clearly to his ears. "I wanted to make sure you were still alive. You were in a crap mood over the holidays."

"I'm fine. Worrying is my job," he said with a glance at Tristan. The kid might pretend not to be listening, but Brandon sensed he was soaking up every word. "Sorry, but I'm in the middle of something."

"Something more important than wishing Vanna a happy birthday?" she asked softly.

"Mia, don't." He pinched the bridge of his nose. Every time he spoke with his sister, she asked questions about Savannah and London. Dodging and prevaricating became exhausting. "I'll text you later. Bye, honey."

"Mia?" Tristan asked as Brandon ended the call.

"My sister."

"I have a sister? How old is she? Can I meet her?"

Brandon shook his head. "She's my sister. Not yours."

A confused look appeared on the kid's face. "If she's your sister then isn't she …?"

"No."

"But—"

"It's not that difficult to figure out, kid. She's not your damn sister." He'd never allow them to meet. Mia already struggled with her mounting losses. Taking away the illusion they shared both parents seemed cruel, as would her seeing the family Darien had created so soon after abandoning them.

"Ohhh." Tristan's voice rose. "Right."

They ate in silence, Tristan sending glances his way every few seconds. "Now what?" he asked as Brandon paid the bill.

"It's late, so I guess you crash on my couch." At this point, Brandon didn't know what else to do. He shoved his arms into the sleeves of his coat, tucking the beanie on his head again.

Tristan followed Brandon onto the icy street, hunching his shoulders against the wind as they trudged down the sidewalk. He crammed his hands into the pockets of his coat.

"I have a roommate, so keep it down." Brandon said as they entered the building. Once inside the apartment, he hung his coat and emptied his backpack as the boy looked around.

"Not very big."

"It's enough." He located the blankets and extra pillow he kept for Mia's visits. "Towels are in the closet there"—he pointed—"and there should be a new toothbrush in the drawer in the bathroom. I call dibs on the shower." He hated the antiseptic hospital smell that clung to him after every shift. "Help yourself to a soda or whatever from the fridge."

Tristan nodded as he stowed his small pack on the floor by the sofa.

Brandon closed the bathroom door behind him, staring at his reflection in the mirror over the sink. *You look like him.* He hated the thought of even remotely resembling the man who'd abandoned him. The best he could hope is he'd never be anything like the guy in words or actions. *Fail.* He was already *that guy.* For the millionth time, his thoughts strayed to Savannah and London.

He showered and slung a towel around his hips, gathering his dirty clothes and heading for his bedroom. "What are you doing?" Brandon stopped short at the sight of Tristan sitting cross-legged on his bed.

The boy held a familiar album in his hands, his head tilted as he bent his head closer, inspecting one of the pages. "Cute kid. And she's really hot," he muttered under his breath.

Brandon tugged the book free from Tristan's hands and snapped it shut. "Don't snoop." He shoved the album into the top drawer of his desk.

"Testy," the boy held up his hands. "I get it. You want nothing to do with me." He glanced at the empty crib against the wall. "Those pictures are your kid?" His head bobbed as his lips twisted. "Yeah. I overheard something about that too."

Brandon could only imagine what else he'd overheard. "He has no right to comment. And neither do you." Anger flashed to the surface. "You met me an hour ago, so keep your shitty judgments and opinions to yourself." He balled his hands into fists, wishing Darien stood in front of him, right here and now. The man had overstepped and dragged Tristan into the middle.

The teenager stared at him, a deep frown on his face. "Why do you hate me? It's not my fault he's been a crappy father to you."

Brandon blew out a long slow breath. Something about this kid irritated him even if it wasn't Tristan's fault. "Get some sleep. Tomorrow, you're on a bus."

"Maybe I should go now."

"Go right ahead. Find yourself an icy snowbank to sleep in." He sighed. "There won't be any buses until tomorrow."

Tristan slouched his way to the living room and flopped onto the couch. "Fine. I'll go in the morning. Some brother you turned out to be."

⌇

The constant thud of a fist against the front door dragged Brandon from his sleep. He yanked on a pair of jeans and glanced toward the boy crashed on his couch as he stumbled toward the entrance.

He peered through the peephole. "Damn it," he said as he struggled with the lock, yanking open the door. "Keep it down. You'll wake the whole building."

"Where's my son?" Darien asked. "Is he here?" The man pushed by, stopping short as he spotted Tristan. "What the hell are you doing?" His eyes blazed as he glared at Brandon. "I thought you wanted to have nothing to do with us."

Brandon folded his arms across his bare chest. "The kid showed up with no money and no place to stay. Would you prefer I let him find a cozy cardboard box in a Boston alley? You're the one who walked away."

"Enough about you."

"I'm not talking about me, you idiot. You left your second family too?"

Darien furrowed his brow. "Is that what he told you?" His tone softened. "You took him in?"

"Dad?" Tristan sat, his hair sticking out at all angles. "What are you doing here?"

"Get dressed. I'm taking you home." Darien shook a finger at the boy. "You, young man, are grounded. What in the hell were you thinking?"

"Okay, okay." Tristan lifted a hand as he pushed off the sofa. "Give me a minute." The kid stumbled into the bathroom. Moments later, the toilet flushed, followed by the sound of the shower.

Brandon glanced at the clock, noting it was barely eight. He'd hoped for several more hours of sleep before his afternoon shift started. "I need caffeine." He sighed as he began the process of brewing coffee. "Want some?"

The man nodded as he looked around the apartment. "Not quite what I expected on a doctor's income."

"Yeah, well, I'm a medical resident with massive loans to repay. How'd you get in the building?"

"I slipped in after a couple of your neighbors left." Darien shrugged out of his coat and hung it over the back of a chair. "I guess I should thank you for watching out for your brother."

Brandon selected cups from the cupboard. "Have a seat." He motioned to the small kitchen table.

Darien planted himself in a chair, scrubbing his hands over his face. "You look like hell."

"Thanks. I do try." Brandon propped himself against the counter. He took in the dark circles under the man's eyes, the rumpled clothing, and rough stubble covering his face. "You don't look so hot yourself."

"As soon as I heard the message, I got in the car."

"How did you know?" Brandon stroked his jaw. "The phone number?"

"It went to voice mail when I called back. I figured Tristan was in Boston." Darien leaned back in his chair. "I had a business trip, and when I got home, he was gone. Madeline was freaking out. The kid's impulsive, and he's bright, so I should have anticipated he'd connect the dots."

"He overheard something."

"Ahh." The man's head bobbed. "Curiosity ruled his head. If it's any consolation, he'll be grounded for months for this stunt. I'm sure you were grounded once or twice during your teenage years."

Brandon scoffed. "I've never been grounded in my life."

"Oh." Darien nodded knowingly. "You were a rule follower, rather than a rule breaker. The good kid."

"Sure. I was a complete fucking angel." Brandon turned away to pour steaming coffee into the two mugs, then set one in front of Darien with a thump. He didn't bother to ask if the man took cream or sugar; he didn't give a damn. All he wanted was for them to get out of his apartment.

"Now he knows about his brother." Darien tipped his chin. "Or not, because you've disowned me. I suppose that means you refuse to acknowledge him or your sister."

Brandon fixed his gaze on a spot on the floor. Typical for the man to turn it around and put it on him. What else could he expect from a guy who thought nothing of abandoning his son for sixteen years?

"This might be my only chance. I'm sorry. For everything. I made a huge mistake. Maybe one day, you'll forgive me." The man dug into his coat. "I never forgot you, Brandon."

A scoff escaped. How was he supposed to believe that?

Darien slid a photo from his wallet. "You probably think I'm full of shit, but I've always carried this with me and wondered. What you looked like, what you were doing. All of that," he said. "Do you remember this?" He pushed the picture across the table.

Brandon lifted his chin enough to survey the faded image, noting the curl of the edges. The two people in the photo seemed complete strangers, yet oddly familiar; a small dark-haired boy and Darien in his younger years. He shook his head, returning his focus to the pattern on the linoleum.

"It's one of my happiest memories. We went to a ballgame in the city to celebrate your eighth birthday. You were so excited, and we ate hot dogs and popcorn. I even bought cotton candy. It turned your tongue blue, but you loved it."

That day for Brandon remained as faded as the photo on the table. His last clear memory of deserving any attention from this man, it occupied a black spot in his mind. That had been the last birthday celebration with his father. A few weeks later, Darien had walked out the door and never returned.

"You don't remember how we used to go camping and roast marshmallows? Or the ball games? Did Carol never show you any of the pictures? Or give you my letter?"

"Nope." He leveled his gaze at the man. "Oh. Maybe she added them to the blazing inferno in the back yard. Who knows?"

He frowned, his lips tugging downward. "She …?"

"Sadly, we didn't roast marshmallows. They would've absorbed an unappealing gasoline flavor. Even though it might have been fun. A fitting send off. Kind of like you never existed."

"You are kidding, aren't you?" The man's voice was low, with an apparent sad note.

Brandon shrugged, turning away. It simply didn't matter whether the man believed him or not. In his mind, the days for amends and apologies were long gone. He'd survived, and this man reappearing with his lame-ass excuses caused painful memories to surface.

"I am so, so, sorry. I never knew."

*Of course, you didn't. You walked away and never bothered looking back.* "As soon as Tristan is ready, you can let yourself out." He set his cup on the counter and headed toward his bedroom. Half-way, he halted. "Don't ever contact me again." The last few steps were covered with leaden feet, an endless effort to lift one after the other. When he reached his room, he shut the door behind him with a soft click.

Brandon crawled under his covers, fighting the visions, the sounds, and the smells that surrounded him. The worst was the stench of burning gasoline that manifested in his mind. Followed by the realization he'd become the man he hated. He'd walked away. And why? *Because I didn't want to be a father to someone else's child?* Was that even the entire truth? Or was he a coward, his fear overwhelming his logic. Did it even matter? He loved them. He missed them. And he'd destroyed everything.

⁓

Brandon curled his arms around his legs, dropping his head against his knees. His head pounded from last night's binge, and he didn't have the energy to even shower.

"Kavanagh called. You're two hours late for your shift. Again," Nate said. "Get your ass in gear."

He shook his head and slid his hands around the back of his neck squeezing his eyes closed.

"Hey." His friend touched his arm. "Pull it together. You've been a train wreck since before Christmas."

"Doesn't matter." Brandon muttered. Everything had spun out of control after Tristan had appeared, followed by Darien. His work performance had suffered. Soon Kavanagh would boot his ass from the program and offer the Fellowship to a more deserving candidate.

Topping it off was losing a child he adored and the woman he both loved and hated. She'd betrayed him. *Or had she?* He couldn't sort real from imagined.

Nate sighed. "I have to go. Are you going to be okay?" After another drawn out sigh, the sound of his footsteps retreated, followed by the thunk as the door shut behind his friend.

*Blessed silence.*

He didn't move, hoping the nausea and headache would fade. Maybe he'd sink into oblivion and disappear.

Sometime later, Brandon became aware of keys in the lock and the sound of footsteps, but he stayed in place.

"Brandon?"

Of all people to appear in his apartment, having this man show up had to be the worst.

Hands rested on his shoulders and squeezed.

"You need to look at me."

Brandon made a small motion, too exhausted to even shake his head.

Aiden pressed two fingers against his inner wrist and then released it.

Brandon became vaguely aware that the man now sat beside him on the floor.

"You've been missing shifts."

*This was it. The moment my career ended.*

"Want to tell me what's happening?"

Brandon swallowed hard and fought the tight feeling in his chest. "Fire me and leave."

"That's not why I'm here." Aiden placed a hand on his arm.

*Then why?* His thoughts jumbled together. Nothing made sense anymore.

"Things seem dark right now, but you can't give up everything you've worked for. You have a promising career ahead. Don't throw it away."

Brandon buried his head deeper in his arms, his eyes burning as he dragged in a breath.

"Let me help."

"I've messed it all up."

A warm hand moved to the back of his neck. Aiden pulled Brandon's head to rest on his shoulder. "It's fixable."

A tear tracked down Brandon's face, and his cheeks reddened, mortification rising, but he couldn't control it. His shoulders shook as the dam broke, the salty river streaming from his eyes. He dragged in long halting breaths, the emotions crashing over him. Loss. Devastation. Anger. Humiliation. The deep pain slicing through his heart.

Eventually, Brandon forced himself upright, his cheeks burning. Crying wasn't something he allowed anyone to see, let alone weeping on another man's shoulder. A shame made worse by having this particular man witness his breakdown. "What you must think." He gathered the courage to look at Aiden as he brushed the dampness from his gritty eyes with his sleeve.

"We've all had these moments." Aiden squeezed his shoulder. "It'll get better."

Brandon massaged his temples, too mortified to look at the man.

Aiden rose, followed by the sound of his footsteps retreating and returning moments later. He pressed a cold glass into Brandon's hands. "You drink. I'll pack."

Brandon sipped at the icy water, tracking the man's movements as he skirted the various piles of clothing on the floor and located a bag in the closet.

Aiden tilted his head at the empty rack of hangers, shooting a silent glance at Brandon before he scanned the room.

Brandon dropped his head onto his knees, refusing to meet Aiden's gaze. He closed his eyes, trying to block it all out, avoiding looking at the expression on the other man's face as he surveyed the disgusting mess.

Thankfully, Aiden said nothing, leaving only the sound of him moving about the room and finally, zipping the bag. "Laptop, keys, wallet. Anything else you can't live without?"

*My family.* The words popped into his head unbidden, but Brandon shook his head. He couldn't voice his longing for Savannah or London when the separation was his fault.

"On your feet." The order, issued in a firm tone, said; *don't bother arguing or I will drag your sorry ass out of here.*

Brandon forced himself upright and yanked on his shoes before shoving his arms in the leather coat Aiden retrieved from the closet. He trailed the man down the stairs and a further few feet along the street to the shiny black sports car.

Aiden hit the remote to unlock the door and motioned for him to get in before stowing the bags in the trunk.

He sank back against the leather seat and closed his eyes as the engine purred to life. His mind wandered as they pulled into traffic, winding their way out of the city.

"Brandon." A gentle shake awoke him. "We're here."

He pried open his bleary eyes and stared at the front of the familiar house.

Aiden hopped out of the car and opened the trunk before Brandon managed to crawl from the passenger seat and follow him through the front door.

The man gave him the once over before heading up the staircase, leading Brandon into the large bright guest room down the hall from Savannah's. He set the case with the laptop and other personal items on the desk. "You know where everything is. Feel free to shower or sleep, or you can come downstairs. I planned to make lunch. Hungry?"

Brandon shook his head. Nausea rose at the thought of food.

"I'll let you get settled. Need anything?"

"No," he whispered.

Aiden patted his shoulder and left the room.

Brandon stripped off his jeans and crawled between the sheets, hugging a pillow to his chest as he closed his eyes.

⌒

Familiar but muffled cries jolted him from his sound sleep. He forced his eyes open, and gazed around the large room. The light had faded into early evening. His stomach growled as he swung his legs over the edge of the bed.

The baby's cries silenced, replaced by the soft murmur of a low voice. Brandon rubbed at his temples, the low-grade ache in his head making him long for relief. *Caffeine.* He craved a strong, hot cup of coffee.

He tugged at the sweaty t-shirt, sniffing at his armpit and grimacing. He couldn't remember the last time he'd showered. After stripping off his clothes, he piled them on the floor and wandered into the bathroom.

After a long steamy shower, he emerged and slung a towel around his hips. He rubbed a spot in the foggy mirror, examining his red eyes and scruffy face. "Such a mess," he muttered.

He moved into the bedroom, searching for his bag. *Do I even own any clean clothing?* He couldn't remember doing laundry in weeks.

The bag was nowhere to be seen, but a neat stack sat on the bench at the end of the bed. The packages of socks and underwear were new, the rest of the clothing he recognized as Aiden's. He yanked on the jeans and one of the sweaters and slunk from the room, sniffing the air and following the fragrant aroma into the kitchen.

He stood in the doorway for a moment, taking in the domestic scene. Cierra in her high chair, cramming pieces of sliced banana into her mouth with chubby fingers. Kellan on a step stool, transferring sliced mushrooms with focused precision onto the top of a pizza, placing each with care. London in her bouncy seat, kicking her feet, and cooing and babbling as she followed the action with bright eyes.

"Done, Papa." The boy grinned and clapped his hands.

"Good job, hijo mio." Aiden kissed the top of his son's head and ruffled his hair. "You want to put the sauce and cheese on the second one?" He looked up. "You're awake."

"Barely." Brandon scrubbed a hand over his stubbly jaw. "Thanks for the clothes."

"No problem. I threw a load of yours in the laundry."

Brandon cringed. "Sorry." He hung his head. "You had to deal with my disgusting clothes."

"It's not a big deal." Aiden opened the wall oven, popped the pizza inside, and set the timer before setting another shell in front of Kellan along with a bowl of sauce and grated cheese. He added coffee beans to the fancy stainless steel machine on the counter and hit the button. "That's enough, Kellan." He swooped in to rescue the bowl of cheese from his son and replaced it with the board of sliced toppings.

"Look, Brandon." Kellan patted the top with a flattened palm. "Pizza."

"Yum. You're a great helper." Brandon smiled at the boy. "Where's Emily?"

"California. She's having a spa weekend with Nat and Jules."

Brandon had met Emily's sisters at one of the holiday functions in Chicago. "And Savannah?"

"New Haven."

His mouth grew dry. Aiden was fully aware of how things ended. How he'd treated Savannah. "How's Yale?"

"She likes it. It's a good fit, and she has friends in her classes."

The pang hit Brandon's heart. He furrowed his brow. "Justin," he muttered. "Should've known."

Aiden leaned back on the counter, crossing his arms as he narrowed his eyes. "Why does that bother you?"

Brandon ducked his head and shrugged.

"Jealousy will get you nowhere." Aiden set two more bowls beside Kellan, watching as the small boy arranged the toppings.

"Doesn't mean I have to like it." Brandon covered his eyes with a hand, taking a deep breath and massaging his temples.

"Good job, Kel." Aiden scooped his son from the chair. "Wash your hands and play until dinner's ready."

The small boy raced down the hall.

Aiden dampened a cloth and wiped Cierra's fingers. "You too, princesa." He freed her from the seat, smiling as she toddled into the living room and dug into the toy box. "Like it or not, you made a choice." Aiden placed his flattened palms on the counter.

"So, now I watch from the sidelines as she hooks up with her ex-boyfriend? Isn't that what's happening?"

Aiden frowned. "Worry about getting your own shit together. You're a damn mess."

Brandon sucked in a breath. "Why are you helping me? Why am I here?"

Aiden shrugged. "You've hit a rough patch, and you need help getting through it."

"Why you?"

"We don't stand by and watch family self-destruct."

The statement hit Brandon in the gut, causing a shiver to run through him. He scoffed. "You don't owe me anything." He glanced at London, who'd begun to fuss.

"It's not about *owing*." He poured a steaming cup of coffee and set it in front of Brandon before he unbuckled London from her seat, cradling her in the crook of his arm. Aiden moved easily, bouncing the little girl as he retrieved a bottle from the fridge and popped it into the warmer.

"You're the last person I'd ask for help."

"Why?" Aiden glanced his way.

Brandon's cheeks burned as he bowed his head. He lifted one shoulder.

"You're not a captive, but I hope you'll talk to me before you walk out that door."

Brandon squeezed his eyes closed, forcing back the imminent tears. He'd fallen apart. He'd cried on this man's shoulder. Even worse, he loved this man's daughter, but he'd ruined everything by abandoning her and *his child?* He avoided looking at the baby girl nestled in Aiden's arms.

"Why won't you accept my help?"

"Savannah," Brandon whispered. "After what I did, how could you consider helping me?"

"No matter what, I care what happens to you."

"Simple as that?" He wrapped a hand around the coffee cup, savoring the slight warmth. "If I were you, I'd kill the guy who did that to my family."

"My experiences are vastly different from yours. But not so different at all."

"You make no sense. You'll pat me on the back and pretend I'm not the useless guy who ruined your daughter's life?"

"You give yourself far too much credit." Aiden scoffed.

Brandon swallowed hard. "So I'm the extra? Savannah doesn't need me. She's gone back to him, even after she told me it was long over."

Aiden studied him, a frown on his face.

"Stupid, right? I freaked out, but she told me to leave. That she didn't need me."

"Or maybe you took the easy out when it was offered."

"So it's my fault?"

"Yes. And no."

Brandon clenched his jaw and blinked hard.

"The situation could have been better handled, but take ownership of your actions," Aiden said. "Do you want to be part of London's life?"

"This isn't how I pictured having a child, and I made a huge mistake."

"That isn't what I asked."

"Yes," Brandon said softly. "I miss her."

"Then you know what to do."

"What if she's not mine?"

Aiden tilted his head and gave Brandon a long cool look. "That's what this mess is about? Just who do you think …?" He squinted. "Never mind. I've got the picture."

"Savannah didn't tell you why we broke up?"

"Not that detail." Aiden gazed down at the little girl in his arms. "Did Vanna tell you London isn't yours?"

"She implied it." Brandon avoided Aiden's searching look.

"But you have guilt written all over your face."

Brandon bowed his head.

"So you asked the deadly question you should never ask. And she reacted and gave you the out you've been waiting for."

"No. I never wanted to leave. From the moment London was born, I've loved her. Not having her in my life has been the hardest part," Brandon said. "Given the circumstances, it seemed justified to ask." He sighed. "I miss them. I love London like a father, even if I'm not."

"You believe you're not London's father?"

"I'm the biggest asshole in history, right? But Vanna spent the entire weekend with Justin. And then I heard some things about her and him, and …" He gave a helpless shrug.

"Problematic." Aiden emitted an exasperated sigh.

"You see my issue."

"Yeah, I see it." The man gave his head a small shake. "Lack of trust combined with the stupidest, most insulting question you could ever ask your girlfriend. Fucking idiot."

"Haven't you ever asked a woman if the kid is yours?"

"If I'd asked my wife that question, I'd be six feet underground." Aiden rocked on his feet, the baby girl cuddled in his arms. "I've never doubted Kellan or Cierra were mine, because I don't doubt Emily."

Brandon dropped his head onto his forearms and closed his eyes. Tiny pinpricks burned behind his eyeballs. "Is London my daughter?"

"Don't drag me into the middle."

"You offered your help."

"But I can't answer that question."

"You never asked whose kid she is?"

"I'm damn sure she's my granddaughter. Besides, you wanted to be involved. It surprised me when you bowed out and decided we couldn't work together."

"You knew?"

"It came down to you or me, isn't that right?"

Brandon sat back on his stool.

"Yet you're throwing it all away. The Fellowship. Years of education and training. An entire family. Every good thing in your life, you've sabotaged."

"Why sacrifice your career for a lowly resident? I expected to be booted."

"Really? I thought you knew better."

Brandon furrowed his brow.

"You're seriously clueless?"

"Savannah asked you?"

"Wrong." Aiden scrubbed a hand through his hair. "What are we to you?"

"I …" Brandon stared at him, unsure what the man wanted to hear. "It'll sound stupid." He shrugged.

Aiden sighed as he snagged the bottle from the warmer.

"I don't know if you're my boss, my mentor, my big brother, or my friend." *Or my substitute father.* A sentiment he didn't have the courage or words to express. "Maybe it's a combination?"

"It's a convoluted dynamic, but lowly resident? That's disappointing."

Brandon pinched the bridge of his nose. "I'm unworthy of the sacrifice." He motioned to London. "There's nothing I can give her, except further disappointment."

"Are you incapable of loving a child?" Aiden tilted his head.

"Savannah said stay away."

"How much do you want to be in your daughter's life?"

"She ordered me to go."

"Or she let you go. There's a difference," Aiden said. "Love means allowing someone their freedom when you think it's what they most desire."

Images of that day flashed before his eyes. The way she'd turned away and told him he didn't have to be there. That she would manage on her own. The devastation when confronted with his accusations. *Had I seen only what I wanted to see?*

"London only needs her father to be part of her life," Aiden said softly. "To love her."

The little girl turned her eyes toward Brandon. They'd darkened into a warm brown, resembling her mother's eyes.

Brandon held out his arms, giving in to his need to hold her. He exhaled a long slow breath as he cradled her against his chest. The soothing sweet baby smell surrounded him as he accepted the bottle. "I've missed so much," he said as the baby wrapped a hand around his finger, gazing at him with curiosity.

"She remembers you." Aiden brushed a hand over the girl's wispy hair. He settled on the stool beside Brandon. "It's for you to decide whether to stay or go."

A sharp pang knifed through his chest.

"You know what to do." Aiden slid from the stool as the timer chimed. "And try having a little trust and faith in people."

Brandon peered at the baby's face, trying to discern her features, wondering if she looked like him at all. Perhaps not, but it didn't really mean anything of significance. Without his own baby pictures—which he'd never have—finding true resemblance in a child so young was near impossible.

The man settled the two kids at the table, feeding Cierra a few small bites of pizza as Kellan nibbled on his own slice. "Come eat."

Brandon moved to a seat at the table, still holding London in the crook of his arm. He'd juggled meals around her before, and he wasn't ready to put her down.

By the end of the meal, London had drifted to sleep, so Brandon placed her in the bassinet.

He cleared some dishes from the table, carrying them into the kitchen. Something tacked to the fridge caught his eye. He squinted at it, the name—*Anderson, Emelia A.*—making his eyes widen as he digested the meaning of the test. "No way. That must be a bit of a shock."

"Yes and no. The baby part was planned. The twin part, well, not so much. We're getting used to the idea. And hey, Iona is thrilled, because she has true job security."

"Until some guy steals her away and she has her own."

"Uh-uh. None of that. Finding a great nanny isn't easy. We need her. Three kids under the age of five running around this house, which is soon to be five under five."

"Damn." Brandon rubbed the back of his neck. The nanny had been instrumental in keeping everyone sane after London's birth, especially with Savannah's move to New Haven. "How much time does London spend here?"

"London is here twice a month, but mostly, she's in New Haven with Vanna. It's tricky, but we make it work. London's here for a few days as Iona needed to make a trip to Ireland."

"Too bad I have to get back to work. To avoid wasting the sacrifice and all."

"No chance. You're a liability in your current state of mind." Aiden rubbed a hand through his hair. "I'll clear some mental health days with Will."

"He'll be thrilled." Brandon blew out a puff of air. "Why would he allow it? His patience must be worn out considering all the time I've had off."

"What's a little more?" Aiden asked. "Anyway, this is medical leave. Will understands stressful personal situations and how it effects people." He leaned against the counter. "I hit that wall when my marriage ended. We'd endured a hellish six months. The pressures of medical school, the pissed off wife, on top of losing our friend Matthias to suicide all added onto the load. When my marriage fell apart, so did I. It didn't get better in one day, that's for damn sure."

"Your friend committed suicide?"

"His name was Matthias LaRousseau." The man returned to his task of wrapping leftovers and loading the dishwasher. "The pressure of medical school and his relationship troubles with his girlfriend and family overwhelmed him."

"I'm sorry," Brandon said. "I can't imagine."

"Really?" Aiden said softly.

"Well ... No. I mean ..." He slid onto one of the stools and rested elbows on the gleaming counter, slouching forward and pressing his palms against his cheeks.

"Does a nap, dinner, and a two-hour visit with London fix your issues?" Aiden asked.

He shook his head without looking up. The thought of returning to his apartment or trying to muddle through hours in a busy ER brought despair rushing in.

"Why don't you hang out here for a few days and get your shit together. Spend some time with London. Schedule a visit with a counselor. Have some decent meals and get some sleep."

"Finish my laundry?"

"Excellent idea."

"What about Vanna? Can I see her?"

"One step at a time." Aiden moved to the small desk at the side of the kitchen and procured a card from a drawer. "You'll require several counseling sessions before you tackle that one." He held out the card. "Non-negotiable, Brandon. You want to clean up your mess, do it right."

"But you'll let me see London? Stay in this house with your kids? But stay away from Vanna? How does that make sense? Half of my problem is her."

"Exactly." Aiden lifted a brow. "You're depressed, angry as hell, and a complete fucking disaster. Dangerous around the kids? No. Dangerous to Savannah and her well-being? No doubt in my mind."

"But if I just—"

"No. If you care about her at all, you'll do this my way. She's worked too damn hard to sort out her own crap and focus on her education. She can't deal with yours too. No calls, no texts, no contact."

Brandon bowed his head, sucking in a long breath.

"Are you registering this? Do not fuck this up for my daughter, or I will end you."

The shock of the harsh tone attached to that final statement shook him. The man had been calm and level through everything, until this moment. He lifted his chin enough to take in the folded arms, the flat, grim set of the man's face, and he understood this wasn't an idle threat, but a clear warning that his grace period had expired.

"I refuse to resort to coddling or pretending or putting a fake rosy glow on the situation. This is all sorts of fucked up. I understand that more than you will ever know. Believe me, I'm doing you a huge favor by giving it to you straight, even if you don't appreciate it. Maybe one day you will."

"I'll do it your way," Brandon said, his voice barely a whisper. "I never meant to hurt her."

"Maybe not." Aiden's tone softened. "But you did."

"I'll leave her be. Thank you for being honest. And for taking me in. Again. You've always helped me."

"I've tried not to show favoritism, but I'm sure I've failed on many levels. Maybe I should have nixed the relationship between you and Vanna from the start."

"Why didn't you?"

"I couldn't bear to disappoint my daughter. My love for her clouds my judgment."

"You're a great dad. Don't let anyone tell you otherwise. Savannah is amazing, in so many ways."

"It's good you recognize it."

"I love her, Aiden. More than I've ever loved anyone, and it scares me," Brandon said. "The magnitude of everything buried me. Some days I couldn't manage to be what she needed." He raked his fingers through his hair. "Maybe it's stupid to think I can be a good father."

"Scared is a normal reaction to taking on the responsibility of a child." Aiden contemplated him. "Emotions run high, everyone has something to gain ... and they all have something to lose. All you can do is ride the wave and live it."

"And if I fail?"

"You won't if you commit from here." He tapped a finger over his heart. "Love isn't a logical equation to be solved. It's about feeling, about allowing yourself to love and to trust, and opening up to the possibilities." Aiden leveled a look at Brandon. "Children don't demand perfection. You'll make plenty of mistakes, but I guarantee you won't regret a single moment."

"You make balancing marriage, kids, and career seem effortless. I've never seen you and Emily fight."

"No, but we do. We get angry, sometimes we even hate each other, just a little. But then we talk it through and forgive each other." He shrugged. "I can't imagine life without Emily. I love her beyond reason, and I never have to pretend to be anyone other than who I am."

"With Tiffany it was different?" Brandon asked in a low voice.

"That woman is a firecracker. One of the main reasons the relationship failed was that we lacked communication."

"But you loved her."

"Without a doubt. She owns a piece of my heart. It's unavoidable; she's the mother of one of my children."

"That's forever," Brandon said softly. "And Emily?"

"My game-changer," he said. "It took us forever to get together. I suspected she was the one, but I wasn't ready to commit. Not long after we started dating, I knew I never wanted to let her go."

Brandon tipped his head back and closed his eyes. Thoughts of Savannnah were never far from the surface. Now the main questions were whether she was the elusive forever love, or the game-changer, and whether or not he had any chance of earning her forgiveness.

No matter the answer, he had plenty of hard work ahead before he even earned the chance to find out.

# Chapter 28

Her keys clanged against the dish as she dropped them in. She hung her coat before wandering into the living room and slumping on the couch.

"It went that well, huh?" Justin peered over the lid of his laptop before tapping at the keyboard. He flipped it closed and propped his ankle on the opposite knee, tucking his hands behind his head. "Tell me."

"Dating sucks." Vanna sighed deeply. "I broke it off."

"Why? You seemed to like him."

"Third date." Savannah twirled her hair around her fingertip. "I'm not ready for what's expected."

"Not sure that's a thing." Justin frowned.

"Tell that to Marco. He invited me to his place and got handsy in the car. It's like a switch flipped the minute he realized we'd hit the magic number. And to make it worse, he acted like I should be grateful he's interested."

"That's ridiculous. You're a beautiful, intelligent woman. He's the one who should be showing gratitude."

"Right. I'm such a catch. Having a six-month-old daughter puts the damper on a relationship in a hurry." Her eyes burned. "Why am I doing this again?"

Justin offered a faint smile. "You believe you need to move on or some such crap. There's an obvious answer, sweetheart."

Savannah wrinkled her nose as she swung a throw pillow at him. "He's not coming back." The familiar pain overtook her every time she thought about life without Brandon. She'd done what she needed to do and let him go, even if she drowned in an ocean of tears. Many nights she'd cried herself to sleep, but at some point, the pain would recede. Or so she hoped. "I'll be alone forever. Who wants to play Daddy to another guy's kid?"

"The right guy will jump at the chance to be with you and your adorable daughter." Justin leaned forward and caught her hands. "You're a long way from the alone forever scenario."

"Promise? Maybe we should make one of those pacts. If we're both single at thirty, we'll marry each other." The plan sounded ludicrous, even to her own ears. "Never mind. Some girl will snap you up long before you get to even And twenty-five. I'll be happy for you."

"You'll be swept off your feet long before me. But if it makes you feel better … it's a deal." Her friend pressed a kiss to her forehead. "In the meantime, your darling daughter has her Uncle Justin."

"She's a lucky girl." Her smile was gentle. The guy was terrific with London, and she appreciated the attention he lavished on her baby girl. But, she still wished her daughter had her father's love.

"It's not the same as having her daddy." Justin leaned in and reached for her hand. "You're still in love with him, honey. Give yourself time. Trying to fit someone else into that space isn't fair to anyone, especially your child."

"You know what's not fair?" Savannah pulled her hand free and straightened. "Promising to never leave, but running at the first opportunity. Not once, Justin," she said, as she raised her index finger, "but twice. Three times if you include the first break up."

"Savannah—"

"No! If he loved me, he'd never have left. If he loved me, he'd never have made assumptions. If he loved me, he'd never have accused me of cheating." She narrowed her eyes. "Why aren't you pissed off? He hates you too!"

"I love you, hon, but Brandon has a fair point. We spent the night together in your hotel room, in the same bed. Can't say I'd love hearing that about my girlfriend."

"That gives him the right to make accusations and check out of his daughter's life?" She bounced from her seat and stomped up the stairs and into her bedroom, throwing herself across the bed. It felt like a familiar position these days, hugging her pillow to her chest while her heart ached for a man who judged her. A man who made no apologies or bothered to see the baby girl he'd professed to love.

Justin appeared in her doorway. "Your dad is trying to reach you." He sat on the edge of her bed "I'm sorry. I hate being the instigator of this mess."

"The real problem is his lack of trust. You're my friend, and I refuse to give you up to make some guy happy." She sniffled.

"I'm not a fan of that plan either, but at least consider there's fault on all sides. I accept my behavior was inappropriate."

"I should make that call." She plucked her phone from Justin's fingers and waved him toward the door.

"You know I'm right." Justin gave her a stern look before he retreated down the hallway.

Vanna opened her laptop and made a video call to her dad. "Everything okay? Where's London?"

"Napping. I'll call you again when she's up, but I wanted to discuss this weekend," Aiden said.

"You can't bring London?" Her heart sank. "It'll be tight timing, but I'll come there."

"No, we'll bring her to you. It's something else, but there's no easy way to say this, so … Brandon is here."

"Here as in …?"

"Staying at the house."

She wrinkled her brow as she opened her mouth, then snapped it closed, unsure of what to say. Her brain refused to work, but she finally managed to ask, "How long?"

"He's been here a few days. Sorry I didn't mention it before, but I didn't want to upset you."

"Why is he there?"

"Long story. He's been spending time with London. He wants to drive her to New Haven."

She bit her lip, shaking her head. "Just like that. After all these months, he just waltzes in the door, and I'm expected to accommodate what he wants? Tell him no. Tell him to leave her alone."

"I'm sorry, but this ridiculous crap has gone on long enough." He steepled his hands under his chin. "Why did he walk away?"

She stared into the camera before dropping her chin and picking at her duvet. As he'd never questioned her before, she assumed Brandon had revealed the true nature of their fight. She was busted. "He told you."

"Uh-huh."

She wrapped a finger in her hair, tugging at it as she blinked hard. "I let him go. He didn't want to be there."

"I'm not so sure about that, honey. Regardless, he's here now." He massaged his temples. "I hate this part, but I'm going to ask, because I have no choice. Is there any valid legal reason to deny Brandon visitation with London?"

"No," she said softly. "He's her father."

"Then I can't and won't deny him access to his daughter."

"He's the one who questioned it in the first place."

"I understand that, but what you led him to believe wasn't right, nor was it fair. Not to Brandon and especially not to London. You can't deny either of them the right to build a relationship. But," he said softly, "you already know that."

"I'm sorry. It was such a mess. I thought he'd be happier without us."

"You two will sort it out." He met her gaze on-screen. "I have many regrets and made my own mistakes," he said. "I wasted so much time. Don't be like me, Vanna."

"I should take him back?"

"That's your decision, but you should work with Brandon, not against him. Find a suitable compromise allowing you both to be happy and be there for London."

"You're coming with him, right?"

He offered a faint smile. "As you are fond of reminding me, you're an adult."

She tacked on a silent *so act like one* to his statement. "I've disappointed you."

"I'd have no right to be, given my history. I'm proud of you. I love you. You've done your best in difficult circumstances, and I'm confident you'll figure it out and make the right choices."

"Have I, though?" Her dad's gentle words made her wonder.

"You've made mistakes, but it's not too late to do the right thing."

"I love you," she said, blowing him a kiss before they signed off.

Her phone buzzed. The text that appeared gave her an approximate arrival time for Brandon on Friday evening. How she would face him, she didn't know. What she would say, she had even less of a clue. What he would to say to her … that unknown caused her gut to clench and a tide of nausea to rise.

The moment of reckoning drew near, but there was nothing she could do to stop it.

⁓

"You're a hot mess." Justin stuffed his laptop into his bag as she checked her reflection. "Calm down."

"Just what I needed to hear." Savannah stared at the barely disguised dark circles under her eyes.

"Ahh, my sweet, beautiful girl. He'll weep when he lays eyes on you." Her friend kissed each cheek in turn. "I'm off. Best make myself scarce, or it'll cause friction."

Savannah nodded as she wrapped a strand of hair around her fingertip, appreciating how her friend volunteered to vacate without being asked.

"Justin?" She bowed her head. "The night at the hotel shouldn't have happened, even if we didn't do anything."

"I'm sorry it's caused trouble. We'll manage boundaries better in the future." Her friend hugged briefly before waggling his phone. "Call in case of emergency." Justin waved over his shoulder and strode down the front walk.

She shut the door, performing a last inspection in the mirror. Drops had reduced the red puffiness around her eyes, but they felt gritty, and her entire body trembled.

The soft rap made her jump. She closed her eyes, repeating her personal mantra to calm her thoughts before she shuffled toward the door.

A smile lit her face at the sight of her daughter. "Mi angelito." She claimed London from Brandon's arms. "I missed you." She peppered kisses on the girl's chubby cheeks as the baby let out a string of babble and wrapped her arms around Vanna's neck.

"Can I …?" Brandon motioned.

"Come in." She stepped back, her palms growing damp as his presence filled the hallway. Savannah hurried into the kitchen.

Brandon followed and set the diaper bag onto one of the stools at the counter. "The place looks good."

"Thanks." She couldn't bear to look at the sexy scruff on his face, knowing she was in imminent danger of giving in to her desire to wrap her arms around him. Savannah set the squirming baby on the floor, smiling as the little girl crawled toward the toy box in the corner of the attached family room. "She's happy to be free."

"She's not fond of the car seat." Brandon leaned on the counter.

"Can I offer you a drink?" Savannah rounded the island, desperate to create a physical barrier between them. She retrieved two sodas from the fridge, colliding with his chest as she turned.

One can slipped from her grasp as she froze and it hit the floor with a thunk. *Damn. The man moved like a jungle cat, sneaking up on me with barely a sound.* The hiss of coke escaping through the broken seal was almost imperceptible above the pounding of her heart.

Brandon's arm slid around her waist, drawing her closer so their faces were only inches apart. Heat radiated from him, warmth seeping through her light blouse, his sweet breath brushing her cheek. "I've missed you." His deep husky voice sent a quiver down her spine.

She lifted her chin, daring to look into his sad gray eyes. His proximity disarmed her, bringing every buried longing to the surface. After these months of being alone, having him say those words set loose a flood of emotions. Half of her wanted to slap him, the other longed to nestle against him and beg forgiveness.

Savannah flattened a palm against his chest, taking a large backward step, breaking his hold. *Distance. Space. A moment to gather my wits and thoughts.* She retreated, one slow step at a time, dipping her head to allow her curtain of hair to obscure her expression, even as she kept a wary eye on him.

Brandon tipped his head and shoved his hands half-way into his pockets, fidgeting and scuffing one foot across the floor. "Why did you cut me out?"

Savannah swayed, reaching out with one hand to steady herself. She closed her eyes, giving the slightest shake of her head. *You didn't want her. Or me.*

"Is London my daughter?"

The words plunged like a dagger into her heart. "Don't you know?"

"You never answered my question." His voice grew firm, little wisps of anger curling around the words.

"Do you even care? You've had one foot out the door our entire relationship. You couldn't wait to leave and be free of the burden."

"Not true." Brandon scrubbed a hand through his hair. "You said she wasn't mine."

"Wrong, asshole. You assumed." Her face flushed and heated. "You heard what you expected."

"Can you imagine how I—"

"Don't even. I absolved you. Allowed you to get on with your precious career. You didn't want her or me. You made that damn clear. Now you act like I've wronged you?" She turned, heading toward the living room. "Why did you bother?"

The hand descending onto her arm brought her to an abrupt halt. "Don't you dare run away." Brandon swung her around.

"But it's okay for you?" Savannah dealt him a resounding slap across the cheek, her palm stinging as he grabbed her wrists, pinning them to her sides. "*Don't* manhandle me."

"Answer the damn question."

Savannah twisted, leveraging her body weight to break his hold, simultaneously raising her knee, making a solid connection with his groin.

"Ooof." Brandon doubled over and dropped to his knees, groaning as he curled up on the floor.

Without a backward glance, she stalked away, rubbing at her wrists. "It's okay," she whispered, kneeling in front of the wide-eyed baby girl and soothing her with her favorite bear.

Brandon grimaced as he dragged himself to his feet, only to lower himself gingerly onto the couch. "This is how it's going to go?" He shifted positions as he rubbed at his reddened cheek.

"You shouldn't have grabbed me." She shot him a scathing look. "I didn't sleep with Justin, but you refuse to believe me. Who even told you that?"

"It's not important."

"It is to me. A fabricated imaginary scenario …" She wrinkled her brow, a vague remembrance of a comment he'd made during their fight surfacing. "Oh." She bit her lip. "Gray? Or Piper?"

He leaned forward, resting his elbows on his knees as he rubbed open hands over his face.

"Now who's avoiding the question?" She rose to her feet, scooping up her daughter. Disappointment and pain swirled through her. He'd allowed their relationship to be poisoned.

She tucked London onto her hip and went to search for a bottle in the fridge, eyeing the sticky puddle oozing across her kitchen floor.

"I'll clean up." Brandon ripped paper towels from the roll on the counter. He sank to his knees, dabbing ineffectually at the mess. "I'm sorry," he said in a low voice. "They messed with my head."

Savannah closed her eyes, clamping her teeth onto her lower lip. Did he really believe his pathetic apology would help? If anything, the admission made his betrayal even more painful. She'd made no secret about her issues with Gray. The man had even witnessed the abuse firsthand.

"Can you say something? Please?"

"How quickly you forget."

Brandon stared at her, not moving a muscle. "Forget what?"

"How he treated me? He's an abusive creep."

"I know," he said softly. "He won't hurt you again. I promise you that."

"Except he already did."

"What?" Brandon rose to his feet in one smooth motion, his jaw clenching. "When?" His hands curled into fists.

"The pain he caused this time was far worse than a few bruises. At least those healed and faded. His lies and deceit will leave permanent scars. Only you can't see them."

Brandon massaged his temples, his shoulders sagging as he hunched forward, dropping his head into his hands. "I'm an idiot." He lifted his chin. "That's why he's with Piper?"

"Who cares?" Savannah had only ever seen the couple together from afar, and she had no way of knowing Gray's intentions. "Piper's a treacherous two-faced little viper with her own agenda. They deserve each other."

"Where does that leave us?"

"With a daughter who needs two parents. Assuming you accept she's yours. You can get DNA testing if you'd like."

"No. I believe you. I'm in … or back in? If you'll allow me to see her. I made a huge mistake, but I won't run, ever again."

"For London's sake, I hope that's true."

"It is. What about you?"

"Don't worry about me. We'll work out a visitation schedule. London stays with Dad and Emily quite often."

"So, you want me to …?" Brandon nodded. "Got it." He seemed fixated on the sweater Justin had left draped over one of the chairs. "He'll be back soon."

"He's staying with a friend. You can sleep in the guest room. If you want. Or not." This tense dance with Brandon was sapping the last of her energy.

"I'll stay. We have more to discuss." He rubbed at the stubble on his jaw, the bloodshot eyes and haggard appearance of his face becoming more apparent.

"London is almost ready for her afternoon nap. I'll feed her, and then I have a paper to finish."

"I'll take care of baby girl. Come on, sunshine." Brandon accepted London and her bottle, cradling her against his shoulder.

"Daaaaa." London lifted her head, patting at his face.

Brandon nibbled at her fingertips, earning a giggle and grin.

Savannah opened her laptop, peering from the corner of her eye as the man carried his daughter upstairs. A few moments later, soft humming drifted through the air, followed by the familiar and slightly magical Spanish lullaby.

An involuntary flicker of hope blossomed in her heart, but she shut it down. Loving this man spelled danger, and she wasn't sure she'd survive him leaving again. He'd broken promises before.

Silence fell, piquing her curiosity. She tiptoed up the stairs and peered into her bedroom. Brandon had curled up on her bed with London beside him. He'd created a semi-circle of pillows, keeping her safely in the middle of the king-sized bed. Both were sound asleep.

The growing bond between father and daughter showed. Brandon had been proven to be loving and gentle with the baby girl from the first moment. Savannah hoped this visit signaled a significant change. That he'd accepted London as his daughter and a permanent part of his life.

# CHAPTER 29

## *Brandon*

BRANDON STARED AT THE GUEST room ceiling, his conversation with Savannah running in an endless loop. The woman pushed him away, but her magnetic pull drew him in, leaving him uncertain and unbalanced. On edge.

*What did she want? Did she even know?*

The evening had passed uneventfully, Savannah preoccupied with dinner, finishing the essay due on Monday, and spending time with her daughter.

He'd tried to help, but she'd been adamant on doing much of it herself. Exerting her independence? Proving to him she didn't need a man at her side? Or was she simply unwilling to let him in?

He didn't have a clue. Whatever her reasons, the easy and comfortable way they'd related to each other had disappeared. Now their interactions seemed stiff and formal. *Forced.*

A small muffled sound carried through the silent house. He slid from the bed, the hardwood cold against his feet as he moved quietly down the hallway to the master bedroom. "Savannah?" he whispered, tapping on her door as he peered into the room. "Are you …?"

"Go back to bed." Her voice sounded choked, the following sniffle giving her away.

He crossed the room and perched on the edge of the bed, plucking a tissue from the box on the bedside table. "What's the matter, sweetheart?"

Vanna dabbed at her eyes. "Embarrassing," she muttered, curling into a ball.

"Why?" He smoothed her hair away from her face. "It's just me."

The tiniest scoff escaped as she buried her face into the pillow. "You hate it when I'm emotional."

Brandon wondered how she'd gotten that impression. Maybe it didn't matter. *I'd caused her endless pain.* He closed his eyes, thinking of the recent hours spent with his new therapist. How she'd encouraged him to show his vulnerable side. To quit hiding from those closest to him.

"I'm sad too." After a brief hesitation, he brushed his fingertips over her silky hair. When she didn't push him away, he stretched out on the bed beside her, looping an arm over her shoulder. The magnitude of his mistakes and the subsequent damage to this precious woman crept over him. Those hidden scars he'd help create.

"I'm sorry." He stroked her hair, hoping the tension would leave her body. "I've been a complete idiot. How do I make it up to you?" He pressed his face into the crook of her neck.

"Commit to being a father to London. Stop worrying about me."

"But I do worry." He tightened his embrace, craving the closeness after the long months apart. "It's important to me that you're okay. That we get past this. That …" *There are so many things I wish you'd say. Like you missed me, even if only a little. Or you forgive me for overreacting and being crazy jealous.* The last wish he had, the words he wanted to hear, they were too much to ask. He'd keep his final wish silent, but close to his heart.

"Do we have to talk? Can't we just …" She burrowed deeper under the covers.

"Mmmhmm." He held her, resisting the urge to delve into the reasons for her tears. Stopping himself from saying anything that might upset her further or get him kicked out of her room.

Eventually, her breathing deepened. The cool night air wafted across his skin, but he didn't dare move for fear of waking her. Finally, his eyelids drooped and slid shut.

⌒

He awoke early the next morning with a blanket draped over him. Sometime in the night, Savannah had been up, tucking London into the space created between them. As he lifted himself from the mattress, the little girl opened her dark eyes, reaching out to him.

"Good morning," he whispered, cuddling her against his bare chest.

Savannah slept on, looking peaceful with her blonde hair fanned across her pillow. Her eyelids twitched, an expression fleeting crossing her face.

He hoped whatever the dream, it was a sweet one.

Brandon tiptoed from the room, pulling the door closed before carrying London downstairs. "Let's feed you breakfast." He moved around the kitchen, easily finding everything he needed before settling into a chair overlooking the backyard.

This house had a cozy, family feel to it. Savannah had chosen her decor with care, leaving it uncluttered, but homey and inviting. Brandon loved being here, despite the upheaval in the current vista of their relationship.

London had almost finished her bottle when the doorbell rang, jolting him out of his peaceful musings.

Brandon tucked London's blanket around her and cradled her against his chest as he opened the door. "Can I help you?" He eyed the blond man standing on the front steps holding two coffee cups and a paper sack recognizable as being from the local bistro.

"You're not Justin." The younger man took a step back, fixated on the bundle in Brandon's arms. "How many guys is she dating?" he muttered.

A flicker of anger raced through Brandon. *How many guys?* That was an interesting question.

"Who is it?" Vanna said as she arrived, dressed in an oversized sweatshirt and sweatpants, her hair adorably tousled. "What are you doing here, Marco?" She ducked around Brandon, planting herself between him and the interloper.

"I brought a peace offering to apologize for the other night, but I see you're"—he cleared his throat—"busy."

"I've got this, Brandon." Vanna waved a hand, dismissing him.

Brandon narrowed his eyes at Marco, but retreated to the living room, straining his ears to hear the conversation.

"Is that your baby daddy? I thought he was out of the picture." Marco asked in a petulant tone. "Is that why you wouldn't—"

"It's none of ..."

London erupted into tears, squirming and fussing, drowning out the conversation.

Brandon swayed and shushed the baby, recognizing the odor emanating from the girl. "You need a change." He carried her upstairs and placed her on the change table. "It's okay, sunshine. Daddy will have you cleaned up in no time."

Savannah appeared in the doorway. "Sorry. I don't know what that was about."

"No?" Brandon focused on securely fastening the diaper. "Some guy shows up on your doorstep first thing in the morning, full of apologies? Seems pretty clear, Savannah. How long have you been seeing him?"

"I'm not." She folded her arms across her chest, her expression turning stony. "Not that it's your business. You called me a tramp and abandoned your daughter."

He scoffed, the flicker of anger re-emerging. "You led me to believe London wasn't mine. After you spent the night with Justin in a hotel room."

"Nothing happened. But you don't care. I'm sorry. I'm sorry. I'm sorry," she said, folding her arms over her chest. "But that's not good enough, is it?"

He shook his head. Not because it wasn't good enough, but because he wished she'd fought like this months ago. That she'd stayed long enough for them to work it out. And … that he'd had enough sense to pursue her.

"Right," she whispered. "You wanted out, so you found a way to blame me." She brushed each eye with the back of her hand. "And now, months later, you show up. Why?" A tear trickled down her cheek.

"I never wanted out." He pressed his palms onto the change table on either side of London, bowing his head. "These last months have been awful. I've missed both of you. Yeah, I'm practically insane with jealousy over Justin. I hate he lives here. But even worse is you allowing that Marco guy to …" The thought made him cringe.

"You don't date?" Defiance reflected in her narrowed eyes and grimly set lips. "You haven't seen anyone since you left?"

"Maybe I should." Retaliating based on his newly learned knowledge that Savannah was seeing and perhaps sleeping with other men was tempting. Maybe he'd harbored hope for their relationship for too long, but pursuing relationships required time and energy; two things in short supply. "Then maybe I'll get over you," he muttered.

Savannah sniffled, but she opened the dresser drawer, digging into the pile of clothing. "It's cold outside. Better dress her in something warm." She set a small stack of clothing within his reach before wandering to stare out the window.

Brandon took his time dressing the baby girl before he cradled her against his chest. "This is getting us nowhere. You don't want me here."

"So, that's it? Ready to run when things get tough? 'Cause that's what you do." She scoffed as she spun and stomped from the room, her footsteps echoing on the stairs.

"Impossible woman," he muttered. With London in his arms, he followed her tracks into the living room, releasing his squirming daughter. "I'm here, damn it. Quit pushing me away."

She skirted the counter, resting her hands on the stone island.

"Talk to me." He rubbed a hand through his hair as she bowed her head, her hair falling forward, hiding her expression.

"I want to believe you're here for the right reasons," she whispered. "I'm trying to keep it together, but it's all coming apart."

"Hey." He circled the counter in three strides. Brandon wrapped her in his arms, pulling her close. "Can we find a way to get past this? I'm sorry for doubting you. I never meant for it to come out like that or create this huge rift. But you left me hanging. I needed for you to say it wasn't true."

"You chose to believe the worst." She pressed a hand to her chest. "That I lied about something so … life altering." Her voice dropped. "You broke my heart."

Brandon closed his eyes, searching for the right thing to say. For the right thing to do. He sank to his knees, wrapping his arms around her slim hips as he rested his forehead against her navel. "I've made huge mistakes. But I love you. Please, please forgive me. Maybe I don't deserve another chance, but I'm begging for one."

Savannah brushed her fingers through his hair, her other hand curling around the nape of his neck. "Is this something you want, with me? You can be London's father even if we aren't together."

"I want our family." He tipped his head, studying her expression. "Remember how it was those first months after London was born? Or our vacation in the vineyard? Our life could be amazing."

"Those are the rosy parts. The happy bits. What about the fights? The breakups? The times you left?" She pried free from his grip. "I can't afford to fall apart. London depends on me."

"You don't have to carry the burden alone." He pushed to his feet, reaching for her. "I'm here."

"Are you? For how long?" Her eyes shimmered as she stepped back, wrapping her arms around herself. "Who do I count on? The man who doesn't have a clue what love or commitment or family even means?"

"There's no way to win," he muttered as he paced back and forth. "You've made up your mind."

"I'm not a possession to be won or lost. And I don't see what's changed from three months ago, except you've decided you want us. Until we hit a rough patch, and you'll make it my fault and leave all over again."

"Or you'll make me go." He glowered at her. "Why don't I save you the trouble?" Brandon spun and stalked to the guest room, tossed his few belongings into the bag, and grabbed the car keys and his wallet. He refused to look at her as he charged down the stairs and exited, slamming the door behind him.

Brandon slung the bag into the back and slid into the leather seat. The engine purred to life at the touch of a button. "Fuck." He pounded his clenched fist on the dashboard. "What are you doing?" He draped himself over the wheel, his eyes burning with unshed tears. A sick feeling grew inside of him. "Running away like a stupid coward," he whispered. *Running. Always running.*

If he left now, there'd be no return. His defining moment was now. The moment he became his father or learned to be a better man. The moment he made a decision that would govern the rest of his life and hers. *And London's.* He cut the engine and retraced his steps to the front door. Silence met him as he stepped inside the house.

Savannah stood in the living room, cradling London against her shoulder, rocking from side to side. "Forget something?" she asked in a low flat voice.

He crossed the floor in slow measured steps to wrap his arms around them both, sucking in a breath at her sob. "You and London are everything. I love you both, so much. Please don't make me leave."

She buried her face against his chest, one arm curling around his back, shoulders shaking as she cried.

Brandon pressed a kiss to her temple, rocking them both in his arms. His heart told him he'd made the right choice. Time to stop fighting the inevitable and find a way to make this work, or he'd regret it forever. "Tell me how to make this right, because I love you."

～

Brandon yawned as he trudged downstairs with London cuddled against his chest. "Hungry, sunshine?"

She crammed a fist into her mouth, sucking at her fingers as she blinked her big brown eyes.

"Your mom does that same thing with her eyes. Between you and me, it gets me every time." He rested his cheek against the baby's hair, swaying on his feet as he popped the bottle in the warmer. "Daddy needs coffee." One press of a button and the coffee maker whirred to life.

Brandon turned to stare through the wall of glass into the back yard. A small patch of early morning sun filtered through the clouds like a beacon. He remembered the day they'd chosen this house; how bright their future had seemed.

The buzzing timer combined with London's low whine reminded him she needed to eat. He settled in the adjoining sunroom, enjoying the peace and quiet with his daughter. The girl twirled a lock of her hair with a tiny hand as she observed him. "How will I go home? I'm going to miss you." His heart sank at the thought he wouldn't see her until the next weekend when Vanna made the trip to Boston.

"Morning." Justin appeared, rubbing a hand through his hair as he moved into the kitchen, pouring a steaming cup of coffee.

"I thought you were at a friend's place."

The other man shrugged as he wandered into the sunroom and dropped into one of the overstuffed chairs. "I planned to be."

"You're checking up on Vanna?"

"Why would I? She's a grown woman."

They stared at each other, neither blinking.

"This is stupid." Justin emitted a low humorless laugh. "There's no competition, except in your deluded mind." His lips settled into a grim line. "Are you planning to stick this time?"

Brandon adjusted London, holding her against his shoulder as he rubbed her back. "I'm not going anywhere." He pressed a kiss to his daughter's downy head. "I'll be the best daddy to my little ray of sunshine."

Justin raised his brow. "Such a familiar tune. If you don't follow through …"

"Living without them is impossible."

"What does Savannah say?"

"Take it slow. I have much atonement and groveling ahead. The distance doesn't make it any easier," he said. "But in less than two months Vanna returns to Boston for the summer."

"Life, four months at a time." Justin nodded. "You knew it wouldn't be easy."

He acknowledged the comment with a lift of his shoulder, more focused on his immediate concerns with this man. "She leans on you. Confides in you. The first rush carries you away, but when it fades, there has to be more. You have the *more* with her."

"Blind idiot." Justin scoffed. "Why are you here if you don't think you have it?"

"Hope."

A contemplative look appeared on Justin's face. He tilted his head and studied Brandon.

The need to break the silence grew. Last night, with Savannah in his arms, he'd felt so sure about everything. Now, with her best friend staring him down, his certainty crumbled.

"What the hell does that even mean?" Justin asked. "You hope you love her?"

Brandon sank his teeth into his bottom lip, dropping his head, the small tremble rippling through his body betraying him. How could he share his doubts and fears? Especially with this man. "The hope is she'll forgive me. That we have enough love to make this work."

Justin nodded slowly, tapping one finger on his knee; a constant steady beat.

Brandon dragged in a breath. "I love her, Justin. She's changed my entire world. But my mother is on her fifth divorce. I've seen few long-term happy relationships. I'm not sure I know how to be what she needs." Brandon looked at the sleeping baby in his arms. "Maybe you're the better man. You know how to be part of a happy family."

"I had the good fortune of two incredible and loving parents, it's true." The younger man met Brandon's gaze without flinching. "You view me as a threat, but I'm not," he said softly. "The power to give Savannah the happiness she deserves and the stability she craves rests with you. Be there. Show her you love and trust her. The happy family will follow."

Happiness. Stability. *Lifetime commitment.* The words made his pulse race and he broke out in a cold sweat, shivering.

"It scares the shit out of you." Justin's eyes narrowed. "It's all over you, which means she smells it. Know this, Brandon. Vanna is extraordinary. A grown woman who needs an emotionally mature man, not an overgrown man-child. Her needs pretty much eliminate most guys my age from the competition. Does it eliminate you too?"

He shook his head.

"I see how you look at her. How you look at London. You have it in you to give her everything," Justin said softly. "Get it together. If you hurt her again, you will receive a severe ass-kicking."

"You'd have plenty of help with that." He scowled. "But what about that tool, Marco?"

"Zero threat." Justin shook his head. "He means nothing. In fact, he blew it before the end of the third date." He quirked a brow. "She's been unsuccessful in reclaiming her heart."

Brandon's own heart thudded as he processed the information.

"Don't blow your final chance." The man glanced toward the stairs as the floorboards upstairs creaked. "If you're giving it another go with Vanna, I'll find another place to live. It pains me that my lack of judgment caused so many issues in your relationship. I'm sorry for my part in this mess."

"And I'm sorry for being a stupid ass." Brandon emitted a deep sigh. "You've been good to Vanna, so please don't move on my account. If she wants you here, it won't interfere in our relationship."

"Finally."

Brandon didn't miss the eye roll and exasperated look on Justin's face. "Yeah, I deserve that."

"You sure do, but I get it. You love her, and I'm the interfering ex-boyfriend. Remember I've been her friend since play school. Admittedly, I have deep feelings for her, but not the kind you need to worry about." Justin rose and stretched at the sound of footsteps on the stairs. "But I will return to my place in the coach house."

"Justin. You're home." Vanna shot looks between the two men. "My dad asked for you to call him." She extended her phone toward Brandon.

Brandon accepted it, transferring the sleeping baby into her arms. He wandered up the stairs to Vanna's room as he dialed.

"Getting it together?" Aiden asked.

"Checking up on me?" He closed the door with a soft click.

"I needed to see what's up for today."

"Me getting my head sorted as I drive home. I need to discuss work with Dr. Kavanagh."

"Stay in New Haven until the end of the week. The work discussion can happen tomorrow over video chat."

"I'd have to see if Vanna … Never mind. You already discussed it with her. And Will, naturally."

"Smart boy." Aiden let out a low laugh before his voice turned serious. "You two are making progress."

He scrubbed at his jaw. "It'll take time."

"Everything worthwhile does."

"Thanks, Aiden." Brandon sank onto the edge of the bed. "You've had my back, but I have no way of repaying you."

"Wrong. Be good to my daughter. Make her happy, and take care of your baby girl. That's your ticket to redemption."

"You have my word."

"I'll hold you to it."

Brandon said goodbye, taking a moment to gather his thoughts. Time to make amends and prove his commitment. With any luck, he'd earn the happy family.

# CHAPTER 30

## *Savannah*

ONDAY MORNING ARRIVED TOO SOON, with a full day of classes scheduled.

Savannah kissed Brandon's cheek before tucking a gurgling, smiling London into bed with him. "She's fed and changed. Bottles are prepped and in the fridge, and—" Her words were cut short by his mouth covering hers, his warm hand tangling in her hair.

"I know her routine, sweetie," he said as he came up for air. "Study hard. We'll be fine." His lips met hers again.

She entwined her fingers into his hair, longing to crawl into the cozy bed with them. To remain wrapped in the cocoon and keep the real world at bay.

"Vanna. We'll be late." Justin's voice carried up the stairs.

"Sorry," she whispered, pressing her forehead against his.

Brandon stroked her cheek with his thumb, before his smile widened. "Go. Learn lots." He patted her butt.

"Be good for Daddy." She kissed her daughter's cheek before waving and dashing down the stairs and then following Justin to the car.

"What?" she asked after silence had reigned for several minutes.

"Nothing." A sly grin appeared. "It seems you two have made up," he said with a snicker, "for lost time."

The burn crept up her neck, her cheeks reddening. "What do you know? You were out half the night."

"And why, I wonder?" Justin chuckled.

"Shut up," she muttered, but her lips twitched. "But thank you."

"Anytime."

She maneuvered the car into a parking spot and they hurried toward their lecture hall.

"Chai latte?" Justin handed her his jacket as they reached the doors.

"Yup. Thanks." She entered the classroom and draped Justin's coat over his usual seat beside hers. As she worked her laptop free from her bag, someone dropped into the chair, their backpack hitting the floor with a thump. "That was quick." But she soon realized it wasn't Justin. "That seat is taken."

"By the invisible man?" Marco squinted.

"So funny." Savannah combed her fingers through her hair. "What do you want?"

"An explanation." The blond man folded his arms across his chest. "You never answered my question. I thought we were getting somewhere with our relationship and then that guy appears out of nowhere."

"That guy is London's father."

"So I gathered, but you said it was over," Marco muttered. "Yet he answered your door, early in the morning, half-naked. Did you sleep with him?"

"Is that your business?" Savannah smothered a snort. Justin had earned leeway on the topic, but this man had no right to comment or inquire. "You're not my boyfriend."

"I suppose not, but that sounds like a yes." Marco bowed his head. "I swear I felt a connection, but you pushed me away. I apologized for the other night, but you didn't want to hear it."

"I heard, but acting like I owed you something made it come across as insincere. For future reference, third date isn't synonymous with feel me up and try to take me to bed."

He opened his mouth, but snapped it closed again. Then he said, "Umm, sorry? I thought you were"—he lifted his hands in a helpless shrug—"into it."

Savannah shifted to face him. "Well, I wasn't. And, for the record, I never lied. I didn't anticipate Brandon showing up, but he did." She didn't know how to explain the convoluted situation, or the current condition of her heart. Nor did she owe it to Marco. They'd only gone on two-and-a-half dates.

"Do you love him?"

"He wants to give our relationship another chance."

Marco met her gaze. "And what do you want?"

"If I don't try, I'll regret it. I really do love him," she said softly. "Besides, I'm a complicated mess. I have a baby to consider in every decision. No guy in his right mind would get involved with me."

"You're amazing, but I don't want to be your fallback position." He picked up his bag. "I'm sorry for misreading the situation. I hope it works out with Brandon."

"Thanks." She bit her lip as Marco selected a seat several rows away. He seemed like a nice guy, and she felt bad, but this weekend convinced her another attempt with Brandon was worthwhile. The feelings, the attraction, the pure adrenaline rush she felt with the man was still there, and it felt like there was more, untapped, lingering just beneath the surface. If only he'd allow her all the way in.

He'd accepted her decisions in order to make her happy. Made an impassioned plea to stay. That had to mean something. Yet, even as they dove into making up, many of the underlying issues remained unvoiced. This weekend didn't eliminate her fears. This could end badly.

And she needed to own up to her part in this disaster. Brandon had made huge mistakes, but she'd misled him. She understood the seriousness of her error. Of the damage she'd caused by depriving London and Brandon of their precious father-daughter bond. If he wanted to spend time with his daughter, she'd facilitate it. Maybe his change of heart boded good things for their future as a couple.

Justin slid into the seat beside her, handing her a cup. He tilted his head. "Tell me," he whispered.

"I've been away for less than half an hour, but I miss them." Tears burned behind her eyes. "I've made such a mess. If I'd taken the time to talk to him, we wouldn't be here. I accused him of running, but he's right. I pushed too hard. I forced my decisions onto him." She pressed the back of her hand against her mouth. "There's so much we haven't resolved."

"He's ten minutes away." Her friend squeezed her arm. "Go home. Spend some time with your family. Sort this out." He smiled faintly. "Ask forgiveness."

Vanna tucked her laptop into her bag, giving Justin a grateful smile. "Take notes?" At his nod, she dashed for the door, retracing her steps to the parking lot.

Within a few minutes, she'd made the return trip. She stepped inside, the first sounds reaching her ears being London's delightful laugh and the clatter of blocks.

"Help me build another tower?" Brandon asked London.

Savannah peeked around the corner, her smile widening at the sight of the grown man sitting cross-legged on the floor with the little girl balanced in front of him.

He pointed to a block. "Blue one next?" He assisted her in balancing it on top of a red one. "Great. How about the yellow one?"

The two repeated the procedure until they had six colorful blocks stacked, and then London swiped at it with a chubby hand, squealing in delight and kicking her feet as it toppled.

"All fall down." He lifted his daughter, laying back and suspending her in the air over his head. "Maybe we should get out of the house." Brandon brought her down, peppering her cheeks with kisses, making exaggerated kissy noises. "I bet you'd like that, wouldn't you, sunshine?"

"Careful, or you'll wear her breakfast."

His eyes widened. "Damn. You startled me. Why aren't you at school?" He rose from the floor, tucking London on his hip.

She shook her head as she set her backpack on the chair, moving to cuddle against him, slipping one arm around his waist and the other around their daughter. "You're good with her."

He rubbed her back. "It's sunny, so London and I were planning to take a walk. Are you done for the day?"

"Yes. Let me grab a couple of things and we'll go."

"I'll change her while you get ready."

Savannah moved efficiently, topping up the baby supplies in the small pack she kept handy for outings. She grinned when Brandon reappeared with the baby snuggled securely against him in the wrap. "You wear it well."

"You know it." He did a slow turn, modeling his dad look for her.

"Adorable. Here." She made a quick adjustment to one of the ties before slinging the pack over her shoulder. "Perfect."

Brandon captured her hand, holding it firmly in his as they strolled down the tree-lined street. "You skipped class."

"I needed to be here."

"What's on your mind?"

"Us," she said in an even voice. "Mostly just wishing we could redo that unfortunate day. I overreacted, and it cost us far too much." She tugged at him, pulling him to a halt. Looking him in the eye was difficult, but she forced herself to do it anyway. "I made decisions without considering how they affected you, and I'm sorry. I just don't know what else I could have done."

"What decisions?" He kept hold of her hand, his voice level and calm.

"I vetoed terminating or putting her up for adoption, both of which you would have preferred. I became a burden, forcing a responsibility onto you. One you never wanted or even agreed to."

"Flip that around."

She stared at him, wide-eyed.

"What if I'd forced my choices onto you? Coerced you to undergo a medical procedure or into giving up your child to avoid responsibility? Isn't that imposing my will onto you?"

She nodded slowly, finding no argument with his logic.

"If I had insisted on either, it would have a profound effect on you, your future, everything in your life from that moment forward. Who knows what regrets that would have brought? Not only for you, but for me." He cupped her cheek in his palm. "I made my own choices. Don't assume you coerced me, or trapped me, or that I consider our child to be a horrible burden. She most certainly isn't. I never thought that for a single minute."

"Then why?"

"Why run?" He rubbed a hand through his hair. "Ryan said something about being there one-hundred-percent, and I allowed the doubts to creep in."

"My Uncle Ryan told you to go?" *Planted doubts in his head?*

"No." His eyes widened. "Oh, sweetie. He never told me to leave. Never blame anyone for my actions but me. The failings are mine alone." He sucked in a breath. "I choose to be here, but you need me less than I need you. Your family surrounded you like your own personal fortress. What difference would it make to anyone if I disappeared entirely?"

"Every difference in the world. London needs you. And so do I." Her heart broke at the thought he'd ever felt this way. "Did I do that? Make you feel unneeded?"

"I did it to myself." His lips tugged downward. "Ridiculous jealousy over Justin, resenting your Dad and Emily for stepping in and backing you from that first moment, fearing the posse of scary uncles … my own good-for-nothing father and alcoholic mother … my whole messed up life. What would either of you need me for? I thought I had nothing to give. Then someone made me realize, maybe I do." His gaze met hers, a gentle smile appearing. "I can love her. I can love you. I can be thankful for arriving in a place I never dreamed possible. When the time is right, maybe I'll achieve the exalted level of trophy husband."

Her pulse raced, her knees trembling. This felt like a previously unmentioned or unacknowledged level of commitment; a promise for their future.

"I'm grateful you refused to consider the other options. Never having known my sunshine is impossible to consider."

"I love you," she whispered, pulling his head down. Her doubts and fears washed away as she clung to him, savoring each gentle kiss they shared. The vulnerability he'd shown told her this was real. This man was worth fighting for, every single moment, of every single day.

"Where do we go from here?" she asked. "Should I move back to Boston?"

"No. We finish what we started. Otherwise, there will be regrets. Maybe not today, or tomorrow, but eventually, it would get between us." He slung an arm around her, drawing her close as he steered her toward the park, his other arm curled protectively around their daughter. "We need to make our sacrifices now. Like my Fellowship. It means a longer separation, but I'll dive back in and work my ass off to make the most of it. If I fail, it won't be for lack of effort."

"And us?"

"Four months at a time, right? One day, not too far into the future, we'll be together as a proper family. It'll take commitment and communication, but I believe we'll make it work. Are you in?"

"One-hundred-percent in."

"It won't be easy."

"I'm still in." She stopped him again, stretching to seal it with a kiss.

"I was hoping you'd say that." A thoughtful look appeared on his face.

"What?"

"Nothing." He released her hand as they arrived at the park. "London has been patient, so we should let her have playtime before her nap."

Vanna helped extract the baby from the wrap. This felt just like it should. Her. Brandon. Their daughter. A happy little family, enjoying time together at the park. Like everything would be okay after all. She could only hope it would last.

# CHAPTER 31

## Brandon

BRANDON RUBBED HIS JAW AS he contemplated the tray of sparkling rings. He picked one, holding it up to the light. The tag caught his eye, causing a streak of panic.

"She'd love a rock like that." Nate stole it from Brandon's fingertips.

"I bet." Brandon shuttered his doubts from the observant eyes of the woman behind the counter. "It needs to be special."

"That one is very special and lovely," she said. "Any woman would wear it proudly."

"I'll think it over," Brandon said. "Thanks for your help."

The sales associate nodded and tucked the tray into the glass display case.

"Aiden has a diamond guy," Nate said in a low voice as they exited onto the street.

"How do I start that conversation? Marriage is a huge step."

"You've been torturing yourself ever since you reconciled. Three months of unnecessary self-inflicted pain." His friend scrutinized him. "Quit stalling. Grow a pair and ask her."

"And if she laughs in my face?"

"She'd never." His friend shook his head. "And hey, marriage is a small thing compared to making babies."

"Two very different things, man." Brandon didn't know how to express his doubts. What if he couldn't persuade Savannah to marry him? It had been a topic he'd hinted at, but never had the courage to broach outright. "It needs to be perfect and," he said as he shot a look toward Nate, daring him to poke fun at his words, "romantic." *And accompanied by a miracle to make her say yes.*

"Hell yeah, it does." Nate patted his shoulder. "Make it memorable. My sister gushes over the proposal from my brother-in-law. Lilly always says it's something a girl never forgets." He snickered. "Do it wrong and you'll end up like my idiot cousin."

"How's that?"

"No matter how small and insignificant the disagreement, his wife brings up his sad and poorly planned proposal."

"Thanks. That makes me feel loads better."

"No problemo. Hey, she said yes in the end, if it's any consolation."

Brandon scowled, but his annoyance faded as he considered the challenge. He tapped a finger against pursed lips, contemplating the advice Ryan received before he proposed to Kaari. Romantic. Private. Special. Never in front of a room full of people. Never in a spot where the pressure could cause embarrassment and ruin the moment.

"Aiden proposed to Emily in Boston. Ryan took Kaari to a fancy hotel during a ski vacation. Tom and Joel proposed to their wives at the Vineyard because …" He frowned as the idea formed. "We've had some great times at the beach house."

Nate grinned. "Now you're on to something."

"Except it'll be Christmas by the time I pay for a ring." A vision of the dollar signs on the dream ring danced through his mind. "Not this one either, but Christmas five years from now. Never mind. I can't do it."

"Wuss. Ask Aiden and it'll be a whole lot sooner," Nate said under his breath. "If I ever find the right girl, he's the guy I'd ask."

"He's already done so much for me. For Mia."

"Which should make it easy. Hey, call her Uncle Ryan and ask him."

"Very funny." After the debacle on the ski trip, and Brandon's confession about Ryan scaring the crap out of him, Nate loved to remind him, often inserting the man's name into random conversation.

"Just trying to help." Nate glanced at his watch. "We'd better head to the court if we're gonna play ball."

By the time they trekked to the park, both Aiden and Will had arrived and were warming up.

"About time you ladies showed. Thought you were afraid of getting your asses kicked." Will dribbled the ball across the court. "Teams? Aiden and I versus you two?" He waved a finger at them.

"Uh-uh." Nate narrowed his eyes. "You two speak in secret code. Better split you up."

Aiden laughed. "All right. Brandon, you're with me. Let's play."

They moved to their spots, which was a well-rehearsed drill, as they'd played on a regular basis all summer.

Within a few minutes of play, Brandon was wiping his forearm across his forehead, catching the droplets of sweat beading on his skin. The day had grown warm, and nobody gave an inch during these games. They always turned into a full-on court battle, the ball moving rapidly between the players.

"Ask him," Nate said as they stopped for a short break in play to rehydrate.

"Later." He picked up the ball, ready to restart the game. Now his mind drifted as he watched his teammate sink a shot. The man who could be his father-in-law one day soon.

"Brandon! Heads up!"

Brandon brought his hands up, barely catching the speeding ball before it slammed into his face. He lunged toward the net, but Nate executed a smooth steal and dashed down the court, sinking another basket.

"Get in the game," Aiden muttered as he passed by. "You almost ate that last pass."

The next few minutes flew by, Brandon struggling through every second of it, mentally kicking his own ineptitude as Will and Nate sank several baskets in quick succession.

"Game point." Nate extended his index finger skyward before he passed the ball to Will.

Aiden intercepted, tossing the basketball neatly to Brandon, who ran it down the court.

Brandon lobbed the ball toward the net, groaning as it rebounded off the rim.

Will caught it, heading down the court to the opposite basket, leaping to sink it with an impressive jump shot. He high-fived Nate before he scooped up his water bottle. "Drinks on you." A grin appeared. "Or maybe it should be dinner."

"Good game," Aiden said. "Pick the place, and we'll meet you guys in a couple of hours. Need to grab a shower and change."

Brandon sank onto the bleachers, dabbing at his face and the back of his neck with a small towel from his sports bag. He followed with a long slug of water and leaned forward to rest his forearms on his knees.

Aiden jogged across the short expanse of court. "What was that?"

Brandon shook his head as he rubbed a hand through his damp hair. "Lost focus. I'll be fine." He pressed the cold bottle to his cheek.

"Well, you cost me dinner and drinks," Aiden said, his tone light and teasing. "And my daughter would have blamed me if I'd broken that pretty face of yours with the ball."

"Sorry."

Aiden dug out his own water bottle and chugged half of it before he sat. "What's the deal?"

Brandon sneaked a look at Aiden from the corner of his eye, unsure how the man would react. "Not sure this is the time or place." Brandon glanced at the court where Nate was practicing free throws.

"Now I am curious." Aiden gave him a searching look. "So?"

He dragged in a long breath, rubbing his sweaty palms against his shorts. "Iwannamarryyerdaughter."

Aiden drew his brows together. "Say again?"

*Calm down.* He gave his head a small shake, combined with a nervous laugh. "I want," he said, enunciating each word clearly, but softly, "to marry Savannah."

"Are you … asking permission?" Aiden's brows shot upward.

"Hell no." Brandon shuddered at the thought of his supremely independent girlfriend catching wind of anything so archaic. "She'd hate it."

"Five points for knowing better than to make that fatal mistake." Aiden leaned back on his elbows, appearing unconcerned. "Does she know this is coming?"

Brandon straightened his spine, meeting Aiden's gaze without blinking. "No, but my girls deserve the security and commitment." He rubbed the back of his neck. "Do you think she'll say yes?"

"I can't speak for Savannah." He lifted a shoulder, a grin twitching his lips. "She'd hate it. But Tiff and I will support her decision one-hundred percent."

"You can speak for Tiffany?" His brows rose. "Wouldn't she hate that?"

"Neither of us would steal our daughter's happiness." Aiden's smile seemed tinged with sadness. "You'll have to trust me on that one."

Brandon nodded slowly, curious about the word *steal*. No matter how much time he spent with Aiden, the man remained an enigma. "You aren't concerned she's too young? You were eighteen when you married Tiffany, and it didn't work."

"Our divorce was a catastrophic meltdown. Almost called a hazmat team to contain the mess," he said with a feigned lightness. "But you aren't me. Savannah isn't her mother."

That was at least half true. Perhaps Savannah wasn't much like Tiffany aside from the physical resemblance, but he related to Aiden on many levels. They were more alike than different.

"If you aren't asking permission, what do you need?"

"A ring?" Brandon gulped a mouthful of water to combat his dry mouth. "I don't have a huge budget. You have a guy, right?"

"My jeweler? He's not inexpensive, but he owes me. He'll produce something amazing with what you've got."

"And use of the beach house?"

"Ah, you were listening." The man's brows rose. "Should I save you some trouble and offer to take London when you visit the Vineyard?"

"It's a lot to ask."

"It's not. She's mi tesoro." He placed a hand over his heart. A thoughtful look appeared on Aiden's face. "About the ring …."

"No to the jeweler?"

"Sorry, I'm thinking out loud."

"About?"

"Is this something you plan soon?"

"As soon as I can afford a decent ring." Brandon fidgeted with his water bottle. "Maybe that's stupid." His mind returned to the day he told Rory he hoped his girl would say yes because she loved him, not because of the ring. But he also had to consider the family he'd marry into. And Savannah in a room with the other wives, wearing the tiniest imaginable diamond—at least in comparison. He heaved a sigh.

"What is?" Aiden shot him a quizzical look. "Wanting to give a woman a nice ring? Or thinking you're ready?"

"If Vanna knows I'm ready to commit one-hundred percent," he said, "dealing with her return to New Haven in September will be easier."

Aiden studied him, scrubbing at his jaw.

Brandon would give anything to know the man's thoughts at this moment. Did he wonder if this was about jealousy? About staking a claim? That he was rushing into this out of fear? Or could he read Brandon's true intentions? "I don't mind a long engagement if she's not ready for a wedding, but she needs to understand how committed I am to making us work."

The silence hung between them, and Brandon shifted on the hard bench. "Damn! Can you say something?" He bowed his head. "Is it wrong?"

Aiden gave a soft laugh. "You remind me … of me. With Emily. Except things between us felt far more complicated. Or maybe just different-complicated."

"So it's not ridiculous?"

"Showing a woman how much you love her could never be ridiculous. Don't stress about the ring. Maybe I'm not one to talk, but it's not all about a big-ass diamond."

"Emily's ring is incredible."

Aiden shrugged. "She loves it, and wears it, but she never expected or demanded it. In fact, she said yes before she even saw it." He held up a hand. "Let's pick up the ring conversation again once I've made a couple of calls."

"Not too long, though?" His heart raced. He'd be a bundle of nerves until he'd sorted out this issue.

"I'm not trying to torture you." The man smiled. "Relax, and make your plans. Leave this part to me, for now." Aiden tucked his water bottle away. "Time to hit the shower and meet Nate and Will at the pub. You can redeem yourself for that crap basketball game at the pool table."

Two days later, Brandon stepped out of the stifling afternoon heat into the cool depths of the house. Arriving at what he considered his second home always relaxed him, especially after a particularly long and grueling day in the ER.

A feminine voice drifted from the patio at the rear, deep in what sounded like a telephone conversation, even though the rest of the house was bathed in silence. He strained his ears to figure out where he'd heard the familiar voice. It wasn't Emily or Savannah, or even Mia.

"Thought I heard someone." Aiden appeared, two tall icy glasses in his hands. "Why don't you change and join us on the patio?"

"I should shower. And I have to eat. You have company?"

"Yes, but you can have lunch outside. I left a plate in the fridge for you." He smiled and continued on his way through the French doors.

*Us who?* Brandon's curiosity was piqued, but he longed to wash away the antiseptic hospital scent. He headed upstairs, stripping off his clothes the moment he reached the bedroom, enjoying the light breeze flowing through the open patio doors.

He spent only five minutes in the shower before dressing and heading to the kitchen. A grin spread across his face as he poured a glass of lemonade from the pitcher and retrieved his plate from the fridge.

"That's why I didn't go—" The beautiful blonde ensconced in the chair across from Aiden smiled as Brandon appeared.

"Tiffany. Hi," he said as he set his glass and plate on the table. "When did you arrive?"

"I flew in this morning." She rose to hug him and to kiss each cheek. "It's good to see you."

Brandon settled in a chair, surveying the two. They appeared comfortable in each other's presence. The perfect couple. Except they weren't, even if he could picture them together. Something that would never be again.

"Where is everyone?" Brandon asked, wondering why they were here. Alone. In this big house. No significant other in sight.

"Em and Vanna took the kids for a playdate at Jenna's." Aiden sipped his drink.

Brandon ate a few bites, chewing slowly, sensing the undercurrent. "No Stefan this trip?"

"Stefan's traveling in the Outback." A soft smile touched her lips. "Given the circumstances, I thought I'd pass."

This tidbit didn't enlighten him as to what circumstances or why she'd shown up unexpectedly. Savannah hadn't said a word about her mother visiting.

"Are you in town for a show?" Brandon asked after he finished his last bite.

"Actually, I'm delivering an important package." Tiffany tucked one leg underneath herself as she angled toward him. "There's a rumor about big changes in the near future."

"You told her?" Brandon's gaze swung to Aiden. "Does anyone else know?"

"Em does," Aiden said, "but otherwise, I haven't shared."

Brandon swallowed a large mouthful of lemonade. Was this the parents joining forces to discourage him? To advise him how things would go with Savannah? Telling him he'd failed their precious daughter too many times to allow a permanent union? He shifted in his seat, waiting for Tiffany to let him in on the secret.

"Don't look so worried." Aiden laughed softly. "There's something we wanted to discuss without Vanna overhearing. Em is our accomplice."

"Is this the parent lecture on how I'd better not mess this up?"

"Now you mention it …" Tiffany smirked.

Brandon gulped another mouthful of lemonade, swallowing hard.

"Give the guy a break, Tiff." Aiden rolled his eyes.

"You ruin all my fun." She wrinkled her nose at her ex-husband, a teasing smile tugging at the corners of her mouth. "And you're bossy."

"Back at ya." He glanced at his watch. "Get to the point before we're overrun with small children."

"Sorry, I couldn't resist." Her expression grew serious. "I shouldn't tease. This is a major event, but it's how I deal with things."

He could understand the need to combat nerves with humor, but he wasn't sure why she'd be on edge. Unless it was bad news. He gripped the arms of his chair, steeling himself for the blow to come.

"I'll never stand in the way of my daughter's happiness," she said. "Our families didn't support our marriage, and the damage was irreversible."

"I'm sorry."

"Ancient history." Tiffany waved a hand.

Ancient, but not forgotten. The look exchanged between Aiden and Tiffany said more than they intended to reveal. The term *steal her happiness* made more sense every time the subject came up.

"I thought I should …." Tiffany sucked in a breath and blinked hard, her eyes shimmering as she produced a velvet box and extended it on her flattened palm.

Brandon eyed it. He shot a glance toward Aiden before accepting it. His breath caught in his chest as he revealed a set of rings—clearly a diamond engagement ring, with a matching wedding band nestled beside it. "Damn."

Tiffany folded her hands in her lap. "What do you think?"

Brandon lifted the larger of the two from the cushion, examining the ornate setting, admiring the sparks of fire emanating from the impressive center diamond. "I'm speechless."

"I … we," she said, giving Aiden a watery smile, "thought the ring should be Savannah's."

"Are you saying …?"

"This was my engagement ring and wedding band. The engagement ring was inherited from Aiden's grandparents, who were happily married for over half a century."

"You could give it to her as is," Aiden said. "Or you could design a modern setting with the diamonds."

"I don't know what to say." Brandon couldn't take his eyes off of the band, which he assumed to be platinum. "It's a generous offer."

Tiffany squeezed his hand. "It's your decision. It's an option we wanted you to have. If you'd prefer to give her something else, it's totally fine."

Brandon turned it, his breath catching as the light hit the facets, creating a prism of color. "Are you sure you don't want to keep this?" He looked at Tiffany, and then at Aiden. "It has to be valuable."

"It's been buried in a storage box for close to fifteen years." A wistful look appeared in the woman's eyes. "Our daughter wearing the rings, or at least the diamonds, would make us happy."

He stroked his jaw, picturing Savannah receiving an engagement ring that was not only stunning, but meant so much to both of her parents.

"The center stone is roughly four carats of high-grade old European diamond." Aiden said. "It's a shame to have it hidden in a safe."

"Thank you." Brandon cleared his throat to dispel the lump forming there. "This is unexpected." He blinked hard. "If I do this, she'll love it, won't she?"

"I believe she will." Tiffany reached over to squeeze Aiden's hand. "It has a special history. Our marriage ended, but the love was real."

"And you're sure? It wouldn't upset anyone?" He clutched the box in his hand. "It feels like cheating to use these," he said under his breath.

"Then I guess I cheated. Somehow, Tiffany didn't seem to mind."

"I loved it." The look in her eyes conveyed her fondness for her ex. "The proposal felt incredibly special. Aiden offered me a piece he treasured."

"It belongs to your family, though. Not mine." Brandon wished his family had handed down something he could treasure. All he'd inherited from them was a need for intense therapy.

"It's Tiffany's to give. Heirloom jewelry is meant to be passed down. To be worn and appreciated."

"It's not something you'd want to give to …" But he knew the answer before he even finished the question. Emily would never wear a ring previously bestowed on her husband's ex-wife, nor could it be truly meaningful to Kellan or Cierra. This heirloom belonged to Savannah; the first-born child. The ring was woven as intricately into her parent's love story as the delicate details were woven into the platinum band.

"Thank you. I could never offer her anything half as incredible. I hope she'll treasure it too." Brandon clutched the box in his hand, deciding he would leave the ring intact. Preserve the beautiful and unique heirloom. Changing anything about it felt like destroying part of Savannah's history.

"I have one request." Tiffany placed a soft hand on Brandon's wrist. "Residency years are tough, and weddings are expensive, but I hope to share her special day. I have this crazy dream about the dress shopping and helping plan the wedding."

"No eloping, huh?" A smile crept onto Brandon's face. He'd entertained it, but only briefly. It would feel wrong if her family weren't present, given how much of their daughter's life they'd missed. Depriving them of the joy of a wedding would seem cruel after their generosity and kindness. "I'm sure she'd love for you to share her big day." He rubbed his damp palms against his shirt. "If she says yes."

The question preyed on his mind. Considering how adamant she'd been about not walking down the aisle when they'd first found out about London, it was far from a sure thing. He hoped her viewpoint had been altered by the past three months. Their renewed commitment to each other.

"She loves you," Tiffany said softly.

"You're all in on this?" Aiden observed him. "She has no clue any of this is coming."

"I am. I can't imagine loving anyone as much as I love her." He lifted the lid, taking another long look at the ring. It seemed too much to take it, but refusing it would feel wrong.

Aiden rose. "Drink anyone?"

"Please," Tiffany said. "Something cold."

Brandon nodded. "Same."

Aiden disappeared into the house.

Tiffany slid forward in her seat. "If this makes you uncomfortable, then no offense will be taken if you don't accept it."

He opened his mouth, but closed it again as she held up her hand, palm facing him.

"But first, let me assure you; you are a part of this family. That"—she pointed to the ring box—"proves Aiden agrees."

"You don't mind giving this up? He's a persuasive guy."

"Oh, no," she said with a small shake of her head. "I mean, he is a smooth talker, but it's a brilliant idea. Savannah is my heart and soul." Her hand rose to rest on her chest. She gave a tiny helpless shrug. "It's fitting they be worn by our daughter."

He contemplated the next step in the process. The final parts of his plan would be easy to implement—the biggest part of the equation had been settled.

# Chapter 32

## Savannah

SAVANNAH SOAKED UP THE SUN, relaxing in the lounger on the patio off the master bedroom, surveying the expanse of blue. *Perfection.* Well, almost perfection. She looked at the picture of her little angel. As promised, a new picture had arrived on her phone that morning, and Aiden had been on time for each of their scheduled daily video chats.

The days were rushing by, and her dad promised to deliver London to the beach house before the weekend, allowing them time with their daughter before Brandon returned to work.

The man in question strolled onto the deck, giving his head a shake as he spotted the picture. "She's doing great. Don't you worry about my sunshine." Brandon handed her a steaming cup of coffee and planted a kiss on her lips before settling into the chair next to her. "Enjoy, and then we'll go sailing. I checked the weather report, and it will be calm and sunny all day."

"My family always takes good care of mi angelito." Her dad had swooped in to her rescue many times during those first months, caring for his granddaughter when things grew too hectic and overwhelming with her school schedule. And he'd arranged for Iona to spend time in New Haven in the early days. Even Tiffany had flown to New Haven on occasion, lending a hand. "How did you know I needed this?"

"Because I needed it too?" He captured her hand, rubbing the back with this thumb. A grin played across his lips before it disappeared. "Yes to sailing?"

She narrowed her eyes, studying him intently, pondering his decidedly strange moodiness. One moment, he acted like a teenage boy planning mischief. The next, he grew serious and straight-faced. In the past, it was her begging to sail, but this time … "You're scaring me."

"Why?" His eyes widened, his pupils dilating, his hand trembling as he set aside his coffee cup.

"I don't know." She tilted her head. "You're on edge. Is there something you need to tell me?"

"Me? Nope. Nothing at all." He shielded his eyes with dark sunglasses, obscuring part of his expression. But his mouth twitched with a glimmer of a self-satisfied grin before his expression settled into a flat, unreadable line.

Savannah slid on her own glasses to hide her furtive glances. The guy had been keyed up for the past two weeks, with his odd behavior growing more noticeable after her mother's surprise visit.

Emily hadn't seemed at all surprised to find the trio lounging on the deck when they'd arrived home after the play date at Jenna's. Even stranger was how her parents were so casual and chummy with each other, laughing and talking like it was the most natural thing in the world. Her mother had even fussed over Kellan and Cierra before claiming London for a cuddle.

"Maybe I should be scared," she mumbled, almost to herself.

"What?" Brandon lifted his sunglasses, turning his head toward her. "You still haven't answered. Should I pack the cooler?"

"Well, duh. When have I ever said no to a sunny day spent on a boat?" She wrinkled her nose, softening her words by blowing him a kiss. "Do I have time to shower?"

"I'll warm it up for you." He leaped from his seat, holding out his hand to pull her up. One arm curved around her waist as he cradled her face with one hand, kissing her deeply.

She curled an arm around his neck, pressing herself against him. The flicker of desire grew, igniting, but she sagged as he stepped back and straightened before ushering her down the hall into their bathroom.

He turned on the water, monitoring the temperature for a moment. "In. I'll pack." He spun, leaving her standing alone, completely stunned, the spark smothered by his seeming indifference.

She hung her light cover-up, playing a hand through the warm spray. As hard as it was to shut down her thoughts, she avoided the inevitable over-analysis of his bizarre exit, instead singing along to the music that filtered in from the speaker in the bedroom. She lathered up with her luxurious scented body wash, bobbing to the beat, her smile widening. The happy upbeat tunes of her favorite morning playlist always put her in a great mood. She could almost forget his odd exit when her boyfriend was acting like the sweetest man in the world.

She reached for a towel and wrapped it around herself, a small laugh escaping at the heart drawn on the steamy mirror, and the *I love you* written in the center.

The bedroom was empty when she shuffled in, but one of her rompers lay across the bed. Maybe a fancier outfit than she'd normally choose for a day on the water, but definitely one she loved to wear.

Fifteen minutes later, she followed the savory aroma wafting through the air, arriving in the kitchen as Brandon piled a plate high with fluffy scrambled eggs, crispy bacon, and sliced fruit.

His long, low whistle made her smile. "You look beautiful, sweetheart."

She did a slow pirouette, lifting her arms gracefully to allow him to admire the outfit he'd chosen, glad she'd spent the extra few minutes styling her hair into a loose updo.

He rounded the counter with her breakfast, setting it down before he wrapped his arms around her from behind. His warm breath tickled her neck as he nuzzled against it and placed tender kisses across her shoulder. "Mmm. You smell delicious." Too soon, he released her, pulling out a stool. "Eat, before it gets cold. I loaded the cooler and the beach bag onto the boat."

"You've been busy." She savored each bite, enjoying watching him as he tidied the kitchen. Only seconds after she finished her last mouthful, he piled her dishes in the sink. "What's the hurry?" she asked as she followed him to the door.

"Just giving you a taste of what it's like to be me when you're eager for a day on the water."

"Ahh." She slipped on her cutest pair of deck shoes and locked the door behind them. "Guess I've trained you well."

And perhaps she had. They prepared to set sail, each moving around the small craft as if performing a well-practiced and efficient dance. Gone were the days when she had to issue instructions.

The moment they hit open water, she relaxed, tipping her face toward the sun. These were the moments she savored, but today seemed extra special. She'd barely lifted a finger, and her man was being attentive and loving.

He sat beside her, an arm looped around her waist. "I love days like this. Wouldn't you enjoy doing this every summer for the rest of your life?"

"This is one of my favorite things in the whole world, in one of the most amazing places. Every year, we add to the special memories. If it could be like this forever, I'd be thrilled." She linked their fingers. "One day, I'll teach London to sail. Maybe she'll love it too."

"I bet she will. She's already so much like you." Brandon pressed his face against hers as he wrapped her in his arms. He held up his phone. "Smile." He snapped a photo, turning it so she could see.

"Oh. My camera." Savannah felt a surge of disappointment as she pictured her expensive equipment sitting on top of the dresser.

"I remembered it." He rose and moved easily into the small cabin, reappearing moments later with her bag.

"You thought of everything."

At lunch time, they anchored in a small familiar cove; the same one they'd visited the first day they'd sailed *Maya* together. A place they'd returned to again and again on each visit they'd made to the island.

Together they spread out the charcuterie and cheese board, Savannah smiling when she found the chilled bottles tucked in the cooler.

"Oh. My favorite. But you know the rules."

"Don't worry. We'll be anchored for a while, and the limit is one each. Or we can share." He patted the deck beside him. "Join me."

She sat cross-legged, setting aside her glass and added some of the morsels to her plate. "This looks delicious."

They ate in comfortable silence, enjoying the gentle rock of the boat and the calls of the birds from overhead. Once they were done and the leftovers were stowed in the cabin, Brandon poured two small glasses of the craft beer and sat cross-legged in front of her, his knees touching hers. He took both of her hands in his.

"What are you thinking?" she whispered.

"Where to begin." His grip tightened. "How fortunate I was that day, not so long ago, to meet an amazing woman at an unexpected time, in an unexpected place. Or how we've managed to arrive here, where I can't imagine my world without her in it."

She closed her eyes, her head bobbing in agreement, her heart telling her the same thing. Her world forever changed, at times spinning out of control, but settling at this spot of perfect bliss. When she reopened her eyes, he was still focused on her, barely blinking as he leaned in to brush his lips against hers.

"These past months have allowed us to learn about each other, and know each other on an unimaginably deep and intimate level," he murmured against her mouth, their breaths intermingling. "Yet, there's much, much more to know about you, Savannah Jayde Phillips Hamilton, and I can't wait."

He brought their linked hands up, grazing his lips across her fingers. "When I look at you, at our daughter, I see everything I've always dreamed. I

love you, Savannah. I want to spend the rest of my life loving you. Here's to us."
He handed her a glass, tapping the rim lightly with his.

"To us." She savored a sip of her icy cold drink. Something about the way
he looked at her made her hesitate and swallow hard. She bowed her head,
swirling the amber liquid, her brow furrowing at the light tinkling sound of
something hitting the side of her glass. "There's something in my ..." Her eyes
widened, her stomach performing a tiny flip as she tipped it, peering into the
depths of her drink. "Oh, Brandon. Is that ...?" She looked his way before
dipping a pinky into the cold liquid, looping it into the metal band.

She pressed her fingers over her mouth, unable to take her eyes off the shiny
circle as he moved onto his knees. Her vision blurred as she held her breath,
frozen in place, anticipating his next words, but also scared to death.

"I love you, so much. Will you"—he lifted her chin, forcing her to look at
him—"marry me?"

Her mouth grew dry as her eyes traveled from his face, to the ring, then
back to his face. The hope and love reflected there caused a sob to break free
from her chest. Words failed her. All she could do was nod and blink hard,
trying not to burst into tears.

His exhale was audible, his hands shaking as he rescued the band suspended
from the tip of her pinky. The ring slid easily onto her finger; a perfect fit.

Still, all she could see was him. This amazing, sweet man who'd changed
her world. She rose onto her own knees, wrapping her arms around him. "I
love you," she whispered, pressing her lips to his, maneuvering her body to
twine her legs around his waist.

Each kiss grew deeper, more passionate, her hair cascading over her
shoulders as he freed it from its pins. He rose in one smooth motion, with her
still clinging to him, wrapping her limbs tighter, unable to let go.

Vaguely, she knew they were moving, descending through the hatch, and he
lowered her onto the bed. She helped him remove his shirt, her hand moving
down to unfasten his shorts, smiling at his satisfied sigh as he unbuttoned her
top, revealing the lacy pink bra she wore underneath.

"My beautiful love," he murmured against her heated skin. "You drive me
mad."

"Get used to it," she whispered against his hair, skimming her hands over
his smooth flesh. "For the rest of your life."

⌒〜

Savannah sighed, completely contented, lulled by the soft rocking of the boat
and the warmth of the arms wrapped around her.

"Do you like it?" he asked as he brought her hand to his lips, kissing her
ring finger.

She suppressed a giggle. "I haven't even taken a proper look."

He let out a hearty laugh. "Not sure how to feel about that."

"Hmm. Flattered, maybe? I was so overwhelmed, nothing registered, aside from the fact it was a ring and you wanted me to marry you. And then we were otherwise occupied." She trickled her fingers over his firm chest, then propped herself up on one elbow, holding out her left hand for an inspection.

"Wait!" She sat, turning her wrist, admiring the sparkling stones. The delicate and ornate design of the band became more visible as she lifted her finger, bringing it closer to her face for inspection. "Holy crap. Where did you get this? It's … wow. Just …." She extended it toward the round window, straining to get a better look, a prism of color catching fire as the light hit it.

"Do you like it?" He sat, bringing her in to rest against his chest.

"I don't like it. I absolutely freakin' love it." She stared for several seconds, her heart sinking as she estimated how much he'd spent on this stunning display of diamonds. It could easily be worth as much as he owed in professional loans. "I can't take this. It's …"

"It's what? Not what you want?" His voice dropped an octave. "Or you just don't want to get married."

She shifted, cradling his face between her palms. "The yes was real, Brandon. But this ring! Did you rob a bank? Sell your sister into bondage?"

He shook his head, staring at her with a perplexed expression.

"Auction a kidney on the black market? 'Cause this cost a fortune. This isn't an average ring, even I can see that. It's too much."

"You've never seen this?" He caught her fingers, turning the ring as if seeing it for the very first time himself. "Just how much do you think …?"

"Seen it? What do you mean?" She examined it, but nothing about it seemed familiar. "Did you get a huge raise you never told me about?" Savannah tipped her head. "Or are you teasing me? Is it an impressive fake? Or from a box of Crackerjacks? Or one of those machines, you know the ones"—she curled her fingers, making little grabbing motions—"with the claw thingy where you fish out a prize?"

"I didn't see this reaction coming." He rubbed his jaw. "So … umm. It's … umm … real. All my body parts are intact, and I promise, no felony convictions are coming anytime soon. No candy boxes or claw thingies either."

"But?"

"I don't know how to even begin." He heaved a sigh. "Okay, when I talked to your dad about—"

She straightened her spine and squinted. "You asked my dad for permission?"

"No. Absolutely not. I only asked who made Emily's ring." He dropped his head into his hands. "This is so not going how I expected. Stupid idea. I wanted it to be special, and I blew it. Even the ring in the glass. Cheesy, right?"

"No." Her heart lurched at the despair in his voice. "I'm sorry." She wrapped her arms around him. "It's been an amazing day. Sweet, memorable, and beautiful. We spent our time doing something we both love in an incredibly special place. But you shouldn't take on huge debt for a ring. I don't need anything fancy. I only need you."

A hopeful smile appeared as he lifted his head, but moments later, it faded. "I didn't go into debt. Please don't freak out." He took her hand. "This was your mom's ring."

"Why would she give you …?" She pressed her palms together, bringing them against her lips, shaking her head as the pieces dropped into place. The comment about her dad. Tiffany's unexpected visit. Brandon's weird behavior. The over-the-top, expensive piece of jewelry now adorning her finger. An impossibility on a resident's puny salary, especially considering the aggressive repayment schedule on his professional loans.

"If you hate the idea, I'll buy you another. Please, just say you'll marry me. That you're not angry I cheated on the ring."

"My mother's engagement ring?" Her eyes sought his, a lump forming in her throat at his nod. She swallowed hard once, and then again to loosen it. "The ring my dad gave her?"

"It was his grandmother's ring. It's been in your family forever." He furrowed his brow. "You've never heard the story?"

She hadn't. Funny how she'd never asked about how or where her dad proposed, or about the ring, or any of the details. It had never occurred to her that her mom might have the ring after so many years. Or that her dad had entrusted Tiffany with a precious heirloom meant to be kept in the family. "No." She looked down at her hand. "She gave you this?"

"They did. Together. And I accepted it, because even though their marriage didn't work, they loved each other. Like … they really, truly loved each other. Your dad never asked her to return the ring, she never let it go, and they both want you to have it. They've blessed our engagement, our entire lives together, with something deeply personal and precious."

She grasped Brandon's left hand with her own, raising them to rest over her heart. "I'll treasure the ring. I love you."

◦◦◦

Two days later, Savannah still couldn't peel her eyes from the glittering diamonds on her finger. It felt slightly foreign and unreal. Each morning she'd awoken, afraid it was a fantastic dream, or that he might take it back.

"Today?" Brandon asked softly as he opened the laptop, preparing for their daily video call.

She shook her head, clamping her teeth onto her bottom lip.

Thankfully, Brandon didn't push. He grinned as London's cherubic face came into view. "Hi, sunshine." He blew kisses to his daughter.

"Da-da-da-da." London pointed and pressed a hand to her mouth. "Mah." She flung her arm out wide, before repeating the move again with another resounding kissy sound.

Savannah giggled at her daughter's sweet attempt to mimic Daddy. "How are you, mi angelito? I miss you. I can't wait to see you."

"Tomorrow, Vanna," Aiden said as he appeared behind London. "I plan to be on the road early to beat the traffic. Anything you need?"

"Groceries," Brandon said. "The market's crazy expensive and the selection isn't nearly as good."

Savannah smothered a giggle.

"What? It's true." He wrapped an arm around her, squeezing her against him.

"He needs midnight snacks, Dad."

"Done." Her dad's gaze rested on her. "How's everything else?"

"Great. The sailing's been amazing." She tucked her left hand under her thigh to avoid flashing the ring.

"Good." He squinted, clearly curious, but he didn't comment further.

They spent a few minutes longer talking to London and then signed off with waves and air kisses.

The moment they were done, Brandon rose. "I'm in the mood for a walk on the beach." He held out his hand. "Let's enjoy our last bit of quiet time."

⌒

Savannah linked her fingers through his, enjoying the soft shush of the waves against the beach as they walked across the sand.

"I'm missing the hectic family evenings, but this is amazing. I love how your family steps in to help with London whenever we need it."

"I swear they thrive on it. Even with twins on the way, Dad and Emily are so calm and collected." Savannah leaned into him as they ambled along the shoreline. "We should take a few days like this every summer."

"I agree." He twirled her ring. "Will you wear your ring tomorrow? Or did we get engaged too soon?"

She blew out a puff of air, not quite sure of the answer.

"We can have a long engagement or I can give the ring back, and we'll never speak of it again. Or buy you something else. Just tell me, because I can't bear this state of limbo."

She turned her head toward him. "I love you. I want to marry you. But wearing this ring has brought up emotions I can't quite process. It's incredibly special that my parents gave this to you."

"So why don't you want your dad to know you're wearing it? Do you want a different ring? Is it too weird? Or you hate the idea? Did I cheat by not buying a ring?"

"No, I don't think any of that. It's like you said. They truly love each other."

"Loved, you mean?"

"No … *love,* Brandon. Even though they're divorced, I still feel it. My dad always says she'll forever own a piece of his heart. I didn't understand how or why for the longest time, and it seemed disloyal to Emily, but now I get it. You can't go through what they did and not have strong feelings. Closure is darn near impossible."

"You think something is going on between them? I don't get that vibe."

"Like an affair?" She shook her head. "It's nothing like that. I can't explain. My dad loves Emily far too much. He'd never cheat, especially not with my mother."

"Funny, because when I realized they were in the house alone, it threw me. Your parents have an interesting dynamic, but so do Emily and Aiden."

"Trust. A deep, unshakable belief in each other. Emily and Aiden have both been through horrible endings to relationships. I swear they have some sort of pact, or they are just damn great at communicating and keeping it real."

"Maybe both." His smile was tinged with sadness. "Are we there yet? Has all that therapy gotten us to where we can keep it real, and be damn great communicators?"

This she knew was her cue. To explain her hesitation. If only she could.

# CHAPTER 33

## *Brandon*

S HE HADN'T EXPLAINED. IT SEEMED she couldn't find the words. He'd given her space. Time to process. Like she'd done for him when he'd needed to sort his emotions. She'd graced him with an abundance of patience and compassion.

*She loves me.* Without a doubt, he knew this to be the truth. Her soft words in the night, affirming they were on solid ground. The way she responded to his touch, giving back as much as she took when they made love; it all led him to the same conclusion. *We are about to embark on a great adventure together; if only we can get to that next important step.*

Her comment on the beach had provided the clue; the answer to the puzzle. Her hesitation. A single phone call was all it took to set the final act in motion. Now, he'd practice patience and wait.

He tightened his embrace, smiling as they sat on the log watching the sunrise over the ocean. Golden rays of light creating a path on the water; one that seemed to lead directly to them.

Savannah rested her head against his shoulder, her face lit by a radiant smile. "Pure bliss. I wish we could stay here forever." Her soft warm fingers slid into his.

"Wouldn't it be amazing?" Brandon played with the exquisite ring, still not used to seeing it on her finger. Later it would disappear into its plush box, hidden from her father's keen eyes. A situation he hoped to rectify. But not now. Right now he intended to prolong the blissful peace of early morning in the arms of the woman he loved; live in the moment, savoring every single second. This vacation would end too soon.

Savannah emitted a happy sigh as she rose and stretched. She held out her hand, inviting him to join her for the customary morning stroll along their beach.

⌒

By early afternoon, Savannah was keyed up, fidgeting and unable to sit still. When the sound of tires crunching against gravel and the hum of an engine carried to where they sat on the deck, she leapt from her seat.

"They're here." She rushed to the railing, craning her neck to peer around the side of the house.

"Let's go down." Brandon held out his hand. Together they descended to the main floor, but she pulled free, bounding through the doors. He hurried after her, eager to see her reaction.

"Emily. Mia. You're both here." She beamed as she skipped across the gravel straight toward Aiden, who cradled London on his hip. "I've missed you." Her shoulders shook as she kissed her daughter, and then pressed her face into her dad's shoulder.

"Hey, munchkin. I didn't know you were coming." Brandon embraced his sister, sending a grateful look toward Aiden. His focus had been on other things, but he should have suggested it himself.

To his surprise, she didn't object to the dreaded nickname, but kissed his cheek and graced him with a bright smile. "Aiden promised to take me sailing."

"Well, you are a lucky girl." He kept an arm looped around her. "Thank you," he mouthed to Aiden.

The man gave him a small nod and half-smile, which Brandon read to mean *you're welcome* and *things are on schedule as planned.*

"Thank you, Dad." Savannah said in a faint voice, stretching to kiss her dad's cheek. She turned, wrapping her arms around her stepmother. "I can't believe you're here. How are you feeling?"

"Wonderful, despite two little monkeys dancing on my bladder." She rested a hand on her belly. "When Aiden suggested we get away for a few days without the kids, I jumped at the chance. I hope you don't mind us joining you for the weekend."

"I'm glad you came. You deserve a break before the babies are born." Savannah grinned. "Are we expecting little girl or little boy monkeys?"

"Uh-uh." Aiden shook a finger at his daughter. He released London, who toddled toward Brandon and Mia.

"I missed you." Brandon lifted his daughter, peppering her face with kisses as the little girl wrapped her arms around his neck. He inhaled the soft baby scent.

"Da-da-da-da." She lay her head on his shoulder, content in his arms.

At the unmistakable sound of a second car coming down the drive, Vanna perked up. "Who could that be?" She gazed steadily at her dad as the vehicle parked beside the Cayenne, the silent *what-are-you-up-to* hanging between them before she bounded around the car.

Tiffany emerged from the passenger side, opening her arms to her daughter.

"Mom. What are you doing here?" A smile lit Vanna's face as she hugged the woman. "How are you?" Her hand traveled to the slight roundness of her mother's belly. "How's my little brother or sister?"

"I can't visit my daughter?" A twinkle appeared in the woman's eyes as she smiled at Brandon over her daughter's shoulder. "And I'm fabulous. As is the baby."

"Great to see you, love." Stefan hugged his stepdaughter, planting a kiss on her cheek before he offered a hand to Brandon, pulling him in for a quick embrace.

Tiffany plucked London from Brandon's arms. "Come to Grandma, sweet angel. Why don't we go with Abuelita and Mommy and find everyone cold drinks?" Tiffany tucked an arm around Savannah, and the group of women disappeared around the corner with Mia trailing them.

"That's our cue to unload the luggage." Stefan chuckled as he opened the trunk of their car.

"The art of being bossy without saying a word." Aiden laughed and handed Brandon a large cooler. "She's a pro."

Stefan grinned and hefted their bags. "I'll take these in and be back to help."

"Get settled, Stefan. Top of the stairs, second door on the right. Brandon and I will handle the few things in our car."

"Few things?" Brandon snickered after they'd made three trips each to carry in three coolers, ten bags of food and the small travel bag Aiden shared with Emily.

"You asked for snacks." Aiden lifted a shoulder as he stowed several boxes in the pantry. "And we'll be feeding a lot of people. Tom confirmed they'd all drive down for the weekend."

"But no pressure."

"They don't know anything, so no, there really isn't."

"Ahh." He felt relieved that news of the intended proposal had been contained to only a few parties. Even though Savannah had technically said yes, until the announcement had been made to her immediate family, he'd prefer to keep it quiet. "Hey, thanks for inviting Mia."

"She's welcome to join us anytime," Aiden said. "Mia's excited about learning to sail."

"Creating more addicts." Brandon chuckled, but underneath, he was thankful. The entire extended family had welcomed his sister and included her in any invitations to their homes during the holidays. Emily and Aiden had gone as far as designating Mia her own bedroom in their home, so she could stay whenever she had time off from school.

As he emptied the last of the contents from the largest cooler, Brandon discovered two bottles of expensive champagne. He held them up, examining the labels.

"Put those away." Aiden waved a hand toward the wine fridge. "Don't want to get you into trouble." He set an ice-cold pitcher of lemonade on the counter. "Why don't you top up the ladies' drinks? It's scorching hot today. And deliver these too." He poured nacho chips into a bowl and set it on the tray with a jar of homemade salsa. "I'm almost done here."

Brandon nodded and headed toward the patio with the refreshments. He arrived to find Tiffany bouncing London on her knee, the baby whining and rubbing at her eyes.

"She's ready for a nap." Brandon set the refreshments on the table and held out his arms. "I'll put her to bed." He smiled as London reached out, the whine fading away as she clung to him. Despite his months away, they'd formed a strong bond. He spent as much time as humanly possible nurturing his relationships with both Savannah and his daughter.

"I'll help." Savannah trailed after him.

"I can manage, sweetie."

"No doubt you can, but I missed her."

They worked in comfortable silence to change their daughter and tuck her into her crib.

"This is amazing," Savannah whispered as they crept into the hall. "It's great to have them here."

"Maybe we should take advantage of it." Brandon caught her hand. "Are you ready to make it official?"

"Ahh." She tilted her head. "It's no coincidence they're here. You set me up? Sneaky. I thought it was my dad."

Brandon blew out a slow breath. This would be the moment he'd know if his assessment of the situation was correct, or if he'd earned big trouble. "Guilty."

"It's a bit frightening how well you know me." She wiggled the fingers of her left hand. "Where is it?"

He extracted the velvet box from his pocket and removed the ring from the cushion. "Last chance to back out."

Her smile widened as she shook her head, her gaze lifting to meet his as he slid the ring onto her finger.

"I love you." He kissed the back of her hand before linking their fingers and leading her downstairs.

The sounds of laughter and ice clinking against the sides of glasses carried in from the patio. The kitchen was now empty, as Aiden had joined the party.

"They get along so well." Savannah hesitated in the doorway, watching as Aiden topped up glasses. "I don't know why I'm nervous. They know, don't they?"

"Well, they suspect, though I neither confirmed nor denied whether the event in question had taken place. Or what the answer might be."

"Nothing like letting the anticipation build," she said. "Thank you for inviting them. Having Mom and Dad here and being able to share our news with everyone … that's exactly what was missing. Now we can celebrate as a family."

"I know you love Emily. She's been a huge part of your life, but the ring came from Aiden and Tiffany, so …" Brandon shrugged.

"See? You understand me. I didn't even realize it until they arrived. Let's not keep them waiting." A smile lit her face. "I'm ready."

Brandon nodded, his own set of nerves taking over. The moment they walked through that door, it would begin for real. He had months of planning a wedding to look forward to.

"Don't look so worried." Savannah caught his hand.

"I'm not." He tugged her onto the patio, keeping the ring hidden as they joined the group.

"London's asleep?" Emily asked.

"Like an angel." Savannah's grip tightened.

A hush fell over the group, a sense of anticipation building as they stood together, hand in hand.

Mia gave him a quizzical look, her brows rising as neither he nor Savannah made any move to sit.

Savannah turned toward him, giving the slightest of nods.

"No point in dragging this out." Brandon looked into the semi-circle of faces, coming to rest on Aiden, the man he'd grown so close to in such a short period of time. A lump formed in his throat, and he cleared it, hoping he could produce the words.

Aiden gave him an encouraging smile and tiny nod.

"Brandon asked me to marry him," Savannah said in a soft voice. "And I said yes." She held up her hand, revealing the dazzling ring.

Brandon held back a soft laugh, grateful she'd taken the pressure off by making the announcement. Somehow, she'd read his emotions and inability to speak. Standing in front of her family, even in these circumstances, was daunting.

"What? You're getting married?" Mia leapt to her feet, a huge smile breaking as she skipped across the patio. "Let me see. You'll be my sister."

Tiffany pressed her palms over her face, tears springing to her eyes as she rose from her seat, heading straight for them.

Brandon found himself surrounded, accepting best wishes and warm hugs from both sets of Savannah's parents and his little sister. Again, he sent a silent thanks to Aiden for ensuring Mia was there to share in the moment. She remained the only family he truly had.

Calling his mother to share his news was out of the question, especially given her cold indifference after she'd signed over guardianship for Mia. Darien … well, that man remained a complete stranger. He hadn't heard a single word from the guy since he'd hauled Tristan back to Albany. Maybe he never would.

～

Brandon kicked harder, picking up the pace as he caught a glimpse of the man just ahead of him. It had become a competition, albeit a friendly one, to see who could reach the dock first during their morning swims. He was determined today would be his first win.

"Crap." He hauled himself out of the water a split-second after Aiden. "Almost had you."

"Ha." Aiden laughed, sweeping a hand through his hair to brush away the droplets of water. "Not even close."

Brandon leaned back on his hands, tipping his head up to the early morning sun. "The rest of the gang is joining us later?"

"Yup. Tom and Jenna arrived late last night, and Joel and Alex should be here sometime later this morning. Ryan and Kaari are flying in this afternoon."

He pictured the complete chaos that would ensue. Of course, the other couples had their own homes, except for Ryan, who planned to stay with Tom. But once they all learned about the proposal, pandemonium would break loose.

"What's that look for?" Aiden chuckled.

"Oh, you know how it'll be. Once the rest of the family gets here, the talk will be about wedding dresses, bridesmaids, and flowers. I don't even know where to start with all of that stuff." He waved a hand in the air. "It'll get way out of control."

"I have two words for you." Aiden swished his feet through the water. "Wedding planner. In your circumstances, planning a wedding is insanity waiting to happen."

He cringed. "I can't afford one."

The man tilted his head toward Brandon. "I'd like to host the wedding."

"Host? Is that Aiden-speak for you want to pay for the entire thing?" Brandon shook his head. "It's too much. We can do something small and affordable."

"What should I spend my money on if not my family? It doesn't have to be an extravaganza with huge white tents, doves, and five hundred guests, but the numbers will add up. We have a large extended family who will insist on being there." Aiden met his gaze. "I've missed too much of my daughter's life. As has her mother. Let Tiffany have this one day, Brandon. She deserves the joy of arranging her daughter's wedding without worrying about the budget."

He was beat. The number of invitations he'd issue would be minuscule in comparison to Savannah's guest list. Not to mention the guilt he'd feel if he robbed either his intended wife or her mother of their happiness. And he had to keep his promise to Tiffany. He hadn't forgotten how emotional she'd become that day they'd presented the ring, or her reveal about how she dreamed about Savannah getting married. "Thank you."

Aiden simply nodded, tipping his head back and closing his eyes. "Not sure you've set a date, but you should bring your best man into the loop soon."

More details, and they hadn't even begun to plan. "I'll probably ask Nate, if he has the time."

"What about Rory?"

Brandon scoffed. "I doubt it. We're not exactly talking. Didn't Savannah tell you?"

Aiden shook his head. "Nope. And Rory didn't say much the day I drove him to the airport. What went down?"

He shrugged, idly kicking at the water.

"Let me guess. A woman?"

Brandon threw Aiden a sideways glance. "How'd you know?"

The man laughed softly. "What else? You were pissed, he acted guilty as fuck. So he moved in on someone, and you weren't impressed. How am I doing so far?"

"Nailed it." He stared at the tiny waves lapping at the dock. "He moved in on my ex-girlfriend. Even admitted he'd lusted after her when we were dating. He sprang it on me, right before he planned to ask her to marry him. It's a betrayal."

A thoughtful look appeared on Aiden's face, but he remained silent.

"He swears nothing happened until after I'd started dating Vanna, but still, after everything we've been through, he had to pick her?"

"Is it a choice?" Aiden asked. "You love who you love. If the relationship didn't develop until after you'd moved on, then what's the big deal?"

"He took forever to tell the truth."

"But he did tell it." The man sighed. "I know what it's like to be at odds with someone you consider family, but there are two sides here. If his friendship is important, you might want to figure out exactly why it bothers you. Maybe you can let it go. Maybe you can't."

"Joel?" His curiosity rose at the mention of being at odds.

"Uh-huh, and that situation got way out of hand. It could have ended badly and destroyed a lot of lives. Don't let your issues with Rory escalate into something more than it is. Anger has a way of building, and over time, it'll eat you alive."

"You got over it."

"We worked through it. Some damage was done, and it may never be the same, but we're more honest about things. That's not necessarily a bad outcome. It's often said forgiveness is more about setting your own mind at rest than absolving someone of their actions. Trust me, I know. I have done a whole lot of forgiving and repairing relationships over the past few years. I guarantee, it's a high body count."

Brandon simply nodded. He'd become close enough to this family to understand the wisdom of Aiden's words. At thirty-six, the man had endured unimaginable pain and loss, but Aiden was also one of the happiest people he knew.

Besides, he missed his friend. The first name that came to mind when he thought about a best man was Rory, even though he'd grown close to Nate over the past years.

Rory had left countless apologetic messages over the last few months, which had finally tapered into silence. Brandon knew the relationship with Autumn had met its demise. A tidbit Vanna had shared not long after they'd reconciled. He didn't know the reason why it ended, but he hoped it had nothing to do with his reaction to the news.

Another name came to mind. Someone to consider while he busied himself with forgiving and letting those chips slide away. Perhaps he should revisit the situation with his father. They may never have a relationship, and initiating contact with the man would mean coming clean with Mia about her unknown father.

But maybe that secret wasn't his to keep. Perhaps he should allow his sister to deal with her own reality sooner, rather than later. It could spare her untold future pain.

Time to move into his new life with his new family, leaving the old burdens behind.

# Chapter 34

## *Savannah*

Savannah let herself out of the house, stretching her arms wide and soaking up the bright morning sun. She headed for the deserted beach, intent on having a peaceful stroll before the demands of a toddler consumed her day.

Usually, Brandon would be out with her dad for a morning swim, but today he'd accepted an early morning call from Rory instead. After these many months, Savannah was thrilled he'd decided to take the first step toward repairing the rift between him and his friend. She wasn't sure what sparked the change of heart, but he'd even mentioned making a call to Darien and having a discussion with Mia, revealing what he'd learned about their family.

When questioned on what had initiated his actions, his answer had been cryptic. She decided not to push the issue. His reasons didn't much matter; it only mattered that he tried.

She understood on a deeply personal level how hard it could be to make amends and to bestow forgiveness. How tough the road ahead would be for Brandon. She'd traveled it herself with her own mother. Even her relationship with Brandon had been tumultuous before evolving into its current form.

She ambled down the beach, stopping now and again to examine the shells and sea glass that washed up overnight. One day, London would be old enough to join her. Maybe next spring, she mused, picturing their blonde angel collecting the small treasures left by the tide. The little girl had an active curiosity, fueled to greater heights by the constant interaction with Savannah's younger siblings and the need to keep up.

Her heart warmed as she thought about their expanding family. Emily and Aiden had revealed they were expecting baby girls during last night's family gathering. Tiffany and Stefan would welcome a baby boy shortly after the New Year, which would increase her total number of siblings to an amazing five.

And someday, another child of her own might be added to the mix. Not right away, but she and Brandon loved being parents and agreed they'd like another baby when the time was right.

She rounded the bend, hesitating as she spotted two figures perched on her favorite log. One she'd visited many times for numerous heart-to-heart conversations in the past few years. This particular place had become the usual stop for her and Brandon to watch the sunrise on their morning walks.

As she ventured closer, she recognized the individuals. "What are you two doing here?"

Tiffany shrugged. "We were both out enjoying the morning and met here by chance." A soft smile touched her lips. "There's nothing quite like sitting on a beautiful beach watching the sun creep over the horizon. I could view it every single day and never tire of it. This morning it was especially magnificent."

Savannah returned the smile, slipping easily into the space her mom and dad had left between them. "It's a perfect spot."

"Sadly, one day, the tides or a storm will take this all away. But then those same forces of nature will create a new place equally as beautiful." Aiden slid an arm around her.

"That's the amazing part of life." Tiffany's arm crept around her from the other side, her mom moving a tiny bit closer. "You never know what will happen next."

Savannah reached out to take her parent's free hands, entwining her fingers with theirs, linking the three of them together. As their lives would forever be linked and interwoven through the good and bad, and the joy and pain even when many miles separated them. They'd traveled an unimaginable distance, forging new connections and renewing bonds that had been broken.

Now, the future stretched out in front of them. Unknown and unpredictable, but unimaginably exciting. She knew they were ready to embrace those futures, whatever they might be.

Enjoy an excerpt from with *Everything We Promised,* Book 6

# CHAPTER 1

## Aiden

A BOY'S SHRILL VOICE PIERCED THE air several rows behind Aiden as the aircraft bumped across the tarmac toward the O'Hare terminal. "Mommy. We're home."

*Home.* Aiden pinched the bridge of his nose, blinking against the burn. He wished he could join the other passengers emerging from flight-induced stupors, smothering smiles, and tapping at chiming phones.

Chicago was simply a distant memory, blurred over three years of exile. He was sorry he was back.

Excited chatter rolled over him as they rolled to stop, and he rose and stretched to work out the kinks. After a moment, he tugged his carry-on from the overhead bin.

He slung his bag over his shoulder and trudged through the jetway, gazing around as he wandered along the concourse, in no hurry to reach the baggage area. By the time he arrived, most of the passengers were already in the arms of their loved ones, and the animated calls and murmurs of family members flowed around him.

"I missed you." A teenage girl threw herself into the arms of an older woman he assumed was her mother.

Aiden turned away from the happy scenario and shuffled toward the carousel. He found a vacant spot and leaned against a pillar, tipping his head back and closing his eyes, blocking out the small but joyful reunions continuing around him.

"Mr. Hamilton?"

Aiden glanced at the uniformed man. "That's me."

"Can I retrieve your bag, sir?" The man's brows lifted.

Aiden motioned to the black case with the distinctive red baggage tag as it slid from above and landed with a soft thunk on the conveyor. "That one."

The man maneuvered through the gathering crowd, scooped up the bag, and wound his way back. "Ready, sir?"

Aiden followed the man to the sleek black sedan and waited for the driver to open his door. *Funny how old habits remained second nature even after all this time.* He settled in the leather seat as the driver stowed his bag.

Moments later, the car pulled from the curb and merged into traffic. He closed his eyes, concentrating on calming his thoughts and relaxing his tense muscles.

Finally, the car slowed and turned through the familiar iron gates. The sedan drew to a smooth stop in the circular drive.

Aiden inhaled a long slow breath as the driver opened his door. "Thank you." He stared at the imposing stone mansion. Nothing had changed. The vines still crept up the South wall, the fountain bubbled merrily in the center of the circular drive, the flowerbeds overflowed with bright blooms, and the lawns were a lush and immaculate green. Even the most meticulous greens keeper would be envious.

The massive wooden doors swung open the moment he set foot on the first step. "Hi, Bernard." He shrugged out of his light coat.

Bernard draped the jacket over his arm. "Welcome home, sir." He nodded before extending his arm toward the study. "Mr. Hamilton requested you report to him upon arrival."

Aiden lifted his chin and tilted his head, listening for sounds of life. *Silence.* Nobody appeared, but this wasn't a surprise. Expecting an enthusiastic or warm welcome for the errant grandson was ridiculous.

"Sir?"

"Thank you, Bernard." He trudged across the gleaming tile. Requested? No. *Summoned.* That was more accurate. And it would be unwise to keep Thomas Hamilton waiting.

Aiden proceeded down the marble-tiled hallway and tapped on the door before entering the dark-paneled room.

The gray-haired man behind the desk fixed a cold gaze on Aiden, not bothering to rise from the leather chair behind the oak desk. He tapped the nib of his pen against the paper, barely blinking as he stared at his grandson.

"Grandfather." Aiden straightened, maintaining a level tone and expressionless visage even as the bitter hatred rose. He longed to vent his rage upon this imperious man, but he bit back the scathing words.

The memory of the last time he'd stood in this spot flooded into his mind and it felt like he was right back to that day. As he had then, he fixed his eyes on the painting behind Thomas's head and clenched his jaw. He forced his hands to relax, doing his utmost not to curl them into fists.

"Dinner will be served at seven sharp." Thomas tapped the manila envelope sitting on the side of his desk twice with the tip of his index finger. "This contains the information on your apartment. Be packed and ready to leave by next Thursday."

Aiden translated this as he smothered the scoff. *Be sure you're out of my house by next Thursday.* That's what the man really meant.

There would be little packing to complete. Even as he stood here, the upstairs maid would be unpacking his bag, sorting his laundry, and boxing up the souvenirs he'd brought home.

That same maid would repack his bags and, he was sure, his few belongings would be on their way to Philadelphia before he left Chicago.

His grandfather narrowed his eyes and pushed the package across the expanse of the oak desk. After a moment of intense scrutiny, the man bent his head and focused on his paperwork. He waved toward the door. "That's all."

Aiden took one step forward to retrieve the information before leaving the room as silently as he'd entered. He headed down the hallway and exited through the French doors at the rear of the house.

It was pointless to head to his room. Instead, he crossed the lawn and slipped into the cool depths of the pool house before pulling out his phone and using his speed dial to make the call.

"Hey. How are you?" Tom asked. "Where are you?"

"Chicago. At least for now." Aiden dropped onto the couch and propped his feet on the coffee table.

"Your grandparents' house?"

"Unfortunately."

"You want to break out?"

"I'd better stick around for dinner, but after they've gone to bed, I'll escape."

"We're heading to the beach later. Do you want me to pick you up?"

Aiden debated on his answer. Having a ride would make things easier, but he had another stop to make. "No. Maybe I'll meet you there, but if not, then tomorrow night for sure. I can't wait to see everybody."

"We're happy you're finally back."

Once he'd finished his call with Tom, he decided to work out and do some laps in the pool. He needed to keep himself occupied, or he'd go crazy.

Hours later, after an excruciating formal dinner, Aiden retreated to his room and flopped onto his bed, covering his eyes with the back of his hand. His grandparents had acted as if nothing had changed. They hadn't inquired about his travels or time overseas. Aside from a light kiss on his cheek from his grandmother, his absence hadn't been acknowledged.

In one short week, he'd move to Philadelphia, and his grandparents could go on as if he'd never been here at all.

He turned on the big screen television affixed to the wall and flipped through the channels. Nothing to do but bide his time. His grandfather insisted on retiring to his room on a strict and predictable schedule, so he'd only have an hour to kill.

By ten-thirty, the house was dark and silent. Aiden crept into the hallway and tiptoed toward the back staircase. Nobody seemed to be around, but one could never tell in this house. His grandparents maintained a large staff, including at least two maids who had a habit of popping up from nowhere. But he supposed no one would prevent him from leaving. He'd turned eighteen in June. A grown up. No longer a child to be ordered about.

Aiden longed to escape the heavy and oppressive atmosphere in this mausoleum. The keys on the rack just inside the garage door beckoned him, and he selected a set without hesitation. The buttery, soft leather welcomed him as he slid into the driver's seat and gripped the wheel, giving a light tap on the garage door opener.

A grin spread across his face as the engine purred to life. After easing the car out of the garage, he navigated the dimly lit drive without the headlights. Once he turned onto the main road, he flicked them on and retracted the convertible's roof. A satisfying roar rose from the precision engine as Aiden pressed the accelerator to the floor. *Ahhh, freedom at last.*

His grandfather would have a coronary if he caught Aiden driving his pride and joy, but … *What the hell?* What could Thomas Hamilton do to him that he hadn't already done?

The luxurious seat suited Aiden, but he grimaced at the jarring country twang that poured from the high-end sound system. "That man still has no taste in music." He stabbed at the controls on the steering wheel and tapped along to an upbeat rock song as he savored the warm evening air sweeping over him.

As he neared his destination, he lowered the volume to a whisper and slowed to a crawl. The smoke-gray sports car blended into the shadows left between the scattered streetlights on this peaceful residential avenue. *Perfect.* No need to disturb the neighbors.

Most of the houses were quiet with darkened windows, signaling the occupants had retired for the evening, including the ones inside the stately colonial home.

After a quick scan of the street, he hopped from the car and trotted down the verge of grass along the sidewalk before veering across the lush green lawn. The familiar trellis beckoned him, and he tugged at it, hoping it wouldn't break free from its anchors when he added the weight of his muscular six foot frame.

The creak of aged wood had him holding his breath as he scaled it one inch at a time. A sigh escaped as he clung to the ledge. Fortunately, the window was open a crack to allow the cool night air into the bedroom.

"Tiff," he whispered as he tapped on the glass. "Wake up."

A rustle came from the direction of the bed, followed by shuffling feet. "Who's there?"

"Tiff. It's me. Hurry up, my fingers are cramping."

"Aiden?" A pale face appeared at the window. The girl's eyes widened as she opened the window further. "You're here. When did you get back?" Tiffany reached out, tugging at him as he slid through the window and landed on the floor with a slight thump. She threw a panicked look over her shoulder. "Shh."

"Get dressed," he whispered. "Come for a ride with me."

"I don't know." She hesitated and glanced toward her door.

"I haven't seen you in forever, Tiff. Please?"

"Shush, they'll hear you. I'll be down in a minute." She motioned him away, still throwing anxious looks toward her bedroom door.

Aiden lowered himself to the ground, stepping into the shadows as he waited. The scrabble of feet against wood alerted him and held up his hands, supporting her as she climbed down.

As soon as her feet touched the grass, she threw her arms around him. "I thought you were never coming home."

Aiden rocked her against his chest. "I'm sorry. I didn't have a choice." A sweet floral scent surrounded him as he buried his face in her hair. Being in her arms made him feel like he was finally home.

"It's been years." Red-rimmed shimmering eyes scanned him as she offered a faint smile. "You're so tall. Mmm," she said as she ran her fingertips over his firm chest, "and muscly."

"Let's get out of here before someone sees." He linked their fingers and tugged her toward the car.

"You're going to be in so much trrrrrouble." A grin spread across her face as she sang out the final word. "Does your grandfather know you have his Porsche?"

"Are you kidding? You know how he is about his cars." Aiden rolled his eyes even as his lips twitched. "He'll never know." He opened her door.

Tiffany smothered a giggle as Aiden guided that car along a familiar and winding route toward their favorite spot by the lake.

As soon as he shut off the car, Tiffany turned toward him. "How have you been? I can't believe you're here." She brushed her fingertips over his cheek. "It's so good to see your face."

"You got my letters?"

"Alex smuggled them to me." Her vibrant blue eyes shone with tears.

Aiden cupped her face in his palms. "It's so good to be here."

They stared at each other for a moment, before their lips met. At first, it was tender and gentle, but it grew, becoming deeper and more passionate.

"Aiden," she murmured as she slid her hands under his shirt, pressing herself against him.

He pulled her closer, luxuriating in the feel of her soft lips on his, plundering her mouth. This visit might seem impulsive, but he couldn't stand another day without seeing her. With her in his arms again, the pain of missing her faded away. He couldn't let go.

"Back seat?" he whispered before capturing her sweet mouth again.

She nodded.

Aiden tumbled over the seat, and then lifted Tiffany, encouraging her to join him.

"Aiden." She giggled as she landed on top of him.

"Shh." He wrapped his arms around her, kissing her as he spanned her tiny waist with his hands.

Tiffany slid a leg over, straddling him. She peered into his eyes and ran her fingers through his hair. "I can't believe you're here."

"Me either." He tangled his hand in her honey-blonde hair and pulled her to him, nuzzling against her neck.

Tiffany leaned back enough to peel her shirt off, then pressed her mouth to his.

Aiden returned her fiery kisses, his heart pounding as he caressed her soft skin. With a flick, he unhooked her bra and tossed it aside, burying his face against her.

"Love me," she whispered against his hair.

⌐≼

As he cuddled with Tiffany on the leather seat, he rested his cheek against her silky hair and savored the feel of her in his arms.

She sighed and snuggled against his chest. "I forgot how amazing we are together."

He dropped a kiss on her temple and closed his eyes, refusing to think about the others who'd been in their lives during their forced separation. He brushed his fingertips up and down her arm. "You're not seeing anyone, right?"

Tiffany shook her head. "No." She blinked her shiny eyes. "Can we not talk about it? We agreed, Aiden. You were gone so long."

"I know." He kissed her lips. "Tiff?"

"What?"

"Have you thought about Philly?"

"What about it?"

"So you didn't get it? I'm moving next week for medical school."

"You only came home."

"Come with me."

"To Philly?" A frown settled on her face. "And do what?"

"Go to school?" Aiden grasped her arms. "Please, Tiff? We've been apart for so long, and you know I've always wanted to be a doctor."

"Dr. Aiden Hamilton." She brushed his hair back from his forehead. "That has a beautiful ring to it." She bit her lip. "I can't. I start classes at the Art Institute next week."

Aiden's heart sank. His hard work over the past three years had paid off, and now his dream to attend medical school had come true. Would he be forced to live without Tiffany? He'd anticipated this moment for so long. Having her in his arms with the knowledge they'd be parted so soon was bittersweet.

Tiffany relaxed against his chest and sighed. "Will we ever be together?"

"We can visit. Long distance relationships aren't ideal, but here we are after three years. Can we try?"

"Philly is much closer than wherever you happened to be overseas on any given day. Do you think it will work? My dad …"

"You'll be eighteen at the end of September. What can he say?"

"He could refuse to pay my tuition. I only have a small scholarship, and if he takes away his support, I can't go. It's all I've ever wanted."

"We'll find a way. We've kept secrets before, Tiffany. What's one more?"

"Please, don't." She pressed her face into his chest and sniffled. "I can't even talk about it. Please don't make me relive it."

"Hey." Wrapping his arms around her, he held her tight. It had been even more difficult for her than it had for him, but he shared her pain. "We don't have to talk about it, honey, but I love you, and I want us to be together. Will you consider it? Maybe I should apply for medical school in Chicago."

"You can't give up your spot. It's a great school. Besides, how could you live in the same house as your grandfather?"

Aiden stared at the stars as silence fell over them. It seemed an impossible situation. Whenever they managed to find their way back into each other's arms, they were torn apart. He'd loved this girl forever, but now he'd have to leave her all over again.

He let his eyes slide shut and snuggled her against him, wishing everything was different.

*Thank you for reading!*

**I always love to hear from readers. I can be contacted at  http://katesmithauthor.ca**

**Follow me on social media:**

https://www.instagram.com/katesmithauthor/

https://twitter.com/KateSmithAuthor/

https://www.facebook.com/katesmithauthor/